Enid Blyton

The
Wishing Chair
Collection

The Adventures of the Wishing Chair first published
in Great Britain in 1937 by Newnes
The Wishing Chair Again first published in Great Britain in 1950 by Newnes
More Wishing Chair Tales first published in Great Britain in 1997 by Dean

This edition first published in Great Britain in 2002 by Dean,
an imprint of Egmont Books Limited, 239 Kensington High Street,
London W8 6SA

ISBN 0 603 56074 1

3 5 7 9 10 8 6 4

Printed and bound in Great Britain by The Bath Press, Bath

CONTENTS

I

THE STRANGE OLD SHOP

The adventures really began on the day that Mollie and Peter went out to spend thirty-five pence on a present for their mother's birthday.

They emptied the money out of their money-box and counted it.

"Thirty-five!" said Peter. "Good! Now, what shall we buy Mother?"

"Mother loves old things," said Mollie. "If we could find an old shop somewhere, full of old things—you know, funny spoons, quaint vases, old glasses, and beads—something of that sort would be lovely for Mother. She would love an old tea-caddy to keep the tea in, I'm sure, or perhaps an old, old vase."

"All right," said Peter. "We'll go and find one of those shops this very day. Put on your hat and come on, Mollie."

Off they went, and ran into the town.

"It's a shop with the word 'Antiques' over it that we want," said Peter. "Antiques means old things. Just look out for that, Mollie."

But there seemed to be no shop with the word "Antiques" printed over it at all. The children left the main street and went down a little turning. There were more shops there, but still not the one they wanted. So on they went and came to a small, narrow street whose houses were so close that there was hardly any light in the road!

And there, tucked away in the middle, was the shop with "Antiques" printed on a label inside the dirty window.

"Good!" said Peter. "Here is a shop that sells old things. Look, Mollie, do you see that strange little vase with swans set all round it? I'm sure Mother would like that. It is marked twenty-five pence. We could buy that *and* some flowers to put in it!"

So into the old dark shop they went. It was so dark that the children stumbled over some piled-up rugs on the floor. Nobody seemed to be about. Peter went to the counter and rapped on it. A tiny door at the back opened and out came the strangest little man, no higher than the counter top. He had pointed ears like a pixie. The children stared at him in surprise. He looked very cross, and spoke sharply.

"What do you want, making a noise like that?"

"We want to buy the vase with swans round it," said Peter.

Muttering and grumbling to himself, the little chap picked up the vase and pushed it across the counter. Peter put down the money. "Can I have some paper to wrap the vase in?" he asked politely. "You see, it's for my mother's birthday, and I don't want her to see me carrying it home."

Grumbling away to himself, the little man went

6

to a pile of boxes at the back of the shop and began
to open one to look for a piece of paper. The
children watched. To their enormous surprise a
large black cat with golden eyes jumped out of
the box and began to spit and snarl at the little
man. He smacked it and put it back again. He
opened another box.

Out of that came a great wreath of green smoke
that wound about the shop and smelt strange. The
little man caught hold of it as if it were a ribbon
and tried to stuff it back into the box again. But
it broke off and went wandering away. How he

7

stamped and raged! The children felt quite frightened.

"We'd better go without the paper," whispered Mollie to Peter, but just then another extraordinary thing happened. Out of the next box came a crowd of blue butterflies. They flew into the air, and the little man shouted with rage again. He darted to the door and shut it, afraid that the butterflies would escape. To the children's horror they saw him lock the door, too, and put the key into his pocket!

"We can't get out till he lets us go!" said Mollie. "Oh dear, why did we ever come here? I'm sure that little man is a gnome or something."

The little fellow opened another box, and, hey presto, out jumped a red fox! It gave a short bark and then began to run about the shop, its nose to the ground. The children were half afraid of being bitten, and they both sat in an old chair together, their legs drawn up off the ground, out of the way of the fox.

It was the most curious shop they had ever been in! Fancy keeping all those queer things in boxes! Really, there must be magic about somewhere. It couldn't be a proper shop.

The children noticed a little stairway leading off the shop about the middle, and suddenly at the top of this, there appeared somebody else! It was somebody tall and thin, with such a long beard that it swept the ground. On his head was a pointed

8

hat that made him seem taller still.

"Look!" said Mollie. "Doesn't he look like a wizard?"

"Tippit, Tippit, what are you doing?" cried the newcomer, in a strange, deep voice, like the rumbling of faraway thunder.

"Looking for a piece of paper!" answered the little man, in a surly tone. "And all I can find is butterflies and foxes, a black cat, and ——"

"What! You've dared to open those boxes!" shouted the other angrily. He stamped down the stairs, and then saw the children.

"And who are *you?*" he asked, staring at them. "How dare you come here?"

"We wanted to buy this vase," said Peter, frightened.

"Well, seeing you are here, you can help Tippit to catch the fox," said the tall man, twisting his beard up into a knot and tying it under his chin. "Come on!"

"I don't want to," said Mollie. "He might bite me. Unlock the door and let us go out."

"Not till the fox and all the butterflies are caught and put into their boxes again," said the tall man.

"Oh dear!" said Peter, making no movement to get out of the chair, in which he and Mollie were still sitting with their legs drawn up. "I do wish we were safely at home!"

And then the most extraordinary thing of all

9

happened! The chair they were in began to creak and groan, and suddenly it rose up in the air, with the two children in it! They held tight, wondering whatever was happening! It flew to the door, but that was shut. It flew to the window, but that was shut too.

Meantime the wizard and Tippit were running after it, crying out in rage. "How dare you use our wishing-chair! Wish it back, wish it back!"

"I shan't!" cried Peter. "Go on, wishing-chair, take us home!"

The chair finding that it could not get out of the door or the window, flew up the little stairway. It nearly got stuck in the doorway at the top, which was rather narrow, but just managed to squeeze itself through. Before the children could see what the room upstairs was like, the chair flew to the window there, which was open, and out it went into the street. It immediately rose up very high indeed, far beyond the housetops, and flew towards the children's home. How amazed they were! And how tightly they clung to the arms! It would be dreadful to fall!

"I say, Mollie, can you hear a flapping noise?" said Peter. "Has the chair got wings anywhere?"

Mollie peeped cautiously over the edge of the chair. "Yes!" she said. "It has a little red wing growing out of each leg, and they make the flapping noise! How queer!"

The chair began to fly downwards. The children

saw that they were just over their garden. "Go to our playroom, chair," said Peter quickly. The chair went to a big shed at the bottom of the garden. Inside was a playroom for the children, and here they kept all their toys and books, and could play any game they liked. The chair flew in at the open door and came to rest on the floor. The children jumped off and looked at one another.

"The first real adventure we've ever had in our lives!" said Mollie, in delight. "Oh, Peter, to think we've got a magic chair—a wishing-chair!"

"Well, it isn't really ours," said Peter, putting the swan vase carefully down on the table. "Perhaps we had better send it back to that shop."

"I suppose we had," said Mollie sadly. "It would be so lovely if we could keep it!"

"Go back to your shop, chair," commanded Peter. The chair didn't move an inch! Peter spoke to it again; still the chair wouldn't move! There it was and there it stayed. And suddenly the children noticed that its little red wings had gone from the legs! It looked just an ordinary chair now!

"See, Mollie! The chair hasn't any wings!" cried Peter. "It can't fly. I expect it is only when it grows wings that it can fly. It must just have grown them when we were sitting in it in the shop. What luck for us!"

"Peter! Let's wait till the chair has grown wings again, and then get in it and see where it goes!" said Mollie, her face red with excitement. "Oh, do let's!"

"Well, it might take us anywhere!" said Peter doubtfully. "Still, we've always wanted adventures, Mollie, haven't we? So we'll try! The very next time our wishing-chair grows wings, we'll sit in it and fly off again!"

"Hurrah!" said Mollie. "I hope it will be to-morrow!"

II

THE GIANT'S CASTLE

Each day Mollie and Peter ran down to their playroom in the garden, and looked at their wishing-chair to see if it had grown wings again. But each time they were disappointed. It hadn't.

"It may grow them in the night," said Peter. "But we can't possibly keep coming here in the dark to see. We must just be patient."

Sometimes the children sat in the chair and wished themselves away, but nothing happened at all. It was really very disappointing.

And then one day the chair grew its wings again. It was a Saturday afternoon, too, which was very jolly, as the children were not at school. They ran down to the playroom and opened the door, and the very first thing they saw was that the chair had grown wings! They couldn't help seeing this, because the chair was flapping its wings about as if it was going to fly off!

"Quick! Quick!" shouted Peter, dragging Mollie to the chair. "Jump in. It's going to fly!"

They were just in time! The chair rose up in the air, flapping its wings strongly, and made for the door. Out it went and rose high into the air at once. The children clung on tightly in the greatest delight.

13

"Where do you suppose it is going?" asked Peter.

"Goodness knows!" said Mollie. "Let it take us wherever it wants to! It will be exciting, anyhow. If it goes back to that funny shop, we can easily jump off and run away when it goes in at the door."

But the chair didn't go to the old shop. Instead it kept on steadily towards the west, where the sun was beginning to sink. By and by a high mountain rose up below, and the children looked down at it in astonishment. On the top was an enormous castle.

"Where's this, I wonder?" said Peter. "Oh, I say, Mollie, the chair is going down to the castle!"

Down it went, flapping its rose-red wings. Soon it came to the castle roof, and instead of going lower and finding a door or a window, the chair found a nice flat piece of roof and settled down there with a sigh, as if it were quite tired out!

"Come on, Mollie! Let's explore!" said Peter excitedly. He jumped off the chair and ran to a flight of enormous steps that led down to the inside of the castle. He peeped down. No one was about.

"This is the biggest castle I ever saw," said Peter. "I wonder who lives here. Let's go and see!"

They went down the steps, and came to a big staircase leading from a landing. On every side

were massive doors, bolted on the outside.

"I hope there are no prisoners inside!" said Mollie, half afraid.

The stairs suddenly ended in a great hall. The children stood and looked in astonishment. Sitting at an enormous table was a giant as big as six men. His eyes were on a book, and he was trying to add up figures.

"Three times seven, three times seven, three times seven!" he muttered to himself. "I never can remember. Where's that miserable little pixie? If he doesn't know, I'll turn him into a black beetle!"

The giant lifted up his head and shouted so loudly that both children put their hands over their ears. "Chinky! Chinky!"

A pixie, not quite so big as the children, came running out of what looked like a scullery. He held an enormous boot in one hand, and a very small boot-brush in the other.

"Stop cleaning my boots and listen to me!" ordered the giant. "I can't do my sums again. I'm adding up all I spent last week and it won't come right. What are three times seven?"

"Three times seven?" said the pixie, with a frightened look on his little pointed face.

"That's what I said," thundered the bad-tempered giant.

"I know they are the same as seven times three," said the pixie.

"Well, I don't know what seven times three are either!" roared the giant. "*You* tell me! What's the good of having a servant who doesn't know his tables? Quick—what are three times seven?"

"I d—d—d—don't know!" stammered the poor pixie.

"Then I'll lock you into the top room of the castle till you *do* know!" cried the giant, in a rage. He picked up the pixie and went to the stairs. Then he saw the children standing there, and he stopped in astonishment.

"Who are you, and what are you doing here?" he asked.

16

"We've just come on a flying visit," said Peter boldly. "*We* know what three times seven are — and seven times three too. So, if you let that pixie go, we'll tell you."

"You tell me, then, you clever children!" cried the giant, delighted.

"They are twenty-one," said Peter.

The giant, still holding the pixie tightly in his hand, went across to the table and added up some figures.

"Yes — twenty-one," he said. "Now why didn't I think of that? Good!"

"Let the pixie go," begged Mollie.

"Oh no!" said the giant, with a wicked grin. "He shall be shut up in the top room of my castle, and *you* shall be my servants instead, and help me to add up my sums! Come along with me whilst I shut up Chinky."

He pushed the two angry children in front of him and made them go all the way up the stairs until they came to the topmost door. The giant unbolted it and pushed the weeping pixie inside. Then he bolted it again and locked it.

"Quick!" whispered Peter to Mollie. "Let's race up these steps to the roof and get on to our magic chair."

So, whilst the giant was locking the door, the two of them shot up the steps to the roof. The giant didn't try to stop them. He stood and roared with laughter.

17

"Well, I don't know how you expect to escape *that* way!" he said. "You'll have to come down the steps again, and I shall be waiting here to catch you. Then what a spanking you'll get!"

The children climbed out on to the flat piece of castle roof. There was their chair, standing just where they had left it, its red wings gleaming in the sun. They threw themselves into it, and Peter cried, "Go to the room where that little pixie Chinky is!"

The chair rose into the air, flew over the castle roof, and then down to a big window. It was open, and the chair squeezed itself inside. Chinky the pixie was there, sitting on the floor, weeping. When he saw the chair coming in, with the two children sitting in it, he was so astonished that he couldn't even get up off the floor!

"Quick!" cried Mollie. "Come into this chair, Chinky. We'll help you to escape!"

"Who's talking in there?" boomed the giant's enormous voice, and the children heard the bolts being undone and the key turned to unlock the door!

"Quick, quick, Chinky!" shouted Peter, and he dragged the amazed pixie to the magic chair. They all three sat in it, huddled together, and Peter shouted, "Take us home!"

The door flew open and the giant rushed in just as the chair sailed out of the window. He ran to the window and made a grab at the chair. His big

hand knocked against a leg, and the chair shook violently. Chinky nearly fell off, but Peter grabbed him and pulled him back safely. Then they sailed high up into the air, far out of reach of the angry giant!

"We've escaped!" shouted Peter. "What an adventure! Cheer up, Chinky! We'll take you home with us! You shall live with us, if you like. We have a fine playroom at the end of our garden. You can live there and no one will know. What fun we'll have with you and the wishing-chair!"

"You are very kind to me," said Chinky

gratefully. "I shall love to live with you. I can take you on many, many adventures!"

"Hurrah!" shouted the two children. "Look, Chinky, we're going down to our garden."

Soon they were safely in the garden, and the chair flew in at the open door of the playroom. Its wings disappeared, and it settled itself down with a long sigh, as if to say, "Home again!"

"You can make a nice bed of the cushions from the sofa," said Mollie to the pixie. "And I'll give you a rug from the hall-chest to cover yourself with. We must go now, because it is past our tea-time. We'll come and see you again to-morrow. Good luck!"

III

THE GRABBIT GNOMES

It was such fun to have a real live pixie to play with! Mollie and Peter went to their playroom every day and talked with Chinky, whom they had so cleverly rescued from the giant's castle. He refused to have anything to eat, because he said he knew the fairies in the garden, and they would bring him anything he needed.

"Chinky, will you do something for us?" asked Mollie. "You know we can't be with the magic chair always to watch when it grows wings, but if you could watch it for us, and come and tell us when you see it has wings, then we could rush to our playroom and go on another adventure. It would be lovely if you'd do that."

"Of course," said Chinky, who was a most obliging, merry little fellow. "I'll never take my eyes off the chair!"

Well, will you believe it, that very night, just as Chinky was going off to sleep, and the playroom was in darkness, he felt a strange little wind blowing from somewhere; it was the chair waving its wings about! Chinky was up in a trice, and ran out of the playroom to the house. He knew which the children's room was, and he climbed up the old pear tree and knocked on the window.

It wasn't long before Mollie and Peter, each in

warm dressing-gowns, were running down to the playroom. They lighted a candle and saw the chair's red wings once more.

"Come on!" cried Peter, jumping into the chair. "Where are we off to this time, I wonder?"

Mollie jumped in too, and Chinky squeezed himself beside them. The chair was indeed very full.

It flew out of the door and up into the air. The moon was up, and the world seemed almost as light as day. The chair flew to the south, and then went downwards into a strange little wood that shone blue and green.

"Hallo, hallo! we're going to visit the Grabbit Gnomes," said the pixie. "I don't like that! They grab everything they can, especially things that don't belong to them! We must be careful they don't grab our wishing-chair!"

The chair came to rest in a small clearing, near to some queer toadstool houses. The doors were in the great thick stalks, and the windows were in the top part. No one was about.

"Oh, do let's explore this strange village!" cried Mollie, in delight. "I do want to!"

"Well, hurry up, then," said Chinky nervously. "If the Grabbit Gnomes see us here, they will soon be trying to grab this, that, and the other."

The two children ran off to the toadstool houses and looked at them. They really were lovely. How Mollie wished she had one at home in the garden!

It would be so lovely to have one to live in.

"Whatever is Chinky doing?" said Peter, turning round to look.

"He's got a rope or something," said Mollie, in surprise. "Oh, don't let's bother about him, Peter. Do look here! There are six little toadstools all laid ready for breakfast! Fancy! They use them for tables as well as for houses!"

Suddenly there was a loud shout from a nearby toadstool house.

"Robbers! Burglars!"

Some one was leaning out of the window of a big toadstool house, pointing to the children. In a trice all the Grabbit Gnomes woke up, and came pouring out of their houses. "Robbers! What are you doing here? Robbers!"

"No, they're not," said Chinky, pushing his way through the crowd of excited gnomes. "They are only children adventuring here."

"How did you come?" asked a gnome at once.

"We came in our wishing-chair," said Mollie, and then she wished she hadn't answered. For the Grabbit Gnomes gave a yell of delight and rushed off to where their chair was standing in the moonlight.

"We've always wanted one, we've always wanted one!" they shouted. "Come on! Let's take it safely to our cave where we hide our treasures!"

"But it's ours!" cried Peter indignantly. "Besides, how shall we get back home if you take our chair?"

But the gnomes didn't pay any attention to him. They raced off to the chair, and soon there wasn't a tiny piece of the chair to be seen, for, to Peter's dismay, all the little gnomes piled themselves into it, and sat there — on the seat, the back, the arms, everywhere!

"Go to our treasure-cave!" they shouted. The chair flapped its red wings and rose up. The gnomes gave a yell of triumphant delight:

"We're off! Good-bye!"

"Oooh! Look!" said Mollie suddenly. "There's something hanging down from the chair. What is it?"

"It's a rope!" said Peter. "Oh, Chinky, you clever old thing! You've tied it to the leg of the

24

chair, and the other end is tied to that tree-trunk over there. The chair can't fly away!"

"No," said Chinky, with a grin. "It can't! I know those Grabbit Gnomes! I may not know what three times seven are, but I *do* know what robbers these gnomes are! Well, they won't find it easy to get away!"

The chair rose up high until the rope was so tightly stretched that it could go no farther. Then the chair came to a stop. There it hovered in the air, flapping its wings, but not moving one scrap. The gnomes shouted at it and yelled, but it was no good. It couldn't go any farther.

"Well, the gnomes are safe for a bit," said Chinky, grinning. "Now what about exploring this village properly, children?"

So the two spent half an hour peeping into the quaint toadstool houses; and Chinky gave them gnome-cake and gnome-lemonade, which were perfectly delicious.

All this time the gnomes were sitting up in the wishing-chair, high above the trees, shaking their fists at the children, and yelling all kinds of threats. They were certainly well caught, for they could go neither up nor down.

"Now, we'd better go home," said Chinky suddenly, pointing to the east. "Look!—it will soon be dawn. Now listen to me. I am going to pull that chair down to earth again with your help. We will pull it down quickly, and it will land on the ground with such a bump that all the gnomes will be thrown off. Whilst they are picking themselves up, we will jump into the chair, and off we'll go."

"Good idea!" grinned Peter. So he and Mollie and Chinky went to the rope and pulled hard, hand over hand. The chair came down from the air rapidly, and when it reached the ground it gave such a bump that every single gnome was thrown off.

"Oooooh!" they cried. "You wait, you wicked children!"

But they *didn't* wait. Instead, the three of them jumped into the chair, and Peter called out, "Take us home, please!"

Before the Grabbit Gnomes could take hold of the chair, it had risen up into the air. But the gnomes pulled at the rope, and down came the chair again.

"Quick! Cut the rope!" shouted Peter to Chinky. Poor Chinky! He was feeling in every one of his many pockets for his knife, and he couldn't find it. The gnomes pulled hard at the rope, and the chair went down still farther.

And then Chinky found the knife! He leaned over the chair-arm, slashed at the rope and cut it. At once the chair bounded up into the air, free!

"Home, home!" sang Peter, delighted. "I say! Talk about adventures! Every one seems more exciting then the last! Wherever shall we go next?"

IV

THE HO-HO WIZARD

One day when Peter and Mollie ran down to see Chinky the pixie in their playroom, they found him reading a letter and groaning loudly.

"What's the matter, Chinky?" said the children, in surprise.

"Oh, I've had a letter from my cousin, Gobo," said Chinky. "Gobo says that my village is very unhappy because a wizard has come to live there, called Ho-Ho. He is a horrid fellow, and walks about saying, 'Ho, ho!' all the time, catching the little pixies to help him in his magic, and putting all kinds of spells on any one that goes against him. I feel very unhappy."

"Oh, Chinky, we're so sorry!" said the children at once. "Can't we help?"

"I don't think so," said Chinky sadly. "But I would very much like to go off in the wishing-chair to my village, next time it grows wings, if you don't mind."

"Of course!" said the children. Then Mollie cried out in delight, and pointed to the magic chair. "Look! It's growing wings now! How lovely! It must have heard what we said."

"We'll all go," said Peter, feeling excited to think that yet another adventure had begun.

"Oh, no," said Chinky at once. "I'd better go

alone. This wizard is a horrid one. He might quite well catch you, as you are clever children, and then think how dreadful I would feel!"

"I don't care!" said Peter. "We're coming!"

He and Mollie went to the chair and sat firmly down in it. Chinky went to it and sat down too, squeezing in between the two. "You are such nice children!" he said happily.

The chair creaked, and before it could fly off, the pixie cried out loudly, "Go to the village of Apple-pie!"

It flew slowly out of the door, flapping its rose-red wings. The children were used to flying off in the magic chair now, but they were just as excited as ever. The village of Apple-pie! How magic it sounded!

It didn't take them very long to get there. The chair put them down in the middle of the village street, and was at once surrounded by an excited crowd of pixies, who shook hands with Chinky and asked him a hundred questions.

He talked at the top of his voice, explained who the children were, and why he had come. Then suddenly there was a great silence, and every one turned pale. The Ho-ho Wizard was coming down the street!

He was a little fellow, with a long flowing cloak that swirled out as he walked and showed its bright golden lining. On his head he wore a round tight cap set with silver bells that tinkled loudly.

He wore three pairs of glasses on his long nose, and a beard that hung in three pieces down to his waist. He really was a queer-looking fellow.

"Ho, ho!" he said, as he came near the pixies. "What have we here? Visitors? And, bless us all, this is a wishing-chair, as sure as dogs have tails! Well, well, well!"

Nobody said anything at all. The wizard prodded the chair with a long stick and then turned to the children.

"Ho, ho!" he said, blinking at them through his pairs of glasses. "Ho, ho! So you have a magic chair. Pray come to have a cup of cocoa with me

this morning, and I will buy your chair from you."

"But we don't want to sell it," began Peter at once. The wizard turned round on him, and from his eyes there came what looked like real sparks. He was very angry.

"How dare you refuse me anything!" he cried. "I will turn you into a——"

"We will come in half an hour," stammered Chinky, pushing Peter behind him. "This boy did not understand how important you are, Sir Wizard."

"Brrrrrrrr!" said the wizard, and stalked off, his cloak flying out behind him.

"*Now* what are we to do?" said Peter, in dismay. "Can't we get into the chair and fly off, Chinky. Do let's!"

"No, no, don't!" cried all the pixies at once. "If you do, Ho-ho will punish the whole village, and that will be terrible. Stay here and help us."

"Come to my cousin Gobo's cottage and let us think," said Chinky. So the two children went with him and Gobo, who was really very like Chinky, to a little crooked cottage at the end of the village. It was beautifully clean and neat, and the children sat down to eat coco-nut cakes and drink lemonade. Every one was rather quiet. Then Peter's eyes began to twinkle, and he leaned over to Gobo.

"I say, Gobo, have you by any chance got a spell to put people to sleep?" he asked.

"Of course!" said Gobo, puzzled. "Why?"

"Well, I have a fine plan," said Peter. "What about putting old Ho-ho to sleep?"

"What's the use of that?" said Chinky and Gobo.

"Well—when he's asleep, we'll pop him into the magic chair, take him off somewhere and leave him, and then go back home ourselves!" said Peter. "That would get rid of him for you, wouldn't it?"

"My goodness! That's an idea!" cried Chinky, jumping up from his seat in excitement. "Gobo! If only we could do it! Listen! Where's the sleepy-spell?"

"Here," said Gobo, opening a drawer and taking out a tiny yellow thing like a mustard seed.

"Well, Peter has a bag of chocolates," said Chinky, "and he could put the sleepy spell into one of them and give it to Ho-ho."

"But how do we know he'd take the right chocolate?" asked Mollie.

"We'll empty out all of them except one," answered Chinky, "and that one Peter shall carry in the bag in his hand, and he must carry it as though it was something very precious indeed, and Ho-ho is sure to ask him what it is, and if Peter says it is a very special chocolate that he is not going to part with, or something like that, the old wizard is sure to be greedy enough to take it from him and eat it. Then he will fall asleep,

31

and we'll take him off in the chair to old Dame Tap-Tap, who will be *so* pleased to have him! He once tried to turn her into a ladybird, so I don't think she will let him go in a hurry!"

"Good idea!" cried every one, and Gobo danced round the room so excitedly that he fell over the coal scuttle and sent the fire-irons clanking to the floor. That made them all laugh, and they felt so excited that they could hardly empty out Peter's bag of chocolates on the table and choose one for the sleepy spell.

They chose a chocolate with a violet on top because it looked so grand. Peter made a little hole in it and popped in the spell. Then he left the rest of the chocolates with Gobo, who said he would enjoy them very much, put the violet one into the bag, and went off to get the wishing-chair with the others.

It was still standing in the market-place, its red wings hanging down, for it was tired. Chinky and Peter thought they might as well carry it to Ho-ho's cottage, which was only in the next street; so off they went, taking it on their shoulders.

Ho-ho was waiting for them, his wily face watching from a window. He opened the door, and they all went in with the chair.

"I see you have brought me the chair," said Ho-ho. "Very sensible of you! Now sit down and have a cup of cocoa."

He poured out some very thin cocoa for them,

made without any milk, and looked at them all sharply. He at once saw that Peter was holding something very carefully in his hand, which he did not even put down when he was drinking his cocoa.

"What have you got in your hand?" he asked.

"Something I want to keep!" said Peter at once.

"Show me," said the wizard eagerly.

"No," said Peter.

"SHOW ME!" ordered the wizard angrily.

Peter pretended to be frightened, and at once put the paper bag on the table. The wizard took it and opened it. He took out the chocolate.

"Ho, ho! The finest chocolate I ever saw!" he said, and licked it to see what it tasted like.

"Don't eat it, oh, don't eat it!" cried Peter at once, pretending to be most upset. "It's mine!"

"Well, now it's *mine!*" said the wizard, and he popped it into his mouth and chewed it up. And no sooner had he swallowed it than his head began to nod, his eyes closed, and he snored like twenty pigs grunting!

"The spell has worked, the spell has worked!" cried Peter, jumping about in excitement.

"Now, Peter, there's no time to jump and yell," said Chinky hurriedly. "The spell may stop at any time, and we don't want to wake up the wizard till we've got him to Dame Tap-Tap's. Help me to put him into the chair."

Between them they dumped the sleeping wizard into the chair. Then Mollie sat on one arm, Peter sat on the other, and Chinky sat right on the top of the back. "To Dame Tap-Tap!" he cried. At once the wishing-chair flapped its idle wings, flew out of the door, and up into the air, cheered by all the pixies in the village. What a thrill that was!

In about five minutes the chair flew downwards again to a small cottage set right on the top of a windy hill. It was Dame Tap-Tap's home. The chair flew down to her front door, outside which there was a wooden bench. The three of them pulled the snoring wizard out of the chair and put him on the bench.

Then Chinky took hold of the knocker and banged it hard, four times. "RAT-TAT-TAT-TAT!"

He yelled at the top of his voice:

"Dame Tap-Tap! Here's a present for you!"

Then he and the children bundled into the wishing-chair again, and off they flew into the air, leaning over to see the old dame crying out in astonishment and delight when she opened the door and found the wizard Ho-ho sleeping outside!

"What a shock for him when he wakes up!" said Chinky, with a grin. "Well, children, many, many thanks for your help. You've saved Apple-pie village from a very nasty fellow. It will be nice to think of him dusting Dame Tap-Tap's kitchen, and getting water for her from the well! I guess she'll make him work hard!"

"Ho, ho!" roared the children, as the chair flew down to their playroom. "Perhaps the wizard won't say 'ho, ho' quite so much to Dame Tap-Tap!"

"No! He might get a spanking if he did," grinned Chinky. "Well, here we are! See you to-morrow, children!"

V

POOR LOST CHINKY

Once a dreadful thing happened when the children were adventuring on the wishing-chair. It had grown its wings most conveniently when all three were in the playroom, so they jumped on, and were soon flying high in the air.

As they were flying they heard a loud droning noise, and looked round.

"It's an aeroplane!" shouted Peter.

"I say! It's very near us!" cried Mollie.

So it was. It didn't seem to see them at all. It flew straight at them, and the edge of one widespread wing just touched their flying chair, giving it a tremendous jerk.

Mollie and Peter were sitting tightly in the seat — but Chinky was on the back, and he was jolted right off the chair.

Mollie clutched at him as he fell — but she only just touched him. The two children watched in the greatest dismay as he fell down — and down — and down.

"Oh, Peter!" cried Mollie, in despair, "poor, poor Chinky! Whatever will happen to him!"

The aeroplane flew on steadily, never guessing that it had touched a wishing-chair. Peter turned pale and looked at Mollie.

"We must make the chair go down and see if

36

Chinky is hurt," he said. "Oh dear! What a dreadful thing to happen! Chair, fly down to earth!"

The chair flapped its red wings and flew slowly down to the ground. It stood there, and the children jumped off. They were in open country with wide fields all around them. There was no sign of Chinky at all.

They heard the sound of some one chanting a song, and saw coming towards them, a round, fat little man carrying a bundle on his head.

"Hi!" called Peter. "Have you seen a little pixie falling out of the sky?"

"Is that a riddle?" said the round little man, grinning stupidly. "I can ask *you* one too! Have you seen a horse that quacks like a duck?"

"Don't be silly," said Mollie. "This is serious. Our friend has fallen out of the sky."

"Well, tell him not to do it again," said the little round man. "All that fell out of the sky to-day was a large snowflake! *Good*-morning!"

He went on his way, his bundle bobbing on his head. The children were very angry.

"Making a joke about a serious thing like poor Chinky falling out of the sky!" said Mollie, with tears in her eyes. "Horrid fellow."

"Here's some one else," said Peter. "Hi! Stop a minute!"

The some one was another round, fat person, also carrying a bundle on her head and singing a little song. She stopped when she saw the children.

"Have you seen a pixie falling out of the sky?" asked Peter.

"No. Have you?" said the round little woman, grinning.

"Of course!" said Mollie impatiently.

"Fibber!" said the round woman. "A big snow-flake fell out of the sky, but nothing else."

"They've got snowflakes on the brain!" said Peter, as the woman went on her way, singing. "Come on, Mollie. We'd better go and look for Chinky ourselves. We know that it was some-where near here that he fell. We'll carry the chair between us so that we may have it safely. I don't trust these stupid people."

They carried the chair along and came to a market-place. It was full of the same round, fat people, all humming and singing. A town-crier was going round the market, ringing a bell, and crying "Oyez! Oyez! Dame Apple-pie has lost her spectacles! Oyez! Oyez!"

Then Peter had a splendid idea. "I say, Mollie! Let's tell the town-crier to shout out about Chinky. We'll offer a reward to any one that can tell us about him. *Some* one must have seen him fall."

So, before very long the town-crier was ringing his bell and crying loudly, "Oyez! Oyez! A reward is offered to any one having news of a pixie who fell from the sky! Oyez!"

Mollie and Peter stood on a platform so that

people might know to whom to go if they had news. To their delight there came quite a crowd of people to them.

"We've news, we've news!" they cried, struggling to get to Peter first.

"Well, where did you see the pixie fall?" asked Peter of the first little man.

"Sir, I saw a big snowflake fall in the Buttercup Field," said he.

"Don't be foolish," said Peter. "I said a *pixie*, not a snowflake. Don't you know the difference between pixies and snowflakes? We all know that snowflakes fall from the sky. That is not news. Next, please!"

But the next person said the same thing—and the next—and the next! It was most annoying and very disappointing.

"We want our reward!" suddenly shouted some one. "We have given you news, but you have given us no reward."

"You haven't given us the right news!" shouted back Peter angrily.

"That doesn't matter!" shouted the little folk, looking angry. They looked rather funny too, because for some reason or other they all carried their bundles and baskets balanced on their heads. "Give us our reward!"

They swarmed towards the platform on which the two children were standing, and Mollie and Peter suddenly felt frightened.

"I don't like this, Mollie," said Peter. "Let's go! These stupid creatures think that pixies and snowflakes are exactly the same—and we certainly can't give them *all* a reward. Climb into the chair!"

40

Mollie jumped into the chair, which was just near them on the platform. Peter sat on the arm and cried out loudly, "Home, chair, quickly!"

The chair flapped its wings and rose up—but it didn't rise very high, only just above the heads of the angry people. Its legs began to jerk in and out, and to Peter's enormous astonishment, the chair kicked off bundles, pots, and baskets from the heads of the furious marketers! Peter began to laugh, for, really, it was most comical to see the chair playing such a trick—but Mollie was in tears.

"What's the matter?" asked Peter, drying her tears with his handkerchief.

"It's Chinky," sobbed Mollie. "I did love him

so. Now I feel we shall never see him again."

Peter's eyes filled with tears too. "He was such a good friend," he said. "Oh, Mollie! It would be so dreadful if we never saw him again."

They flew home in silence. The chair flew in at the playroom door and the children jumped off.

"It will never be so nice going on adventures again," said Mollie.

"Why ever not?" said a merry little voice – and the children turned round in joy – for there was Chinky, the pixie, sitting on the floor, reading a book!

"Chinky! We thought you were lost for ever when you fell from the chair!" cried Mollie, hugging him hard.

"Don't break me in half!" said Chinky. "I wasn't hurt at all! I just changed myself into a big snow-flake and fell into the Buttercup Field. Then I caught the next bus back to the bottom of the garden, and here I am. I've been waiting simply ages for you!"

"A snowflake!" cried Peter. "So that's why everyone talked about snowflakes! *Now* I understand!"

He told Chinky all about their adventures – and *how* the pixie laughed when he heard about the chair kicking the bundles off the heads of the angry people!

"I wish I'd been there!" he said. "Come on, now – what about a game of ludo?"

VI

THE LAND OF DREAMS

"Mollie! Peter! Come quickly! The chair is growing its wings again!" whispered Chinky, peeping in at the dining-room window. The children were busy drawing and painting, but they at once put away their things and scampered down the garden to their playroom.

"Goody!" cried Peter, as he saw the red wings of the chair slowly flapping to and fro. "Come on, every one. Where shall we go to this time?"

"We'll let the chair take us where it wants to," said Chinky, sitting on the top of the back as usual. "Off we go — and mind you don't get worried if I fall off, Mollie!"

"Oh, I shan't worry any more!" laughed Mollie. "You can look after yourself all right, Chinky!"

Off they went into the air.

"Where's the chair going, Chinky?" asked Mollie, presently.

"I think it's going to the Land of Dreams," said Chinky. "Oh! I don't know that I like that! Strange things happen there! Perhaps we'd better not go!"

"Oh, do let's!" said Peter. "*We'll* be all right!"

Down to the Land of Dreams flew the chair and came to rest outside a small sweet shop. Peter felt in his pocket and found a penny there. "I'll buy

43

some toffee!" he cried. He went into the shop, and saw a large old sheep sitting there, knitting. He stared at her in surprise and then asked for a pennyworth of toffee. She gave him some in a bag and he ran out. He opened the bag and offered the toffee to the others.

But when they tried to take some they found that the bag was full of green peas! How extraordinary!

"I told you strange things happened here," said Chinky. "Come on. Let's carry the chair in case it runs away or something!" He turned to pick it up, and gave a shout!

It had turned into a little dog, and its red wings were now red ribbons round the dog's neck!

"I say! Look at that! What are we going to do now?" said Chinky in dismay. They all stared at the dog, which wagged its tail hard.

Suddenly there came an angry shout behind them.

"Spot! Spot! Come here, sir!"

The children turned and saw a clown running down the road, calling to the dog.

"Quick! We must run off with the dog before the clown gets it," said Chinky. "It may change back into a chair again at any moment, and we can't let any one else have it."

He caught up the surprised dog, and the three of them raced down the street at top speed.

"Stop thief, stop thief!" shouted the clown, and

ran after them. He caught them up and took hold of Chinky. To the children's amazement the clown then turned into a large fat policeman!

"I arrest you for stealing a dog!" said the policeman solemnly. Chinky stared at him in despair. But Mollie cried out loudly: "What do you mean, policeman? We haven't any dog!"

And sure enough the dog had changed into a yellow duck! There it was, under Chinky's arm, quacking away for all it was worth! The policeman stared at it, looked very blue, and in a trice had changed into a blue motor-van that trundled itself down the street!

"I don't like this land," said Mollie. "Things are never the same two minutes running!"

"Nor are they in dreams!" said Chinky. "You can't expect anything else here. *I* didn't want to come, you know. I say, won't one of you carry this duck? It's awfully heavy."

He handed it to Peter, a great yellow bird—but even as Peter took it, something strange happened! The bird's beak, legs, and tail disappeared, and all that was left was a great pile of yellow stuff that slithered about in Peter's hands!

"Ow!" he cried, "it's cold! It's ice-cream! I can't hold it!"

"You must, you must!" shouted Chinky, and he and Mollie did their best to hold the slippery mass together. But it was no good—it slithered to the ground and began to melt!

"There goes our chair!" said Chinky sorrowfully. "It looks as if we are here for ever now! First it turned into a dog, then into a duck, and now into ice-cream! This is a horrid adventure!"

They left the melting ice-cream and went on down the street. Peter took out his bag of green peas and looked at them again. They had turned into tiny balloons, ready to be blown up. He gave one to Chinky and one to Mollie. They began to blow them up—but, oh dear, dear, dear! instead of blowing up the balloons, they blew themselves up! Yes, they really did! Peter stared in dismay, but he couldn't stop them! There they were,

Mollie and Chinky, two big balloons swaying about in the air—and they even had strings tied to them! Peter was afraid they might blow away, so he took hold of the strings.

He wandered down the street alone, very puzzled and unhappy. Nothing seemed real. The Land of Dreams was very peculiar indeed! The two enormous balloons floated along behind him, and when he turned to look at them what a shock he had!

They were not in the least like Chinky and Mollie any more! One was green and one was blue —and even as Peter stared at them, the air began to escape from each balloon! They rapidly grew smaller – and smaller – and smaller – and soon they were just tiny lumps of coloured rubber, hanging from the string. Peter looked at them sadly.

"All that's left of Mollie and Chinky!" he thought unhappily. "No wishing-chair either! Only me! Oh dear, oh dear! Whatever will be the end of this strange adventure?"

He put the balloons into his pocket, and went on. He came to a large hall, where a concert seemed to be going on. He slipped inside and sat down on a chair. He suddenly felt very tired indeed. He shut his eyes and yawned.

The chair began to rock softly. Peter opened his eyes, and saw that it had changed into a rocking-horse! But things no longer astonished him in the Land of Dreams. It would be surprising if peculiar things *didn't* happen, not if they did!

Soon he was fast asleep on the rocking-horse. It rose up into the air and flew out of the door. Peter slept on. He didn't wake up until hours afterwards, and when at last he opened his eyes, what a surprise!

He was in the playroom at home, lying on the rug by the window! He sat up at once, and remembered everything. Sorrowfully he put his hands into his pockets and pulled out the two air balloons.

"Mollie and Chinky!" said Peter sadly.

"Yes! Do you want us?" said Mollie's voice, and to his astonishment and delight he saw both Mollie and Chinky sitting in the wishing-chair nearby, both yawning, just waking up from a sleep.

"Oh!" he said, "I must have dreamt it all then! Listen, you two! I had such a funny dream! I went to the Land of Dreams and—"

"Yes, yes, yes!" said Chinky impatiently. "We've all been there. It was a real adventure. I don't want to go there again. Ooooh! It was a horrid feeling turning into a balloon! It was a good thing you put us into your pocket, Peter!"

"Was it a *real* adventure then?" cried Peter, in amazement.

"As real as adventures ever are in the Land of Dreams," said Chinky. "Now, what about some *real* toffee—that won't turn into green peas or balloons? Get some treacle from your cook, Mollie, and we'll make some. We deserve a treat after that horrid adventure!"

VII

THE RUNAWAY CHAIR

One morning, when the two children went down to their playroom to have a game with Chinky the pixie, they found him fast asleep.

"Wake up!" cried Peter, rolling him over. But Chinky didn't wake up! He was breathing very deeply, and had quite nice, red cheeks—but he simply would *not* wake up!

"What's the matter with him?" said Mollie, puzzled.

"Oh, he's just pretending," said Peter. "I'll get a wet sponge! He'll soon wake then!"

But even the sponge didn't wake him up.

"There must be a spell on him or something," said Mollie, rather frightened. "What shall we do, Peter? If only we knew where to get help. But we mustn't tell any one about Chinky—he'd be so cross when he woke up. And we don't know how to find any fairies, or we could ask *them* for help!"

Suddenly the wishing-chair gave a creak, and Mollie looked round. "It's growing its wings!" she cried. "Don't let it fly away, Peter! We don't want an adventure without Chinky!"

Peter ran to the chair—but it dodged him and flew straight out of the door, its wings flapping swiftly. Peter stared after it in dismay.

"Oh, Peter!" said Mollie. "Isn't this dreadful! Here's Chinky under a spell, or something—and now the chair's run away! What an unlucky day!"

"Well, it's gone," said Peter gloomily. "Now what *are* we going to do about Chinky, Mollie?"

Just then there came the sound of a cautious tiptoe noise. Peter turned—just in time to see an ugly goblin slipping out of the door! "I put him under the sleepy spell!" shouted the goblin. "I meant to steal the chair before he woke up—but *you* came! Now I'm going to find the chair! If you don't find the way to wake up that pixie before twelve o'clock to-night, he will vanish altogether! Ho, ho!"

"Horrid thing!" said Mollie, as the goblin disappeared into the garden. "I suppose he will go after our chair and have it for himself—and here he's left Chinky in a magic sleep and we don't know how to wake him! If only, only, only we knew how to find a fairy who might help us!"

"I'll go and call for one in the garden," said Peter. So he went out and called softly here and there. "Fairies! If you are there, come and help me!"

But he had no answer at all, and he went sadly back to the playroom where Mollie sat by the sleeping pixie.

"No good," said Peter. "I didn't see a single fairy. I really don't know what we are to do!"

"If only we had the chair we could go off in it

and find a fairy somewhere to help us," said Mollie. "But even that's gone and left us—run away on the very day we needed its help!"

They went back to the house for dinner and for tea, and Mother exclaimed at their long faces. They very nearly told her about Chinky, but didn't like to, for they had solemnly promised the pixie never to mention his name to the grown-ups.

When it was their bed-time, Chinky was still asleep!

"Fancy! He hasn't had anything to eat all day!" said Mollie. "Oh, Peter, do you really think he will disappear at midnight, if we can't wake him up?"

"We *must* wake him!" said Peter. So he got two drums and two trumpets, and he and Mollie made as much noise as ever they could until Jane, the housemaid, was sent down the garden to stop them. But Chinky didn't even stir in his sleep!

Then they poured cold water down his neck— but that only made him wet, and didn't make him flicker so much as an eyelash! Then they found a hen's feather, set it alight, and let it smoulder just under the pixie's nose—but the strong smell did not even make him turn away. He slept on peacefully.

A bell rang in the distance.

"Oh dear! There's our bedtime bell!" said Mollie, in dismay. "Peter, I'm coming back to the playroom to-night, somehow. There surely must

be something we can do!"

"We've tried everything!" said Peter, and looked very miserable. They went off to bed, first covering up Chinky warmly. In an hour's time they were back again, in their dressing-gowns! They had slipped out of bed, run out of the garden door, and gone to the playroom without being seen!

Chinky was still fast asleep. Mollie looked at the clock. "Half-past eight!" she said. "Oh dear!"

They tried to think of more ways to waken up the sleeping pixie, and Mollie squeezed a sponge over his head with icy-cold water, and then with hot water—but neither had any effect at all. The hands of the clock stole round and round—and at last it was only ten minutes to midnight. The children were quite in despair.

Suddenly there came a curious sound of knocking at the door. It sounded more like kicking. Peter ran to it. Outside was their wishing-chair, wet through, for it was raining! It had found the door shut and had kicked at it with one of its front legs. Sitting in it was a jolly-faced gnome with a silvery beard and enormous nose, two pairs of spectacles, and a large umbrella to keep off the rain.

"Who are you?" said Peter, in surprise.

"Oh, don't bother him with questions!" said Mollie anxiously. "He's a fairy of some sort. Perhaps he has come to make Chinky better."

"Yes," said the gnome, putting on a third pair of spectacles. "This chair knew where I lived, and flew one hundred and thirty-three miles to fetch me! I am only just in time."

"There are only seven minutes till midnight," said Mollie. "Do be quick!"

The little gnome doctor rolled up his sleeves, took a towel and a piece of soap from the air, and with them washed Chinky's face very carefully. Then he brushed the sleeping pixie's eyes with a peacock's feather that he also took most conveniently from the air, and smeared them with a peculiar-smelling yellow ointment.

"Do hurry!" said Mollie. "It's almost midnight. The clock's going to strike!"

"It's one minute fast," said the doctor. He took a black ball from the air, opened it, put a blue

54

powder inside it, struck a match, and put it to the black ball. At once there was a loud explosion and the playroom rocked and shook. Smoke covered the room. It had a very pleasant smell. When it cleared, the two children saw, to their delight, that Chinky was sitting up, looking most astonished.

"Who made that horrible noise?" he said crossly. "Hallo, doctor! What are *you* doing here?"

"Just going, so good-bye!" grinned the little gnome. "See you some day!"

He jumped into the wishing-chair, which at once flew off with him again. Chinky ran his finger round his collar and frowned.

"Who's been wetting me?" he asked.

"Oh, Chinky, don't be cross!" begged Mollie. "We've been quite anxious about you. A goblin put you under a sleepy spell — and the clever wishing-chair went to fetch that gnome doctor you saw — only just in time, too!"

"So *that's* it, is it!" said Chinky. "No wonder I feel so hungry. I've been asleep all day, I suppose. Can you find me anything to eat?"

"There are some buns and apples in the cupboard," said Peter, delighted to see Chinky awake again. "We'll have a fine feast!"

So they did — and they didn't go back to bed till the cock crew! No wonder they slept late the next morning. Chinky didn't, though! He was up bright and early. He had quite enough of sleeping!

VIII

THE LOST CAT

One morning it was very wet, and Mollie, Peter, and Chinky were playing a very noisy game of snap in the playroom together. Whiskers, the cat, had come with them and had curled herself up on a cushion in the wishing-chair, where she had gone fast asleep.

"Snap! Snap! SNAP!" yelled the children — and were so interested in their game that they didn't hear a little flapping sound. The wishing-chair had grown its wings and was flapping them gently to and fro. Before any one noticed the chair rose silently into the air and flew out of the open door — taking the puss-cat with it, still fast asleep!

"Snap!" yelled Chinky, and took the last pile of cards in glee. "I've won!"

"Good," said Peter. He looked round the play-room to see what game to play next — and then he looked rather surprised and scared.

"I say!" he said. "Where's the chair gone?"

Chinky and Mollie looked round too. Mollie went pale.

"It's gone!" she said.

"It was here when we began our game," said Chinky. "It must have slipped out without us noticing. I sort of remember feeling a little draught. It must have been its wings flapping."

56

"Whiskers has gone too!" said Mollie, in alarm. "She was asleep on the cushion. Oh, Chinky—will she come back?"

"Depends where she has gone to," said Chinky. "She's a black cat, you know—and if a witch should see her she might take her to help in her spells. Black cats are clever with spells."

Mollie began to cry. She was very fond of Whiskers. "Oh, why did we let Whiskers go to sleep on that chair?" she wept.

"Well, it's no good crying," said Chinky, patting Mollie's shoulder. "We must just wait and see. Perhaps old Whiskers will come back still fast asleep when the chair returns!"

They waited for an hour or two with the door wide open—but no wishing-chair came back. The two children left Chinky and went to their dinner. They hunted about the house just in case Whiskers should have got off the chair cushion and wandered home—but no one had seen her.

After dinner they ran down the garden to their playroom again. Chinky was there, looking gloomy.

"The chair hasn't come back," he said.

But, just as he spoke, Peter gave a shout and pointed up into the sky. There was the chair, flapping its way back, all its red wings twinkling up and down.

"Look! There's the chair! Oh, I do hope Whiskers is on her cushion. Suppose she has fallen out!"

The chair flapped its way downwards, and flew in at the open door. It came to rest in its usual place and gave a sigh and a creak. The children rushed to it.

There was no cat there! The cushion was still in its place, with a dent in the middle where Whiskers had lain – but that was all!

The three stared at one another in dismay.

"Whiskers has been caught by a witch," said Chinky. "There's no doubt about it. Look at this!"

He picked up a tiny silver star that lay on the seat of the chair. "This little star has fallen off a witch's embroidered cloak."

"Poor Whiskers!" wept Mollie. "I do want her back. Oh, Chinky, what shall we do?"

"Well, we'd better find out first where she's gone," said Chinky. "Then, the next time the chair grows its wings we'll go and rescue her."

"How can we find out where she's gone?" asked Mollie, drying her eyes.

"I'll have to work a spell to find that out," said Chinky. "I'll have to get a few pixies in to help me. Go and sit down on the couch, Mollie and Peter, and don't speak a word until I've finished. The pixies won't help me if you interfere. They are very shy just about here."

Mollie and Peter did as they were told. They sat down on the couch feeling rather excited. Chinky went to the open door and clapped his hands softly three times, then loudly seven times. He

whistled like a blackbird, and then called a magic word that sounded like "Looma, looma, looma, loo."

In a minute or two four little pixies, a bit smaller than Chinky, who was himself a pixie, came running in at the door. They stopped when they saw the two children, but Chinky said they were his friends.

"They won't interfere," he said. "I want to do a spell to find out where this wishing-chair has just been to. Will you help me?"

The pixies twittered like swallows and nodded their heads. Chinky sat down in the wishing-chair, holding in his hands a mirror that he had borrowed from Mollie. The four little pixies joined hands and danced round the chair, first one way and then another, chanting a magic song that got higher and higher and quicker and quicker as they danced round in time to their singing.

Chinky looked intently into the mirror, and the children watched, wondering what he would see there.

Suddenly the four dancing pixies stopped their singing and fell to the floor, panting and crying, "Now look and tell what you see, Chinky!"

Chinky stared into the mirror and then gave a shout.

"I see her! It's the witch Kirri-Kirri! *She* has got Whiskers. Here she is, cooking her dinner for her!"

The two children sprang up from the couch and hurried to look into the mirror that Chinky held. To their great amazement, instead of seeing their own faces, they saw a picture of Whiskers, their cat, stirring a soup-pot on a big stove – and behind her was an old witch, clad in a long, black cloak embroidered with silver stars and moons!

"See her!" said Chinky, pointing. "That's the

witch Kirri-Kirri. I know where she lives. We'll go and rescue Whiskers this very night — even if we have to go on foot!"

The four little pixies twittered good-bye and ran out. The picture in the mirror faded away. The children and the pixie looked at one another.

"What a marvellous spell!" said Mollie. "Oh, I did enjoy that, Chinky! Shall we really go and fetch Whiskers to-night?"

"Yes," said Chinky. "Come here at midnight, ready dressed. If the chair has grown its wings, we'll go in it — if not, we'll take the underground train to the witch's house."

"Ooh!" said Mollie. "What an adventure!"

IX

THE WITCH KIRRI-KIRRI

The children dressed themselves again after they had been to bed and slept. Mollie had a little alarm-clock and she set it for a quarter to twelve, so they awoke in good time for their adventure. Chinky was waiting for them.

"We can't go in the wishing-chair," he said. "It hasn't grown its wings again. I think it's asleep, because it gave a tiny snore just now!"

"How funny!" said Mollie. "Oh, Chinky—I do feel excited!"

"Come on," said the pixie. "There's no time to lose if we want to catch the underground train."

He led the children to a big tree at the bottom of the garden. He twisted a piece of the bark and a door slid open. There was a narrow stairway in the tree going downwards. Mollie and Peter were so surprised to see it.

"Go down the stairs," Chinky said to them. "I'll just shut the door behind us."

They climbed down and came to a small passage. Chinky joined them and they went along it until they came to a big turnstile, where a solemn grey rabbit sat holding a bundle of tickets.

"We want tickets for Witch Kirri-Kirri's," said Chinky. The rabbit gave them three yellow tickets and let them through the turnstile. There was a little platform beyond with a railway line running by it. Almost at once a train appeared out of the darkness. Its lamps gleamed like two eyes. There were no carriages — just open trucks with cushions in. The train was very crowded, and the children and Chinky found it difficult to get seats.

Gnomes, brownies, rabbits, moles, elves, and hedgehogs sat in the trucks, chattering and laughing. The two hedgehogs had a truck to themselves for they were so prickly that no one wanted to sit by them.

The train set off with much clattering. It stopped at station after station, and at last came to one labelled "Kirri-Kirri Station."

Chinky and the children got out.

"Kirri-Kirri is such a rich and powerful witch that she has a station of her own," explained Chinky. "Now listen — this is my plan, children. It's no use us asking the witch for Whiskers, our cat — she just won't let us have her. And it's no use trying to get her by magic, because the witch's magic is much stronger than mine. We must get her by a trick."

"What trick?" asked the children.

"We'll creep into her little garden," said Chinky, "and we'll make scrapey noises on the wall, like mice. We'll squeak like mice too — and the witch will hear us and send Whiskers out to catch the mice. Then we'll get her, run back to the station, and catch the next train home!"

"What a fine plan!" said Peter. "It's so simple too! It can't go wrong!"

"Sh!" said Chinky, pointing to a large house in the distance. "That's Kirri-Kirri's house."

They had left the station behind and had come up into the open air again. The moonlight was bright enough to show them the road, and they could see everything very clearly indeed.

They slipped inside the witch's wicket-gate. "You go to that end of the house and I'll go to the other," said Chinky. So Peter and Mollie crept to one end and began to scratch against the wall with bits of stick, whilst Chinky did the same the other end. Then they squeaked as high as they could, exactly like mice.

They heard a window being thrown up, and saw the witch's head outlined against the lamp-light.

"Mice again!" she grumbled. "Hie, Whiskers, come here! Catch them, catch them!"

Whiskers jumped down into the garden. The witch slammed down the window and drew the blind. Mollie made a dash for the big black cat and lifted her into her arms. Whiskers purred nine-teen to the dozen and rubbed her soft head against Mollie's hand. Chinky and Peter came up in delight.

"The plan worked beautifully!" said Peter. "Come on — let's go to the station!"

And then a most unfortunate thing happened!

Peter fell over a bush and came down with a loud clatter on the path! At once the window flew up again and Kirri-Kirri looked out. She shouted a very magic word and slammed the window down again.

"Oh dear, oh dear, oh dear!" groaned Chinky at once.

"What's the matter?" asked Mollie, scared.

"She's put a spell round the garden!" said the pixie. "We can't get out! She'll find us here in the morning!"

"Can't get out!" said Peter, going to the gate. "What nonsense! *I'm* going, anyway!"

But although he opened the gate he couldn't walk out. It was as if there was an invisible wall all round the garden! The children couldn't get out anywhere. They forced their way through the hedge—but still the invisible wall seemed to be just beyond, and there was no way of getting out at all!

"Whatever shall we do?" asked Mollie.

"We can't do anything," said Chinky gloomily. "Peter was an awful silly to go and fall over like that, just when we had done everything so well."

"I'm terribly sorry," said poor Peter. "I do wish I hadn't. I didn't mean to."

"Well, we'd better go and sit down in the porch," said Chinky, who was shivering. "It's warmer there."

They sat huddled together in the porch and Mollie took Whiskers on her knee, saying she would make a nice hot-water bottle.

They were nodding off to sleep, for they were all very tired, when Whiskers suddenly began to snarl and spit. The children and Chinky woke up in a fright. They saw something flying round the garden, like a big black bird! Mollie stared—and then she leapt up and whispered as loudly as she dared—"It isn't a bird! It's the dear old wishing-chair! It's come to find us!"

Chinky gave a chuckle of delight. He ran to the chair and took hold of it.

"Come on!" he said to the others. "The only way out of this bewitched garden is by flying up and up. We can't get out any other way! The wishing-chair is just what we want!"

They all got into the chair. Whiskers was on Mollie's knee. The chair flapped its wings, rose up into the air and flew almost to the clouds!

"What will old Kirri-Kirri say in the morning when she finds *no* one in her garden, not even Whiskers!" giggled Chinky. "She'll think she's been dreaming! I wish I could see her face!"

The chair flew to the playroom. The children said good-night to Chinky, and, with Whiskers in her arms, Mollie ran with Peter up the path to their house. They were soon in bed and asleep. As for Whiskers, you may be sure she never went to sleep in the wishing-chair again!

X

THE DISAPPEARING ISLAND

It happened once that the children and Chinky had a most unpleasant adventure, and it was all Mollie's fault.

The wishing-chair grew its wings one bright sunny morning just as the three of them were planning a game of pirates. Mollie saw the red wings growing from the legs of the chair and cried out in delight.

"Look! The chair's off again! Let's get in and have an adventure!"

They all crowded into it, and in a trice the chair was off through the door and into the air. It was such fun, for the day was clear and sunny, and the children could see for miles.

The chair flew on and on, and came to the towers and spires of Fairyland. They glittered in the sun and Peter wanted to go down and visit the Prince and Princess they had once rescued. But the chair still flew on. It flew over the Land of Gnomes, and over the Land of Toadstools, and at last came to a bright blue sea.

"Hallo, hallo!" said Chinky, peering over the edge of the chair. "I've never been as far as this before. I don't know if we ought to fly over the sea. The chair might get tired—and then what would happen to us if we all came down in the sea!"

"We shan't do that!" said Mollie, pointing to a blue island far away on the horizon. "I think the chair is making for that land over there."

The chair flew steadily towards it, and the children saw that the land they had seen in the distance was a small and beautiful island. It was packed with flowers, and the sound of bells came faintly up from the fields and hills.

"We mustn't go there," said Chinky suddenly. "That's Disappearing Island!"

"Well, why shouldn't we go there?" said Mollie.

"Because it suddenly disappears," said Chinky. "I've heard of it before. It's a horrid place. You get there and think it's all as beautiful as can be — and then it suddenly disappears and takes you with it."

"It can't be horrid," said Mollie longingly, looking down at the sunny, flower-spread island. "Oh, Chinky, you must be mistaken. It's the most beautiful island I ever saw! I do want to go. There are some lovely birds there too. I can hear them singing."

"I tell you, Mollie, it's dangerous to go to Disappearing Island," said Chinky crossly. "You might believe me."

"You're not always right!" said Mollie obstinately. "I *want* to go there! Wishing-chair, fly down to that lovely island."

At once the chair began to fly downwards. Chinky glared at Mollie, but the words were said.

69

He couldn't unsay them. Down they flew and down and down and down!

The brilliant island came nearer and nearer. Mollie shouted in delight to see such glorious bright flowers, such shiny-winged birds, such plump, soft rabbits. The chair flew swiftly towards them.

And then, just as they were about to land in a field spread with buttercups as large as poppies, among soft-eyed bunnies and singing birds, a most strange and peculiar thing happened.

The island disappeared! One moment it was there, and the sun was shining on its fields—and the next moment there was only a faint blue mist! The chair flew through the mist—and then SPLASH! They were all in the sea!

Mollie and Peter were flung off the chair into the water. Chinky grabbed the back of the chair, and reached his hand out to the children. They clambered back on to the chair, which was bobbing about on the waves, soaking wet.

"What did I tell you?" said Chinky angrily. "Didn't I say it was Disappearing Island? Now see what's happened! It's gone and disappeared, and we've fallen into the sea! A nice pickle we are in—all wet and shivery! Just like a girl to get us into this mess!"

Mollie went red. How she wished she hadn't wanted to go to Disappearing Island!

"Well, I didn't know it was going to disappear

so suddenly," she said. "I'm very sorry."

"Not much good being sorry," said Peter gloomily, squeezing the water out of his clothes. "How are we going to get to land? As far as I can see there is water all round us for miles! The chair's wings are wet, and it can't fly."

The three of them were indeed in a dreadful fix! It was fortunate for them that the chair was made of wood, or they would not have had anything to cling to!

They bobbed up and down for some time, wondering what to do. Suddenly, to their great surprise, a little head popped out of the sea.

"Hallo!" it said. "Are you wanting help?"
"Yes," said Chinky. "Are you a merman?"
"I am!" said the little fellow. The children looked down at him, and through the green water they could see his fish-like body covered with scales from the waist downwards and ending in a silvery tail. "Do you want to be towed to land?"

"Yes, please," said Chinky joyfully.

"That will cost you a piece of gold," said the merman.

"I haven't any with me, but we will send it to you as soon as we get home," promised Chinky. The merman swam off and came back riding on a big fish. He threw a rope of seaweed around the back of the chair and shouted to Chinky to hold on to it. Then the fish set off at a great speed, towing the chair behind it with Chinky and the children safely on it! The merman rode on the fish all the way, singing a funny little watery song. It was a strange ride!

Soon they came to land, and the children dragged the chair out of the water on to the sun-baked sand. "Thank you," they said to the merman. "We will send you the money as soon as we can."

The merman jumped on the fish again, waved his wet hand, and dived into the waves with a splash.

"We'll wait till the sun has dried the chair's wings, and we'll dry our own clothes," said Chinky. "Then we'll go home. I think that was a most unpleasant adventure. We might have been bobbing about for days on the sea!"

Mollie didn't say anything. She knew it was all her fault. They dried their clothes, and as soon as the wings of the chair were quite dry too, they sat in it, and Chinky cried, "Home, wishing-chair, home!"

They flew home. Mollie jumped off the chair as soon as it arrived in the playroom and ran to her money-box. She tipped out all her money.

"Here you are, Chinky," she said. "I'm going to pay for that fish-ride myself. It was all my fault. I'm very sorry, and I won't be so silly again. Do forgive me!"

"Oh! That's very nice of you, Mollie!" said Chinky, and he gave her a hug. "Of course we forgive you! All's well that ends well! We're home again safe and sound!"

He changed Mollie's money into a big gold piece and gave it to the blackbird in the garden, asking him to take it to the merman.

"That's the end of *that* adventure!" said Chinky. "Well, let's hope our next one will be much, much nicer!"

XI

THE MAGICIAN'S PARTY

One afternoon, when the children and Chinky were reading stories, there came a timid knock at the door. "Come in!" called Mollie. The door opened and in came two small elves.

"May we speak to Chinky?" they asked. Chinky waved them to a chair.

"Sit down," he said. "What do you want?"

"Please, may we borrow your wishing-chair to go to the Magician Greatheart's party," said the bigger elf.

"Well, it doesn't belong to me," said Chinky. "It belongs to these two children."

"Would you let us borrow it?" asked the little elves.

"Certainly," said Mollie and Peter.

"What reward do you ask?" said the elves.

"Oh, you can have the chair for nothing," said Mollie. "Bring it back safely, that's all."

"I suppose you wouldn't like to come to the party?" asked the elves. "We are very small, and there are only five of us to go. There would be plenty of room for you and for Chinky too in the chair."

"Stars and moon, what a treat!" cried Chinky in delight. "Yes, we'll all go! Thanks very much! Greatheart's parties are glorious! My word, this

is luck! When is the party, elves?"

"To-morrow night," said the elves. "Sharp at midnight. We'll be here at half-past eleven."

"Right," said Chinky. The little elves said good-bye and ran out. Chinky rubbed his hands and turned to the two delighted children.

"The magician is a marvellous fellow," he said. "He is a good magician, and the enchantments and magic he knows are perfectly wonderful. I hope he does a few tricks! Put on your best clothes and be here at half-past eleven to-morrow night, won't you!"

The children were most excited. They talked about nothing else all day long and the next day too. They dressed themselves in their best clothes and ran down to the playroom at half-past eleven the next night. Chinky was there too, looking very grand indeed, for he had on a suit that seemed to be made of silver moonbeams sewn with pearls.

The elves were there waiting, all dressed daintily in flower petals, sewn with spider thread. Even the wishing-chair looked smart, for Chinky had tied a big bow on each of its arms! Its red wings were lazily flapping.

The children got in and Chinky sat on the back. The five little elves easily found room on the two arms. Off they went, flying through the moonlight to their great and wonderful party!

The magician's palace was set on top of a high hill. The chair did not take long to get there. It flew down and took its place among the long line of carriages that were drawing up one by one at the big front door. When their turn came the children and the elves jumped off the chair and ran up the steps. They were shown into a great hall and there they shook hands with Magician Greatheart, a tall and handsome enchanter, whose cloak rippled out as he walked, as if it were made of blue water. His eyes were kind and looked right through every one.

A band was playing merrily in the big hall, and Chinky caught hold of Mollie and danced with her. Peter found a small, shy fairy and danced with her too, though she was so light that he couldn't make up his mind if she was real or not!

There were hundreds of fairy folk there of all kinds—gnomes, goblins, brownies, fairies, elves, pixies—but only two children, so Mollie and Peter felt most honoured.

Then came the supper. It was so queer. The long, long table was spread with plates and glasses and dishes, but there was no food at all, no, not even a yellow jelly.

The magician took his place at the end of the table.

"Will you each wish for what you like best to eat?" he said in his kind, deep voice. "Take it in turn, please!"

A brownie next to him said, "I wish for honey-lemonade and sugar biscuits!"

At once a jug of yellow lemonade appeared by him and a plate of delicious sugar biscuits! The fairy next to the brownie wished for chocolate blanc-mange and a cream ice. They appeared even as she spoke the words! It was such fun to see them come.

Mollie and Peter watched in amazement as all the dishes and jugs on the table became full of the most exciting things when each little creature wished his or her wish. They had their turns too!

"I wish for cream buns and ginger-beer!" said Mollie.

"And I wish for treacle pudding and lemon-ade!" said Peter. A dish of cream buns and a bottle of fizzy ginger-beer appeared in front of Mollie, and a dish with a steaming hot treacle pudding and a jug of lemonade appeared by Peter. It was just like a dream!

Every one ate and drank and was merry as could be. Then, after the supper, the magician spoke one strange word, and the long, long table, with its dishes and plates, vanished into thin air!

"Now we will have some magic!" said the magician, beaming at his excited guests.

They all sat down on the floor. The magician took a silver stick and tapped three times on the floor. A spire of green smoke came up and made a crackling noise. It shot up into the air, turned over and over and wound its way among the guests, dropping tiny bunches of sweet-smelling flowers as it passed—buttonholes for every one!

The smoke went. The magician tapped the floor again and up rose five black cats, each with a violin except the last one, and he had a drum. After the cats came six plump rabbits, who danced to the tunes that the cats played. One rabbit turned upside down and danced on his ears, and that made Peter laugh so much that he had to get out his handkerchief to wipe his tears of laughter away.

Then an even stranger thing happened next. The magician tapped the floor once more, and up came a great flower of yellow. It opened, and in the middle of it the guests could see five red eggs. The eggs broke and out came tiny chicks. They grew—and grew—and grew—and became great brilliant birds with long drooping tails. Then they opened their beaks and sang so sweetly that not a sound could be heard in the great hall but their voices.

The birds flew away. The flower faded. The magician tapped the floor for the last time. A gnome appeared, whose long beard floated round him like a mist. He handed Greatheart a big dish with a lid. The magician took off the lid and lifted out a silver spoon. He stirred in the air and a bubbling sound came. Round the spoon grew a glass bowl. The children could see the spoon shining in it. But suddenly the spoon turned to gold and swam about—a live goldfish.

Greatheart took the goldfish neatly into his hand and threw it into the air. It disappeared.

"Who has it?" asked Greatheart. Every one looked about—but no one had the fish. Greatheart laughed and went over to Mollie. He put his hand into her right ear and pulled out the goldfish! Then he took up Peter's hand and opened it—and will you believe it, Peter had a little yellow chick there, cheeping away merrily!

Oh, the tricks that the magician did! No one would ever believe them! Peter and Mollie rubbed their eyes several times and wondered if they were dreaming.

Best of all came the last trick. The magician,

as he said good-night to his guests, gave each a tiny egg.

"It will hatch to-morrow," he said, "Keep it safely!" The children thanked him very much for a marvellous evening, and then got sleepily into the wishing-chair with Chinky and the elves. How they got home they never knew—for there must have been magic about that took them home, undressed them, and popped them into bed without their knowing. Anyway, they found themselves there the next morning when they awoke, although they did not remember at all how they got there!

"I believe it was all a beautiful dream," said Mollie.

"It wasn't!" said Peter, putting his hand under his pillow. He brought out his little egg. As he looked at it, it broke—and there, in his hand, was a tiny silver watch, ticking away merrily!

Mollie gave a scream of delight and put her hand under her pillow to get her egg too. It broke in her hand—and out of it came a necklace of beads that looked exactly like bubbles! It was the loveliest one Mollie had ever seen!

"Hurry up and dress and we'll see what Chinky got," said Mollie. They hurried—and when they saw Chinky, he showed them *his* present—golden buckles for his shoes. Didn't they look grand!

"That was the loveliest party I've ever been to!" said Mollie happily. "I wish *all* our wishing-chair adventures were like that!"

XII

THE WISHING-CHAIR IS FOOLISH

Once the wishing-chair was very foolish, and nearly landed the children and Chinky in a dreadful fix!

It grew its wings one morning when the children were playing snakes and ladders. Chinky saw the red wings flapping and jumped up in excitement.

"Come on!" he cried. "I'm longing for another adventure!"

They all jumped on to the chair. It flew out of the door in a great hurry, and then up into the air. It was a beautiful day and the children and Chinky could see for miles. The chair seemed in a rather silly mood. It swung to and fro as it flew, and even jiggled about once or twice.

"I say!" said Chinky. "I don't like this! Hold on tightly, children, in case the chair turns head-over-heels, or something silly. It's in a dangerous mood."

"Shall we go back home?" asked Mollie, in alarm.

"Of course not!" said Peter. "We'll never turn our backs on an adventure!"

So on they went, the chair still doing its little tricks. At last Chinky really did get a bit frightened, for once Peter nearly fell off.

"Go down to earth at once, chair!" he

commanded. The chair seemed cross. It didn't want to go down—but it had to. So down it went, jiggling every now and again as if it really did mean to jerk the children off.

Peter looked down to see where they were going. There was a village below them, and they seemed to be going down towards the roof of a house.

"Hope the chair doesn't land on the roof!" said Peter. "It looks just as if it's going to!"

But it did something even worse than land on the roof! What do you suppose it did?

It tried to go down the large red chimney belonging to the house! It really *was* behaving very foolishly!

Of course, it couldn't possibly go down—and it stuck fast, three legs in, and one out, and there it was, all sideways, with the children getting covered with soot and smoke!

Chinky climbed out first, and helped Peter and Mollie out too.

They sat on the roof, holding on to the chimney, which felt rather hot, because warm smoke was coming out of it.

Chinky was very angry.

"I never thought the chair would be so silly!" he said. "It has acted so sensibly up to now. Now look what it's done! It's gone and stuck itself in somebody's chimney, and goodness knows how we're going to get it out! And here we are up on a roof in a village we don't know!"

"It's too bad," said Mollie. "Look at my frock!
All over soot."

"We'd better shout and see if some one will get
us down," said Peter. So they shouted.

"Hie, hie, hie! Help! Hie, hie, hie!"

Soon a gnome heard their shouting, and came
out to see what it was all about. When he saw
the three children up on the roof and the chair in
the chimney he was amazed. He shouted to his
friends, and soon the whole village was staring
upwards.

"Get a ladder and help us down!" shouted

Peter. "Our chair has landed us in this fix!"

In a few minutes a long ladder was brought, and the children and Chinky climbed carefully down it to the ground. Chinky explained what had happened, and the village folk exclaimed in astonishment.

"The thing is," said Peter, "*how* are we going to get the chair out? It can't stay there for the rest of its life, cooking in a chimney pot! Who would have thought it would have been so silly?"

"It's trying to get out!" said Mollie suddenly. "Look, it's wriggling!"

So it was. It did look funny! It tried its hardest to get out, but it was stuck much too tightly.

"It's no good," said Peter gloomily. "It will have to stay there. I don't see how we can possibly get it out."

"Of course we can!" said Chinky. "We'll get the village sweep to come along and put his long brush up the chimney! Then the silly old chair will be swept out of the chimney! We will get into it when it comes to earth, and go home immediately before it has time to do anything silly again!"

"I'll fetch the sweep!" said a round-faced gnome at once. "He lives next door to me."

He ran off, and in a few minutes came back with a little sweep, looking rather black, carrying his bundle of poles. He stared in astonishment at the chair in the chimney.

"Can you push it out for us?" asked Chinky anxiously.

"I'll try," said the sweep. He went into the house and fitted the big round brush on to the first pole. He pushed it up the chimney. Then he fitted another pole on to the first one, and pushed that up the chimney too. So he went on until the brush was almost at the top. Then he fitted on his last pole, and prepared to give a good push.

Chinky, Mollie, and Peter were outside the house, watching the chair in the chimney. All the gnome villagers were with them too. It was really rather exciting.

The chair gave a jolt!

"The sweep is pushing it!" yelled Chinky, dancing about excitedly. "Ooh, look! He's pushing it hard—the chair is coming out! It's nearly out!"

So it was! The sweep was pushing and pushing with his round brush, and the chair was getting loose as it was jerked farther up. Suddenly it came right out of the chimney with a rush! The sweep's brush came out too, and twiddled round in the air in a funny manner.

"There it comes, there it comes!" shouted Mollie. "Hie, chair, come to earth!"

But to the children's dismay, that naughty wishing-chair flapped its red wings and flew right up into the air! It didn't go *near* the ground!

"Oh, I say!" said Chinky. "*Isn't* it behaving badly!"

85

They all watched it fly away till they could no longer see it. It was gone!

"Well," said Mollie, "we'll have to get home another way, that's all. I'm afraid we've lost the chair now."

"We'll catch the bus that leaves here in five minutes' time," said Chinky, looking at a bus time-table set out on a wall near. "It won't be long before we're home."

"I'm sorry about the chair," said Peter sadly. "It gave us some fine adventures, you know. It has behaved very badly to-day, it's true—but once or twice it has been very good to us—like when it fetched us from Witch Kirri-Kirri's."

"Yes," said Chinky, "We mustn't forget the good things just because it has once been bad. Come on—here's the bus."

They got into the bus, which was very peculiar, because the driver was a duck and the conductor a rabbit. However, Chinky didn't seem surprised, so Mollie and Peter said nothing, but just stared. In ten minutes they found themselves outside a cave in a hillside.

"This is where we get off," said Chinky, much to their surprise. They followed him into the cave and up some steps. Chinky opened a door—and to the children's amazement they found themselves climbing out of a tree in the wood near to their home!

"You simply never know where an entrance to

86

Fairyland is!" said Mollie, staring at the tree, as Chinky shut the bark door.

They ran home—and the very first thing they saw in their playroom was—guess! Yes, their wishing-chair. They stared in astonishment.

"Why, it's come back home after all!" said Peter, delighted. "It's wings have gone. Oh, fancy, it's come back to us! Isn't that lovely!"

"Good old chair!" said Mollie, running to it and sitting down in it. "I'm glad it's back. I expect it's sorry now. I don't mind having nearly gone down a chimney now it's all over—it's so exciting to think of!"

"Don't say things like that in front of the chair," said Chinky. "There's no knowing what it might do next."

"Let's brush our clothes clean," said Peter, getting a brush. "We'll get into trouble if we don't —and certainly no one would believe us if we said we'd been stuck in a chimney!"

"Whatever shall we do *next*?" said Mollie. Aha! Wait and see!

XIII

THE POLITE GOBLIN

The next time the chair grew its wings again, Chinky looked at it sternly.

"Last time you were very badly behaved!" he said. "If you want us to come with you this time, just behave yourself. If not, I'll sell you to the Jumble-Man, and you won't like that!"

The chair flapped its wings violently, and Chinky grinned at the others. "That will make it behave itself this time," he said. "It wouldn't like to be given to the Jumble-Man! Come on, let's get in."

They all got in. The chair rose very slowly, and flew out of the door, taking care not to jerk or jolt the children at all. It flew so very slowly and carefully that Chinky got quite impatient.

"Now you're being silly!" he said to the chair. "Do fly properly. You're hardly moving."

The chair flew faster. It flew very high and the children could hardly see the houses below them. They even flew above the clouds – and suddenly, to the children's great astonishment, they saw a big castle built on a cloud!

"I say! Look!" said Peter, in amazement. "A castle on a cloud! Who lives there, Chinky?"

"I don't know," said Chinky. "I hope it's

someone nice. I don't want to meet a giant this morning!"

The chair flew to the castle. There was a big front door standing open. The chair flew inside.

"Goodness!" said Mollie, in alarm. "This isn't very polite. We ought to have knocked!"

The chair came to rest in a big kitchen. A small goblin, with pointed ears, green eyes, and bony legs and arms, was sitting in a chair reading a paper. When the wishing-chair flew in with Chinky, Mollie, and Peter in it, he jumped up in astonishment.

The children and Chinky got out of their chair. "Good morning," said Chinky. "I'm so sorry to come in like this—but our chair didn't wait to knock."

The goblin bowed politely. "It doesn't matter at all!" he said. "What a marvellous chair you have, and how pleased I am to see you! Pray sit down and let me give you some lemonade!"

They all sat down on stools. The goblin rushed to a cupboard and brought out a big jug of lemonade.

"It is so nice to see such pleasant visitors," said the goblin, putting a glass of lemonade before each of them. "And now, will you have biscuits?"

"Thank you," said Mollie and Peter and Chinky. They felt that it was kind of the goblin to welcome them—but they didn't like him at all. He seemed *much* too polite!

"Another glass of lemonade?" asked the goblin, taking Chinky's empty glass. "Oh do! It is a pleasure, I assure you, to have you here! Another biscuit, little girl? I make them myself, and only save them for *special* visitors."

"But we aren't very special," said Peter, thinking that the goblin was really silly to say such things.

"Oh yes, you are *very* special," said the goblin, smiling politely at them all. "*So* good of you to come and see an ugly little goblin like me!"

"But we didn't *mean* to come and see you," said Mollie truthfully. Chinky frowned at her. He

didn't want her to offend the goblin. He did not trust him at all. He wanted to get away as soon as he could.

"Well," said Chinky, finishing his biscuit, "it is kind of you to have welcomed us like this. But now we must go."

"Good-bye and thank you," said the polite goblin. He shook hands with each of them and bowed very low. They turned to go to the wishing-chair.

And then they had a most *terrible* shock! The wishing-chair was not there! It was gone.

"I say! Where's the wishing-chair?" shouted

Chinky. "Goblin, where's our chair?"

"Oh, pixie, how should *I* know?" said the goblin. "Haven't I been looking after you every minute? It must have flown away when you were not looking."

"Well, it's funny if it has," said Chinky. "We should have seen it, or at least felt the wind of its wings flapping. I don't believe you, goblin. You have done something with our chair—your servants have taken it away! Tell me quickly, or I will punish you!"

"*Punish* me!" said the goblin. "And how would you do that, pray? You had better be careful, pixie—how are you going to get away from my castle without a wishing-chair? I live here by myself in the clouds!"

"Be careful, Chinky," said Peter. "Don't make him angry. Goodness knows how we'd escape from here if he didn't help us!"

Mollie looked frightened. The little goblin smiled at her politely, and said, "Don't be afraid, pretty little girl. I will treat you as an honoured guest for as long as you like to stay with me in my castle."

"We don't want to stay with you at all," said Chinky. "We want our wishing-chair! What have you DONE with it?"

But he could get no answer from the polite goblin. It was most tiresome. What in the world were they to do?

Chinky suddenly lost his temper. He rushed at the goblin to catch him and shake him. The goblin looked scared. He turned to run and sped out of the big kitchen into the hall. Chinky ran after him. Mollie and Peter looked at one another.

"Chinky will get us all into trouble," said Mollie. "He really is a silly-billy. If he makes the goblin angry, he certainly won't help us to get away. I suppose that naughty wishing-chair flew away home."

"I'm quite sure it didn't," said Peter. "I know I would have seen it moving."

The goblin came running into the room followed by Chinky. "Catch him, catch him!" yelled Chinky. Peter tried to—but the goblin was like an eel. He dodged this way, he dodged that way—and then a funny thing happened. Peter fell over something that wasn't there!

He crashed right into something and fell over, bang! And yet, when he looked, there was nothing at all to fall over! He felt very much astonished. He sat up and stared round. "What did I fall over?" he said. Chinky stopped chasing the goblin and ran to him. He put out his arms and felt round about in the air by Peter—and his hands closed on something hard—that couldn't be seen!

"Oh!" he yelled joyfully, "it's the wishing-chair! That deceitful goblin made it invisible, so that we couldn't see it, even though it was really here! And he meant to help us home all right—and

93

as soon as we had gone he meant to use our wishing-chair for himself, and we'd never know!"

"Then it hasn't flown away!" cried Mollie, running over and feeling it too. "Oh goody, goody! We can get into it and go home even if we can't see what we're sitting on! Get up, Peter, and let's fly off before that nasty little polite goblin does any more spells!"

They all sat in the chair they couldn't see. "Home, wishing-chair, home!" cried Chinky. The invisible chair rose in the air and flew out of the door. The goblin ran to the door and bowed. "So pleased to have seen you!" he called politely.

"Nasty little polite creature!" said Chinky. "My goodness — we nearly lost the chair, children! Now we've got to find a way of making it visible again. It's no fun having a chair and not knowing if it's really there or not! I don't like feeling I'm sitting on nothing! I like to *see* what I'm sitting on!"

They flew home. They got out of the chair and looked at one another.

"Well, we do have adventures!" said Peter, grinning.

XIV

THE SPINNING HOUSE

It was most annoying not being able to see the wishing-chair. The children kept forgetting where it was and falling over it.

"Oh dear!" groaned Peter, picking himself up for the fourth time, "I really can't bear this chair being invisible. I keep walking into it and bumping myself."

"I'll tie a ribbon on it!" said Mollie. "Then we shall see the ribbon in the air, and we'll know the chair is there!"

"That's a good idea," said Chinky. "Girls always think of good ideas."

"So do boys," said Peter. "I say! How queer that ribbon looks all by itself in the air! We can see it, but we can't see the chair it's tied on! People *would* stare if they came in here and saw it!"

It certainly did look funny. It stuck there in mid-air—and it did act as a warning to the children and Chinky that they must be careful not to walk into the invisible chair. It saved them many a bump.

"I've been asking the fairies how we can get the chair made visible again," said Chinky the next day. "They say there is a funny old witch who lives in a little spinning house in Jiffy Wood, who is very, very clever at making things invisible *or* visible! So if we fly there next time the chair grows wings, we may be able to have it put right."

"But how shall we know when it grows its wings if we can't see them?" said Mollie.

"I never thought of that!" said Chinky.

"I know!" said Peter. "Let's tear up little bits of paper and put them round the legs of the chair on the floor! Then, when its wings grow, the bits will all fly about in the draught the wings make with their flapping—and we shall see them and know the chair is ready to go off adventuring again!"

The children tore up the bits of paper and put them on the floor near the legs of the chair.

"Really, it does look funny!" said Mollie. "A ribbon balanced in mid-air—and bits of paper below, on the floor! Mother would think us very untidy if she came in."

"Let's play tiddly-winks now," said Peter. "I'll get out the cup and the counters."

Soon the three of them were playing tiddly-winks on the floor. Mollie flipped her counters into the cup very cleverly, and had just won, when Chinky gave a shout:

"Look! Those bits of paper are fluttering into the air! The chair must have grown its wings!"

Mollie and Peter turned to look. Sure enough, the scraps of paper they had put on the floor were all dancing up and down as if a wind was blowing them. The children could feel a draught too, and knew that the wishing-chair had once again grown its red wings.

"That was a good idea of yours, Peter," said Chinky. "Boys have good ideas as well as girls, I can see! Come on, let's get into the chair and see if it will fly to Jiffy Wood to the old witch's."

They climbed on to the chair. It was really very strange climbing on to something they couldn't see, but could only feel. Chinky sat on the back, as usual, and the children squeezed into the seat.

"Go to Jiffy Wood, to the little Spinning House," Chinky said to the chair. It rose up into the air, flew out of the door, and was up high before the children could say another word! They must have looked very queer, sitting in a chair that couldn't be seen!

It was raining. Mollie wished they had brought an umbrella. "Tell the chair to fly above the clouds, Chinky," she said. "It's the clouds that drop the rain on to us. If we fly beyond them, we shan't get wet because there won't be any rain."

"Fly higher than the clouds, chair," said Chinky. The chair rose higher and higher. It flew right through the misty grey clouds and came out above them. The sun was shining brightly! It made the other side of the clouds quite dazzling to look at!

"This is better," said Mollie. "The sun will dry our clothes."

They flew on and on in the sunshine, above the

great white clouds. Then they suddenly flew downwards again, and the children saw that they were over a thick wood.

"Jiffy Wood!" said Chinky, peering down. "We shall soon be there!"

Down they flew and down, and at last came to a little clearing. The chair flew down to it, and came to rest on some grass. A little way off was a most peculiar house. It had one leg, like a short pole, and it spun round and round and round on this leg! It did not go very fast, and the children could see that it had a door on one side and a window on each of the other three sides. It had one chimney which was smoking away merrily—but the smoke was green, a sign that a witch lived in the house.

"Well, here we are," said Chinky, getting out of the chair. "I'd better carry the chair, I think. I don't like leaving it about here when we can't see it. We shouldn't know where it was if any one came along and untied the ribbon."

"Is the old witch a fierce sort of person?" asked Mollie.

"No, she's a good sort," said Chinky. "She will do all she can to help us, I know. You needn't be afraid. She won't harm us. My grandmother knew her very well."

"How are we going to get into the house?" asked Peter, looking at the strange house going round and round and round. "It's like getting on a roundabout that's going! Our mother always says that's a dangerous thing to do."

"Well, we'll try and get the witch to stop the house spinning round for a minute, so that we can hop in with the chair," said Chinky. "Come on. I've got the chair."

Off they went towards the queer little house. As it went round the smoke went round too, and made green rings. It was very peculiar.

"Witch Snippit, Witch Snippit!" called Chinky. "Stop your house and let us in!"

Some one opened a window and looked out. It was an old woman with a red shawl on and a

pretty white cap. She had a hooky nose and a pair of large spectacles over her eyes. She seemed surprised to see them.

"Wait a minute!" she called. "I'll stop the house. But you'll have to be very quick getting in at the door because it won't stop for long!"

The house slowed down — it went round more and more slowly — and at last it stopped. The door was facing the children, and the witch opened it and beckoned to them. Mollie shot inside, and so did Peter. Chinky was trying to get in, with the chair too, when suddenly the house began to spin round fast again! Poor Chinky fell out of the doorway with the chair!

Mollie and Peter really couldn't help laughing, he looked so funny! The witch stopped the house again, and then Peter helped Chinky in quickly. They put the wishing-chair down and then turned to greet the witch.

"Good-morning," she said, with a nice smile. "And what can I do for you?"

XV

WITCH SNIPPIT

The children and Chinky looked at the smiling witch. They liked her very much. She had kind blue eyes, as bright as forget-me-nots. At first they felt rather giddy, for the house they were in spun round and round all the time—but they soon got used to it.

"We've brought our wishing-chair to you," said Chinky. "We went to the cloud-goblin's castle the other day, and he made our chair invisible. It's such a nuisance to have a chair we can't see—so, as we knew you were clever at all kinds of visible and invisible spells, we thought we would bring it to you. Could you make our chair seeable, please?"

"Certainly," said Witch Snippit. "I have some very strong magic paint. If you use it, you will make your chair easily seen."

She went to a cupboard. The children stared round the room.

It was a very strange room indeed. The clock on the mantelpiece had legs, and for every tick it gave, it walked a step along the mantelpiece. When it got to the end it turned and walked back again. Then it suddenly disappeared!

"Ooh!" said Mollie, surprised. "Your clock's gone, Witch Snippit!"

101

"Oh, don't take any notice of that," said the witch. "It's just showing off!"

The clock said "Urrrrrrrrr!" and came back again. Up and down it walked, and the children thought it was the strangest one they had ever seen.

Other things in the cottage were most peculiar too. There was a chair that had four legs and a back, but no seat. Mollie wondered if it really *had* got a seat that couldn't be seen. She went to sit down on it and found that it *had* got a seat, but it was quite invisible. There was a table, too, that had a top but no legs.

On the dresser there were cups with no handles, and lids balanced in the air but no dishes below. Mollie put out her hand and felt the dishes, but she couldn't see them. She turned round to Witch Snippit.

"You *have* got a funny home," she began — and then she stopped in surprise. Witch Snippit was all there except her middle! Oh dear, she did look so funny!

"Don't be worried," she said to Mollie. "I'm quite all right. My middle is really there, but it's vanished for a few minutes. You can't meddle about with visible and invisible magic without having things like this happen to you at times."

As she spoke, her middle came back again, and, oh dear, her hands and feet went! Mollie began to laugh. "Whatever will go next!" she said.

All of the witch disappeared then—and the children and Chinky couldn't see her anywhere! They knew she was in the room, because they could hear her laughing.

"Don't look so surprised," she said. "You should never be astonished at anything that happens in a witch's house."

"I say! The floor's gone!" said Peter, in alarm, looking down at his feet. "Oooh! I feel as if I'm falling! Where's the floor?"

"Oh, it's there all the time," said Witch Snippit, coming back in bits. "It's only disappeared from sight. Don't worry, it's there!"

She put a tin of paint on the table. "Would

you like to paint your chair and get it right again?" she asked. "It's quite easy. There are three brushes for you. It's good paint. It will make invisible things visible, or visible things *in*visible. I'm rather busy to-day, so if you'll do the job yourself, I'll be glad."

"We'd love to!" said Chinky. He took off the lid of the paint tin and picked up a brush. "It's going to be funny painting something you can't see!" he said.

He felt for the legs of the chair and dipped his brush into the paint, which was a queer silvery colour and seemed as thin as smoke. He painted along one of the chair's invisible legs – and hey presto! it came into sight, as brown and solid as ever!

"I've got a leg back!" said Chinky, in excitement, and waved his brush in the air. A drop of paint flew on to Peter's nose.

"Don't," said Peter. Mollie stared at him in horror. His nose had disappeared!

"Peter, your nose has gone!" she said. "A drop of the paint went on to it! Oh, whatever shall we do?"

"Get it back again, of course," said Chinky. "Didn't you hear Witch Snippit say that this paint acted either way? It makes things seen that can't be seen, and it makes things that are seeable *un*seeable! Come here, Peter – I'll paint where your nose should be, and it'll come back again!"

104

He dabbed some paint where he thought Peter's nose should be—and sure enough, it *did* come back again! Mollie was so glad. Peter looked horrid without a nose.

"I'll teach you to make my nose disappear!" said Peter to Chinky. He dipped his brush in the paint and dabbed at Chinky's pointed ears. They vanished in a trice.

"Don't!" said Chinky crossly. He threw some paint at Peter's feet and they disappeared at once!

"Oh!" said Peter, surprised. "I don't like having no feet. I shall paint them back! There they are! Stop it, Chinky. I don't like this game. It would be awful if something *didn't* come back!"

Chinky was naughty. He dipped his brush in the magic paint, and ran it round Mollie's neck. How queer she looked with a head and a body but no neck! Peter couldn't bear it. He painted her neck in again at once, and frowned at Chinky.

"If you're not careful I'll paint you from top to toe and then take away the tin of paint!" he said.

"Now listen to me," suddenly said Witch Snippit's voice above them. "I didn't give you that paint to waste. If you are not careful there will not be enough to finish painting your wishing-chair, and then you will find there is a bit still left invisible, that you cannot see. So be sensible."

Chinky and Peter went red. They began to paint the chair busily, and Mollie joined them. The clock on the mantelpiece was so interested in what they were doing that it walked right off the mantelpiece and fell into the coal-scuttle.

"It can stay there," said the witch. "It is much too curious—always poking its nose where it isn't wanted."

"Urrrrrrrrr!" said the clock, and disappeared. Mollie was glad her clock at home didn't behave like that.

In an hour's time the wishing-chair was itself again, and all the paint in the tin was finished. There it stood before them, their same old wishing-chair. It had been very strange to see it gradually becoming visible to their eyes.

"There's a bit at the back here that can't be seen," said Mollie, pointing to a bit that hadn't come back again. But there was no paint to finish that bit, and the children didn't like to ask for any more. So that tiny piece of the chair had to remain invisible. It looked like a hole!

"Thank you very much, Witch Snippit," said Chinky politely. "We've finished now, and had better be getting home. Could you stop your house spinning and let us go out?"

"Very well," said Witch Snippit. She called out a magic word and the spinning house slowed down. "Good-bye," she said to Chinky and the children. "Come and see me again another time. Hurry, now, or the house will start spinning again!"

The three squeezed into the wishing-chair. The

house stopped and the witch opened the door.

"Home, wishing-chair!" shouted Chinky—and the chair flew straight out of the door and up into the air.

"Good-bye, good-bye!" called Mollie and Peter, looking down at the house, which was already spinning fast again. "I say, that was a pretty good adventure, wasn't it!"

"I wish we'd got some of that magic paint with us," said Chinky. "We could have some fun with it!"

"I'm glad we haven't!" said Mollie. "I don't know *what* mischief you'd get into, Chinky!"

XVI

THE SILLY BOY

The children were cross because Mother had said that the painters were to paint the walls of the playroom and mend a window—and this meant that they couldn't play there for some time.

Their playroom was built right at the bottom of the garden, and it was quite safe for their friend, Chinky, the pixie, to live there, for no one ever went to the garden playroom except themselves. But now the painters would be there for a week. How tiresome!

"It's a good thing it's summer-time, Chinky, so that you can live in the garden for a bit," said Mollie.

"Oh, don't worry about *me*," said Chinky. "I've a nice cosy place in the hollow of an oak tree. It's the chair I'm thinking about. Where shall we keep that? We can't have it flying about whilst the painters are there."

"We'd better put it in the boxroom, indoors," said Peter. "That room's just been repainted so I don't expect Mother or any one will think it must be turned out just yet. It will be safe there."

So, when no one was looking, Peter and Mollie carried the wishing-chair up to the boxroom and stood it safely in a corner. They shut the window up tightly, so that it couldn't fly out if its wings grew suddenly.

They couldn't have Chinky to play with them in the house, because he didn't want any one to know about him. So they asked Thomas, the little boy over the road, to come and play soldiers, on a rainy afternoon.

They didn't like him very much, but he was better than nobody.

Thomas came. He soon got tired of playing soldiers. He began turning head-over-heels down the nursery floor. He could do it very well.

"I can make awful faces, too," he said to Mollie and Peter — and he began to pull such dreadful faces that the two children gazed at him in surprise and horror.

"Our mother says that if you pull faces and the wind happens to change you may get stuck like that," said Mollie. "Do stop it, Thomas."

But Thomas wouldn't. He wrinkled up his nose and his forehead and blew out his cheeks — and do you know, the wind changed that very minute! And poor Thomas couldn't get his face right again! he tried and he tried, but he couldn't. It was dreadful! Whatever was he to do?

"Oh, Thomas, the wind changed — I saw the weather-cock swing round that very moment!" cried Mollie. "I did warn you! I do think you're silly."

"He can't go home like that," said Peter. "Let's

wash his face in hot water – then perhaps it will go right again."

So they washed Thomas's face well – but it was as bad as ever when they had finished! Screwed-up nose and forehead and blown-out cheeks . . . oh dear!

"Do you suppose Chinky would know what to do?" said Peter at last.

"Who's Chinky?" asked Thomas.

"Never you mind," said Mollie. "Peter, go and find Chinky and see what he says. I'll stay here with Thomas. He mustn't go out of the nursery, because if he meets Mother or Jane, they will think he's making faces at them and will be ever so cross.

Peter ran downstairs. He went into the garden and whistled a little tune that Chinky had taught him. He had to whistle this whenever he wanted the pixie.

Chinky whistled back. Peter saw him under a big hawthorn bush, mending a hole in his coat.

"What's up?" asked Chinky, sewing away.

"We've got a boy in our nursery who's been making dreadful faces," explained Peter. "And the wind changed just as he was making a specially horrible one – and now he can't get his face right again. So Mollie sent me to ask you if you could do anything to help."

"A boy as silly as that doesn't deserve help," said Chinky, breaking off his cotton and threading

110

his needle again. "You go and tell him so."

"Oh no, Chinky, we really *must* help him," said Peter. "His mother may think *we* made his face like that, and we'll get into trouble. You don't want us to be sent to bed for a week, do you?"

"No, I don't," said Chinky, putting on his coat. "I'll help *you* because you're my friends. There's only one thing to be done for a person who's been making faces when the wind changed."

"What's that?" asked Peter.

"You've got to get a bit of the wind that blew just then, and puff it into his face," said Chinky. "Then he'll be all right—but it's dreadfully difficult to get a bit of the same wind."

"How can we?" asked Peter, in dismay.

"We'd better go in the wishing-chair to the Windy Wizard," said Chinky. "He knows all the ins and outs of every wind that blows. I've seen the old wishing-chair looking out of the window this afternoon, trying to get out, so I'm sure it's grown its wings again. Go and see, and if it has, tell Mollie, and we'll go and get help from the old wizard."

"Oh, thank you, Chinky," said Peter, and he ran indoors. He whispered to Mollie all that Chinky had said.

"I think the chair *must* have grown its wings," Mollie said, "because there have been such queer sounds going on in the boxroom this afternoon — you know, knockings and bumping. I expect it's the chair trying to get out."

"I'll go and see," said Peter. He ran up the topmost flight of stairs and opened the boxroom door. The wishing-chair was standing by it, ready to fly out — but Peter caught hold of it just as it was slipping out of the door.

"Now just wait a minute," he said. But the chair wouldn't! It forced its way past Peter and the little boy jumped into it. "Go to Chinky!" he called hoping that the chair wouldn't meet any one on the way.

The chair flew down the stairs and out into the garden. It went to where Chinky was standing by the hawthorn bush. It was flapping its red wings madly and Chinky jumped into it at once.

"To the Windy Wizard's!" he shouted. "I say, Peter, isn't it in a hurry! It must have got tired of being shut up in the boxroom!"

Mollie was looking out of the window. She had heard the chair flying downstairs. She saw it up in the air, carrying Peter and Chinky, and she wished she were in it too!

"Some one's got to stay with Thomas, though," she thought to herself. "He'd only run home or go and find our mother or something, if we left him quite alone. What an ugly face he has now! I do hope Peter and Chinky find something to put it right!"

XVII

THE WINDY WIZARD

The wishing-chair rose high into the air, carrying Peter and Chinky. It had stopped raining and was a hot sunny day and the wind the chair made rushing through the air was very pleasant. Peter wished Mollie was with them. It was much more fun to go on adventures all together.

Presently the chair came into a very windy sky. Goodness, how the wind blew! It blew the white clouds to rags. It blew Peter's hair nearly off his head! It blew the chair's wings so that it could hardly flap them.

"The Windy Wizard lives somewhere about here," said Chinky, looking down. "Look! Do you see that hill over there, golden with butter-cups? There's a house there. It's the Windy Wizard's, I'm sure, because it's rocking about in all directions as if the wind lived inside it!"

Down flew the wishing-chair. It came to rest outside the cottage, which was certainly rocking about in a most alarming manner. Peter and Chinky jumped off and ran to the cottage door. They knocked.

"Come in!" cried a voice. They opened the door and went in. Oooh! The wind rushed out at them and nearly blew them off their feet!

"Good-day!" said the Windy Wizard. He was a

most peculiar-looking person, for he had long hair and a very long beard and a cloak that swept to the ground, but, as the wind blew his hair and beard and cloak up and down and round and about all the time, it was very difficult to see what he was really like!

"Good-day," said Peter and Chinky, staring at the wizard. He hadn't a very comfortable house to live in, Peter thought, because there were draughts everywhere, round his legs, down his neck, behind his knees! And all the cottage was full of a whispering, sighing sound as if a wind was talking to itself all the time.

"Have you come to buy a little wind?" asked the wizard.

"No," said Chinky. "I've come about a boy who made faces when the wind changed — and he can't get right again. So we thought perhaps you could help us. I know that if we could get a little of the wind that blew at that time, and puff it into his face, he'll be all right — but how can we get the wind?"

"What a foolish boy!" said the Windy Wizard, his cloak blowing out and hiding him completely. "What time did this happen?"

"At half-past three this afternoon," said Peter. "I heard the nursery clock strike."

"It's difficult, very difficult," said the wizard, smoothing down his cloak. "You see, the wind blows and is gone in a trice! Now let me think for

115

a moment—who is likely to have kept a little of that wind?"

"What about the birds that were flying in the air at that moment?" asked Chinky. "They may have some in their feathers, you know."

"Yes, so they may," said the wizard. He took a feather from a jar that was full of them, and flung it out of the door.

> "Come, birds, and bring
> The breeze from your wing!"

he chanted.

Peter and Chinky looked out of the door, hoping that dozens of birds would come—but only one appeared, and that was a blackbird.

"Only one bird was flying in the air with the wind at that moment," said the wizard. "Come, blackbird, shake your feathers. I want the wind from them!"

The blackbird shook his glossy feathers out and the wizard held a green paper bag under them to catch the wind in them. The bag blew up a little, like a balloon.

"Not enough wind here to change your friend's face back again!" said the wizard, looking at it. "I wonder if there were any kites using the wind at that moment!"

He went to a cupboard and took the tail of a kite out of it. He threw it up into the air just outside the door.

116

"Come, kites, and bring
The breeze from your wing!"

he called.

Peter and Chinky watched eagerly—and to their
delight saw two kites sailing down from the sky.
One was a green one and one was a red. They fell
at the wizard's feet.

He shook each one to get the wind into his
green bag. It blew up just a little more.

"Still not enough," said the wizard. "I'll get
the little ships along. There will surely be enough
then!"

117

He ran to the mantelpiece and took a tiny sailor doll from it. He threw it up into the air and it disappeared.

"Come, ships, and bring
The breeze from your wing!"

sang the old wizard, his hair and beard streaming out like smoke.

Then, sailing up a tinkling stream that ran down the hillside came six little toy sailing ships, their sails full of the wind. They sailed right up to the wizard's front door, for the stream suddenly seemed to run there—and quickly and neatly the old wizard seized each ship, shook its sails into the green paper bag, and then popped it back on the stream. Away sailed the ships again and Peter and Chinky saw them no more.

The paper bag was quite fat and full now.

"That's about enough, I think," said the wizard. "Now I'll put the wind into a pair of bellows for you!"

He took a small pair of bellows from his fireside and put the tip of them into the green paper bag. He opened the bellows and they sucked in all the air from the bag. The wizard handed them to Peter and Chinky.

"Now don't puff with these bellows until you reach your friend," he said. "Then use them hard and puff all the air into his face! It will come right again in a twink!"

"Thank you so much for your help," said Chinky gratefully. He and Peter ran to the wishing-chair again and climbed into it, holding the bellows carefully. The chair rose up into the air as Chinky cried, "Home, chair, home!"

In a few minutes it was flying in at the boxroom window, for Mollie had run up and opened it, ready for the chair when it came back again. Peter and Chinky shut the window after them, ran down to the nursery and burst in at the door.

Thomas was still there, his face screwed up and his cheeks blown out!

"I'm so glad you're back!" said Mollie. "It's horrid being here with Thomas. His face is so nasty to look at, it makes me feel I'm in a dream! Have you got something to make it right?"

"Yes," said Chinky, showing her the bellows.

"The Windy Wizard has filled these bellows full of the wind that blew when Thomas made that face. If we puff it at him, his face will be all right again!"

"Go on then, puff!" said Mollie. So Chinky lifted up the bellows and puffed them right into Thomas's face—phoooooof! Thomas gasped and spluttered. He shut his eyes and coughed—and when he opened them, his face had gone right again! His nose and forehead were no longer screwed up, and his cheeks were quite flat, not a bit blown up!

"You're right again now, Thomas," said Chinky. "But let it be a lesson to you not to be silly any more."

"I'll never pull faces again," said Thomas, who had really had a dreadful fright. "But who are you? Are you a fairy?"

"Never mind who I am, and don't say a word about me or what has happened this afternoon!" said Chinky, and Thomas promised. He ran home feeling puzzled, but very happy to think that he had got his face its right shape again.

"Well, that was an exciting sort of adventure, Mollie!" said Peter, and he told her all about it. "The Windy Wizard was *so* nice. I say—what about giving him back his bellows?"

"I'll manage that," said Chinky, taking them. "I must go now or some one will come into the nursery and see me! Good-bye till next time!"

XVIII

MR. TWISTY

One day, when the two children and Chinky were in their playroom at the bottom of the garden, reading quietly, a knock sounded at the door.

They looked up. A small man stood there, with his straw hat in his hand and a sly look on his face.

"Have you anything old to sell?" he asked. "I buy old clothes, furniture, carpets—anything you like. I'll give you a good price for it too."

"No, thank you," said Mollie. "We couldn't sell anything unless our mother said so."

"What about that old chair there?" said the man, pointing to the wishing-chair. "It can't be wanted or you wouldn't have it in your playroom. I like the look of that. I'll give you a good price for that."

"Certainly not!" said Peter. "Please go away, or I'll call the gardener."

The little man put on his straw hat, grinned at them all, and went. Chinky looked uncomfortable. "I don't like the look of him," he said to the children. "He may make trouble for us. I think I'll hop out into the garden to-day. I don't like people seeing me here."

So he hopped out and went to play with the fairy folk there—and a good thing he did too—for in about ten minutes Mother came down the garden followed by the little man in the straw hat.

"Are you there, Peter and Mollie?" she said. "Oh, this man, Mr. Twisty, says he will buy anything old—and he saw an old chair here he would like to buy. I couldn't remember it—which is it?"

Poor Mollie and Peter! They had kept their wishing-chair such a secret—and now the secret was out! They really didn't know what to say.

Mother saw the chair and looked puzzled. "I don't remember that chair at all," she said.

"I'll give you two pounds for it," said Mr. Twisty. "'Tisn't worth it—but I'll take it for that."

"That seems a lot of money for a playroom chair," said Mother. "Well, fetch it to-night, and you can have it."

"Oh, Mother, Mother!" shrieked the two children in despair. "You don't understand. It's our own, very own chair. We love it. It's a very precious sort of chair."

"Whatever do you mean?" said Mother, in surprise. "It doesn't look at all precious to me."

Well, Mollie and Peter knew quite well that they couldn't say it was a wishing-chair and grew wings. It would be taken away from them at once, then, and put into a museum or something. Whatever were they to do?

"Two pounds for that dirty old chair," said Mr. Twisty, looking slyly at Mother.

"Very well," said Mother.

"I'll send for it to-night," said Mr. Twisty, and he bowed and went off up the garden path.

"Don't look so upset, silly-billies!" said Mother. "I'll buy you a nice comfy wicker-chair instead."

Mollie and Peter said nothing. Mollie burst into tears as soon as Mother had gone. "It's too bad!" she sobbed. "It's our own wishing-chair — and that horrible Mr. Twisty is buying it for two pounds."

Chinky came in, and they told him what had happened. He grinned at them, and put his arm round Mollie. "Don't cry," he said. "I've got a good plan."

"What?" asked Mollie.

"I can get Mr. Knobbles, the pixie carpenter who lives out in the field over there, to make me a chair almost exactly like the wishing-chair!" said Chinky. "We'll let Mr. Twisty have that one — not ours! He won't know the difference. He doesn't know ours is a wishing-chair — he just thinks it's an old and valuable chair. Well, he can buy one just like it — without the magic in it!"

"Ooh!" said Mollie and Peter, pleased. "Can you really get one made in time?"

"I think so," said Chinky. "Come along with me and see."

So they squeezed under the hedge at the bottom of the garden and crossed the field beyond to where a big oak tree stood. Chinky pulled a root aside, that stuck out above the ground, and under it was a trap-door!

"You simply *never* know where the little folk live!" said Mollie excitedly.

Chinky rapped on the door. It flew up and a bald-headed pixie with enormous ears popped his head out. Chinky explained what he wanted and the pixie invited them into his workshop underground. It was a dear little place, scattered with small tables, chairs, and stools that the carpenter had been making.

"Do you think you could make us the chair in time?" asked Mollie eagerly.

"Well, if I could get a quick-spell, I could," said the pixie. "A quick-spell makes you work three times as fast as usual, you know. But they are so expensive."

"Oh," said Mollie and Peter, in dismay. "Well, we've hardly any money."

"Wait!" said Chinky, grinning at them in his wicked way. "Remember that Mr. Twisty is paying two pounds for the chair! Can you make the chair and buy the quick-spell for two pounds, Mr. Knobbles?"

Mr. Knobbles worked out a sum on a bit of paper and said he just could. He came back to the playroom with the children and saw their own chair. He nodded his head and said he could easily make one just the same. The children were so pleased. They hugged Chinky and said he was the cleverest person they had ever known. He always knew just how to get them out of any difficulty.

"Now, we'd better hide our own chair," said Chinky. "Where shall we put it?"

"In the gardener's shed!" said Mollie. "Gardener will be gone at five. We'll put it there, then."

So they did, and covered it up with sacks. Just as they came back from the shed, they met Mr. Knobbles carrying on his back a new chair, just *exactly* like their old one! It was marvellous!

"The quick-spell worked quickly!" he said. "Here's the chair. You can bring me the money any time."

The children thanked him and put the chair in their playroom. Then they waited for Mr. Twisty.

He turned up for it at half-past six, his straw hat in his hand, and the usual wide smile on his sly face. "Ah, there's the chair!" he said. "Here's the money! Thank you very much!"

He took the chair on his back, paid over the money and went, whistling a tune.

"Well, he's got a marvellous pixie-chair for his money," said Chinky, "but he hasn't got a wishing-chair! He can sell that chair for twenty pounds, I should think—for Mr. Knobbles has made it beautifully—hasn't used a single nail—stuck everything with magic glue!"

"And *we've* got our own dear chair still!" cried the two children, and sat down in it for joy.

Just then Mother popped her head in — and saw the chair! Chinky only *just* had time to hide himself behind the sofa!

"Why!" she said, "the chair isn't sold after all! I'm quite glad, because it really is a pretty chair. I can't imagine how I came to let you have it in your playroom. I think I will have it in the house. Bring it up with you to-night, Peter."

Mother went away again. Chinky popped out from his hiding-place and looked at the others in dismay.

"I say!" he said. "That's bad news. You'll have to do as you're told, Peter. Take the chair up to the house with you when you go to-night — and we'll try and think of some way out of this new fix. Oh dear! Why can't we have our own chair!"

So Peter took it up to the house with him — and Mother put it into the study. Suppose it grew wings there! Whatever would happen?

XIX

TWO BAD CHILDREN

Mollie and Peter were very upset. Mother had got their wishing-chair in the study—and if it grew its wings there the grown-ups might see them—and then their great secret would be known. Whatever could be done about it?

Chinky had no ideas at all. He simply didn't know how to get the chair back into the playroom. If they just took it back, Mother would notice and would have it brought to the house again.

Peter and Mollie thought very hard how to get the chair for their own again—and at last Mollie had an idea. She and Peter ran down to the play-room to tell Chinky.

"This is my idea," said Mollie. "It's a very naughty one and we shall get into trouble—but I don't see how we can help it. After all, it *is* our chair!"

"Go on, tell us your plan," said Peter.

"It's this," said Mollie. "Let's spill things over the chair—and tear the seat or something—and scratch the legs! Then, when Mother sees how dirty and scratched and torn it is, she won't think it is good enough for the study—and perhaps we can have it back again!"

"I say! That's a really good idea!" said Peter and Chinky together.

"But we *shall* get into trouble!" said Peter. "You know how Mother hates us to mess things —that's why we have this playroom at the bottom of the garden—so that we can do as we like and not spoil things in the dining-room or drawing-room or study up at the house."

"Well, even if we do get into trouble it will be worth it if we can get back our chair," said Mollie. "I don't mind being punished if we can only go for some more adventures."

"All right," said Peter. "I don't either. What shall we do first?"

"We'll spill some ink across the seat," said Mollie.

"Come on, then," said Peter. So they shouted goodbye to Chinky, who wished them good luck, and ran up to the house. They went into the study. The wishing-chair stood there, looking very good and proper. Mother had put a fine new cushion into it. Mollie took it out. She didn't want to spoil anything that belonged to Mother.

Peter got the ink-bottle, and the two children emptied ink across the seat of the chair. Then they went to tell Mother.

She *was* cross! "How very, very careless of you!" she scolded. "You shall not go out to tea to-day, Peter and Mollie. I am very much annoyed with you. It's a good thing the ink didn't get on to my new cushion."

Mollie and Peter said nothing. They did not go

129

out to tea that day, and they were sad about it—but they kept thinking that perhaps they might get their wishing-chair back—so they did not get too unhappy.

The next day Peter sat in the wishing-chair and kicked his boots against the legs as hard as he could, so that they were scratched and dented. Mother heard him kicking and put her head into the study to see what was going on there.

"Peter!" she cried, "why aren't you out in the garden on this fine day—and do stop kicking your feet against that chair! Oh, you bad boy, see what you have done!"

She ran over to the chair and looked at the legs. They *were* scratched!

"This is very naughty, Peter," said Mother. "Yesterday you and Mollie spilt ink on this chair—and now you have kicked it like this. You will go to bed for the rest of the day!"

Poor Peter! He went very red, but he marched upstairs without a word. It was horrid to have to be so careless with a chair, especially one he loved so much—but still, somehow or other he *had* to get it back to the playroom! Suppose it grew its wings when Mother was sitting in it and flew away with her. Whatever would she do? She would be so frightened!

Mollie was sorry that Peter had been sent to bed. She crept into his room and gave him a piece of chocolate to eat.

130

"I'm going to slit the seat now," she whispered. "I expect I'll be sent to bed too—but surely after that Mother will say the chair isn't good enough for the study and we'll have it back again!"

So Mollie went downstairs, and took her work-basket into the study. She got out her scissors and began to cut out some dolls' clothes—and then, oh dear, she ran her scissors into the seat of the chair and made a big cut there!

Mother came in after a while—and she saw the slit at once. She stared in horror.

"Mollie! Did you do that?"

"I'm afraid I did, Mother," said Mollie.

131

"Then you are as bad as Peter," said Mother crossly. "Go to bed too. This chair is simply dreadful now—inky, torn, and scratched! It will have to go back to the playroom. I can't have it in the study. You are two bad children, and I am ashamed of you both."

It was dreadful to have Mother so cross. Mollie cried when she got into bed—but she was comforted when she thought that the wishing-chair was really going back to the playroom. She and Peter had to stay in bed all day, and they were very tired of it. But when the next day came, they carried the chair back to their playroom and called Chinky.

"We've got the chair, Chinky!" they cried. "Hurrah! But we did get into trouble. We both went to bed for the day, and Mother was dreadfully cross. We shall have to be extra nice to her now to make up—because we didn't really mean to vex her. Only we *had* to get the chair back some-how!"

"Good for you!" said Chinky, pleased. He looked at the chair and grinned.

"My word!" he said. "You did do some damage to it, didn't you! What a mess it's in! Mollie, you'd better get your needle and cotton and mend the seat—and Peter and I had better polish up the legs a bit and try and hide the scratches!"

So that morning the children and Chinky worked hard at the chair and by dinner-time it really looked very much better. Mollie put back into it the cushion they always had there, and then clapped her hands for joy.

"Dear old wishing-chair!" she said. "It's nice to have you again! Mr. Twisty nearly got you—and Mother nearly had you too—but now we've got you back again at last!"

"And *I'm* longing for another adventure!" said Peter. "I wish it would grow its wings again!"

"It soon will!" said Chinky. "I expect it wants another adventure as much as we do!"

XX

THE HORRID QUARREL

One morning Mollie, Peter, and Chinky were playing in the playroom at the bottom of the garden. It had been raining all morning, which was horrid in the summer-time. The children and the pixie were very tired of staying indoors.

They had played ludo and snap and draughts and snakes-and-ladders and dominoes. Now there didn't seem any other game to play, and they were getting cross and bored.

"Cheer up, Peter!" said Mollie, looking at Peter's cross face. "You look like a monkey that's lost its tail."

"And you look like a giraffe with a sore throat," said Peter rudely.

"Don't be horrid!" said Mollie.

"Well, don't you, then," said Peter.

"I'm not," said Mollie.

"You are," said Peter.

"Now be quiet, you two," said Chinky. "I don't like to hear you quarrelling. You only get silly."

"Don't interfere," said Peter crossly. "You talk too much, Chinky."

"Yes, remember we've been given two ears but only one mouth—so you should talk only half as much as you hear," said Mollie.

"Same to you," said Chinky. "All girls talk too much."

"They *don't*!" said Mollie. "How horrid of you to say that, Chinky."

"You're horrid this morning, too," said Chinky. "You're both horrid."

"Well, if you think that, just go away and play somewhere else," said Mollie at once. "*We* don't want you!"

"All right then, I will!" said Chinky, offended — and to the children's dismay he got up and walked out of the playroom!

"There! Now see what you've done!" said Peter, getting up. "Sent Chinky away! Suppose he doesn't come back!"

He ran to the door and called. "Chinky! Hie, Chinky! Come back a minute!"

But there was no answer. Chinky had gone. There was no sign of him anywhere.

"I do think you are horrid and silly," said Peter to Mollie. "Fancy sending Chinky away like that!"

"I didn't mean to," said Mollie, almost in tears. "He was being horrid, so I was too. We were all being horrid."

"*I* wasn't," said Peter.

"Yes, you were," said Mollie.

"No, I wasn't," said Peter.

"Yes, you were," said Mollie. "I shall smack you in a minute."

135

"Now, now!" said a voice, and Mother looked in at the door. "You are silly to quarrel like that! Uncle Jack is here and wants to know if you would like to go with him to the farm. They have some puppies there, and he wants to choose one for himself. Would you like to go and help him?"

"Oh yes!" cried Peter and Mollie. "We'll put on our macs and rubber boots and go with him!"

So off they ran, forgetting all about their quarrel —and all about Chinky too! They went to the farm with Uncle Jack and chose a lovely black puppy with him. Then back home they went, chattering and laughing, forgetting all about how horrid they had been, and enjoying their lovely walk.

It was dinner-time when they got home. They had dinner and ran down to the playroom afterwards, meaning to ask Chinky to play with them in the field outside the garden.

But Chinky wasn't in the playroom. Peter and Mollie looked at one another and went red.

"Do you suppose he has *really* gone?" said Mollie, feeling upset.

"I don't know," said Peter. "I'll whistle for him outside and see if he comes trotting out of the bushes!"

So Peter went to the door and whistled the little pixie tune that Chinky had taught him. But no Chinky came trotting up. It was really horrid.

"Suppose he never, never comes again!" said

Mollie, crying. "Oh, I do, do wish I'd never said that to him—telling him to go away. I didn't really mean it."

"I shan't like going on adventures in the wishing-chair unless Chinky is with us," said Peter. "It isn't any fun without him."

"Peter, do you suppose he will *never* come and see us again?" asked Mollie.

"I shouldn't be surprised," said Peter. "Pixies are funny, you know—not quite like ordinary people."

The two children would have been very unhappy indeed if something hadn't suddenly happened to take their minds away from their disappointment. The wishing-chair suddenly grew its wings again!

"Look!" said Mollie excitedly. "The chair is ready to fly off again. Shall we go, Peter?"

"I don't feel as if I want to, now Chinky's not here," said Peter gloomily.

"But, Peter, I've such a good idea!" said Mollie, running to him. "Listen! Let's get in the wishing-chair and tell it to go to Chinky's home, wherever it is. I expect he's gone back there, don't you? Then we can say we're sorry and ask him to come back again."

"That's a fine idea," said Peter, at once. "Come on, Mollie. Get in! We'll go at once."

So the two children squeezed into the wishing-chair. It had grown its four red wings round its legs and was lazily flapping them to and fro,

longing to be off into the air once more.

"Go to Chinky's home," commanded Peter. The chair rose up into the air, flew out of the door and rose high above the trees. It was fun to fly again. The two children looked down on the gardens and fields, and wished 'Chinky were with them, sitting in his usual place on the top of the chair!

"I wonder where Chinky's home *is*," said Peter. "He has never told us."

"We shall soon see," said Mollie.

The chair flew on and on, just below the clouds. Soon it came to the towers and spires of Fairyland.

Then it suddenly flew downwards to a little village of quaint crooked houses, all of them small, and all of them with bright flowery gardens. The chair flew down into one of the gardens and rested there. The children jumped off at once.

They went to the little red door of the house and knocked.

"Won't Chinky be surprised to see us!" said Mollie.

The door opened. An old pixie woman, with a very sweet face and bright eyes, looked out at them.

"Oh!" said Mollie, in disappointment. "We thought this was Chinky's home."

"So it is when he is at home!" said the pixie woman. "I'm his mother. Come in, please."

They went into a neat and spotless little kitchen. Chinky's mother set ginger buns and lemonade in front of them.

"Thank you," said Peter. "Do you know where Chinky is?"

"He came and asked me to make up his bed for to-night," said the pixie woman. "He said he had quarrelled with you, and wanted to come and live at home again."

The children went red. "I didn't mean what I said," said Mollie, in a little voice.

"I expect Chinky was to blame too," said his mother. "He went out to buy himself a new hand-kerchief—and though I've been waiting and waiting for him he hasn't come back—so I wondered if he had gone back to you again."

"No, he didn't come back," said Peter. "I wonder what's happened to him. We'll stay a little while, if you don't mind, and see if he comes back."

Chinky didn't come back—but in a short while a round, fat pixie came running up the path and into the kitchen, puffing and panting.

"Oh, Mrs. Twinkle!" he cried, when he saw Chinky's mother. "A dreadful thing has happened to Chinky!"

"What!" cried every one in alarm.

"He had bought himself a nice new red handkerchief and was walking down the lane home again when a big yellow bird swooped down from the air, caught hold of Chinky by the belt, and flew off with him!" cried the pixie.

"Oh my, oh my!" wept Mrs. Twinkle. "I know that bird. It belongs to the enchanter Clip-clap. He always sends that bird of his out when he wants to capture some one to help him. Poor Chinky!"

"Don't cry!" said Peter, putting his arms round the old woman. "We'll go and look for Chinky. The magic chair we have will take us. We will try to bring him back safely. It's a very good thing we came to look for him! Come on, Mollie — get into the wishing-chair and we'll tell it to go to wherever Chinky is!"

In they both got. Peter told the chair to go to Chinky, and it rose into the air.

"Another adventure!" said Mollie. "I do hope it turns out all right!"

XXI

THE ENCHANTER CLIP-CLAP

The wishing-chair rose high up and flew steadily towards the west. It had a long way to go so it flew faster than usual, and all its four wings flapped swiftly.

"I wonder where the enchanter lives," said Mollie. "I hope he won't capture us too!"

"Well, all this would never have happened if we hadn't quarrelled with Chinky," said Peter. "He wouldn't have gone back home then—and wouldn't have gone out to buy a new handkerchief —and wouldn't have been captured by the yellow bird that swooped down on him and took him away!"

"I shall never quarrel again," said Mollie. It made her very sad when she remembered the unkind things she had said that morning.

The chair flew over a wood. Mollie leaned over the arm of the chair and looked down.

"Look, Peter," she said. "What is that funny thing sticking out of the wood?"

Peter looked. "It's a very, very high stone tower," he said. "Isn't it strange? It's just a tower by itself. It doesn't seem to be part of a castle or anything. I say! The chair is flying down to it! Do you suppose that is where the enchanter lives?"

"It must be," said Mollie. The children looked

142

eagerly downwards to see what sort of tower this was. It certainly was very queer. It had a pointed roof but no chimneys at all. The chair circled all round it as it flew downwards, trying to find a window. But there was not a single window to be seen!

"This really is a very magic sort of tower!" said Mollie. "Not a window anywhere! Well, there must be a door at the bottom to get in by."

The chair flew to the ground and stayed there. The children jumped off. They went to the tower and looked for a door. There was not one to be seen!

The tower was quite round, and very tall indeed, higher than the highest tree — but it had no doors and no windows, so it seemed quite impossible to get into it. Mollie and Peter walked round and round it a great many times, but no matter how they looked, they could see no way to get in.

"Do you suppose Chinky is in there," said Mollie at last.

"Sure to be," said Peter gloomily. "We told the chair to take us to where Chinky was, you know."

"Well, what are we going to do?" asked Mollie. "Shall we call for Chinky loudly?"

"No," said Peter at once. "If you do that the enchanter will know we are here and may capture us too. Don't do anything like that, Mollie."

"Well, how else are we to tell Chinky we are

here?" said Mollie. "We must *do* something, Peter. It's no good standing here looking for doors and windows that aren't there."

"Sh!" said Peter suddenly, and he pulled Mollie behind a tree. He had heard a noise.

Mollie caught hold of the wishing-chair and pulled that behind the tree too—and only just in time!

There came a loud noise, like the clip-clapping of thunder. A great door appeared in the round tower, half as high as the tower itself. It opened—and out came the enchanter Clip-clap! He was very tall and thin, and he had a long beard that reached the ground. He wore it in a plait and it looked very queer.

"See you finish that spell properly!" he called to some one in the tower. Then there came another loud clapping noise, just like a roll and crash of thunder, and the door in the tower closed—and vanished! The enchanter strode away through the wood, his head almost as high as the trees!

"Goodness!" said Mollie. "We only just got behind this tree in time. It's impossible to get into that tower, Peter. We should never know how to make that door appear."

"What *are* we to do!" sighed Peter. "I hate to think of poor old Chinky a prisoner in there—and all because we quarrelled with him, too."

"Let's hide the chair under a bush and see if we can find any one living near here," said Mollie.

"We might find some one who could help us."

So they carefully hid the chair under a bramble-bush, and piled bracken over it too. Then they found a little path and went down it, wondering where it led to.

It led to a small and pretty cottage. The name was on the gate . . . Dimple Cottage. Mollie liked the sound of it. She thought they would be quite safe in going there.

They knocked. To their enormous surprise the door was opened by a brown mouse! She wore a check apron and cap, and large slippers on her feet. The children stared. They could never get used to this sort of thing, although they had seen many strange sights by now.

"Good afternoon," said Peter, and then didn't know what else to say.

"Do you want to see my mistress?" asked the mouse.

"Well, yes, perhaps it would be a good idea," said Peter. So the mouse asked them in and showed them into a tiny drawing-room.

"What are we going to *say*?" whispered Peter — but before Mollie had time to answer, some one came into the room.

It was a small elf, with neat silvery wings, silvery golden hair, and a big dimple in her cheek when she smiled. Mollie and Peter liked her at once.

"Good afternoon," she said. "What can I do for you?"

Both talking at once, the two children told her their troubles—how they had quarrelled with Chinky—and he had gone home—and been caught by the yellow bird belonging to the enchanter Clip-clap—and how their wishing-chair had brought them to the strange tower.

"But we don't know how to get into it and we are afraid of being caught by Clip-clap too," said Peter. "I don't know if you can help us?"

"I don't think I can," said the elf, whose name was Dimple. "No one knows a spell powerful enough to get into the enchanter's tower. I've lived here for three hundred years and no one has ever got into that tower except the enchanter and his servants and friends. I wouldn't try if I were you."

"We *must*," said Mollie. "You see, Chinky is our own friend—and we must help him."

"Yes—we have to help our friends," said the elf. "Wait a minute—I wonder if my mouse knows anything that might help us. Harriet! Harriet!"

The little servant mouse came running in. "Yes, Madam," she said.

"Harriet, these children want to get into the enchanter's tower," said Dimple. "Do you know of any way in?"

"Well yes, Madam, I do," said Harriet.

"Oh, do you!" cried Mollie, in delight. "Do, do tell us, Harriet!"

"My auntie lives down in the cellars of the tower," said the little mouse. "Sometimes, on my afternoon off, I go to see her."

"And how do you get into the tower?" asked Dimple.

"Down the mouse-hole, of course," said Harriet. "There's one on the far side of the tower. I always scamper down there."

"Oh," said the children, in disappointment, looking at the small mouse. "*We* couldn't get down a mousehole. We are too big. You are a big mouse, but even so, the mouse-hole would not take us!"

Mollie was so disappointed that she cried into her handkerchief. Dimple patted her on the back.

"Don't do that," she said. "I can give you a spell to make you small. Then you can slip down the mouse-hole with Harriet, and see if you can find Chinky."

"Oh thank you, thank you!" cried the children, in delight. "That *is* kind of you!"

Dimple went to a shelf and took down a box. Out of it she shook two pills. They were queer because they were green one side and red the other!

"Here you are," she said. "Eat these and you will be small enough to go down the hole. They taste horrid, but never mind."

The children each chewed up a pill. They certainly had a funny taste—but they were very magic indeed, and no sooner were they eaten than Mollie and Peter felt as though they were going

147

down in a lift—for they suddenly grew very tiny indeed! They looked up at Dimple, and she seemed enormous to them!

"Harriet, take off your apron and cap and take these children to your auntie," said Dimple. So Harriet carefully folded up her cap and apron and then went out with the children. She took them to the tower and showed them a small hole under the wall.

"Down here!" she said—and down they all went!

XXII

THE STRANGE TOWER

The hole was dark and smelt a bit funny. Mollie clung tightly to Peter's hand. It was strange being so small.

Harriet the mouse went on in front, and they could see her little gleaming eyes as she turned round now and again. Once Peter trod on her tail and she gave an angry squeal.

"So sorry," said Peter. "I keep forgetting you have such a long tail, Harriet."

At last they came to a place where the tunnel widened out into a room. It was very warm there. A large mouse pounced on Harriet and gave her a hug.

"Oh, Auntie, you're at home!" said Harriet. "See, I've brought you two children. They wanted to get into the tower, so I thought they might as well use our mouse-tunnel. It's the only way in."

"Good afternoon," said Harriet's aunt. She seemed just an ordinary mouse except that she wore large spectacles. Her home was chiefly made of paper, it seemed. There were hundreds of little bits of it, neatly made into beds and tables.

"What are the children going to do?" said Harriet's aunt.

"We would like to know how to get into the

149

cellars," said Peter. "You see, if you show us the way there we can get into the tower above and perhaps find the friend we are looking for."

"Well, come this way then," said the aunt. "But look out for the cat, won't you? She sometimes waits about in the cellar and you don't want her to catch you."

She took them down another narrow passage, and then the children found themselves walking out of a hole into a dark, damp cellar.

"Good-bye," said the mouse. "I'll put a little candle just inside this hole, so that you will know the way back, children. I hope you find your friend."

Mollie took Peter's hand. The cellar was very dark. A chink of light came from somewhere to the right.

"The cellar steps must go up towards that chink of light," said Peter. "Come on. Walk carefully in case we bump into anything. And look out for the cat! We are very small, you know."

They found the steps. They seemed very, very big to the children, now that they were so tiny, and Peter had to help Mollie up each one. At last they got to the top. They looked under the door that stood at the top of the steps. Beyond was a kitchen.

"Do you suppose the enchanter is back yet?" whispered Mollie.

"No," said Peter. "We should have heard that clip-clapping noise if he had come back. I think

we are safe at the moment. But we must hide at once if we hear him coming. And look out for the cat, Mollie."

"Can we squeeze under the door, do you think?" asked Mollie. But they couldn't. The crack was not big enough. However, the door was not quite closed, and by pushing with all their might the two children managed to get it just enough open to squeeze through.

They looked round. They were in a very big kitchen—or it seemed big to them, because they were so tiny. They could not see Chinky anywhere.

"Come on," said Peter, giving Mollie his hand. "We'll go into the next room."

"Meow!" suddenly came a voice, and a large tabby cat with green eyes came out from behind a chair. Mollie felt quite shaky at the knees. She knew what a mouse must feel like when it saw a cat! What a giant of an animal it seemed!

"Don't show it you are frightened," said Peter. "It has smelt us, and we don't smell like mice. Stay here a moment, Mollie, and I'll go over to it and stroke what I can reach of it."

"Oh, Peter, you *are* brave!" said Mollie. Peter walked boldly over to the cat and stroked her legs. She seemed very pleased and purred loudly. Peter beckoned to Mollie. She ran over and stroked the cat too. It was a friendly creature.

It went into the next room, purring to Mollie and Peter, who followed her. This room was very small and was lighted by a candle. No daylight came into the tower, for there were no windows.

No one was in this little room either. A dish stood on the floor with some milk in it, and a large round basket with a fat cushion in it stood nearby.

"This must be the cat's room," said Mollie. "There is no furniture in it. I do wonder where Chinky is."

There were some stairs going upwards from the cat's little room. The children climbed them with great difficulty for they were very small, and the stairs seemed very big.

152

Before they got to the top they heard the sound of crying. It was Chinky! He must indeed be very unhappy if he were crying! He hardly ever cried.

How Mollie and Peter tried to climb those stairs quickly! At last they reached the top and found themselves before a big open door. They ran in. Chinky was lying on a small bed, crying as if his heart would break!

"Chinky! Chinky! Don't cry! We are here to rescue you!" shouted Peter, hoping that Chinky would hear his voice, for it was a very small one now.

Chinky did hear it. He sat up at once, with the tears still running down his cheeks. He saw Mollie and Peter and stared at them in surprise.

"Chinky!" cried Mollie, running over to him. "We've come to save you. Cheer up! We got in through a mouse-hole after an elf had made us small. How can we save you?"

"Oh, you are good, good friends to come and look for me," said Chinky, drying his eyes. "I hate being here. I hate this enchanter. He wants me to do bad spells, and I won't. I was afraid I would be here for hundreds of years and never see you again."

"Tell us how we can get away," said Peter.

"Well, the only way in seems to be the mouse-hole you came by," said Chinky. "So I suppose the only way out is the mouse-hole too. But I'm too big to go that way."

153

"Well, I'll go back to Dimple's cottage and ask her for a pill to make you small like us," said Peter, at once. "Then when I bring it back you can take it, and we'll all go down the hole, get Dimple to make us the right size again, find the wishing-chair, and go home. See?"

"It sounds easy enough," said Chinky. "But I don't somehow think it will all go quite so nicely as that. Still, we can but try. Leave Mollie here with me, Peter, and you go down the mouse-hole again."

"We'll see him safely to the cellar door," said Mollie. So they all went down the stairs again, and were just going through the cat's little room when Chinky turned pale.

"The enchanter's coming back!" he said. "Oh, where can you hide?"

"Quick, quick, think of somewhere!" cried Mollie. There came a clip-clapping noise, like thunder, as she spoke. The tower split in half and a door came. It opened, and in strode the enchanter, tall and thin, his plaited beard sweeping the ground.

But before he had seen the two children Peter had pulled Mollie over to the cat's basket. The big cat was lying there comfortably. The children scrambled in and lay down by the cat, hiding in her thick fur. Chinky was left by himself.

"I smell children!" said the enchanter.

"How could children get into your tower,

154

master?" said Chinky with a look of surprise.

The enchanter sniffed and began to look all round the two rooms. The cat did not stir. Clipclap stroked her as he passed, and she purred — but she stayed in her basket, and Mollie and Peter cuddled close into her fur, hoping she would not move at all.

The enchanter did not think of looking in the cat's basket. He soon gave up the hunt and ran up the stairs, calling to Chinky to go with him.

"Go quickly now, Peter," whispered Chinky, before he followed Clip-clap. "Mollie can stay with the cat. She is safe there."

Quick as could be Peter slipped across the floor to the cellar door, squeezed through the small opening, and made his way down the steps. He saw the tiny candlelight burning at the entrance to the mouse-hole and ran across to it. In he went and made his way up to the mouse-room. Harriet the mouse was still there, talking to her auntie.

"Please, will you take me back to Dimple?" asked Peter. "It is very important."

Harriet gave him her paw and took him up the hole out into the open air again. Then they hurried together to Dimple's cottage. Soon Peter had told Dimple all that had happened. She gave him another red-and-green pill, and warned him to be careful not to let Clip-clap see him.

Then off went Peter to the mouse-hole again. Ah! Chinky would soon be safe!

XXIII

THE GREAT ESCAPE

Peter hurried from Dimple's cottage, holding the pill in his hand that was to make Chinky as small as he was—then they could all escape down the mouse-hole!

He ran down the hole and made his way to the cellar. He climbed up the steps to the kitchen. He peeped under the door. There was no one in the kitchen.

He ran over the floor to the little room belonging to the cat. The big grey tabby was still in the basket, and Mollie was there too, hiding safely under the thick fur. Good!

"Chinky is still upstairs with the enchanter," she whispered. Just at that moment there came footsteps down the stairs, and the enchanter came in.

The cat jumped out of her basket and went to greet him, rubbing against Clip-clap's legs and purring loudly. Mollie and Peter crouched down in the basket and tried to hide under the cushion —but, alas! The enchanter saw them!

"Aha! I *thought* I sniffed children!" he said. He came over to the basket and looked down.

"How small you are!" he said. "I did not know there were such small children to be found. What have you got in your hand, little boy?"

Oh dear! What Peter was holding so tightly was the little green-and-red pill that was to make Chinky small enough to go down the mouse-hole! Peter put his hand behind his back and glared at the tall enchanter.

But it was no use. He had to show Clip-clap what he had—and no sooner did the enchanter see the little green-and-red pill than he guessed what it was for!

"Oho!" he said. "So you made yourselves small first, did you—and came in through a mouse-hole, I guess—thinking to make Chinky small too, so that he might escape the same way! Well—I'll spoil all that! You shall grow big again—and you won't be able to creep down *any* mouse-holes! You can stay here and help Chinky work for me!"

He tapped Mollie on the head and then Peter. They shot up to their own size again, and stared at Clip-clap in alarm and dismay. What a horrid ending to all their plans! They had thought themselves so clever, too.

"Well," said Clip-clap, looking at them. "You won't escape in a hurry now, I promise you! No one knows the secret of making the door come in this tower but me! Chinky! Chinky! Come and see your fine friends now!"

Chinky came running down the stairs and stopped in the greatest dismay when he saw Peter and Mollie, both their right size, standing in front of the enchanter.

157

"So you had all laid fine plans for escape, had you?" said Clip-clap. "Well, now you can just settle down to working hard for me, and using those good brains of yours for my spells! Go and help Chinky to polish my bedroom floor, and after that you can clean all the silver wands I use for my magic!"

The three went upstairs very sadly and in silence.

Chinky handed each child a large yellow duster and all three went down on their hands and knees and began to polish the wooden floor.

"Don't say a word till we hear Clip-clap go out again," whispered Chinky. "He has ears as sharp as a hare's."

So nobody said a word until they heard the clip-clap crashing noise, and knew that the enchanter had gone out again. Then they stood up and looked at one another.

"What *are* we to do now?" groaned Peter.

"Listen!" said Chinky quickly. "I have a plan. Where's the wishing-chair?"

"Under a bramble bush outside the tower," said Peter. "But what's the good of that? We can't get out to it, and certainly the chair can't get in!"

"I'm not so sure of that!" said Chinky. "You know that mouse you told me about—Dimple's servant? Well, if you could speak to her, Peter, and tell her to go to Dimple and tell her what's

158

happened, she might be able to make the wishing-chair small enough for Harriet to get it down the mouse-hole and into the cellar. *I* know a spell to make it the right size—and then, when Clip-clap does his disappearing act and goes out through the tower door, we'll fly out too! See?"

"Oh Chinky, Chinky, you *are* clever!" cried Mollie, in delight. "Peter, go down to the cellar and call Harriet. She may be somewhere about. If not, her auntie will surely be there!"

So Peter hurried down to the cellar and called Harriet.

She wasn't there, but her auntie came—the brown mouse with spectacles on. Peter told her all that had happened, and begged her to go and tell Dimple, the elf. She hurried off at once, and Peter waited anxiously to see what would happen next.

But Clip-clap came back before anything else had happened. He set the three to work polishing his magic wands—but took the magic out of them first! He wasn't going to have Chinky doing any magic with them, not he!

After tea Clip-clap went out again, and Peter hurried down to the cellar. To his great delight he found Harriet there—and just inside the mouse-hole she had their wishing-chair! It was as small as a doll's house chair.

"My auntie told me all that had happened," whispered Harriet. "I told Dimple, my mistress, and we found the wishing-chair. Dimple made it small enough for me to take down the mouse-hole. Here it is. Good luck!"

She pushed the tiny wishing-chair out of the hole.

Peter picked it up gladly and ran up the cellar-steps with it. How glad Chinky and Mollie were to see it!

"Now," said Chinky, "I must make it big again." He felt in his pockets and took out a duster coloured yellow and green. It had a queer-smelling polish in the middle in a great smear. Chinky began to polish the chair as hard as he could.

As he polished it, it grew bigger – and bigger – and bigger! The children watched in amazement.

At last it was its usual size. "Where shall we hide it?" asked Mollie.

"I say! Don't let's hide it anywhere!" said Peter suddenly. "What about us all getting into it, and waiting till Clip-clap comes back? Then, as soon as he opens the door to come in, we'll yell to the chair to fly out – and off we'll go! The enchanter won't know what's happening till it's too late to stop us!"

"That's a splendid idea!" said Chinky, at once. "We'll do it. Come on – get in, you two – the enchanter may be in at any moment! We must be ready!"

"The good old wishing-chair still has its wings," said Mollie, thankfully. "Wouldn't it be awful if they went, and we couldn't fly away?"

"Don't say things like that in front of the chair," said Peter. "You know how silly it can be sometimes. Have you forgotten the time it landed us all into a chimney?"

"'Sh!" said Chinky. "I can hear Clip-clap coming."

Crash! The tower split in two, and a great door appeared in the slit. It opened – and in strode Clip-clap, calling Chinky. "Hi, Chinky, Chinky!"

"Home, wishing-chair, home!" yelled Chinky. "Hallo, Clip-clap – here I am!"

161

The chair rose up into the air, flew past the left ear of the astonished enchanter and shot out of the door before Clip-clap could shut it! They were safely out in the wood again!

"There's Dimple and Harriet below, waving like mad!" said Peter. "Wave back, you two!"

They all waved to Dimple and Harriet and called good-bye. "We'll send them a postcard when we get back," said Chinky. "They were very good to help us."

"Won't Clip-clap be angry to think we've escaped after all!" said Mollie.

"I say! Oughtn't you to go and tell your mother you are safe?" said Peter. "She was very worried about you."

"I'll go to-night when you are both in bed," said Chinky. "I'll take you home safely first. My, what adventures we've had since this morning!"

"I'm not going to quarrel ever again," said Mollie, as the chair flew in at the playroom door. She jumped off and flung her arms round Chinky. "It was horrid when you didn't come back. I didn't mean what I said. You will always be our friend, won't you, Chinky?"

"Of course," said Chinky, grinning all over his cheeky pixie face. "I would have come back the next day. I was just in a bad temper. We all were."

"I'm sorry about it, too," said Peter. "Anyway, we're all together again, friends as much as before."

162

"You'd better run in and show your mother you're all right," said Chinky. "Mothers are such worriers, you know. You've not been in to tea, so yours will wonder if you're all right. Good-bye! Thanks so much for rescuing me."

Peter and Mollie ran off happily.

Thank goodness everything was all right again! Good old wishing-chair—what *would* they do without it?

XXIV

BIG-EARS THE GOBLIN

One day, when Mollie and Peter were playing with Chinky in the playroom, they heard footsteps running down the garden.

"Quick! Hide, Chinky! There is some one coming!" cried Mollie. The pixie always hid when any one was about. He ran to a cupboard and got inside. Peter shut the door just as Mother came into the playroom.

"Children!" she said, "I've lost my ring! I must have dropped it in the garden somewhere. Please look for it, and see if you can find it."

Peter and Mollie were upset. They knew that their mother was very fond of her best ring. It was a very pretty one, set with diamonds and rubies. They ran out into the garden and began to hunt —but no matter where they looked they could see no sign of any ring!

"Let's go and ask Chinky to help," said Mollie. So they ran back to the playroom. Chinky was sitting reading. They told him how they had hunted for the ring.

"I'll soon find out if it's in the garden," he said, shutting his book. "Is your mother certain she dropped it there?"

"Quite certain," said Peter. "How are you going to find out where it is, Chinky?"

"You'll see in a minute!" said the pixie, with a grin. He went to the door of the playroom and looked round. There was no one about. He whistled softly a strange little twittering tune. A freckled thrush flew down to his hand and stood on his outstretched fingers.

"Listen, Freckles," said Chinky. "There is a ring lost in this garden. Get all the birds together and tell them to hunt for it."

Freckles gave a chirrup and flew off. In a few minutes all the birds in the garden were gathered together in a thick lilac bush. Mollie and Peter could hear the thrush singing away, just as if he were telling a story in a song. They knew he must be telling the birds what to do.

In a few seconds every sparrow, starling, thrush, blackbird, robin, and finch was hopping about the ground, under bushes and in the beds, under the hedges and over the grass. They pecked here and there, they turned over every leaf, and they hunted for that ring as neither Mollie nor Peter could possibly have hunted.

At last Freckles the thrush came back. He flew down on to Chinky's shoulder and chirruped a long and pretty song into his ear. Then he flew off.

"What does he say?" asked Mollie.

"He says that your mother's ring is nowhere here at all," said Chinky. "She can't have dropped it in the garden."

"But she knows she *did*," said Mollie.

"Well, some one must have found it already, then," said Chinky. "I wonder if any goblin was about last night! They are not honest if they find any beautiful jewel. Wait! I'll find out!"

He went to the lawn near the playroom. It was well hidden from the house, so he could not be seen. He drew a ring on the grass in blue chalk.

"Keep away from this ring," he said to the watching children. "When I say the goblin spell, you will see blue flames and smoke come up from the ring if goblins have been this way during the last few hours. Don't go too near. If nothing happens we shall know that no goblins have been this way."

Mollie and Peter watched whilst Chinky danced slowly round the ring, chanting a string of curious, magic-sounding words.

"Look! Look! Smoke is coming—and blue flames!" shrieked Mollie excitedly. "Oh, Chinky, don't go too near!"

Sure enough, as they watched, the ring began to smoke as if it were on fire, and small blue flames flickered all around. Chinky stopped singing. He threw a pinch of dust over the ring. Smoke, flames, and chalk ring vanished as if they had never been there!

"Yes," said Chinky, "a goblin has been here all right! When a blue chalk ring flames like that it's a sure sign of goblins. I wonder which one it was. I'll just go and ask the fairies at the bottom of the garden – they'll know."

He ran off. The children didn't follow, for they knew that Chinky didn't like them to see the fairies, who were very shy. He came back, running fast, his face red with excitement.

"Yes – the fairies saw Big-Ears the goblin pass by here last night – so he must have found the ring and taken it. They said that he seemed very pleased about something."

"Oh dear! How can we get it back for Mother?" asked Mollie in despair.

"We'll get it back all right. Don't worry," said Chinky. "As soon as the wishing-chair grows its wings again we'll go off to old Big-Ears. He'll soon give it back. He's an old coward."

"Good!" said the children in delight. "Oh, won't it be fun to have an adventure again! Where does Big-Ears live?"

"Not very far away," said Chinky. "In Goblin Town. Listen – there's your dinner-bell. You go in to dinner and I'll see if I can get the wishing-chair to grow its wings again. Sometimes a little singing helps it."

The children ran indoors, bubbling with excitement. What fun if the chair grew its wings that afternoon.

After dinner they ran back to their playroom. Chinky met them at the door with a grin.

"The chair's grown its wings!" he said. "It is in a great hurry to get away, so come on!"

Peter and Mollie ran into the playroom. The wishing-chair certainly seemed in a great hurry to go. Its wings were flapping merrily, and it was giving little hops about the floor.

"It thinks it's a bird or something!" said Chinky, grinning. "It will twitter soon!"

The children sat down on the seat. Chinky climbed on to the back. "To Goblin Town!" he cried.

The chair rose into the air and flew out of the door with such a rush that the children were nearly thrown out of their seats.

"Steady, chair, steady!" said Chinky. "There's not such a dreadful hurry, you know."

The chair flew so high in the air that the children were above the clouds, and could see nothing below them but the rolling white mist, like a great dazzling snowfield.

"Where are we now?" asked Mollie, peering down. "Are we getting near Goblin Town?"

"We must be," said Chinky. "But we shan't know till the chair dives down through the clouds again. Ah! Here we go!"

Down went the chair through the cold white clouds. The children looked to see if Goblin Town was below.

"Look at those funny, crooked little houses!" cried Mollie in delight. "And look at the goblins! Oh, it's a market, or something!"

The chair flew down to a busy market-place.

The goblins crowded round it in surprise.

"Good afternoon," said Chinky, getting down from the back of the chair. "Can you tell me where Big-Ears lives?"

"He lives in the yellow cottage at the foot of the hill," said a little green goblin, pointing. The children carried the chair down the hill, for it had stopped flapping its wings and seemed tired. They came to the yellow cottage, and Chinky knocked loudly.

The door opened. There stood a goblin with yellow eyes and great big pointed ears that stuck above the top of his head.

"Good morning, Big-Ears," said Chinky. "We have come for that ring you picked up in our garden the other night."

"W-w-w-what r-r-r-ring?" stammered the goblin, going pale with fright. "I d-d-d-didn't see any ring."

"Oh yes, you did," said Chinky firmly. "And if you don't give it back AT ONCE I'll turn you into a wriggling worm."

"No, no, no!" cried Big-Ears, falling to his knees. "Don't do that. Yes—I did take the ring—but I have given it to the Snoogle, who lives in that castle over there."

"Off to the Snoogle then!" shouted Chinky, and he jumped into the wishing-chair. The children followed—and up went the chair into the air. They were off to the Snoogle—whatever he might be!

169

XXV

THE SNOOGLE

The wishing-chair was off to find the Snoogle!

"If the Snoogle has your mother's ring, we shall have to find some way of getting it back," said Chinky. "I wonder who or what he is. I've never heard of him before."

The chair flew on. Soon, in the distance, the three could see an enormous castle set on a hill-top. At the bottom, all round the foot, was a great moat full of water. A drawbridge stretched across the moat—but, even as the children looked at it, it was drawn up into the gateway on the castle side of the moat.

"There's no way of getting in the Snoogle's castle except by flying, that's plain," said Chinky. "Fly on to the roof, wishing-chair."

The wishing-chair flew to the roof of the castle. It was turreted, and the chair flew over the turrets and down on to a flat part behind.

Sitting on the roof basking in the sunshine was the Snoogle.

The children stared at him in astonishment. He was the funniest-looking creature they had ever seen. He had the body of a dragon, the tail of a cat always twirling and twisting, and the head of a yellow duck!

He was sitting in a deck-chair fast asleep. The

wishing-chair flew down beside his chair, and the children stared at the Snoogle. They did not get out of the chair, because, really, they hardly liked the look of the Snoogle. But Chinky jumped down and went to have a good stare at him.

"Snore-r-r-r-r-r!" went the sleeping Snoogle. "Snore-r-r-r-r-r!"

"Hie! Wake up, Snoogle!" shouted Chinky, and he gave the Snoogle a poke in the chest. The Snoogle woke up in a fright and quacked loudly.

"Quack, quack, quack, quack, quack!" He leapt to his two pairs of dragon feet and glared at Chinky.

"I've come to fetch the ring that Big-Ears the

goblin gave you," said Chinky boldly. "Will you get it, please?"

"You'd better get it yourself," said the Snoogle sulkily.

"Where is it, then?" asked Chinky.

"Go down the stairs there, and walk down two hundred steps," said Snoogle. "You will come to a bolted door. Unbolt it and walk in. You will see my bedroom there. In a big box on the mantelpiece you will find the ring. It was given to me by Big-Ears, and I think you should give me something in return for it."

"You shall have nothing!" cried Chinky. "You knew quite well that Big-Ears should not have taken that ring from our garden. I believe you were just keeping it for him till people had forgotten it and had given up hunting for it. You are just as dishonest as Big-Ears!"

The Snoogle waved its cat-like tail to and fro in anger. It gave a few loud quacks, but Chinky only laughed. He didn't seem a bit afraid of the Snoogle.

"I'll go down and get the ring," he said to the others. "Stay here."

He ran down the steps—but no sooner had he disappeared down them than the Snoogle also went down—following softly behind Chinky.

"Oh! He's gone to catch Chinky!" cried Mollie. "Shout, Peter; shout, and warn him!"

So Peter shouted with all his might—but

Chinky was too far down the steps to hear. The Snoogle waited for him to unbolt the bedroom door—and then, when Chinky was safely inside looking for the box on the mantelpiece, he slammed the door and bolted it.

"Quack!" he cried, with a deep chuckle. "Now you are caught, you cheeky little pixie."

Mollie and Peter were running down the steps, shouting to Chinky. They suddenly heard the sound of the bedroom door being slammed, and the bolts driven home.

"Stop, Mollie," said Peter, clutching hold of her arm. "Chinky is caught. It's no use us running straight into the Snoogle as he comes back. Slip into this room here, and perhaps he will go past us up to the roof again."

They slipped into a nearby room. They hid behind the door—and as he passed, the Snoogle popped his head into the room and looked round it—but he did not see the two children squeezed tightly behind the door.

"Quack!" he said loudly, and went on up the steps.

Mollie and Peter slipped out of the room as soon as it was safe and ran to where Chinky was hammering on the inside of the bolted door in a furious rage. "Let me out, let me out!" he was shouting.

"Chinky, Chinky, hush!" said Peter. "We're just going to unbolt the door."

173

The bolts were big and heavy. It took both Mollie and Peter to pull them back. They opened the door — and there was Chinky, looking as angry as could be.

"To think I should have been trapped so easily!" said Chinky, in a fury. "Anyway — I've got the ring! Look!"

He showed them a ring — and sure enough it was the very one their mother had lost! Mollie and Peter were so pleased.

"Now I'll just go and tell that Snoogle what I think of him!" said Chinky fiercely. "*I'm* not afraid of any Snoogle — silly, duck-headed creature!"

"Oh, Chinky, do be careful," said Mollie, half afraid. "We've got the ring. Can't we just go quietly up to the roof, get into our chair, and go away? I'd much rather do that."

"We'll get into the chair and fly away all right," said Chinky. "But I'm just going to tell the Snoogle a few things first."

The children had never seen the little pixie look so angry. He marched up the steps and out on the roof. Mollie and Peter followed.

The Snoogle was looking all round for the two children, quacking angrily. He was surprised to see them coming up the steps — and even more surprised to see Chinky, whom he thought was safely bolted in the room below.

"Now, look here, Snoogle," said Chinky boldly,

174

walking right up to the surprised creature, "how *dare* you try to capture me like that? I am a pixie — yes, and a powerful one too. I can do spells that would frighten you. Shall I turn you into a black-beetle — or a tadpole — or a wasp without a sting?"

To the children's surprise, the Snoogle looked very much frightened. He was such a big creature compared with Chinky — it seemed strange that he should be so scared of him.

"I've a good mind to fly off in our chair to the Pixie King and complain of you," said Chinky. "You will have your castle taken away from you then, for daring to interfere with a pixie."

"No one can get me out of my castle," said the Snoogle, in a quacking sort of voice. "I have a big moat round — and a drawbridge that I can keep drawn up for months on end. Do your worst, stupid little pixie!"

"Very well, then, I will!" said Chinky. "But just to go on with — take that, you silly Snoogle!"

Chinky took hold of the Snoogle's waving tail and pulled it hard. Naughty Chinky! There was no need to do a thing like that. It made the Snoogle very angry indeed . . . but he did not dare to touch Chinky or the children, for he really was afraid of Chinky's magic.

But the Snoogle was not afraid of the wishing-chair. He ran to it and stood by it. "You shall not fly off in your chair now!" he quacked loudly. "Aha! That will punish you."

"Oh yes, we will!" shouted Chinky, and he ran to push the Snoogle away—but, oh dear, oh dear, whatever do you suppose the Snoogle did? With four hard pecks he pecked off the red wings of the poor wishing-chair! There they lay on the ground, four bunches of red feathers!

"Oh! You wicked creature!" shouted Mollie, in a rage. "You have spoilt our lovely, lovely wishing-chair! Oh, how could you do a thing like that! Oh, Chinky, why did you make the Snoogle angry? Look what he's done!"

Mollie burst into tears. She couldn't bear to see the wings of the wishing-chair on the ground, instead of flapping away merrily on its legs. Peter turned pale. He did not know how they would get home now.

Chinky was full of horror. He had not thought that such a thing would happen—but it was done now!

"Well, I think you'll agree that you can't fly away now," said the Snoogle, with a grin. "Take your chair and go down into the kitchen. You can live there now. No one ever comes here—and you can't get out—so we shall be nice company for one another!"

Chinky picked up the chair. The three of them walked down the steps very sorrowfully.

"We are in a pretty fix now!" said Peter gloomily. "I don't know what we are going to do now that our wishing-chair can't fly!"

XXVI

THE SNOOGLE'S CASTLE

The children and Chinky carried the wishing-chair down to the Snoogle's kitchen. This was a big bare stone place with a huge fire roaring in the grate.

Chinky stood the chair down on the stone floor and sat in it, looking very gloomy.

"I know it was my fault that the wishing-chair's wings were pecked off," he said to the others. "Don't cry, Mollie. There must be some way of getting out of the Snoogle's castle."

"I'm not crying because I'm afraid we can't escape," said Mollie. "I'm crying because of the poor wishing-chair. Is this the end of all our flying adventures? It is horrid to think we may never go any more!"

"Don't think about that," said Chinky. "The first thing is—can we possibly get out of here? Where is the Snoogle, I wonder?"

"Here!" said the quacking voice of the duck-headed Snoogle, and he looked into the kitchen. "If you want any tea, there are cakes in the larder—and you might make some tea and put some cakes on a plate for me too."

"I suppose we might as well do what he says," said Peter. He went to the larder and looked inside. He saw a tin there with CAKES printed on it.

Inside there were some fine chocolate buns. The children put some on a plate for themselves and some on a plate for the Snoogle. Mollie put the kettle on the fire to boil. They all waited for the steam to come out — but nobody said a word. They were too unhappy.

When the kettle boiled Mollie made tea in two teapots. She took one teapot, cup and saucer, and plate of cakes to the Snoogle, who was sitting in the dining-room reading a newspaper. It was upside down, so Mollie didn't think it was much use to him. But she was too polite to say so. She couldn't help feeling, too, that it would be much better for all of them if they tried to be friendly with the Snoogle.

She put the tray down by the Snoogle and left him. He opened his great beak before she was out of the room and gobbled up one cake after another. Mollie thought he must be a very greedy creature.

She went back to the kitchen, and she and the others munched chocolate buns and drank hot tea, wondering gloomily what to do next.

"Perhaps we could swim across that moat," said Mollie at last.

"We'll look and see, when we can creep away for a few minutes," said Peter.

"Listen," said Chinky. "What's that noise?"

"Snore-r-r-r-r-r! Snore-r-r-r-r-r!" went the Snoogle in the dining-room. The three looked at one another.

"What about poking all round to see if there's any way of escape now?" whispered Peter.

"Come on, then!" said Chinky. They all got up. They went to the kitchen door and opened it. It looked straight on to the moat. How wide and deep and cold it looked!

"Ooh!" said Mollie. "I'd never be able to swim across that, I'm sure. Nor would you, Peter!"

"And look!" said Chinky, pointing down into the water. "There are giant frogs there—they would bite us, I expect!"

Sure enough, as Mollie and Peter peered down into the water they saw the blunt snouts of many

179

giant frogs. "Oooh!" said Mollie. "I'm not going to jump in there!"

"I say!" said Peter. "What about the draw-bridge? Couldn't we let that down ourselves and escape that way?"

"Of course!" said Chinky. "Come on. We'll find it before the old Snoogle awakes."

They went through the kitchen and into a big wide hall. They swung open the great front door. A path led down to a gateway that overlooked the moat. The door of the gateway was the drawbridge, drawn up over the entrance.

The three ran down to the gate. Chinky looked carefully at the chains that held up the drawbridge.

"Look!" he said to the others. "These chains are fastened by a padlock. The drawbridge cannot be let down unless the key is fitted into the pad-lock and the lock is turned. Then the drawbridge will be let down over the moat."

"Where is the key to the padlock, I wonder," said Mollie.

"I know," said Peter. "The Snoogle has it. I saw a big key hanging from him somewhere."

"Can't we get it?" asked Mollie. "He's asleep. Let's try."

They tiptoed into the dining-room. The Snoogle was certainly very fast asleep.

"I guess we can get the key without waking him!" whispered Chinky, in delight. "Where is it?"

They looked all round the Snoogle for the key — but they couldn't see it. And then, at last, Peter saw it — or part of it. The Snoogle was sitting on it! They could just see the head of the key sticking out from underneath him.

"No good," said Chinky, shaking his head and tip-toeing out. "We should certainly wake him if we tried to pull that key out, as he's sitting on it. I suppose that's why he sat on it, to stop us getting it!"

"Anyway, I expect the drawbridge would have made an awful noise rattling down on its chains," said Peter gloomily. "The Snoogle would have heard it and woken up and come after us."

"What shall we do now?" said Mollie, in despair. "We can't swim the moat. We can't unlock the drawbridge and let it down."

"There's one thing we might try," said Chinky. "I might try to whistle one of the birds down to a windowsill and tell it of our dreadful fix. It would fly back to pixie-land and perhaps the King would send to rescue us. You never know."

"Yes — do that," said Mollie, cheering up. The children and the pixie went up the stairs and into a bedroom. They leaned out of the open window. Below lay the silvery moat.

Chinky began to whistle. It was a soft whistle, but a very piercing one. Mollie felt sure that if she had been a bird she would have come in answer to Chinky's whistle.

181

Chinky stopped his whistling. He looked anxiously into the sky and waited. No bird came. No bird was to be seen.

"I'll try again," said Chinky. He whistled once more. They waited, looking everywhere for the sign of a bird.

"There are no birds in this Snoogle country," said the pixie, with a sigh. "One would have come if it could."

"Well," said Mollie, looking worried, "whatever can we do now? There doesn't seem to be any way of escape at all—nor any way of getting people to help us."

"Let's go into each of the rooms, upstairs, and downstairs, and see if there is any one there," said Chinky. "We might find a servant or some one—they might help us. You never know!"

So the children and the pixie went into each room, one by one. They were queer, untidy rooms. It looked as if the Snoogle lived in one for a bit and then, when it became too untidy, went into another one and lived there until the same thing happened!

There was no one at all in any of the rooms. Only the Snoogle lived in the castle, that was plain.

"Well, we've been in many fixes," said the pixie gloomily, "but this is about the tightest fix we've ever been in. How I hate the Snoogle for pecking the wings off our dear old wishing-chair!"

The children and Chinky went down into the kitchen again. The Snoogle was no longer snoring in the dining-room. He must be awake!

He was. He came into the kitchen, snapping his duck-beak and waving his cat's tail.

"Well," he said, with a grin. "Been all over the castle to find a way of escape? Aha! You won't find that in a hurry! Well, as you're here, you may as well wait on me. I'm tired of doing my own cooking and washing-up. You can do it for me."

"We won't, then!" said Peter furiously. "It is bad enough to have to be here, without waiting on a duck-headed creature like you!"

"Hush, Peter," said Mollie suddenly. "Hush! Very well, Snoogle, we will do as you say. Where would you like your supper? There is a cloth in the drawer, but it is dirty. Have you a clean one, so that I can begin to get your supper for you?"

"You are a sensible girl," said the Snoogle, pleased. "I have a clean cloth upstairs. I will get it."

He went out of the room. Chinky and Peter turned and stared at Mollie in amazement. What did she mean by giving in so meekly to the horrid Snoogle?

"Peter! Chinky! Look!" said Mollie, and she pointed to the wishing-chair, where it stood in a corner of the kitchen. The others looked — and whatever do you suppose they saw? Guess?

The wishing-chair was growing new wings! Yes,

183

really! Tiny red buds were forming on its legs. They grew fast. They burst into feathers. They were growing into new, strong wings!

"Goodness!" said Peter and Chinky, amazed. "Who would have thought of that! Good old wishing-chair!"

"Quick—here comes the Snoogle. Put the chair behind the table, where he can't see its wings growing," said Mollie. So Chinky pushed it behind the table just in time. The Snoogle pattered in, and held out a clean cloth to Mollie.

"Thank you," said the little girl politely. "And have you got some egg-cups, please? I will boil you some eggs for supper."

The Snoogle trotted out to fetch some egg-cups. As soon as he was gone, Mollie, Peter, and Chinky crowded into the wishing-chair.

"Home, as quickly as you can, wishing-chair!" shouted Chinky. The chair flapped its new red wings and rose into the air. The Snoogle came running into the kitchen. He quacked with rage. He tried to get hold of the chair as it flew past him.

Chinky kicked out at him and caught him on his big yellow beak. The Snoogle gave a squawk and sat down suddenly.

"Good-bye, good-bye, dear Snoogle!" yelled Chinky, waving his hand. "*Do* call in and see us when you are passing, and we'll give you a clean cloth for tea and boil you some eggs!"

The chair flew home at a great rate. At last it

came to the playroom and flew into it. It set itself down on the floor, and its wings gave one more flap and vanished.

"Ha! The old wishing-chair is tired!" said Chinky. "I don't wonder! I hope it will soon grow its wings again. We do have some adventures, don't we, children!"

"Where's Mother's ring, Chinky?" asked Peter, suddenly remembering why they had gone adventuring—to get his mother's lost ring!

"Here you are," said Chinky, and he gave Peter the ring. "Won't your mother be pleased! She won't guess what a lot of adventures we had getting back her ring for her!"

Peter and Mollie ran off happily. They called their mother and gave her her ring. "You *had* dropped it in the garden, Mother," said Peter.

"Thank you! You *are* kind children to find it for me!" said Mother. But she didn't guess that Big-Ears the goblin had stolen it—and that the Snoogle had had it too! No—that was the children's secret.

BOOK TWO

The Wishing Chair Again

I

HOME FOR THE HOLIDAYS

Mollie and Peter had just arrived home for the holidays. Their schools had broken up the same day, which was very lucky, and Mother had met them at the station.

They hugged her hard. "Mother! It's grand to see you again. How's everyone?"

"Fine," said Mother. "The garden's looking lovely, your bedrooms are all ready for you, and your playroom at the bottom of the garden is longing for you to go there and play as usual."

The two children looked at one another. They had a big Secret. One they couldn't possibly mention even in their letters to one another at school. How they were longing to talk about it now!

"Can we just pop down to our playroom first of all?" asked Peter when they got home.

"Oh, no, dear!" said Mother. "You must come upstairs and wash—and help me to unpack your things. You will have plenty of time to spend in your playroom these holidays."

The children's Secret was in their playroom—and they so badly wanted to see it again. They went upstairs and washed and then went down to tea.

"Can we go to our playroom after we've helped you to unpack?" asked Peter.

Mother laughed. "Very well—leave me to unpack, and go along. I expect you want to see if

I've given away any of your things. Well, I haven't. I never do that without asking you."

After tea Peter spoke to Mollie in a low voice.

"Mollie! Do you think Chinky will be down in our playroom waiting for us—with the Wishing-Chair?"

"I do hope so," said Mollie. "Oh, Peter, it was dreadful trying to keep our Secret all the term long and never saying anything to anyone."

"Well, it's such a marvellous Secret it's worth keeping well," said Peter. "Do you remember when we first got the Wishing-Chair, Mollie?"

"Yes," said Mollie. "We went to a funny little shop that sold old, old things to get something for Mother's birthday, and we saw heaps of queer enchanted things there. And we were frightened and huddled together in an old chair . . ."

"And we wished we were safe back at home," said Peter, "and, hey presto! the chair grew little red wings on its legs, and flew out of a window with us, and took us back to our playroom!"

"Yes. And it wouldn't go back to the shop even when we commanded it to," said Mollie. "So we had to keep it—our very own Wishing-Chair."

"And do you remember how we went off in it again, and came to a castle where there was a giant who kept a little servant called Chinky?" said Peter. "And we rescued him and took him home in the Wishing-Chair with us."

"That was lovely," said Mollie. "And after that Chinky lived down in our playroom and looked after the chair for us . . ."

"And told us when it grew its wings so that we could all fly off in it again and have wonderful adventures," said Peter. "Then we had to go to school and leave it."

"But it didn't matter really, because Chinky took the chair home to his mother's cottage and lived with her and took care of it for us," said Mollie.

"And he said he'd come back as soon as we came home for the holidays, and bring the chair with him so that we could go adventuring again," finished Peter. "If Mother only knew that's the reason we want to get down to the playroom— to see if Chinky is there, and to see the dear old Wishing-Chair again."

Peter found the key. "Come on, Mollie—let's go and see all our toys again."

"And the Wishing-Chair," said Mollie in a whisper. "*And* Chinky."

They rushed downstairs and out into the garden. It was the end of July and the garden was full of flowers; it was lovely to be home! No more lessons for eight weeks, no more preps.

They raced down to the playroom, which was really a big, airy shed at the bottom of the garden. Peter slid the key into the lock. "Chinky!" he called. "Are you here?"

He unlocked the door. The children went into the playroom and looked round. It was a nice room, with a big rug on the floor, shelves for their books and toys, a cot with Mollie's old dolls in it, and a large dolls' house in the corner.

But there was no Wishing-Chair and no Chinky the pixie! The children stared round in dismay.

"He's not here," said Peter. "He said he would come to-day with the chair. I gave him the date and he wrote it down in his note-book."

"I hope he's not ill," said Mollie. They looked all round the playroom, set the musical box going and opened the windows.

They felt disappointed. They had so looked forward to seeing Chinky, and to sitting once more in the Wishing-Chair. Suddenly a little face looked in at the door.

Mollie gave a shout. "Chinky! It's you! We were so worried about you! We hoped you'd be here."

Both children gave the little pixie a hug. Chinky grinned. "Well, how could I be here waiting for you if the door was locked and the windows fastened, silly? I may be a pixie, but I can't fly through locked doors. I *have* missed you. Were you very bored away at school?"

"Oh, *no*," said Peter. "Boarding school is simply lovely. We both loved it—but we're jolly glad to be home again."

"Chinky, where's the Wishing-Chair?" asked Mollie anxiously. "Nothing's happened to it, has it? Have you got it with you?"

"Well, I brought it here this morning," said Chinky, "but when I found the door of the playroom was locked and couldn't get in I hid it under the hedge at the bottom of the garden. But you'd be surprised how many people nearly found it!"

"But nobody goes to the bottom of the garden!"
said Peter.

"Oh, don't they!" said Chinky. "Well, first of
all your gardener thought he'd cut the hedge there
to-day, and I had an awful job dragging the chair
from one hiding place to another. Then an old
gipsy woman came by, and she almost saw it,
but I barked like a dog and she ran away."

The children laughed. "Poor old Chinky! You
must have been glad when we got here at last."

"Let's go and get it," said Peter. "I'm hoping
to sit in it again. Has it grown its wings much
since we left it with you, Chinky?"

"Not once," said Chinky. "Funny, isn't it?

It's just stood in my mother's kitchen like any ordinary chair, and never grown even one red wing! I think it was waiting for you to come back."

"I hope it was—because then it may grow its wings heaps of times," said Peter, "and we'll go off on lots of adventures."

They went to the hedge. "There it is!" said Mollie in excitement. "I can see one of its legs sticking out."

They dragged out the old chair. "Just the same!" said Peter in delight. "And how well you've kept it, Chinky. It's polished so brightly."

"Ah, that was my mother did that," said Chinky. "She said such a wonderful chair should have a wonderful polish, and she was at it every day, rub, rub, rub till the chair groaned!"

Peter carried the chair back to the playroom. Chinky went in front to make sure there was nobody looking. They didn't want any questions asked about why chairs should be hidden in hedges. They set it down in its old place in the playroom. Then they all climbed into it.

"It's just the same," said Peter. "We feel a bit more squashed than usual because Mollie and I seem to have grown at school. But *you* haven't grown, Chinky."

"No. I shan't grow any more," said Chinky. "Don't you wish the chair would grow its wings and go flapping off somewhere with us now?"

"Oh, *yes*," said Mollie. "Chair, do grow your wings—just to please us! Even if it's only to take us a little way up into the air and back."

But the chair didn't. The children looked anxiously down at its legs to see if the red buds were forming that sprouted into wings, but there was nothing there.

"It's no good," said Chinky. "It won't grow its wings just because it's asked. It can be very obstinate, you know. All I hope is that it hasn't forgotten *how* to grow wings after being still so long. I shouldn't like the magic to fade away."

This was a dreadful thought. The children patted the arms of the chair. "Dear Wishing-Chair! You haven't forgotten how to grow wings, have you?"

The chair gave a remarkable creak, a very long one. Everyone laughed. "It's all right!" said Chinky. "That's its way of telling us it hasn't forgotten. A creak is the only voice it's got!"

Mother came down the garden. "Children! Daddy's home. He wants to see you!"

"Right!" called back Peter. He turned to Chinky. "See you to-morrow, Chinky. You can cuddle up on the old sofa as usual, with the rug and the cushion, for the night. You'll live in our playroom, won't you, as you did before, and tell us when the chair grows its wings?"

"Yes. I shall like to live here once more," said Chinky.

The children ran back to the house. They had a very nice evening indeed telling their parents everything that had happened in the term. Then off they went to bed, glad to be in their own dear little rooms again.

But they hadn't been asleep very long before Peter began to dream that he was a rat being shaken by a dog. It was a very unpleasant dream, and he woke up with a jump.

It was Chinky shaking him by the arm. "Wake up!" whispered the pixie. "The chair's grown its wings already. They're big, strong ones, and they're flapping like anything. If you want an adventure hurry up!"

Well! What a thrill! Peter woke Mollie and they pulled on their clothes very quickly and ran down the garden. They heard a loud flapping noise as they reached the playroom shed. "It's the chair's wings," panted Chinky. "Come on—we'll just sit in it before it goes flying off!"

II

OFF ON AN ADVENTURE

The children raced in at the playroom door and made for the Wishing-Chair. They could see it easily in the bright moonlight. It was just about to fly off when they flung themselves in it. Chinky squeezed between them, sitting on the top of the back of the chair.

"Good old Wishing-Chair!" said Peter. "You didn't take long to grow your wings! Where are we going?"

"Where would you like to go?" said Chinky.

"Wish, and we'll go wherever you wish."

"Well—let me see—oh dear, I simply can't think of anywhere," said Mollie. "Peter, you wish —quickly."

"Er—Wishing-Chair, take us to—to—oh, goodness knows where I want it to go!" cried Peter. "I simply don't . . ."

But dear me, the Wishing-Chair was off! It flapped its wings very strongly indeed, rose up into the air, flew towards the door and out of it— then up into the air it went, flapping its red wings in the moonlight.

Chinky giggled. "Oh, Peter—you said 'Take us to Goodness Knows Where'," said the pixie. "And that's just about where we're going!"

"Gracious!—is there *really* a land called Goodness Knows Where?" said Peter, in surprise.

"Yes. Don't you remember when we went to the Land of Scallywags once, the Prince of Goodness Knows Where came to see me," said Chinky. "I was pretending to be a King. Well, I suppose it's *his* Land we're going to."

"Where is it?" said Mollie.

"Goodness knows!" said Chinky. "I don't. I've never met anyone who did, either."

"The Wishing-Chair seems to know," said Peter, as it flew higher and higher in the air.

But it didn't know, really. It dropped downwards after a time and came to a tiny village. Peter leaned out of the chair and gazed with great interest at it. "Look at that bridge," he said. "Hey, Chair, whatever are you doing now?"

The chair hadn't landed in the village. It had flown a few feet above the queer little houses and had then shot upwards again.

The chair flew on again, and then came to a heaving mass of water. Was it the sea? Or a lake? The children didn't know. "Look at that lovely silver moon-path on the sea," said Mollie, leaning out of the chair. "I'm sure it leads to the moon!"

The chair seemed to think so, too. It flew down to the water, got on the moon-path and followed it steadily, up and up and up.

"Hey! This isn't the way to Goodness Knows Where!" said Chinky, in alarm. "It's the way to the moon. Don't be silly, Chair!"

The chair stopped and hovered in mid-air as if it had heard Chinky and was changing its mind. To the children's great relief it left the moon-path and flew on till it came to a little island. This was perfectly round and flat, and had one big tree standing up in the middle of it. Under the tree was a boat and someone was fast asleep in it.

"Oh, that's my cousin, Sleep-Alone," said Chinky, in surprise. "He's a funny fellow, you know—can't bear to sleep if anyone else is within miles of him. So he has a boat and an aeroplane, and each night he takes one or the other and goes off to some lonely place to sleep. Hey there, Sleep-Alone!"

Chinky's shout made the children jump. The chair jumped, too, and Mollie was almost jerked off. She clutched at the arm.

The little man in the boat awoke. He was more

197

like a brownie than a pixie and had a very long beard, which he had wound neatly round his neck like a scarf. He was most surprised to see the Wishing-Chair landing on the island just near him. He scowled at Chinky.

"What's all this? Coming and shouting at me in the middle of the night! Can't I ever sleep alone?"

"You always do!" said Chinky. "Don't be so cross. Aren't you surprised to see us?"

"Not a bit," said Sleep-Alone. "You're always turning up when I don't want to have company. Go away. I've a cold coming on and I feel gloomy."

"Is that why you've got your beard wound round your neck – to keep it warm?" asked Mollie. "How long is it when it unwinds?"

"I've no idea," said Sleep-Alone, who seemed a disagreeable fellow. "Where are you going in the middle of the night? Are you quite mad?"

"We're going to Goodness Knows Where," said Chinky. "But the chair doesn't seem to know the way. Do *you* know it?"

"Goodness knows where it is," said Sleep-Alone, pulling his beard tighter round his neck. "Better ask her."

The children and Chinky stared. "Ask who?" said Chinky.

"Goodness, of course," said Sleep-Alone, settling down in his boat again.

"Oh – is Goodness the name of a person then?" said Mollie, suddenly seeing light.

"You are a very stupid little girl, I think," said Sleep-Alone. "Am I to go on and on saying the same thing over and over again? Now good night, and go and find Goodness if you want to disturb someone else."

"Where does she live?" bellowed Chinky in Sleep-Alone's ear, afraid that he would go to sleep before he told them anything else.

That was too much for Sleep-Alone. He shot up and reached for an oar. Before Chinky could get out of the way he had given him such a slap with the oar blade that Chinky yelled at the top of his voice. Then Sleep-Alone turned on the two children, waving the oar in a most alarming manner.

Peter pulled Mollie to the chair. He put out a hand and dragged Chinky to it too, shouting, "Go to Goodness, Chair, go to Goodness, wherever she is!" Up rose the chair so very suddenly that Chinky fell off and had to be dragged up again.

Sleep-Alone roared after them. "Now I'm thoroughly awake and I shan't go to sleep to-night. You wait until I see you again, Chinky, I'll fly you off in my aeroplane to the Land of Rubbish and drop you in the biggest dustbin there!"

"He's not a very nice cousin to have, is he?" said Mollie, when they had left Sleep-Alone well behind. "I hope we don't see him again."

"Who is this Goodness, I wonder?" said Peter.

"Never heard of her," said Chinky. "But the chair really seems to know where it's going this time, so I suppose it knows Goodness all right!"

The Wishing-Chair was flying steadily to the east now. It had left the water behind and was now over some land that lay shining in the moonlight. The children could see towers and pinnacles, but they were too high up to. see anything clearly.

The chair suddenly flew downwards. It came to a small cottage. All three of its chimneys were smoking. The smoke was green, and the children knew that was a sign that a witch lived there.

"I say—that's witch-smoke," said Peter, nervously. He had met witches before on his adventures, and he knew quite a bit about them.

"I hope the chair has come to the right place," said Mollie, as it landed gently on the path just outside the door of the little cottage.

They jumped off the chair, dragged it under a tree and went to knock at the door. A little old woman opened it. She looked so ordinary that the children felt sure she wasn't a witch.

"Please, is this where Goodness lives?" asked Chinky, politely.

"Not exactly. But I keep a Book of Goodness," said the old woman. "Have you come to seek advice from it?"

"Well—we rather wanted to know where the Land of Goodness Knows Where is," said Chinky. "And we were told that only Goodness knew where it was!"

"Ah, well—you will have to consult my Goodness Book then," said the old woman. "Wait till I get on my things."

She left them in a tiny kitchen and disappeared. When she came back, what a difference in her! She had on a tall, pointed hat, the kind witches and wizards wear, and a great cloak that kept blowing out round her as if she kept a wind under its folds. She no longer looked an ordinary little old woman—she was a proper witch, but her eyes were kind and smiling.

She took down from a shelf a very big book indeed. It seemed to be full of names and very tiny writing. "What are your names?" she asked. "I must look you up in my Goodness Book before you can be told what you want to know."

They told her, and she ran her finger down column after column. "Ah—Peter—helped a boy with his homework for a whole week last term—remembered his mother's birthday—owned up when he did something wrong—my word, there's a whole list of goodness here. And Mollie, too—gave up her half-holiday to stay in with a friend who was ill—told the truth when she knew she would get into trouble for doing so—quite a long list of goodness for her, too."

"Now me," said Chinky. "I've been living with my mother. I do try to be good to her." The old woman ran her finger down the list again and nodded her head. "Yes—did his mother's shopping and never grumbled—took her breakfast in bed each day—never forgot to feed the dog—yes, you're all right, Chinky."

"What happens next?" said Peter. The witch

took her Book of Goodness to a curious hole in the middle of the kitchen floor. It suddenly glowed as if it were full of shining water. The witch held the book over it, and out of it slid little gleaming streaks of colour. "That's your Goodness going into the magic pool," she said. "Now, ask what you want to know."

Chinky asked, in rather a trembling voice, "We want to know where the Land of Goodness Knows Where is."

And dear me, a very extraordinary thing happened! On the top of the shining water appeared a shimmering map. In the middle of it was marked "Land of Goodness Knows Where." The children and Chinky leaned over it eagerly, trying to see how to get there.

"Look—we fly due east to the rising sun," began Chinky; then he stopped. They had all heard a very peculiar noise outside. A loud creaking noise.

"The chair's calling to us!" cried Chinky and he rushed to the door. "Oh, look—it's flying away—and somebody else is in it. Somebody's stolen the Wishing-Chair! Whatever shall we do?"

III

WHERE CAN THE WISHING-CHAIR BE?

"Who's taken our chair?" cried Peter, in despair. "We can't get back home now. Come back, Chair!"

But the chair was under somebody else's commands now, and it took no notice. It rose higher and higher and was soon no more than a speck in the moonlight. The three stared at one another, very upset indeed.

"Our very first adventure—and the chair's gone," said Mollie, in a shaky voice. "It's too bad. Right at the very beginning of the holidays, too."

"Who was that taking our chair—do you know?" Chinky asked the witch, who was busy smoothing the surface of the water in the hole in the floor with what looked like a fine brush. The map that had shone there was now gone, and the water was empty of reflection or picture. The children wondered what would appear there next.

The witch shook her head. "No—I don't know," she said. "I didn't hear anyone out there because I was so busy in here with you. All kinds of people come to ask me questions, you know, just as you did, and watch to see what appears in my magic pool. Some of the people are very queer. I expect it was one of them—and he saw your chair, knew what it was and flew off in it at once. It would be very valuable to him."

203

"I do think it's bad luck," said Mollie, tears coming into her eyes. "Our very first night. And how are we to get back home again?"

"You can catch the Dawn Bus if you like," said the witch. "It will be along here in a few minutes' time. As soon as the sky turns silver in the east it comes rumbling along. Now, listen, I can hear the bus."

Wondering whatever kind of people caught the Dawn Bus, Mollie and the others went out to catch it. It came rumbling along, looking more like a toy bus than a real one. It was crammed with little folk of all kinds! Brownies with long beards leaned against one another, fast asleep. Two tiny fairies slept with their arms round each other. A wizard nodded off to sleep, his pointed hat getting more and more crooked each moment —and three goblins yawned so widely that their mischievous little faces seemed all mouth!

"The bus is full," said Mollie, in dismay.

"Sit in front with the driver, then," said the witch. "Go on, or you'll miss it!"

So Mollie, Peter and Chinky squashed themselves in front with the driver. He was a brownie, and wore his beard tied round his waist and made into a bow behind. It looked very odd.

"Plenty of room," he said, and moved up so far that he couldn't reach the wheel to drive the bus. "You drive it," he said to Chinky, and, very pleased indeed, Chinky took the wheel.

But, goodness gracious me, Chinky was no good at all at driving buses! He nearly hit a tree, swerved violently and went into an enormous puddle that splashed everyone from head to foot, and then went into a ditch and out of it at top speed.

By this time all the passengers were wide awake and shouting in alarm. "Stop him! He's mad! Fetch a policeman!"

The bus-driver was upset to hear all the shouting. He moved back to his wheel so quickly that Chinky was flung out into the road. He got up and ran after the bus, shouting.

But the bus-driver wouldn't stop. He drove on at top speed, though Mollie and Peter begged him to go back for Chinky.

"I don't know how to back this bus," said the brownie driver, solemnly. "I keep meaning to learn but I never seem to have time. Most annoying. Still, I hardly ever want to back."

"Well, *stop* if you don't know how to back," cried Peter, but the brownie looked really horrified.

"What—stop before I come to a stopping-place? You must be mad. No, no—full speed ahead is my motto. I've got to get all these tired passengers back home as soon as possible."

"Why are they so tired?" said Mollie, seeing the wizard beginning to nod again.

"Well, they've all been to a moonlight dance," said the driver. "Very nice dance, too. I went to it. Last time I went to one I was so tired when I drove my bus home that I fell asleep when I was driving it. Found myself in the Land of Dreamland in no time, and used up every drop of my petrol."

This all sounded rather extraordinary. Mollie

and Peter looked at him nervously, hoping that he wouldn't fall asleep this time. Mollie could hardly keep her eyes open. She worried about Chinky. Would he find his way back to the play-room all right? And, oh dear, what were they going to do about the Wishing-Chair?

Just as she was thinking that she fell sound asleep. Peter was already asleep. The driver looked at them, gave a grunt, and fell asleep himself.

So, of course, the bus went straight on to Dreamland again, and when Peter and Mollie awoke, they were not in the bus at all but in their own beds! Mollie tried to remember all that had happened. Was it real or was it a dream? She thought she had better go and ask Peter.

She went to his room. He was sitting up in bed and rubbing his eyes. "I know what you've come to ask me," he said. "The same question I was coming to ask *you*. Did we dream it or didn't we? And how did we get back here?"

"That bus must have gone to the Land of Dreamland again," said Mollie. "But how we got here I don't know. I'm still in my day-clothes — look!"

"So am I," said Peter, astonished. "Well, that shows it was real then. Oh, dear — do you suppose Chinky is back yet?"

"Shall we go and see now?" said Mollie.

But the breakfast bell rang just then. They cleaned their teeth, did their hair, washed and tidied their crumpled clothes — then down they went.

After breakfast they ran down to the playroom at the bottom of the garden.

Chinky was there! He was lying on the sofa fast asleep.

"Chinky, wake up!" shouted Mollie.

He didn't stir. Mollie shook him.

"Don't wake me, Mother," murmured Chinky, trying to turn over. "Let me sleep."

"Chinky—you're not at home, you're here," said Peter, shaking him again.

Chinky rolled over on his other side—and fell right off the sofa!

That woke him up with a jerk. He gave a shout of alarm, opened his eyes and sat up.

"I say, did you tip me off the sofa?" he said. "You needn't have done that."

"We didn't. You rolled off yourself," said Mollie with a laugh. "How did you get back last night, Chinky?"

"I walked all the way—so no wonder I'm tired this morning," said Chinky, his eyes beginning to close again. "I did think you might have stopped the bus and picked me up."

"The driver wouldn't stop," explained Peter. "He was awfully silly, really. We were very upset at leaving you behind."

"The thing is, Chinky—how are we going to find out where the Wishing-Chair has gone?" said Peter, seriously. "It's only the beginning of the holidays, you know, and if we don't get it back the holidays will be very dull indeed."

"I'm too sleepy to think," said Chinky, and fell

asleep again. Mollie shook him impatiently.

"Chinky, do wake up. We really are very worried about the Wishing-Chair."

But there was no waking Chinky this time! He was so sound asleep that he didn't even stir when Mollie tickled him under the arms.

The two children were disappointed. They stayed in the playroom till dinner-time, but Chinky didn't wake up. They went indoors to have their dinner and then came down to see if Chinky was awake yet. He wasn't!

Just then there came a soft tapping at the door and a little voice said: "Chinky! Are you there?"

Peter opened the door. Outside stood a small elf, looking rather alarmed. He held a leaflet in his hand.

"Oh, I'm very sorry," he said. "I didn't know you were here. I wanted Chinky."

"He's so fast asleep we can't wake him," said Peter. "Can we give him a message?"

"Yes. Tell him I saw this notice of his," said the little elf, and showed it to the children. It was a little card, printed in Chinky's writing:

"Lost or stolen. Genuine Wishing-Chair.
Please give any information about it to
CHINKY.
(I shall be in the playroom.)"

"Anything else?" asked Peter.

"Well—you might tell him I think I know where the chair is," said the little elf, shyly.

"*Do* you?" cried both children. "Well, tell us, then—it's our chair!"

"There's to be a sale of furniture at a brownie's shop not far away," said the elf, "and there are six old chairs to be sold. Now, I know he only had five—so where did the sixth come from? Look, here's a picture of them."

The children looked at the picture. Peter gave a cry. "Why, they're *exactly* like our chair. Are they *all* wishing-chairs, then?"

"Oh, no. Your chair is very unusual. I expect what happened is that the thief who flew off on your chair wondered how to hide it. He remembered somebody who had five chairs just like it and offered it to him to make the set complete."

"I don't see why he should do that," said Mollie, puzzled.

"Wait," said the elf. "Nobody would suspect that one of the six chairs was a wishing-chair— and I've no doubt that the thief will send someone to bid a price for all six; and when he gets them he will suddenly say that he has discovered one of them is a wishing-chair, and sell it to a wizard for a sack of gold!"

"I think that's a horrid trick," said Mollie, in disgust. "Well, it looks as if we'll have to go along to this furniture shop and have a look at the chairs, to see if we can find out which one is ours. Oh, dear, I do wish Chinky would wake up."

"You'd better go as soon as you can," said the elf. "The thief won't lose much time in buying it back, with the other chairs thrown in!"

So they tried to wake Chinky again—but he just wouldn't wake up! "We'll have to go by ourselves," said Peter at last. "Elf, will you show us the way? You will? Right, then off we go! Leave your message on the table for Chinky to see, then he'll guess where we've gone!"

IV

HUNTING FOR THE CHAIR!

The elf took them a very surprising way. He guided them to the bottom of the garden and through a gap in the hedge. Then he took them to the end of the field and showed them a dark ring of grass.

"We call that a fairy ring," said Mollie. "Sometimes it has little toadstools all the way round it."

"Yes," said the elf. "Well, I'll show you a use for fairy rings. Sit down on the dark grass, please."

Mollie and Peter sat down. They had to squeeze very close together indeed, because the ring of grass was not large. The elf felt about in it as if he was looking for something. He found it—and pressed hard!

And down shot the ring of grass as if it were a lift! The children, taken by surprise, gasped and held on to one another. They stopped with such a bump that they were shaken off the circle of grass and rolled away from it, over and over.

"So sorry," said the elf. "I'm afraid I pressed the button rather hard! Are you hurt?"

"No—not really," said Mollie. As she spoke she saw the circle of grass shoot up again and fit itself neatly back into the field.

"Well—we do learn surprising things," she said. "What next, elf?"

"Along this passage," said the elf, and trotted in front of them. It was quite light underground, though neither of the children could see where the lighting came from. They passed little, brightly-painted doors on their way, and Peter longed to rat-tat at the knockers and see who answered.

They came to some steps and went up them, round and round in a spiral stairway. Wherever were they coming to? At the top was a door. The elf opened it—and there they were, in a small round room, very cosy indeed.

"What a queer, round room," said Peter, surprised. "Oh—I know why it's round. It's inside the trunk of a tree! I've been in a tree-house before!"

"Guessed right first time!" said the elf. "This is where I live. I'd ask you to stop and have a cup of tea with me, but I think we'd better get on and see those chairs before anything happens to them."

"Yes. So do I," said Peter. "Where's the door out of the tree?"

It was fitted in so cunningly that it was impossible to see it unless you knew where it

211

was. The elf went to it at once, of course, and
opened it. They all stepped out into a wood. The
elf shut the door. The children looked back at it.
No — they couldn't possibly, possibly tell where
it was now — it was so much part of the tree!

"Come along," said the elf and they followed
him through the wood. They came to a lane and
then to a very neat village, all the houses set in
tiny rows, with a little square green in the middle,
and four white ducks looking very clean on a
round pond in the centre of the green.

"How very proper!" said Peter. "Not a blade of
grass out of place."

"This is Pin Village," said the elf. "You've

heard the saying, 'As neat as a pin,' I suppose? Well, this is Pin—always very neat and tidy and the people of the village, the Pins, never have a button missing or a hair blowing loose."

The children saw that it was just as the elf said —the people were so tidy and neat that the children felt dirty and untidy at once. "They all look a bit like pins dressed up and walking about," said Mollie with a giggle. "Well, I'm glad I know what 'neat as a pin' really means. Do they ever run, or make a noise, or laugh?"

"Sh! Don't laugh at them," said the elf. "Now look—do you see that shop at the corner? It isn't kept by a Pin; it's kept by Mr. Polish. He sells furniture."

"And he's called Polish because he's always polishing it, I suppose," said Mollie with a laugh.

"Don't be too clever!" said the elf. "He doesn't do any polishing at all—his daughter Polly does that."

"Here's the shop," said Mollie, and they stood and looked at it. She nudged Peter. "Look," she whispered, "six chairs—all exactly alike. How are we to tell which is ours?"

"Come and have a look," said Peter, and they went inside with the elf. A brownie girl was busy polishing away at the chairs, making them shine and gleam.

"There's Polly Polish," said Mollie to Peter. She must have heard what they said and looked up. She smiled. She was a nice little thing, with pointed ears like Chinky, and very green eyes.

"Hallo," she said.

Mollie smiled back. "These are nice chairs, aren't they?" she said. "You've got a whole set of them!"

"Yes — my father, Mr. Polish, was very pleased," said Polly. "He's only had five for a long time, and people want to buy chairs in sixes, you know."

"How did he manage to get the sixth one?" asked Peter.

"It was a great bit of luck," said Polly. "There's a goblin called Tricky who came along and said he wanted to sell an old chair that had once belonged to his grandmother — and when he showed it to us, lo and behold, it was the missing sixth chair of our set! So we bought it from him, and there it is. I expect now we shall be able to sell the whole set. Someone is sure to come along and buy it."

"Which chair did the goblin bring you?" asked Peter, looking hard at them all.

"I don't know now," said Polly, putting more polish on her duster and rubbing very hard at a chair. "I've been cleaning them and moving them about, you know — and they're all mixed up."

The children stared at them in despair. They all looked exactly alike to them! Oh, dear — how could they possibly tell which was their chair?

Then Polly said something very helpful, though she didn't know it! "You know," she said, "there's something queer about one of these chairs. I've polished and polished the back of it, but it seems to have a little hole there, or something. Anyway,

214

I can't make that little bit come bright and shining."

The children pricked up their ears at once. "Which chair?" said Peter. Polly showed them the one. It certainly seemed as if it had a hole in the back of it. Peter put his finger there—but the hole wasn't a hole! He could feel quite solid wood there!

And then he knew it was their own chair. He whispered to Mollie.

"Do you remember last year, when somebody made our Wishing-Chair invisible? And we had to get some paint to make it visible again?"

"Oh, yes!" whispered back Mollie. "I do remember—and we hadn't enough paint to make one little bit at the back of the chair become visible again, so it always looked as if there was a hole there, though there wasn't really!"

"Yes—and that's the place that poor Polly has been polishing and polishing," said Peter. "Well —now we know that this is our chair all right! If only it would grow its wings we could sit on it straight away and wish ourselves home again!" He ran his fingers down the legs of the chair to see if by any chance there were some bumps growing, that would mean wings were coming once more. But there weren't.

"Perhaps the wings will grow again this evening," said Mollie. "Let's go and have tea with the elf in his tree-house and then come back here again and see if the chair has grown its wings."

The elf was very pleased to think they would come back to tea with him. Before they went Peter looked hard at the chairs. "You know," he said to Mollie, "I think we'd better just tie a ribbon round our own chair, so that if by any chance we decided to take it and go home with it quickly before anyone could stop us, we'd know immediately which it was."

"That's a good idea," said Mollie. She had no hair-ribbon, so she took her little blue handkerchief and knotted it round the right arm of the chair.

"What are you doing that for?" asked Polly Polish in surprise.

"We'll tell you some other time, Polly," said Mollie. "Don't untie it, will you? It's to remind us of something. We'll come back again after tea."

They went off with the elf. He asked them to see if they could find his door-handle and turn it to get into his tree-house—but, however much they looked and felt about, neither of them could make out where the closely-fitting door was! It's no wonder nobody ever knows which the tree-houses are!

The elf had to open the door for them himself, and in they went. He got them a lovely tea, with pink jellies that shone like a sunset, and blancmange that he had made in the shape of a little castle.

"I do wonder if Chinky's woken up yet," said Mollie, at last. "No, thank you, elf, I can't possibly eat any more. It was a really lovely tea."

"Now what about going back to the shop and

seeing if we can't take our chair away?" said Peter. "We'll send Chinky to explain about it later—the thing is, we really must take it quickly, or that goblin called Tricky will send someone to buy all the set—and our chair with it!"

So off they went to the shop—and will you believe it, there were no chairs there! They were all gone from the window! The children stared in dismay.

They went into the shop. "What's happened to the chairs?" they asked Polly.

"Oh, we had such a bit of luck just after you had gone," said Polly. "Somebody came by, noticed the chairs, said that the goblin Tricky had advised him to buy them—and paid us for them straight away!"

"Who was he?" asked Peter, his heart sinking.

"Let me see—his name was Mr. Spells," said Polly, looking in a book. "And his address is Wizard Cottage. He seemed very nice indeed."

"Oh dear," said Peter, leading Mollie out of the shop. "Now we've *really* lost our dear old chair."

"Don't give up!" said Mollie. "We'll go back to Chinky and tell him the whole story—and maybe he will know something about this Mr. Spells and be able to get our chair back for us. Chinky's very clever."

"Yes—but before we can get it back from Mr. Spells, that wretched goblin Tricky will be after it again," said Peter. "He's sure to go and take it from Mr. Spells."

The elf took them home again. They went into the playroom. Chinky wasn't there! There was a note on the table.

It said: "Fancy you going off without me! I've gone to look for you—Chinky."

"Bother!" said Mollie. "How annoying! Here we've come back to look for him and he's gone to look for us. Now we'll have to wait till to-morrow!"

V

OFF TO MR. SPELLS OF WIZARD COTTAGE

Mollie and Peter certainly could do no more that day, because their mother was already wondering why they hadn't been in to tea. They heard her calling as they read Chinky's note saying he had gone to look for them.

"It's a pity Chinky didn't wait for us," said Peter. "We could have sent him to Mr. Spells to keep guard on the chair. Come on, Mollie—we'll have to go in. We've hardly seen Mother all day!"

Their mother didn't know anything about the Wishing-Chair at all, of course, because the children kept it a strict secret.

"If we tell anyone, the grown-ups will come and take our precious chair and put it in a museum or something," said Peter. "I couldn't bear to think of the Wishing-Chair growing its wings in a museum and not being able to get out of a glass case."

218

So they hadn't said a word to anyone. Now they ran indoors, and offered to help their mother shell peas. They sat and wondered where Chinky was. They felt very sleepy, and Mollie suddenly gave an enormous yawn.

"You look very tired, Mollie," said Mother, looking at her pale face. "Didn't you sleep well last night?"

"Well—I didn't sleep a *lot*," said Mollie truthfully, remembering her long flight in the Wishing-Chair and the strange bus ride afterwards.

"I think you had both better get off early to bed," said Mother. "I'll bring your suppers up to you in bed for a treat—raspberries and cream, and bread and butter—would you like that?"

In the ordinary way the children would have said no thank you to any idea of going to bed early —but they really were so sleepy that they both yawned together and said yes, that sounded nice, thank you, Mother!

So upstairs they went and fell asleep immediately after the raspberries and cream. Mother was really very surprised when she peeped in to see them.

"Poor children—I expect all the excitement of coming home from school has tired them out," she said. "I'll make them up sandwiches to-morrow and send them out on a picnic."

They woke up early the next morning and their first thought was about the Wishing-Chair.

"Let's go down and see Chinky," said Mollie. "We've got time before breakfast."

So they dressed quickly and ran down to their

playroom. But no Chinky was there — and no note either. He hadn't been back, then. Wherever could he be?

"Oh dear, first the Wishing-Chair goes, and now Chinky," said Mollie. "What's happened to him? I think we'd better go and ask that elf if he's seen him, Peter."

"We shan't have time before breakfast," said Peter. "We'll come down as soon as we've done any jobs Mother wants us to do."

They were both delighted when Mother suggested that they should take their lunch with them and go out for a day's picnicking. Why — that would be just right! They could go and hunt out the elf — and find Chinky — and perhaps go to Mr. Spells with him. Splendid!

So they eagerly took the packets of sandwiches, cake and chocolate that Mother made up for them, and Peter put them into a little satchel to carry. Off they went. They peeped into their playroom just to make sure that Chinky still hadn't come back.

No, he hadn't. "Better leave a note for him, then," said Peter.

"What have you said?" asked Mollie, glancing over her shoulder.

"I've said: 'Why didn't you wait for us, silly? Now we've got to go and look for you whilst you're still looking for us!'"

Mollie laughed. "Oh dear — this really is getting ridiculous. Come on — let's go to the tree-house and see if the elf is in."

So off they went, down the garden, through the hedge, and across the field to where the dark patch of grass was—the "fairy-ring." They sat down in the middle of it and Mollie felt about for the button to press. She found something that felt like a little knob of earth and pressed it. Yes—it was the right button!

Down they went, not nearly as fast as the day before, because Mollie didn't press the button so hard. Then along the passage, past the queer bright little doors, and up the spiral stairway. They knocked on the door.

"It's us—Mollie and Peter. Can we come in?"

The door flew open and there stood the elf. He looked very pleased. "Well, this is really friendly of you. Come in."

"We've come to ask you something," said Mollie. "Have you seen Chinky?"

"Oh, yes—he came to me yesterday, after I'd said good-bye to you, and I told him all you'd told me—and off he went to find Polly Polish and get the latest news," said the elf.

"Well, he hasn't come back yet," said Mollie. "Where do you suppose he is?"

"Gone to see his mother, perhaps?" suggested the elf. "I really don't know. It's not much good looking for him, really, you know—he might be anywhere."

"Yes—that's true," said Peter. "Well, what shall we do, Mollie? Try and find Mr. Spells of Wizard Cottage by ourselves?"

"Oh, I know where *he* lives," said the elf. "He's

221

quite a nice fellow. I'll tell you the way. You want to take the bus through the Tall Hill, and then take the boat to the Mill. Not far off on the top of a hill you'll see a large cottage in the shape of a castle—only you can't call it a castle because it's not big enough. Mr. Spells lives there."

"Oh, thank you," said Peter, and off they went to catch the bus. It was one like they had caught the other night, but it had a different driver, and was not nearly so crowded. In fact there would have been plenty of room inside for Peter and Mollie if they hadn't noticed that one of the passengers happened to be Mr. Sleep-Alone, Chinky's strange and bad-tempered cousin.

"We'd better travel with the driver on the outside seat again," said Peter. "Sleep-Alone might recognize us and lose his temper again."

The bus travelled fast down the lane, going round corners in a hair-raising style. "Do you like going round corners on two wheels?" asked Peter, clutching at Mollie to prevent her from falling off.

"Well, it saves wear and tear on the others," said the driver.

The bus suddenly ran straight at a very steep hill and disappeared into a black hole, which proved to be a long and bumpy tunnel. It came out again and stopped dead beside a little blue river, its front wheels almost touching the water.

"I always do that to give the passengers a fright," said the driver. "Must give them something for their money's worth!"

The children were really very glad to get out. They looked for a boat and saw plenty cruising about on the water, all by themselves. "Look at that!" said Peter. "They must go by magic or something."

One little yellow boat sailed over to them and rocked gently beside them. They got into it. The boat didn't move.

"Tell it where to go, silly!" called the bus-driver, who was watching them with great interest.

"To the Mill," said Peter, and immediately the boat shot off down-stream, doing little zigzags now and again in a very light-hearted manner. It wasn't long before they came to an old Mill. Its big water-wheel was working and made a loud noise. Behind it was a hill, and on the top was what looked like a small castle.

"That's where Mr. Spells lives," said Peter. "Come on—out we get, and up the hill we go."

So up the hill they went and came at last to the curious castle-like house.

But when they got near they heard loud shouts and thumps and yells, and they stopped in alarm.

"Whatever's going on?" said Mollie. "Is somebody quarrelling?"

The children tiptoed to the house and peeped in at one of the windows, the one where the noise seemed to be coming from. They saw a peculiar sight!

Chinky and a nasty-looking little goblin seemed to be playing musical chairs! The children saw the six chairs there that they had seen the day

223

before in Mr. Polish's shop, and first Chinky would dart at one and look at it carefully and try to pull it away, and then the goblin would. Then Mr. Spells, who looked a very grand kind of enchanter, would pull the chairs away from each and then smack both the goblin and Chinky with his stick.

Roars and bellows came from the goblin and howls from Chinky. Oh, dear. Whatever was happening?

"Chinky must have found out that the chairs had gone to Mr. Spells, and gone to get our own chair," said Peter. "And the goblin must have gone to get it at the same time. Can you see the blue handkerchief we tied on our own chair, Mollie?"

"No. It's gone. Somebody took it off," said Mollie. "I believe I can see it sticking out of Chinky's pocket — I expect he guessed we marked the chair that way and took the hanky off in case the goblin or Mr. Spells guessed there was something unusual about that particular chair."

"Sir!" cried Chinky suddenly, turning to Mr. Spells, "I tell you once more that I am only here to fetch back one of these chairs, a wishing-chair, which belongs to me and my friends. This goblin stole it from us — and now he's come to get it back again from you. He'll sell it again, and steal it — he's a bad fellow."

Smack! The goblin thumped Chinky hard and he yelled. Mr. Spells roared like a lion. "I don't believe either of you. You're a couple of rogues. These chairs are MY CHAIRS, all of them, and

I don't believe any of them is a wishing-chair. Wishing-chairs have wings, and not one of these has."

"But I tell you . . ." began Chinky, and then stopped as the enchanter struck him lightly with his wand, and then struck the goblin, too.

Chinky sank down into a deep sleep and so did the goblin. "Now I shall have a little peace at last," said Mr. Spells. "And I'll find out which chair is a wishing-chair—if these fellows are speaking the truth!"

He went out of the room, and the children heard him stirring something somewhere. He was probably making a "Find-out" spell!

"Come on—let's get into the room and drag Chinky out whilst he's gone," said Peter. "We simply must rescue him!"

So they crept in through the window and bent over Chinky. And just at that very moment they felt a strong draught blowing round them!

They looked at each of the chairs—yes, one of them had grown wings, and was flapping them, making 'quite a wind! Hurray—now they could fly off in the Wishing-Chair, and cram Chinky in with them, fast asleep.

"Quick, oh, quick—Mr. Spells is coming back!" said Peter. "Help me with Chinky—quick, Mollie, QUICK!"

MR. SPELLS IS VERY MAGIC

The Wishing-Chair stood with the other five chairs, its red wings flapping strongly. The children caught hold of the sleeping pixie and dragged him to the chair. He felt as heavy as lead! If only he would wake up.

"He's in a terribly magic sleep," said Mollie in despair. "Now – lift him, Peter – that's right – and put him safely on the seat of the chair. Oh dear, he's rolling off again. Do, do be quick!"

They could hear Mr. Spells muttering in the next room, stirring something in a pot. In a few moments he would have made his find-out spell to see which was the Wishing-Chair, and would come back into the room. They *must* get away first!

The chair's wings were now fully grown, and it was doing little hops on the ground as if it were impatient to be off. The children sat down in it, holding Chinky tightly. Tricky the goblin was still lying on the floor, fast asleep. Good!

"Fly home, chair, fly home!" commanded Peter. Just in time, too, because as he spoke the children could hear the wizard's steps coming towards them from the next room. He appeared at the door, carrying something in a shining bottle.

The chair had now risen in the air, flapping its wings, and was trying to get out of the window.

It was an awkward shape for the chair to get through, and it turned itself sideways so that the children and Chinky almost fell out! They clung to the arms in fright, trying to stop Chinky from rolling off.

"Hey!" cried the wizard in the greatest astonishment. "What are you doing? Why, the chair's grown wings! Who are you, children — and what are you doing with my chair? Come back."

But by this time the chair was out of the window and was the right way up again, much to the children's relief. It flew up into the air.

"Good! We've escaped — and we've got both the chair *and* Chinky," said Peter, pleased. "Even if he *is* asleep, we've got him. We'll have to ask the elf if he knows how to wake him up."

But Peter spoke too soon. Mr. Spells was too clever to let the chair escape quite so easily. He came running out into the little garden in front of his castle-like cottage, carrying something over his arm.

"What's he going to do?" said Mollie. "What's he got, Peter?"

They soon knew! It was a very, very long rope, with a loop at the end to lasso them with! Mr. Spells swung the loops of rope round for a second or two, then flung the rope up into the air. The loops unwound and the last loop of all almost touched them. But not quite! The chair gave a jump of fright and rose a little higher.

"Oh, do go quickly, chair!" begged Mollie.

"The wizard is gathering up the rope to throw it
again. Look out—here it comes! Oh, Peter, it's
going to catch us—it's longer than ever!"

The rope sped up to them like a long, thin snake.
The last loop of all fell neatly round the chair,
but, before it could tighten, Peter caught hold of
it and threw it off. He really did it very cleverly
indeed.

"Oh, Peter—you *are* marvellous!" cried Mollie.
"I really thought we were caught that time.
Surely we are out of reach now—the wizard looks
very small and far away."

Once more the rope came flying towards the
Wishing-Chair, and it tried to dodge it, almost

upsetting the children altogether. The rope darted after the chair, fell firmly round it—and before Peter could throw it off it had tightened itself round the chair and the children too!

Peter struggled hard to get a knife to cut the rope—but his arms were pinned tightly to his sides and he couldn't put his hands into his pockets. Mollie tried to help him, but it was no use. Mr. Spells was hauling on the rope and the chair was going gradually down and down and down.

"Oh dear—we're caught!" said Mollie in despair. "Just when we had so nearly escaped, too! Peter, do think of something."

But Peter couldn't. Chinky might have been able to think of some spell to get rid of the rope but he was still fast asleep. Mollie had to use both hands to hold him on the chair in case he fell off.

Down went the chair, pulling against the rope and making things as difficult as possible for the wizard, who was in a fine old temper when at last he had the chair on the ground.

"What do you mean by this?" he said sternly. "What kind of behaviour is this—coming to my house, stealing one of the chairs I bought—the Wishing-Chair, too, the best of the lot? I didn't even know one of the chairs was a magic chair when I bought the set."

Mollie was almost crying. Peter looked sulky as he tried to free his arms from the tight rope.

"You'll keep that rope round you for the rest

of the day," said Mr. Spells. "Just to teach you that you can't steal from a wizard."

"Let me free," said Peter. "I'm not a thief, and I haven't stolen this chair—unless you call taking something that really belongs to us *stealing*. I don't!"

"What do you mean?" said Mr. Spells. "I'm tired of hearing people say this chair is theirs. Tricky said it—Chinky said it—and now you say it! It can't belong to all of you—and, anyway, I bought it with my money."

"Mr. Spells, this Wishing-Chair is ours," said Peter patiently. "It lives in our playroom, and Chinky the pixie shares it with us and looks after it. Tricky stole it and sold it to Mr. Polish, who had five other chairs like it."

"And then Tricky told you about the six old chairs and you went and bought them," said Mollie. "And Tricky came to-night to get back the Wishing-Chair because it's valuable and he can sell it to somebody else!"

"And then Chinky came to try and tell you about it before Tricky stole it," went on Peter. "And I suppose they came at the same time and quarrelled about it."

"Well, well!" said Mr. Spells, who had been listening in surprise. "This is a queer story, I must say. It's true that I came in from the garden to find the goblin and the pixie behaving most peculiarly. They kept sitting down first on one chair and then on another—trying to find out which was the Wishing-Chair, I suppose—and shouting at one another all the time."

"I'd tied my blue hanky on the right arm of the Wishing-Chair," said Mollie.

"Yes—I saw it there and wondered why," said Mr. Spells. "I can see it in Chinky's pocket now— he must have recognized it as yours and taken it off. Well, I suppose you came in just at the moment when I was angry with them both, and put them into a magic sleep."

"Yes," said Peter. "Then you went out and we thought we'd escape if we could, taking Chinky with us. The chair suddenly grew its wings, you see."

"Mr. Spells, can we have back our chair, please, now that you've heard our story?" begged Mollie. "I know you've paid some money to Mr. Polish for it—but couldn't you get it back from Tricky the goblin? After all, he's the rogue in all this, isn't he—not us or Chinky?"

"You're quite right," said Mr. Spells. "And I think it was very brave of you to come to rescue Chinky. I'm sorry I put him into a magic sleep now—but I'll wake him up again. And now I'll take the rope off and set you free!"

He took the rope off Peter and then lifted Chinky from the Wishing-Chair and laid him down on the floor. He drew a white ring of chalk round him and then a ring of blue inside the white circle. Then he called loudly.

"Cinders! Where are you? Dear me, that cat is never about when he's wanted!"

There was a loud miaow outside the window.

In jumped a big black cat with green eyes that shone like traffic signals! He ran to Mr. Spells.

"Cinders, I'm going to do a wake-up spell," said the wizard. "Go and sit in the magic ring and sing with me whilst I chant the spell."

Cinders leapt lightly over the chalk rings and sat down close to the sleeping Chinky. Mr. Spells began to walk round and round, just outside the ring, chanting a curious song. It sounded like:—

> "Birriloola-kummi-pool,
> Rimminy, romminy, rye,
> Tibbynooka-falli-lool,
> Open your sleepy eye!"

All the time the wizard chanted this queer song the cat kept up a loud miaowing as if he were joining in too.

The spell was a very good one, because at the end of the chant, Chinky opened first one eye and then the other. He sat up, looking extremely surprised.

"I say," he began, "what's happened? Where am I? Oh, hallo, Peter and Mollie! I've been looking for you everywhere!"

"And *we've* been looking for you!" said Mollie. "You've been in a magic sleep. Get up and come home with us. The Wishing-Chair has grown its wings again."

Then Chinky saw Mr. Spells standing nearby, tall and commanding, and he went rather pale. "But, I say—what does Mr. Spells think about all this?" he said, nervously.

232

"I have heard the children's story and it is quite plain that the chair really does belong to you," he said. "I'll get the money back from Tricky."

"Well, he's *very* tricky, so be careful of him," said Chinky, sitting down in the Wishing-Chair with the children.

"He'll get a shock when he wakes up," said Mr. Spells, and he suddenly touched the sleeping goblin with the toe of his foot. "Dimini, dimini, dimini, diminish!" he cried suddenly, and lo and behold the goblin shrank swiftly to a very tiny creature indeed, diminishing rapidly before the astonished eyes of the watching children.

Mr. Spells picked up the tiny goblin, took a matchbox off the mantelpiece, popped him into it, shut the box and put it back on the mantelpiece.

"He won't cause me any trouble when he wakes up!" he said. "No, not a bit! Well, good-bye. I'm glad this has all ended well—but I do wish that chair was mine."

The children waved good-bye and the chair rose into the air. "Shall we go home?" said Peter.

"No," said Mollie, suddenly remembering the satchel of sandwiches and cake that Peter still carried. "We'll take Chinky off for the day, picnicking! We deserve a nice peaceful day after such a thrilling adventure."

"Right!" said Peter, and Chinky nodded happily. "Wishing-Chair, take us to the nicest picnic spot you know!" And off they flew at once, to have a very happy day together.

VII

OFF ON ANOTHER ADVENTURE!

For a whole week the children watched and waited for the Wishing-Chair to grow its wings again. It didn't sprout them at all! The wings had vanished as soon as it had arrived safely back in the playroom.

"I hope its magic isn't getting less," said Mollie, one day, as they sat in the playroom, playing ludo together. It was their very favourite game, and they always laughed at Chinky because he made such a fuss when he didn't get "home" before they did.

As they sat playing together they felt a welcome draught. "Oh, lovely! A breeze at last!" said Mollie thankfully. "I do really think this is just about the hottest day we've had these holidays!"

"The wind must have got up a bit at last," said Peter. "Blow, wind, blow—you are making us lovely and cool."

"Funny that the leaves on the trees aren't moving, isn't it?" said Chinky.

Mollie looked out of the open door at the trees in the garden. They were perfectly still! "But there *isn't* a breeze," she said, and then a sudden thought struck her. She looked round at the Wishing-Chair, which was standing just behind them.

"Look!" she cried. "How silly we are! It isn't

the wind—it's the Wishing-Chair that has grown its wings again. They are flapping like anything!"

So they were. The children and Chinky sprang up in delight. "Good! We could just do with a lovely cool ride up in the air to-day," said Peter. "Wishing-Chair, we are very pleased with you!"

The Wishing-Chair flapped its wings very strongly again and gave a creak. Then Chinky noticed something.

"I say, look—it's only grown *three* wings instead of four. What's happened? It's never done that before."

They all stared at the chair. One of its front legs hadn't grown a wing. It looked rather queer without it.

Chinky looked at the chair rather doubtfully. "Do you think it can fly with only three wings?" he said. "This is rather a peculiar thing to happen, really. I wonder if we ought to fly off in the chair if it's only got three wings instead of four."

"I don't see why not," said Mollie. "After all, an aeroplane can fly with three engines, if the fourth one stops."

The chair gave a little hop up in the air as if to say it could fly perfectly well. "Oh, come along!" said Chinky. "We'll try. I'm sure it will be all right. But I wish I knew what to do to get the fourth wing to grow. Something has gone wrong, it's plain."

They got into the chair, Chinky as usual sitting on the back, holding on to their shoulders. The chair flew to the door.

"Where shall we go?" said Chinky.

"Well—we never did get to the Land of Goodness Knows Where after all," said Mollie. "Shall we try to get there again? We know it's a good way away, so it should be a nice long flight, very cool and windy high up in the air."

"We may as well," said Chinky. "Fly to the Land of Goodness Knows Where, Chair. We saw it on the map—it's due east from here, straight towards where the sun rises—you go over the Tiptop Mountains, past the Crazy Valley and then down by the Zigzag Coast."

"It sounds exciting," said Mollie. "Oh, isn't it lovely to be cool again? It's so very hot to-day."

They were now high up in the air, and a lovely breeze blew past them as they flew. Little clouds, like puffs of cotton wool, floated below them. Mollie leaned out to get hold of one as they passed.

"This is fun," she said. "Chinky, is there a land of ice-creams? If so, I'd like to go there sometime!"

"I don't know. I've never heard of one," said Chinky. "There's a Land of Goodies though, I know that. It once came to the top of the Faraway Tree, and I went there. It was lovely—biscuits growing on trees, and chocolates sprouting on bushes."

"Oh—did you see Moon-Face and Silky and the old Saucepan Man?" asked Mollie, in excitement. "I've read the books about the Faraway Tree, and I've always wished I could climb it."

"Yes, I saw them all," said Chinky. "Silky is

sweet, you'd love her. But Moon-Face was cross because somebody had taken all his slippery-slip cushions — you know, the cushions he keeps in his room at the top of the tree for people to sit on when they slide down from the top to the bottom."

"I wouldn't mind going to the Land of Goodies at all," said Peter. "It sounds really fine. I almost wish we'd told the chair to go there instead of the Land of Goodness Knows Where."

"Well, don't change its mind for it," said Chinky. "It doesn't like that. Look, there are the Tip-Top Mountains."

They all leaned out to look. They were very extraordinary mountains, running up into high, jagged peaks as if somebody had drawn them higgledy-piggledy with a pencil, up and down, up and down.

On they went, through a batch of tiny little clouds; but Mollie didn't try to catch any of these because, just in time, she saw that baby elves were fast asleep on them, one to each cloud.

"They make good cradles for a hot day like this," explained Chinky.

After a while, Mollie noticed that Chinky was leaning rather hard on her shoulder, and that Peter seemed to be leaning against her, too. She pushed them back.

"Don't lean so heavily on me," she said.

"We don't mean to," said Peter. "But I seem to be leaning that way all the time! I do try not to."

"Why are we, I wonder?" said Chinky. Then he

237

gave a cry. "Why, the chair's all on one side. No wonder Peter and I keep going over on to you, Mollie. Look—it's tipped sideways!"

"What's the matter with it?" said Mollie. She tried to shake the chair upright by swinging herself about in it, but it always over-balanced to the left side as soon as she had stopped swinging it to and fro.

They all looked in alarm at one another as the chair began to tip more and more to one side. It was very difficult to sit in it when it tipped like that.

"It's because it's only got three wings!" said Chinky, suddenly. "Of course—that's it! The one wing on this side is tired out, and so the chair is flying with only two wings really, and it's tipping over. It will soon be on its side in the air!"

"Gracious! Then for goodness' sake let's go down to the ground at once," said Mollie, in alarm. "We shall fall out if we don't."

"Go down to the ground, Chair," commanded Peter, feeling the chair going over to one side even more. He looked over the side. The one wing there had already stopped flapping. The chair was using only two wings—they would soon be tired out, too!

The chair flew heavily down to the ground and landed with rather a bump. Its wings stopped flapping and hung limp. It creaked dolefully. It was quite exhausted, that was plain!

"We shouldn't have flown off on it when it only

238

had three wings," said Chinky. "It was wrong of us. After all, Peter and Mollie, you have grown bigger since last holidays, and must be heavier. The chair can't possibly take us all unless it has *four* wings to fly with."

They stood and looked at the poor, tired Wishing-Chair. "What are we going to do about it?" said Peter.

"Well—we must try to find out where we are first," said Chinky, looking round. "And then we must ask if there is a witch or wizard or magician anywhere about that can give us something to make the chair grow another wing. Then we'd better take it straight home for a rest."

"Look," said Mollie, pointing to a nearby sign-post. "It says, 'To the Village of Slipperies.' Do you know that village, Chinky?"

"No. But I've heard of it," said Chinky. "The people there aren't very nice—slippery as eels—can't trust them or believe a word they say. I don't think we'll go that way."

He went to look at the other arm of the sign-post and came back looking very pleased.

"It says 'Dame Quick-Fingers'," he said. "She's my great-aunt. She'll help us all right. She'll be sure to know a spell for growing wings. She keeps a pack of flying dogs, you know, because of the Slipperies—they simply fly after them when they come to steal her chickens and ducks."

"Goodness—I'd love to see some flying dogs," said Mollie. "Where does this aunt of yours live?"

"Just down the road, round a corner, and by a big rowan tree," said Chinky. "She's really nice. I dare say she'd ask us to tea if we are as polite as possible. She loves good manners."

"Well—you go and ask her if she knows how to grow an extra wing on our chair," said Mollie. "We'd better stay here with the chair, I think, in case anyone thinks of stealing it again. We can easily bring it along to your aunt's cottage, if she's in. We won't carry it all the way there in case she's not."

"Right. I'll go," said Chinky. "I won't be long. You just sit in the chair till I come back—and don't you let anyone steal it."

He ran off down the road and disappeared round a corner. Mollie and Peter sat down in the chair to wait. The chair creaked. It sounded very tired indeed. Mollie patted its arms. "You'll soon be all right once you have got a fourth wing," she said. "Cheer up."

Chinky hadn't been gone very long before the sound of footsteps made the children look round. Five little people were coming along the road from the Village of Slipperies. They looked most peculiar.

"They must be Slipperies," said Peter, sitting up. "Now we must be careful they don't play a trick on us and get the chair away. Aren't they queer-looking?"

The five little creatures came up and bowed low. "Good-day," they said. "We come to greet you and to ask you to visit our village."

VIII

THE SLIPPERIES PLAY A TRICK!

Peter and Mollie looked hard at the five Slipperies. Each Slippery had one blue eye and one green, and not one of them looked straight at the children! Their hair was slick and smooth, their mouths smiled without stopping, and they rubbed their bony hands together all the time.

"I'm sorry," said Peter, "but we don't want to leave our chair. We're waiting here with it till our friend Chinky comes back from seeing his Great-Aunt Quick-Fingers."

"Oh, she's gone to market," said one of the Slipperies. "She always goes on Thursdays."

"Oh dear," said Peter. "How tiresome! Now we shan't be able to get a fourth wing for our Wishing-Chair."

"Dear me—is this a Wishing-Chair?" said the Slipperies, in great interest. "It's the first time we've seen one. Do let us sit in it."

"Certainly not," said Peter, feeling certain that if he let them sit in the chair they would try to fly off in it.

"I hear that Great-Aunt Quick-Fingers has some flying dogs," said Mollie, hoping that the Slipperies would look frightened at the mention of them. But they didn't.

They rubbed their slippery hands together again and went on smiling. "Ah, yes—wonderful dogs

241

they are. If you stand up on your chair, and look over the field yonder, you may see some of them flying around," said one Slippery.

The children stood on the seat of the chair. The Slipperies clustered round them. "Now look right down over that field," began one of them. "Do you see a tall tree?"

"Yes," said Mollie.

"Well, look to the right of it and you'll see the roof of a house. And then to the right of that and you'll see another tree," said the Slippery.

"Can't you tell me *exactly* where to look?" said Mollie, getting impatient. "I can't see a single flying dog. Only a rook or two."

"Well, now look to the left and . . ." began another Slippery, when Peter jumped down from the chair.

"You're just making it all up," he said. "Go on, be off with you! I don't like any of you."

The Slipperies lost their smiles, and looked nasty. They laid hands on the Wishing-Chair.

"I shall whistle for the flying dogs," said Peter suddenly. "Now let me see—what is the whistle, ah, yes . . ." And he suddenly whistled a very shrill whistle indeed.

The Slipperies shot off at once as if a hundred of the flying dogs were after them! Mollie laughed.

"Peter! That's not really a whistle for flying dogs, is it?"

"No, of course not. But I had to get rid of them somehow," said Peter. "I had a feeling they were going to trick us with their silly smiles and rubbing hands and odd eyes—so I had to think of some way of tricking *them* instead."

"I wish Chinky would come," said Mollie, sitting down in the chair again. "He's been ages. And it's all a waste of time, his going to find his Great-Aunt, if she's at the market. We shall have to go there, I expect, and carry the chair all the way."

"Why, there *is* Chinky!" said Peter, waving. "Oh, good, he's dancing and smiling. He's got the spell to make another wing grow."

"Then his Great-Aunt couldn't have gone to market!" said Mollie. "Hey, Chinky! Have you got the spell? Was your Great-Aunt Quick-Fingers in?"

"Yes—and awfully pleased to see me," said Chinky, running up. "And she gave me just enough magic to make another wing grow, so we shan't be long now."

"Five Slipperies came up, and they said your Great-Aunt always goes to market on Thursdays," said Mollie.

"You can't believe a word they say," said Chinky. "I told you that. My word, I'm glad they didn't trick you in any way. They usually trick everyone, no matter how clever they may be."

"Well, they didn't trick *us*," said Peter. "We were much too smart for them—weren't we, Mollie?"

"Yes. They wanted to sit in the chair when they knew it was a Wishing-Chair," said Mollie.

"But we wouldn't let them."

"I should think not," said Chinky. He showed the children a little blue box. "Look—I've got a smear of ointment here that is just enough to grow a red wing to match the other wings. Then the chair will be quite all right."

"Well, let's rub it on," said Peter. Chinky knelt down by the chair—and then he gave a cry of horror.

"What's the matter?" said the children.

"Look—somebody has cut off the other three wings of the chair!" groaned Chinky. "Cut them right off short. There's only a stump left of each."

Mollie and Peter stared in horror. Sure enough

the other three wings had been cut right off. But how? And when? Who could have done it? The children had been with the chair the whole time.

"I do think you might have kept a better guard on the chair," said Chinky crossly. "I really do. Didn't I warn you about the ways of the Slipperies? Didn't I say you couldn't trust them? Didn't I . . ."

"Oh, Chinky—but when could it have been done?" cried Mollie. "I tell you, we were here the whole of the time."

"Standing by the chair?" asked Chinky.

"Yes—or *on* it," said Peter.

"*On* it! Whatever did you stand *on* it, for?" said Chinky, puzzled. "To stop the Slipperies sitting down?"

"No—to see your Great-Aunt's flying-dogs," said Peter. "The Slipperies said they were over there, and if we would stand up on the chair seat we could just see them flying around. But we couldn't."

"Of course you couldn't," said Chinky. "And for a very good reason, too—they're all at the cottage with my Great-Aunt. I saw them!"

"Oh—the dreadful story-tellers!" cried Mollie. "Peter—it was a trick! Whilst we were standing up there trying to see the dogs, one of the Slipperies must have quietly snipped off the three wings and put them in his pocket."

"Of course!" said Chinky. "Very simple—and you're a pair of simpletons to get taken in by such a silly trick."

Mollie and Peter went very red. "What shall we do?" asked Peter. "I'm very sorry about it. Poor old chair — one wing not grown and the other three snipped away. It's a shame."

"Thank goodness Chinky has the Growing Ointment for wings," said Mollie.

"Yes — but I've only got just enough for *one* wing," said Chinky. "One wing isn't going to take us very far, is it?"

"No," said Mollie. "Whatever are we going to do?"

"I shall have to ask Great-Aunt Quick-Fingers for some more Growing Ointment, that's all," said Chinky, gloomily. "And this time you can come with me, *and* bring the chair too. If I leave you here alone with it, you'll get tricked again, and I shall come back and find the *legs* are gone next time, and I can't even grow wings on them!"

"It's not nice of you to keep on and on about it, Chinky," said Mollie, lifting up the chair with Peter. "We're very sorry. We didn't know quite how clever the Slipperies were. Oooh — horrid creatures, with their odd eyes and deceitful smiles."

They followed Chinky down the road and along a lane. Soon he came to his Great-Aunt's cottage. It was very snug and small. To Mollie's enormous delight, five or six little brown dogs, rather like spaniels, were flying about the garden on small white wings. They barked loudly and flew to the three of them.

"Now, now — these are friends of mine," said

Chinky, and patted the nearest dog, which was flying round his head.

It was strange to have the little dogs sailing about the air like gulls! One flew up to Mollie and rested its front paws on her shoulder. She laughed, and the dog licked her face. Then off it flew again, and chased after a sparrow, barking madly.

Great-Aunt Quick-Fingers came to the door, looking surprised. "Why, Chinky—back again so soon!" she said. "What's happened?"

Chinky told her. "So you see, Great-Aunt, now that the poor chair has lost *all* its wings, I'm afraid that the Growing Ointment you gave me won't be enough," said Chinky. "I'm so sorry."

"Well, well—it takes a very clever person to see through the Slippery ways," said his Great-Aunt. "You'd better come in and have tea now you're all here!"

The children put down the Wishing-Chair and Great-Aunt Quick-Fingers got the little treacle tarts out of the oven. "There you are," she said. "Get your fingers nice and sticky with those! I'll go and make some more Growing Ointment for you. It won't take long."

She disappeared, and the children sat and munched the lovely treacle tarts.

Just at that moment she came back, with a fairly large jar. She handed it to Chinky. "There you are. Use that and see what happens. But remember, you can only use it once on anything. The spell doesn't act twice. It's no good trying to use the ointment another time on the chair, to make it grow wings, because it won't be any use."

Chinky dipped his finger into the jar of ointment. It was curious stuff, bright yellow with green streaks in it.

He rubbed some on to a chair leg and immediately a most wonderful wing sprouted out, big and strong!

"I say—it isn't red, as it always is!" cried Mollie. "It's green and yellow—and a much bigger wing than before. I say, Chair, you *will* look grand. Make another wing come, Chinky."

Soon the Wishing-Chair had four grand green and yellow wings, much bigger than its old red ones. It waved them about proudly.

"You'd better get in the chair and go before it tries its new wings out by itself," said Great-Aunt Quick-Fingers. So in they all got, Chinky on the back, as usual—and off they went!

"Home, Chair, home!" cried everyone, and it rose high in the air, and flew off to the west. "Good-bye and thank you very much," cried Chinky and the children, and Great-Aunt waved till they were out of sight.

"Well, that was quite a nice little adventure," said Peter. "And the chair's got some wonderful new wings. I do hope they'll always grow like this in future—big and strong, and all green and yellow!"

IX

MOLLIE AND THE GROWING OINTMENT

The children were very pleased with the chair's beautiful new green and yellow wings. "They're much better than the little red ones it used to grow," said Peter. "Your Great-Aunt's Growing Ointment is marvellous stuff, Chinky. I only hope the chair will grow its wings more often now."

The green and yellow wings disappeared, of course, as soon as they were all safely at home again. The chair stood still in its place, looking quite ordinary. The children patted it.

"Good old Wishing-Chair. Grow your wings again soon. You haven't taken us to the Land of Goodness Knows Where yet, you know!"

The chair didn't grow its wings again that week. Friday came, Saturday, Sunday, Monday. The children grew tired of asking Chinky if the chair was growing its wings yet.

On Tuesday a spell of rainy weather began. It really was too wet to play any games out of doors at all. The children went down to their playroom day after day to play with Chinky, and that was fun. But on Friday Chinky said he really must go and see how his dear old mother was.

"I haven't seen her since I came back to you with the chair," he said. "I must go to-day."

"Oh, bother! We shall have to do without you," said Mollie. "Just suppose the chair grows its wings, Chinky, and you're not here."

"Well, that's easy," said Chinky, with a grin. "Simply sit in it and wish it to go to my mother's. She will be very pleased to see you, and then we can all three of us go adventuring somewhere."

"Oh, yes — we'll do that, if only the chair grows wings," said Peter. "Well, good-bye, Chinky. Will you be back to-night?"

"Yes," said Chinky. "I'll be sleeping on the old sofa as usual, don't worry. I'm not taking my wand with me, by the way, so keep an eye on it, will you?"

Chinky had just bought a new wand, a very useful one that had quite a bit of magic in it. He was very proud of it, and kept it in the cupboard with the toys and games.

"Yes — we'll look after it for you," said Peter. "And we won't use it, we promise."

"I know you won't," said Chinky. "Well, see you to-night."

Off he went to catch the bus to his mother's cottage, dressed in his mackintosh and sou'wester. The children felt decidedly dull when he had gone.

"Game of ludo, Mollie?" said Peter.

"No. I'm bored with ludo to-day," said Mollie.

"Well, you're not going to be very good company, then," said Peter, taking down a book. "I'll read. You can tell me when you've finished being bored and we'll think up an exciting game."

Mollie lay down on the rug and shut her eyes. What a pity it had rained and rained so long. Even if the Wishing-Chair grew its wings, it wouldn't be much fun going out in the rain. They would have to take an umbrella with them.

Mollie opened her eyes and looked out of the window. Why, the sun was shining—and yet it was still raining.

"I say, Peter, look at this rainbow," said Mollie. "It's glorious. Oh—wouldn't it be lovely to fly off to a rainbow in the Wishing-Chair! If it looks as beautiful as this far away, whatever would it look like very near to us? Oh, I do wish the Wishing-Chair would grow its wings this very afternoon."

Peter took no notice. He was deep in his book. Mollie felt cross. She wandered round the room and opened a little cupboard where Chinky kept some of his things. There on the shelf was the jar of Growing Ointment that Great-Aunt Quick-Fingers had given him to make the wings of the Wishing-Chair sprout again.

Mollie took down the jar and opened the lid. There was plenty of ointment left—yellow with streaks of green in it. She wondered if perhaps it *would* make the chair's wings grow again, although Chinky's Great-Aunt had said it only acted once on anything.

"I'll try it," thought Mollie. "And I won't tell Peter! If the wings grow, I'll fly off in the Wishing-Chair without him, and go to Chinky's alone. That will serve him right for not answering when I speak to him!"

She went over to the Wishing-Chair and rubbed

251

a little of the ointment on one of the front legs. Nothing happened at all. She couldn't feel even a tiny bud of a wing beginning to grow; the Growing Ointment certainly didn't act twice. Great-Aunt Quick-Fingers was right.

Then a wonderful thought came to Mollie. Why shouldn't she try a little of the magic ointment on something else? She looked round. Her dolls, for instance! Oh, if only she could make wings grow on Rosebud, her prettiest doll. That would be really wonderful.

Feeling very excited, Mollie took her doll Rosebud from her cot. She rubbed a little of the green and yellow ointment on to her back – and, hey presto, wing-buds began to form – and little green and yellow wings sprouted out on the doll's back.

And she suddenly left Mollie's knee and flew – yes, *flew* – round the playroom. She flew near Peter and he felt the wind of her little wings. He looked up – and his eyes almost dropped out of his head as he saw Rosebud flying gaily round the room!

Mollie laughed in delight and tried to catch the doll as she flew past. "I've put some of the Growing Ointment on her back," she said. "You know – what Chinky's Great-Aunt gave him for growing wings on the Wishing-Chair. And Rosebud grew wings!"

"Well, I never!" said Peter in amazement. "I say – do you think my engine would grow wings, too?" said Peter suddenly. He had a wonderful

252

clockwork engine, a perfect model that he was very proud of.

"Oh, *yes*—let's try and see," said Mollie. So they got the engine and Peter smeared a little of the ointment on to it. It sprouted out small wings at once!

It flew from Peter's hand and joined the doll. The children laughed till their sides ached to see the two toys behaving like this. They really did look extraordinary.

And then Mollie and Peter went quite mad with the ointment. They smeared it on to a top and that flew round the room, spinning as it went! They smeared the skittles and they all shot round and round, some of them bumping into one another in the air.

They made some of the little toy soldiers fly, and they even gave the bricks in their brick box wings to fly with. All these things flapped their way round the room, and Mollie and Peter screamed with laughter as they tried to dodge the flying toys.

Mollie went to the toy cupboard to see if any toy was there that could be made to fly as well. She picked up Chinky's new wand and put it on one side—but, dear me, her fingers were smeared with the Growing Ointment and the wand at once grew tiny, graceful green and yellow wings, too! It flew out of the cupboard and joined the flying toys.

"Oh dear—there goes the wand," said Mollie. "I do hope Chinky won't mind. I just touched it by accident with the ointment smeared on my fingers, and it grew wings."

"Look—I've made the teapot fly," said Peter, and roared with laughter to see it flapping its way round the room. "Look at the skittles colliding again."

The wind suddenly blew the door wide open. Then a dreadful thing happened. Rosebud the doll, the railway engine, the skittles, the bricks, the top, the teapot, the wand; in fact everything that had grown wings shot straight out of the open door, flew down to the bottom of the garden and vanished!

"Ooooh!" said Mollie in fright.

"They've gone," said Peter, and rushed to the open door. But he could see nothing. No Rosebud was there, no engine, nothing. They had all vanished into the blue.

"Oh dear—shall we get them back?" said Mollie. "Why did I ever begin to smear the Growing Ointment on anything? It was a very silly idea. Now I've lost Rosebud."

"And what about my lovely model engine?" said Peter. "And I *say*—Chinky's magic wand has gone, too!"

They stared at one another in dismay. Chinky's new wand, that he had saved up for and was so proud of! It had grown wings and now it had flown out of the door and vanished, too. This was dreadful.

"We shall have to tell Chinky when he gets back to-night, and ask him if we can possibly get the things back," said Mollie. "If we knew where they had gone we could go and fetch them. Do you suppose they've gone to Great-Aunt Quick-Fingers?"

They said no more to one another, but sat solemnly side by side, hoping and hoping that the things would fly back as unexpectedly as they had flown away. But they didn't.

Chinky came back at half-past six, looking very merry and bright, and bringing a big chocolate cake from his mother. He stopped when he saw their doleful faces.

"What's up?" he said. "Anything happened?"

They told him, and Chinky listened in astonishment. He leapt to his feet when they spoke about his wand.

"WHAT! You don't mean to tell me you were silly enough to meddle with my wand — surely you didn't make my *wand* grow wings, too!"

"It was an accident," said poor Mollie. "I must have had some of the ointment on my fingers when I moved it — and so it grew wings, too. I'm so sorry, Chinky."

"Where have the things gone, Chinky?" asked Peter.

"I don't know," said Chinky. "I haven't the least idea. All I can say is — the next time the Wishing-Chair grows its wings, we'll have to tell it to go wherever the toys have gone — but goodness knows where it will take us to!"

X

OFF TO FIND THE TOYS

Chinky was gloomy and cross that evening. The children were sad, and felt ashamed that they had gone quite so mad with the Growing Ointment. They felt very guilty indeed about Chinky's wand.

"Will you come and tell us if the Wishing-Chair grows its wings again to-night, Chinky?" asked Mollie when it was time for them to go back to the house.

"I might," said Chinky gruffly. "And I might not. I might go off by myself in it."

"Oh, no, don't do that," begged Mollie. "That would be horrid of you. Dear Chinky, please be nice and forgive us for losing your wand."

"All right," said Chinky, cheering up a little.

"I really do feel very upset about losing my doll Rosebud, you know," went on poor Mollie. "I feel just as upset about her as you feel about your wand."

"And I'm miserable about my engine," said Peter. "It was the finest I ever had."

"Well—we'll hope the Wishing-Chair grows its wings again to-night, then, and we can go and fetch everything," said Chinky. "I'll come and tap on your windows if it grows its wings."

But Chinky didn't tap on their windows at all. The chair didn't grow any wings in the night. Mollie sighed.

256

"Just when we so badly want it to fly, it won't grow wings! Now to-day we've got to behave nicely and be on our best behaviour, because Mother's got visitors. Perhaps we shan't be able to go down to the playroom at all."

At eleven o'clock, when the visitors had arrived and Mother was giving them coffee and the children were handing round plates of biscuits and buns, Chinky appeared at the window.

He was horrified when he saw so many people there and disappeared at once. The children caught sight of him.

They looked at one another in despair. Now what were they to do? There was only one thing. They must do something to make Mother send them out of the room.

So Mollie suddenly spilt the plate of biscuits all over the floor, and Peter spilt a cup of coffee.

Mother looked vexed. "Oh, dear—how clumsy of you!" she said. "Go and ask Jane if she will please bring a cloth, Mollie. And I think you and Peter had better go now. I don't want anything else spilt."

"Sorry, Mother," said Peter.

They shot out of the room. Mollie called to Jane to take a cloth to wipe up the coffee, and then both children raced down to the playroom.

"I hope Chinky hasn't gone off in the chair by himself," panted Peter. "If he saw us with all those visitors he might think we couldn't possibly come—and then he'd fly off alone."

They got to the playroom door just as Chinky

was flying out in the Wishing-Chair. They bumped into one another, and Peter caught hold of one of the chair's legs.

"Just in time!" he cried. "Help us up, Chinky!"

Chinky pulled them up with him. Then the chair flapped its green and yellow wings and flew strongly up into the air.

"I was afraid you wouldn't be able to come," said Chinky. "I was just setting off by myself. The chair had only grown its wings a few minutes before I peeped in at the window."

"What fine, big, strong wings it's got now," said Peter. "They make quite a draught round my legs. It will be able to fly faster now."

"Where are we going?" asked Mollie.

"I don't know," said Chinky. "I just said to the chair, 'Go and find my wand, and Rosebud, and the rest of the toys,' and it seemed to know the place I meant, because it rose up at once. I've no idea where we shall land. I only hope it's somewhere nice. It would be awful to go to the Village of Slipperies, or to the Land of Rubbish, or somewhere like that."

"Oh dear—I hope it's somewhere nice, too," said Mollie. "The chair is flying very high, isn't it?"

"Do you think it may be going to Toyland?" asked Peter. "I wouldn't mind that at all. After all, most of the things were toys. I think it's very likely they may have gone there."

"It certainly seems to be taking the way to Toyland as far as I remember," said Chinky, peering down. "I know we pass over the Village of Golliwogs before we reach Toyland, and we're very near that now. There's Toyland, far over there. That must be where we're going."

But it wasn't. The chair suddenly began to fly down and down at a great rate, and it was plain that it was going to land.

"Well! This isn't Toyland!" said Chinky in surprise. "Good gracious! I do believe it's the school run by Mister Grim, for Bad Brownies. Surely the toys haven't gone there!"

The chair landed in the grounds of a big house, just near a wall. Chinky and the children got off. They pushed the chair under a bush to hide it. Then they looked cautiously round.

From the big building in the distance came a chanting noise. The children and Chinky listened.

"I mustn't scream or whistle or shout
Because Mister Grim is always about,
I mustn't stamp or slam any door
Or jump or slide on the schoolroom floor,
I mustn't be greedy, untidy or lazy
Because Mister Grim would be driven
        quite crazy,
I mustn't be slow, and I MUST be quick,
Because Mister Grim has a very BIG
        STICK!"

"Ooooh!" said Mollie. "I don't like the sound of that. That must be the poor Bad Brownies learning verses for Mr. Grim."

"Yes," said Chinky. "I do wish we hadn't come here. I've half a mind to get in the Wishing-Chair and go off again. I've always been told that Mister Grim is a very hard master. We don't want to be caught by him."

"*Caught!*" said Peter. "But we're two children and a pixie—we're not brownies—and this is a school for brownies."

"I know," said Chinky. "I just don't like the feel of this place, that's all. If you think it's all right, we'll stay and see if we can possibly find where our toys are."

"I think we'd better," said Peter. "Well—what's the first thing to do?"

"Listen—is that the brownies coming out to play?" said Mollie as a perfect babel of noise reached them. Then came the sound of feet running and in a trice about fifty small brownies surrounded them. They all looked merry, mischievous little fellows, too young to have grown their brownie beards yet.

"Who are you? Are you new pupils for this awful school?" asked a small brownie, pushing himself forward. "My name's Winks. What's yours?"

All the little brownies crowded round, listening eagerly. Chinky pushed them back.

"Don't crowd so. No, we haven't come to your school. We came because we're looking for things we've lost, and we think they may be somewhere here. My name's Chinky. These are real children, Peter and Mollie."

"Well, be careful Mister Grim doesn't see you," said Winks. "He's in a very bad temper these days—worse than he's ever been."

"Why?" asked Peter.

"Because we found the cupboard where he kept his canes and we broke the whole lot!" chuckled the brownie. "Every one of them."

"Can't he slap you or smack you, though?" said Peter.

"Oh, yes—but we dodge," said Winks. "Can't dodge a cane very well, though. I say—do be careful he doesn't catch you."

"What are you looking for?" asked another brownie. "I'm Hoho; you can trust me."

"Well," said Chinky, "we came here to look for a lot of flying toys—and my new wand. It had wings, too."

"Flying toys!" said Winks. "And a flying wand. Well! Have we seen anything like that, boys?"

"Yes!" shouted Hoho at once. "Don't you remember? Yesterday evening we saw something very peculiar—we thought they were curious birds flying about in the air. They must have been your toys."

"What happened to them?" asked Peter.

"Well, old Grim was out in the garden smoking his evening pipe," said Hoho. "And he suddenly looked up and saw them, too. He was very excited, and called out some words we couldn't hear. . . ."

"And what we thought were the peculiar birds came right down to him," said Winks. "But they must have been your toys on the way to Toyland!

He caught sight of them and made them come to him!"

"Well, whatever can *he* do with them?" said Hoho. "We are never allowed any toys at all. I suppose he will sell them to his friend the Magician Sly-Boots."

"Oh dear," said Mollie. "Well, we must try and get them before he does. Will you show us where you think Mister Grim might have hidden our toys?"

"Yes, we'll show you!" shouted the brownies. "But do be careful you aren't caught!"

They took Chinky and the children to the big building, all walking on tiptoe and shushing each other.

Hoho led them inside. He pointed to a winding stair. "Go up there," he whispered. "You'll come to a little landing. On the left side is a door. That's the storeroom, where I expect Mister Grim has put the toys."

"Creep in—and see if you can find them," whispered Winks.

"Come on," said Chinky to the others. "It's now or never! If we find our things we'll take them and rush down and out into the garden, and be off in the Wishing-Chair before Mister Grim even knows we're here!"

"Sh!" said Mollie, and they all began to go up the stairs on tiptoe. "Shhhhhhh!"

XI

MISTER GRIM'S SCHOOL FOR
BAD BROWNIES

Up the stairs went the three, treading very quietly indeed, hoping that not one of the stairs would creak or crack.

The brownies crowded round the door at the bottom of the stairs, holding their breath and watching. Up and up and up—and there was the landing at last! Now for the door on the left.

They saw the door. They tiptoed to it and Peter turned the handle. Would it be locked? No, it wasn't!

They peeped inside. Yes, it was the storeroom, and stacks of books, pencils, rulers, ink-bottles, old desks, and all kinds of things were there.

"Can't see our toys," whispered Chinky. "Or my wand. Let's look in all the drawers and all the cupboards."

So they began opening the drawers and hunting in them, and pulling open the cupboard doors and peering in at the shelves. But they could find nothing more exciting than books and pens and rubbers.

And then Chinky gave a soft cry. "Look here," he said. "Here they are!"

The others ran quickly over to him. He had opened a big chest—and there, lying quietly in the top of it, their wings vanished, lay all the toys they had lost—yes, Rosebud was there, and

Peter's engine, and the top and the soldiers — everything.

But wait — no, not quite everything. "I can't see my wand anywhere," said Chinky, hunting desperately. "Oh, where is it?"

They hunted all through the chest, but there didn't seem to be any wand there. They looked in despair at one another. They simply *must* find Chinky's wand.

"I'm glad we've found the toys," whispered Chinky, "but it's dreadful that I can't find my wand. It's got a lot of magic in it, you know. I wouldn't want Mister Grim to use that."

Then the children heard a noise that froze them to the floor. Footsteps — footsteps coming slowly and heavily up the stairs. Not light, quick, brownie steps, but slow, ponderous ones. Would the footsteps come to the storeroom?

In panic the children and Chinky squeezed themselves into a cupboard, not having time to put away the toys they had pulled out of the chest. The door opened — and somebody walked in!

The children hardly dared to breathe and Chinky almost choked. Then a voice spoke.

"SOMEONE has been here. SOMEONE has tried to steal toys. And that SOMEONE is here still. Come out!"

The children didn't move. They were much too scared to do a thing. And then poor Chinky choked! He choked again, then coughed loudly.

Footsteps marched to the cupboard and the door was flung wide open.

There stood Mister Grim—exactly like his name! He was a big, burly brownie, with a tremendous beard falling to the floor. He had pointed ears and shaggy eyebrows that almost hid his eyes.

"HO!" he said in a booming voice. "So the SOMEONE is not one person, but three!"

Peter, Mollie and Chinky came out, poor Chinky still coughing. Mister Grim took them each firmly by the back of the neck and sat them down on the window-seat.

"And now will you kindly tell me why you came to steal my toys?" he said. "How did you know they were there, and who told you about them?"

"They're not your toys, sir," Peter said at last in rather a trembling voice. "They're ours. We let them grow wings yesterday by using Growing Ointment on them—and they flew away. We came to fetch them."

"A very likely story indeed," said Mister Grim scornfully. "And how did you come here?"

"Up the stairs," said Mollie.

Mister Grim frowned a fierce frown. "Don't be foolish, girl," he said. "I mean, how did you arrive here—by bus or train—and how did you get into the grounds?"

Chinky gave the others a sharp nudge. Mollie had just been going to say that they had come in their Wishing-Chair, but she shut her mouth again tightly. Of course she mustn't give that away! Why, Mister Grim would search the grounds and find it!

265

"Well?" said Mister Grim. "I am asking you a question—and when I ask questions I expect them to be answered."

Still no reply from any of the three. Mister Grim leaned forward. "Shall I tell you how you came? You must have friends here among the brownies —and they helped you to climb the wall, and told you to take the toys! Aha! Don't try to say you didn't do that."

They didn't say a word. Mister Grim got up and put the toys back in the chest. "You," he said to Chinky, "*you* are a pixie, and I don't usually take pixies into my school. But you are a very bad pixie, I can see, and I shall keep you here. And I shall keep these two as well. I'm not sure what they are—but even if they are real, proper children, which I very much doubt, they deserve to be punished by being my pupils here for a term."

"Oh, no!" said Mollie in horror. "What will our mother say? You can't do that."

"You will see," said Mister Grim. "Now go downstairs, find the brownie called Winks, and tell him you are to come into class when the bell rings. He will give you books and pencils and tell you where to sit."

The three of them had to go downstairs in a row, Mister Grim behind them. They were frightened! Unless they could manage somehow to get to their Wishing-Chair, they would simply *have* to stay at Mister Grim's school!

They found Winks and told him quickly what had happened. He was very sorry. "Bad luck!" he said. "Very bad luck. Come on—I'll get you your books and things. Sit by me in class and I'll try and help you all I can."

He took them into a big room and gave them books and pencils. Almost at once a bell rang loudly and all the brownies trooped in quickly. Not one of them spoke a word. They took their places quietly and waited.

"Why were you sent here, Winks?" whispered Chinky as they all waited for Mister Grim to appear.

"Because I used my grandmother's Blue Spell and turned all her pigs blue," whispered back Winks.

"And I was sent here because I put a spell into my father's shoe-tongues and they were rude to him all the way down our street and back," whispered Hoho.

"And I was sent because . . ." began another brownie, when slow and heavy footsteps were heard. In came Mister Grim and stood at his big desk.

"Sit!" he said, as if the brownies were all little dogs. They sat.

"We have three new pupils," said Mister Grim. "I regret to say that I caught them stealing— STEALING—from my storeroom. If I find out who helped them into this school and told them about the toys they came to steal, I shall take my stick to him. Brrrrrr!"

This was very frightening. Mollie didn't even dare to cry. She comforted herself by thinking of the Wishing-Chair hidden under the bush in the garden. They would run to it as soon as ever they could!

"Now we will have mental numbers," said Mister Grim, and a little groan ran round the class. "You, boy, what number is left when you take eighty-two and sixty-four from one hundred and three?"

He was pointing at poor Peter. Peter went red. What a silly question! You couldn't take eighty-two and sixty-four from one hundred and three.

"Say six hundred and fifty," whispered Winks. "He doesn't know the answer himself!"

"Six hundred and fifty," said Peter boldly. Everyone clapped as if he were right.

"Er—very good," said Mister Grim. Then he pointed to Mollie. "How many pips are there in seven pounds of raspberry jam?"

"Seven pounds of raspberry jam?" repeated Mollie, wondering if she had heard aright. "Er— well . . ."

"Say none at all, because your mother only makes raspberry jelly and strains the pips out," whispered Winks.

"Er—none at all," said Mollie.

"How do you make that out?" thundered Mister Grim in a very frightening voice.

"Because my mother makes raspberry jelly and strains all the pips out," said Mollie. Everyone clapped again.

"Silence!" said Mister Grim. "Now you, pixie—and see you are very, very careful in your answer. If I take fifty-two hairs from my beard, how many will there be left?"

Chinky stared desperately at the long beard that swept down to the floor. "Well," he began . . . and then Winks whispered to him.

"Say 'the rest'!" he hissed.

"Er—well, the rest of the hair will be left," he said.

Mister Grim suddenly pounded on the desk with his hand. "You, Winks!" he shouted. "I heard you whispering then—you told him the answer—and I believe you told the others the answers, too. Come here! I'll give you the stick. Aha, you think because all my canes were broken that I haven't got one—but I have! You just wait."

"Please, sir, I'm sorry," said Winks. "I just thought I'd help them as they were new. I was trying to be good, sir, and helpful, I really was. You're always telling us to be that, sir."

"No excuses," said Mister Grim, and he turned to a cupboard behind him. He unlocked it and took out a long, thin stick.

"Come up here, Winks," he said, and poor Winks went up. He got two strokes on his hands. Mollie was very upset, but Hoho whispered, "Don't worry—Winks always puts a little spell in his hands and he doesn't mind a bit if he's whacked. He doesn't feel it!"

Mollie felt comforted. Winks winked at her as he went back to his seat. Mister Grim went to take a book from a shelf—and as he turned his back Chinky clutched Peter by the elbow.

269

"Peter," he hissed, "do you see what his stick is? It's my WAND!"

Peter stared. Yes—the stick on the desk was Chinky's little wand. Oh, if only it had wings now and could fly to Chinky!

But it hadn't. Chinky never took his eyes off it as the class went on and on. "I must get it," he kept saying to himself. "I MUST get it! But how can I? Oh, for a really good idea!"

XII

CHINKY IS NAUGHTY

Morning school came to an end at last. Mister Grim rapped on his desk with his stick—Chinky's wand!

"Attention, all of you!" he said. "Dinner will be in ten minutes' time. Anyone who is late or who has dirty hands or untidy hair will go without."

Winks groaned. "It's awful," he said to Peter when Mister Grim had gone out. "There's never enough dinner for everyone, so Mister Grim just says, 'Here, you, your hair is untidy,' or 'Here, you, your nails aren't clean,' and about a dozen of us have to go without our dinner."

"What a dreadful school!" said Peter. "Why don't you run away?"

"How can we?" said Winks. "You've seen the

270

high wall round the grounds, and all the gates are locked. I wish I could get out of here; it's a horrid place, and I really would be good if I could escape."

"Would there be room for him in the Wishing-Chair, do you think?" whispered Mollie to Chinky. "He's so nice. I'd like to help him, Chinky."

"So would I," whispered back Chinky. "Well, we'll see."

Poor Chinky was one of those who had to go without his dinner. Mister Grim stood at the door of the dining-hall as each brownie walked in. Every so often he pounced on one and roared at him.

"Here, you, you haven't washed behind your ears! No dinner! Here, you, why aren't your nails scrubbed? No dinner!" And when Chinky tried to slip past him he hit him hard on the shoulder with his hand and roared: "Here, you, why haven't you brushed your hair? No dinner!"

"I did brush it," said Chinky indignantly, "but it's the kind of hair that won't lie down."

"No dinner to-day for untidy hair, and no dinner to-morrow for answering back," said Mister Grim.

"Oh, I say, that's not fair," said Chinky.

"And no dinner for the third day for being rude," said Mister Grim. "Another word from you and I'll cane you with this new stick of mine!"

He slapped the wand down so hard on a nearby table that Chinky was afraid it would break in half. But fortunately it didn't.

Chinky went out of the room, looking angry

and sulky. Horrid Mister Grim! He joined all the brownies who were also to go without their dinner.

Peter and Mollie were very sorry for Chinky. When the pudding came they tried to stuff two tarts into their pockets to take to him. But the pastry fell to pieces and their pockets were all jammy and horrid. Mister Grim saw the crumbs of pastry around their pockets as they marched past him after dinner. He tapped them with the wand.

"Aha! Trying to stuff food into your pockets. Greedy children! No dinner for you to-morrow!"

Peter tried to snatch the wand away from Mister Grim, hoping to run and give it to Chinky,

but Mister Grim was too quick for him. Up in the air it went, and poor Peter got a stinging slash on his arm. Fortunately his sleeve was nice and thick, so he didn't feel it much.

"Bad boy!" roared Mister Grim. "Stay in after school this afternoon and write out one thousand times 'I must not snatch'."

There was a little time before afternoon school. Peter, Chinky, Mollie and Winks had a meeting in a far corner of the grounds.

"Winks, that's my wand Mister Grim has got and is using for a stick," said Chinky.

Winks whistled. "I *say*! That's a fine bit of news. We ought to be able to do something about that."

"But what?" asked Chinky. "I'm so afraid he will break my wand, and then it will be no use. Somehow or other we've got to get it back."

"Now listen," said Winks. "A wand will never hit its owner, you know that. Well, what about being very naughty in class this afternoon and having to go up to Mister Grim to be punished — and your wand will refuse to cane you, of course — and surely you can easily get it back then, and do a bit of magic to get yourselves free?"

"Oooh, yes," said Chinky, looking very cheerful. "That's an awfully good idea of yours, Winks. I'd forgotten that a wand never turns against its owner. I'll be very naughty — and then we'll see what happens."

They all went in to afternoon school feeling rather excited. What would happen? It would certainly be fun to see Chinky being very naughty, to begin with—and even greater fun to see the wand refusing to punish him!

Chinky began by yawning very loudly indeed. Mister Grim heard him and tapped hard on his desk with the wand—crack! crack!

"Chinky? You are most impolite. Stand up during the rest of the class instead of sitting."

Chinky stood—but he stood with his back to Mister Grim.

Mister Grim glared. "Bad pixie! You are being impolite again. Stand round the other way!"

Chinky immediately stood on his hands and waved his feet in the air. All the brownies laughed and clapped.

Mister Grim looked as black as thunder. "Come here!" he cried, and Chinky began to walk towards him on his hands. He really looked very funny indeed. Winks laughed till the tears rolled down his cheeks.

But Mister Grim didn't try to cane him that time. He told him to go and stand in the corner—the right way up.

So Chinky stood in the corner the right way up, turning every now and then to grin at the others. Mister Grim began firing questions at the class. "Hands up those who know why brownies have long beards. Hands up those who know the magic word for 'disappear.' Hands up those who know why green smoke always comes out of chimneys of witches' houses. Hands up . . ."

He didn't even wait for anyone to answer, so the

brownies just shot up their hands at each question and then put them down again and waited for the next. Peter and Mollie thought it was the silliest class they had ever attended!

"And now—can anyone ask me a question *I* can't answer?" said Mister Grim. "Aha! It would take a clever brownie to do that! Be careful— because if I *can* answer it, you'll have to come up and be punished. Now, who will ask me a question I can't answer?"

The brownies had all been caught by this trick before, so nobody put up his hand.

Mister Grim pounced on poor Winks. "You, brownie! Can't you think of a question?"

"Yes, sir," said Winks at once. "I'd like to know why gooseberries wear whiskers. Do they belong to the brownie family?"

Everybody roared at this ridiculous question. Except Mister Grim. He looked as grim as his name. He rapped with his stick on the desk.

"Come up here, Winks. I will not have you upsetting the class like this with your silly remarks." And Winks went up, grinning. He got three strokes of the wand, but it didn't hurt him, of course, as he had still got the spell in his hands that prevented the stick from hurting him.

"I've got a question; I've got a question!" suddenly called out Chinky, seeing a chance to get his wand.

"What is it?" said Mister Grim, frowning.

"Mister Grim, why do horses wear hooves instead of feet?" cried Chinky.

"Come up here," said Mister Grim sternly. "That's another silly question."

Chinky went. "Hold out your hand," said Mister Grim. Chinky held it out. Mister Grim brought down the wand as hard as he could—but, dear me, he missed Chinky's hand altogether. The wand simply slipped to one side and didn't touch Chinky's hand at all.

Mister Grim tried again—and again—and again—but each time the wand slid away from Chinky's outstretched hand and hit the desk instead. It was very puzzling indeed for Mister Grim.

The brownies were all laughing. So were Peter and Mollie. Mister Grim's face was so comical to watch as he tried to hit Chinky's hand and couldn't.

"I shall break this stick in two!" he cried suddenly in a rage.

That gave Chinky a shock. "No," he shouted. "No, you mustn't do that! You mustn't!"

"Why not?" said Mister Grim, and he put both hands on the wand as if to break it.

Peter, Mollie and Chinky watched in despair, waiting for the crack.

But the wand wasn't going to let itself be broken! It slid out of Mister Grim's big hands and shot over to Chinky, who caught it as it came.

"Ha!" shouted Chinky in delight. "I've got it again—my lovely wand—I've got it!"

"What! Is it a wand?" cried Mister Grim in astonishment. "I didn't know that. Give it back to me!"

He snatched at it, but Chinky was skipping down the room, waving it.

"I'll give you all a half-holiday! Yes, I will! See my wand waving to give you all a half-holiday! Go into the garden and play, all of you!"

The brownies didn't wait. They rushed out of the room at top speed, shouting and laughing. Soon only Peter, Mollie and Chinky were left with Mister Grim. Winks was peeping round the door.

"How DARE you treat me like this!" shouted Mister Grim, marching towards Chinky. "I'll——"

"Go back, go back!" chanted Chinky, and waved his wand at Mister Grim, whose feet at once took him six steps backwards, much to his surprise. "You see, I've got magic in my wand," cried the pixie. "Aha! I may have powerful magic, Mister Grim, so be careful!"

"Come on, Chinky," whispered Peter. "Let's go and find the Wishing-Chair and fly off."

"But I want my doll Rosebud before we go," said Mollie. "And have you forgotten your engine and all the other toys, Peter? We must take those with us. Mister Grim, give us our toys!"

"Certainly not," said Mister Grim, and he shook a large key at them. "See this key? It's the key of the storeroom, which I've locked. You can't get your toys and you never shall!"

"We'll see about that," said Chinky. "We'll just see about that, Mister Grim!"

XIII

HOME, WISHING-CHAIR, HOME!

Mister Grim stared angrily at Chinky, who was still waving his wand to keep the teacher from coming any nearer to him.

"You can't get your toys, so make up your mind about that," he said. "And stop waving that ridiculous wand. Its magic will soon run out."

Chinky himself was a bit afraid that it would. It was a very new wand and hadn't very powerful magic in it yet. "I think we'd better go before the wand's magic wears out," he said in a low voice to Peter and Mollie.

They darted out of the door and Mister Grim followed. But just outside the door he ran into a crowd of brownies that popped up from nowhere quite suddenly, and over he went! When he got up the children and Chinky were nowhere to be seen.

He began to run down the garden again, but once more he tripped over a mass of brownies. They weren't a bit afraid of him now because Chinky had taken his stick—the wand!

Chinky and the others raced to find the Wishing-Chair. Where was the bush they had hidden it in? Ah, there it was! They ran to the bush—but, oh dear, the chair wasn't there!

"One of the brownies must have found it and taken it," said Chinky. Just then Winks ran up and pulled at his arm.

"I found your Wishing-Chair and hid it in the shed," he said. "I was afraid Mister Grim might see it if he walked round the garden. Come along — I'll show you where it is."

He took the three to an old broken-down shed. The roof had fallen in at one end. There were no windows to the shed, so it was very dark inside. Chinky groped his way in — and immediately fell over the Wishing-Chair. He felt the legs anxiously to see if the chair still had its wings. Yes — thank goodness — it had!

The wings waved gently as they felt Chinky's anxious hands. The chair creaked softly. Chinky knew it was glad to have him again.

"Wishing-Chair, we must go quickly," said Chinky, and he climbed on to the seat. "Come on, Peter and Mollie — quickly, before Mister Grim comes!"

"What about Winks? Aren't we going to take him, too?" said Mollie.

"Oh — would you really?" said Winks, in delight. "You really are very kind. I hate this school. I've been trying to escape for ages."

He was just about to squeeze in the chair with the others when somebody appeared at the doorway. It was Mister Grim!

"So here you are!" he said, peering in. "All complete with a Wishing-Chair, too! I might have guessed that that was how you came. Well, I'm going to lock this door, so you won't be able to fly out — and there are no windows at all!"

Winks leapt off the chair and ran to him. He

tried to take the key from Mister Grim's hand, and the two struggled at the door.

"Fly out where the roof has fallen in, fly out there!" suddenly shouted Winks. "The chair can just squeeze through it!"

And the chair rose up into the air and flew to where the roof had fallen in! It got stuck half-way through, but Peter broke away a bit more roof and the chair suddenly shot through and out into the open air.

"Oh, poor Winks—we've left him there," cried Mollie, almost in tears. "We can't leave him!"

"Go on, Chair, fly off with them!" shouted Winks from below in the shed. "Don't mind me! Escape while you can."

The chair flew out of hearing. Chinky and Peter were very silent. Mollie wiped her eyes with her hanky. "I think you two should have taken the chair down and tried to help Winks," she said. "It was wrong of you to leave him."

"We'll go back for him," said Chinky, taking Mollie's hand. "But, dear Mollie, you see we had *you* to think of, and both Peter and I know we have to look after you, because you're a girl. We had to think of you—didn't we, Peter?"

"Of course," said Peter. "You're my sister, Mollie, and you know that brothers must always look after their sisters. I couldn't possibly risk taking you down into danger again just then, when I knew Mister Grim was so angry. We'll go back for Winks, don't worry."

"And what about our toys, too?" said Mollie,

with a sniff. "I think it's very nice of you both to want to take care of me like this—but I do feel so sorry for Winks, and it's dreadful to have to leave Rosebud behind, too."

"And my engine," said Peter, gloomily, "and the skittles and soldiers."

"We'll get them all back," said Chinky, comfortingly. "You wait and see."

The chair took them back to the playroom, flapping its wings strongly. They really were beautiful big wings. Mollie was glad they were, because now that she and Peter had grown heavier she felt that the chair really did need to be stronger.

They arrived at the playroom and flew in at the door. The chair gave a creaking sort of sigh and set itself down in its place. Its wings at once vanished.

"There! Its wings have gone already," said Mollie, ready to cry again. "So now we can't go and rescue Winks to-day."

"Well—that's a pity," said Chinky. "We shall just have to wait till its wings grow again. Anyway, it will give us time to make a plan for getting back our toys, too. That will be difficult, you know, because if the storeroom is locked and Mister Grim keeps the key on his key-ring, and carries it about with him, I don't see at present how we can rescue the toys."

Mother's voice was heard calling down the garden. "Children! It's past tea-time—and you didn't come in to dinner either. Where are you?"

"Oh, dear—now we shall have to go," said Mollie. "And we haven't planned anything. Chinky, come and tell us AT ONCE if the chair grows its wings again—and do, do try to think of a good plan."

"Come and see me again to-night if you can," called Chinky. "I may have a visitor here who will help us."

Mother called again, rather impatiently. The children fled. Fortunately, Mother seemed to think they had had a picnic lunch down in the playroom, and she didn't ask any difficult questions.

"I was sorry to send you out of the room this morning," she said. "Especially as I expect you were not really naughty, but just nervous, and so dropped the biscuits and the coffee. Never mind—I expect you were glad not to have to stay with my visitors!"

"We were rather," said Mollie, honestly, "and I expect *you* were glad we kept out of your way to-day, Mother, really."

"Now have your tea," said Mother.

The children wished that Chinky was with them. He had had to go without his dinner at Mister Grim's school, so he must be very hungry. Perhaps he would go out to tea with one of his pixie friends in the garden, and have a good meal.

"Now, Daddy and I are going out to-night," said Mother, when they had finished. "Put yourselves to bed at the right time, half an hour after your supper, and don't lie awake waiting for us, because we shall be very late."

282

"Right, Mother," said Peter, at once making up his mind to go down to the playroom after his supper, just before they went to bed. Chinky's visitor might be there, and it would be fun to see him. Chinky's visitors were always interesting, and sometimes very exciting.

Mother put on her lovely evening frock, and then she and Daddy said good-bye and went. The children did some jobs that Mother had asked them to do, and then found that it was supper-time. Jane brought them in bananas cut into small slices, scattered with sugar, and covered with creamy milk.

"Oooh!" said Mollie. "This is one of my favourite suppers."

After supper they slipped down to the playroom. Chinky wasn't there. There was a note left on the table, though.

"Gone to have supper with Tickles. Felt very hungry after having no dinner. Be back later. Can you come and meet my visitor at half-past nine if you're not asleep? VERY IMPORTANT.
            "Love from Chinky."

"I know, Peter," said Mollie, "let's go to bed now, then we can slip out for half an hour and meet Chinky's visitor without feeling guilty. We simply must meet him if it's important."

So they put themselves to bed half an hour earlier than usual.

Both children went to sleep—but Peter awoke

at half-past nine because he had set the alarm-clock for that time and put it under his pillow. When the alarm went off, muffled by the pillow, he awoke at once. He slipped on his dressing-gown and went to wake Mollie.

"Come on!" he whispered. "It's half-past nine. Buck up!"

Mollie put on her dressing-gown, too, and the two of them slipped out of the garden door and down to the playroom. They peeped in at the door. Yes—Chinky's visitor was there—but, dear me, what a very, very surprising one!

XIV

MISTER BLACKY'S STRANGE ARMY

Chinky saw the children peeping in. He got up from the sofa and called them. "Hallo! I'm so glad you've come. Come along in. I've got an old friend here, and I want you to meet him."

The old friend stood up—and what do you think he was? He was a tall golliwog, so old that his black hair had turned grey! He was not as tall as they were, but a bit taller than Chinky.

"This is Mister Blacky, the ruler of Golliwog Village," said Chinky. The golliwog bowed politely, and shook hands. Everyone sat down, the children and Chinky on the sofa and the golliwog in the Wishing-Chair.

"I hope you don't mind my sitting in your Wishing-Chair," he said, politely, to the children. "But it is really such a treat and a privilege. I have never even *seen* one before."

"Not at all. We're very pleased," said Peter. "I only wish it would grow its wings, then it could take you for a short ride. It feels funny at first but it's lovely when you get used to it."

"I've been telling Mister Blacky about your toys that Mister Grim has got, and won't give you back," said Chinky.

"I think Mister Grim should be forced to give them up to you," said Mister Blacky earnestly. "I propose that I raise a little army from Toyland and march on the school."

Peter and Mollie gazed at him in wonder and astonishment. It all sounded like a dream to them—but a very exciting and interesting dream. An army from Toyland! Good gracious—whoever heard of such a thing?

"Mister Blacky has very great influence in Toyland," explained Chinky. "As I told you, he is head of Golliwog Village and very much respected and admired. In fact, he has now ruled over it for nearly a hundred years."

"Are you really a hundred years old?" asked Mollie, amazed.

"One hundred and fifty-three, to be exact," said Mister Blacky, with a polite little bow. "I became head when I was fifty-four."

"Is it difficult to be head of Golliwog Village?" asked Peter.

"Well, no—not really, so long as you are very firm with the *young* golliwogs," said Mister Blacky. "They are rather wild, you know. Now, what I suggest is this. I will send to the wooden soldiers, the clockwork animals and the sailor dolls—and also my golliwogs, of course, and tell them to meet me at a certain place. They will make a very fine army."

"And you'll march on the school, I suppose?" said Chinky. "And when you have defeated Mister Grim you will rescue Rosebud, the doll, and the other toys?"

"Exactly," said Mister Blacky.

"Can we come, too?" said Peter, excited. "I'd simply love to see all this."

"If only the Wishing-Chair would grow its wings when your army is on the march, we could hover above the battle and watch," said Mollie. "But it never does grow its wings exactly when we want it to."

"I'll send you word when we mean to march," said the golliwog. "It will probably be to-morrow evening. Well, I must go now. Thank you for a very pleasant evening, Mister Chinky."

He shook hands with all three of them and went out of the door.

"Isn't he nice?" said Chinky. "He's a very old friend of my Great-Aunt Quick-Fingers, you know, and I've often met him at her house. I thought I'd tell him about Rosebud and the other toys, and how Mister Grim wouldn't give them back. I guessed he would help."

The playroom clock struck ten. "We must get back," said Mollie, with a sigh. "We only meant to come for half an hour. It's been lovely, Chinky. I do think we're lucky, having you for a friend, and meeting all *your* friends and having such an interesting time."

They went back to bed, hoping that the Wishing-Chair would grow its wings the next night if the golliwog gathered together his curious little army.

They couldn't go down to the playroom till after tea, because Mother took them to see their Granny. They raced down as soon as they could and were met by a very excited Chinky.

"I'm so glad you've come. The Wishing-Chair has grown little buds of wings already—they'll sprout properly in a minute! And the golliwog has sent to say that his army is on the march!"

"Oh—*what* a bit of luck!" cried the children, and ran to the chair. Just as they got to it the knob-like buds on its legs burst open—and out spread the lovely green and yellow wings again! They began to flap at once and made quite a wind.

"Come on," said Peter, sitting in the chair. "Let's go! And, Chinky, don't let's forget to take Winks away from that horrid school, if we can. He can live with you here in the playroom if he hasn't got a home to go to."

Mollie got in and Chinky sat on the back of the chair. Out of the door they flew at top speed.

The Wishing-Chair was told to go to Mister Grim's. "But *don't* go down into the grounds," commanded Chinky. "Just hover about somewhere so that we can see what's going on, and can dart down if we need to."

It wasn't really very long before the chair was hovering over the front gate of Mister Grim's school. Not far off were all the brownies, marching up and down in the big school yard, doing drill with Mister Grim.

Then the marching brownies suddenly caught sight of the Wishing-Chair hovering in the air, and they set up a great shout.

"Look! They've come back! Hurrah for Chinky and Peter and Mollie!"

Mister Grim stared up, too. He looked really furious, and, to the children's dismay, he bent down and picked up a big stone. It came whizzing through the air at them, but the Wishing-Chair did a little leap to one side and the stone passed harmlessly by.

Then Chinky gave the others a nudge. "Here comes the army! DO look!"

The children looked — and, dear me, up the lane marched the strangest little army the children had ever imagined. First came the grey-haired golliwog, swinging a little sword. Then came a row of wooden soldiers, beating drums. Then another row blowing trumpets. After them came a whole collection of clockwork animals.

"There's a jumping kangaroo!" cried Chinky in glee. "And a dancing bear!"

"And a running dog — and a walking elephant!" said Mollie in delight.

"And look—a pig that turns head-over-heels, and a duck that waddles!" shouted Peter, almost falling out of the chair in his excitement. "And behind them all are the sailor dolls. Don't they look smart!"

The strange army came to the gate. The clockwork kangaroo jumped right over it to the other side. He undid the gate and opened it for the army to walk through.

The brownies saw the toys before Mister Grim did and shouted in joy. They ran to meet them. "Who are you? Where have you come from?" they called. "Can we play with you? We never have any toys here!"

> "We've come for Mister Grim,
> We don't like Mister Grim,
> We've come to capture him,
> We've come for Mister Grim!"

chanted all the toys.

Mister Grim stared at them as if he couldn't believe his eyes. "After him!" shouted the golliwog, and after him they went! He turned to run—but the jumping kangaroo got between his legs and tripped him up, and there he was, bumping his nose on the ground, yelling for mercy!

The toys swarmed all over him in delight.

"Don't pull my hair! Don't cut off my beautiful beard," begged Mister Grim. The golliwog seemed just about to saw the long beard off with his sword! The children and Chinky saw it all from their seat up in the Wishing-Chair and were just as excited as the toys and the brownies.

"I'll leave you your beard on one condition," said the golliwog, solemnly. "Go and get the toys you have imprisoned here and bring them out to us."

Mister Grim got up, looking very frightened, and went indoors.

He came out with all the toys. Mollie gave a scream of delight when she saw Rosebud.

"He's even got the teapot that grew wings, too," said Peter, pleased. The chair flew down to Mister Grim, and the children took all their toys from him. Mollie cuddled Rosebud happily.

"Thank you," she said to the grey-haired golliwog. "You and your army have done very, very well. Do please bring any of them to see us whenever you can."

The brownies crowded round the chair. "Take us back with you, take us back."

"We've only room for one of you, and that's Winks," said Chinky, firmly. "Come on, Winks."

Up got Winks, grinning all over his little brownie face. The Wishing-Chair rose up in the air. "Good-bye, good-bye!" shouted Chinky and the others. "Let us know if Mister Grim behaves too badly to you and we'll send the army once again! Good-bye!"

Off they went, with all the toys and brownies waving madly. Mister Grim didn't wave. He looked very down in the mouth indeed—but nobody was sorry for him, not even Mollie!

XV

OFF TO THE LAND OF GOODIES!

The summer days went on and on. The Wishing-Chair seemed to have had enough of adventures for a time, and stayed quietly in its corner, without sprouting so much as one wing.

One day Chinky came tapping at the children's window. They came to it at once.

"Has the Wishing-Chair grown its wings again?" asked Peter, in excitement. Chinky shook his head.

"No. I haven't come to tell you that. I've just come to show you this."

He pushed a piece of paper into their hands. This is what it said:

"DEAR COUSIN CHINKY,

"You haven't been to see my new house yet, so do come. I expect you have heard that I have moved to the Land of Goodies. It's simply lovely. Do come and see me soon. I have a biscuit tree growing in my garden, just coming into fruit, and a jelly plant growing round my front door.

"Yours ever,
"PIPKIN."

"Well! Does your cousin *really* live there?" said Mollie, in wonder. "How lucky you are, Chinky. Now you can go and eat as many goodies as you like. I only wish we could come too."

"I came to ask if you'd like to go with me," said Chinky. "My cousin Pipkin won't mind. He's a very nice fellow, though I always thought he was a bit greedy. I expect that's why he bought a house in the Land of Goodies really—so that he could always have lots of things to eat. Why, if you pass a hedge you'll probably see that it's growing bars of chocolate."

This sounded so exciting that the children felt they wanted to go at once.

"We can't," said Chinky. "We'll have to wait for the Wishing-Chair to grow its wings again. The Land of Goodies is too far unless we go by Wishing-Chair."

"How disappointing!" said Mollie. "I feel awfully hungry even at the thought of going. What about Winks, Chinky? Is he coming, too?"

Winks had come back with them to the playroom, and had stayed a night with Chinky, and then gone to tell his people that he wasn't going back to Mister Grim's again. He meant to bring back some of his things with him, and spend some of the time with Chinky in the playroom and some with his other friends. He was very pleased indeed at being free.

"Winks can come if he's back in time," said Chinky. "I don't know where he is at the moment. He's really rather naughty, you know, although he's nice, and very good fun. I hear that he met my Cousin Sleep-Alone the other evening and, as soon as poor old Sleep-Alone was fast asleep in a little shed in the middle of a field, Winks took along two donkeys that had lost themselves and told them to cuddle up to Sleep-Alone."

"Oh, dear — what happened?" said Mollie.

"Well, Sleep-Alone woke up, of course, and tried to throw the donkeys out," said Chinky, "but one of them gave him such a kick with its hind legs that he flew into the clouds, got caught on a big one, and hung there for a long time."

"Well, it would certainly be a good place to sleep alone in," said Mollie. "What a monkey Winks is!"

"Yes. I'm not surprised really that his family sent him to Mister Grim's school," said Chinky. "Well, will you come with me to the Land of Goodies, then?"

"Of *course*," said the children. "You needn't ask us that again."

The next day was rainy. The children went down to the playroom as usual, but Mother made them take a big umbrella to walk under. "It really is such a downpour," she said.

They shook the raindrops off the umbrella as soon as they reached the playroom door. Chinky's voice came to them, raised in joy. "Is that you, Mollie and Peter? The Wishing-Chair has *just* grown its wings."

"Oh, good!" cried Mollie, and ran in. Sure enough the chair was already waving its green and yellow wings.

"But it's pouring with rain," said Peter, looking in at the door as he struggled to put down the big umbrella. "We shall get soaked if we go miles through this rain."

"We'll take the umbrella," said Mollie. "It will cover all three of us easily."

"*Four* of us," said Winks, and he popped out of the cupboard and grinned at them. "I've come back for a day or two. I hid in the cupboard in case it was your mother or somebody coming."

"Oh, Winks, I'm so glad you're coming, too," said Mollie. "Can we go now, this very minute, Chinky?"

"I don't see why not," said Chinky. "Don't put down that umbrella, Peter; we'll come now and you can hold it over us as we fly."

So very soon all four were sitting in the Wishing-Chair, flying through the rain. Peter held the big umbrella over them, and although their legs got a bit wet, the rest of them was quite dry.

"It's quite a long journey, so I hope the chair will fly fast," said Chinky. "It will be a bit dull because the rain clouds stop us from seeing anything."

The chair suddenly began to rise high. It went right through the purple-grey clouds, higher and higher and higher—and then at last it was through the very last of them, and the children found themselves far above the topmost clouds, full in the blazing sun!

"Well," said Peter, trying to shut the umbrella, "what a brainy idea of yours, Wishing-Chair. Now we shall soon be warm and dry again. Blow this umbrella! I simply *can't* shut it."

So it had to remain open; and, as it happened, it was a very good thing it did, because Winks tried to catch a swallow going past at sixty miles an hour, and overbalanced out of the chair! He clutched at the umbrella as he fell and down he went, with the umbrella acting just like a parachute!

"Very clever of you, Winks!" said Chinky, as the chair swooped down and hovered by the umbrella for Winks to climb on to the seat again. "I hope you only do this sort of thing when there's an open umbrella to catch hold of!"

Winks looked rather pale. He sat panting on the seat. "I got a fright," he said. "I really did."

"Well, don't be frightened if you do fall," said Mollie. "Do what Chinky did when he once fell! He changed himself into a large snow-flake and fell gently to earth! He hadn't even a bruise when he changed back to himself again."

"Very clever. I must remember that," said Winks. "I say, doesn't this Wishing-Chair fly fast?"

It certainly did. It flew even faster than the swallows, and passed over miles and miles of country, which lay spread out like a coloured map far below. The children caught glimpses of it through openings in the clouds.

"What's your cousin Pipkin like?" asked Mollie.

"Well, he was a bit plump," said Chinky. "And I expect he's plumper still now that he lives in the Land of Goodies. He's very generous and kind, though he's rather greedy, too. He could easily beat Mollie at eating ice-creams."

"Could he really?" said Mollie. "Oh, look, Chinky—we're going downwards. Are we there?"

They went down and down through layers of clouds. When they came below them they found that the rain had stopped. Chinky peered down.

"Yes—we're there. Now just remember this, all of you—you can eat whatever is growing on bushes, hedges, or trees, but you mustn't eat anybody's house."

Peter and Mollie stared at him in wonder. "*Eat* anybody's house! Are the houses made of eatable things, then?"

"Good gracious, yes," said Chinky. "Everything is eatable in the Land of Goodies—even the chimneys! They are usually made of marzipan."

The Wishing-Chair landed on the ground. The children jumped off quickly, anxious to see this wonderful land. They looked around.

Mollie's eyes grew wide. "Look—look, Peter—there's a bush growing currant buns. It is really. And look, there's a hedge with a funny-looking fruit—it's bars of chocolate!"

"And look at that house!" cried Peter. "It's all decorated with icing sugar—isn't it pretty? And it's got little silver balls here and there in its walls—and all down its front door too."

"Look at these funny flowers in the grass!" cried Mollie. "I do believe they are jam tarts! Chinky, can I pick one?"

"Pick a whole bunch if you like," said Chinky. "They're growing wild."

Mollie picked two. "One's got a yellow middle —it's lemon curd—and the other's got a red middle—it's raspberry jam," she said, tasting them.

"Better come and find my cousin Pipkin," said Chinky. "We're not supposed to come to the Land of Goodies except by invitation, so we'd better find him, so that he can say we are his guests. We don't want to be turned out before we've picked a nice bunch of jam tarts, currant buns and chocolate biscuits!"

Chinky asked a passer-by where his cousin Pipkin lived. Luckily, it was very near. They hurried along till they came to a kind of bungalow. It was round and its roof was quite flat.

"Why, it's built the shape of a cake!" cried Mollie. "And look, it's got cherries sticking out of the walls—and aren't those nuts on the roof— sticking up like they do in some cakes? Oh, Chinky, I believe your cousin lives in a cakehouse!"

"Well, he won't need to do much shopping then," said Chinky, with a grin. "He can just stay indoors and nibble at his walls!"

They went in at a gate that looked as if it were made of barley sugar. Chinky knocked at the door. It was opened by a very, very fat pixie indeed! He fell on Chinky in delight, almost knocked him over, and kissed him soundly on his cheek.

"Cousin Chinky! You've come to see me after

297

all!" he cried. "And who are these nice people with you?"

"Mollie and Peter and Winks," said Chinky.

"Glad to meet you," said Pipkin. "Now—how would you like to see my Biscuit Tree to begin with? And after that we'll go a nice hungry walk, and see what we can find!"

XVI

AN AFTERNOON WITH COUSIN PIPKIN

Pipkin took them to see his Biscuit Tree. This was really marvellous. It had buds that opened out into brown biscuits—chocolate ones! There they hung on the tree, looking most delicious.

"Pick as many as you like," said Pipkin, generously. "It goes on flowering for months."

"Aren't you lucky to have a Chocolate Biscuit Tree," said Mollie, picking two or three biscuits and eating them.

"Well—it's not so good when the sun is really hot," said Pipkin. "The chocolate melts then, you know. It was most annoying the other afternoon. It was very hot and I sat down under my Biscuit Tree for shade—and I fell asleep. The sun melted the chocolate on the biscuits and it all dripped over me, from top to bottom. I *was* a sight when I got up!"

Everyone laughed. They ate a lot of the biscuits and then Mollie remembered something else.

"You said in your letter to Chinky that you had a jelly plant," said Mollie. "Could we see that, too?"

Pipkin led the way round to his front door. Then the children saw something they had not noticed when they had first arrived. A climbing plant trailed over the door. It had curious big, flat flowers, shaped like white plates.

"The middle of the white flowers is full of coloured jelly!" cried Mollie. "Gracious — you want to walk about with spoons and forks hanging at your belt in this land!"

"Well, we do, usually," said Pipkin. "I'll get you a spoon each — then you can taste the jelly in my jelly plant."

It was really lovely jelly. "I should like to eat two or three," said Mollie, "but I do so want to leave room for something else. Can we go for a walk now, Pipkin?"

"Certainly," said Pipkin. So off they went, each carrying a spoon. It was a most exciting walk. They picked bunches of boiled sweets growing on a hedge like grapes, they came to a stream that ran ginger-beer instead of water and they actually found meat-pies growing on a bush.

The ginger-beer was lovely, but as they had no glasses they had to lie down and lap like dogs. "I should have remembered to bring one or two enamel mugs," said Pipkin. "We shall pass a lemonade stream soon."

"Is any ice-cream growing anywhere?" asked Mollie longingly.

"Oh, yes," said Pipkin. "But you'll have to go down into the cool valley for that. It's too hot here in the sun—the ice-cream melts as soon as it comes into flower."

"Where's the valley?" said Mollie. "Oh—down there. I'm going there, then."

Mollie found a sturdy-stemmed plant with flat green leaves, in the middle of which grew pink, brown or yellow buds, shaped like cornets.

"Ice-creams!" cried Mollie, and picked one. "Oooh! This is a vanilla one. I shall pick a pink flower next and that will be strawberry."

"I've got a chocolate ice," said Peter.

Pipkin and Chinky ate as many as the others. Chinky could quite well see why his cousin had grown so fat. Anyone would, in the Land of Goodies. He felt rather fat himself!

"Now let's go to the village," said Pipkin. "I'm sure you'd all like to see the food in the shops there, really delicious."

"Is there tomato soup?" asked Peter; it was his very favourite soup.

"I'll take you to the soup shop," said Pipkin, and he did. It was a most exciting shop. It had a row of taps in it, all marked with names—such as tomato, potato, chicken, onion, pea—and you chose which you wanted to turn, and out came soup—tomato, chicken, or whatever you wanted!

"There isn't the soup *I* like best," said Winks, sadly. "I like pepper soup."

"You don't!" said Chinky. "It would be terribly, terribly hot."

"Well, I like it—and there isn't any," said Winks.

"There's a tap over there without any name," said Pipkin. "It will produce whatever soup you want that isn't here."

He took a soup-plate and went to the tap without a name. "Pepper soup," he said, and a stream of hot soup came out, red in colour.

"There you are, *red* pepper soup," he said, and handed it to Winks. "Now we'll see if it really is your favourite soup or not!"

"'Course it is!" said Winks, and took a large spoonful. But, oh dear, oh dear, how he choked and how he spluttered! He had to be banged on the back, and had to be given a drink of cold water.

"It serves you right for saying what isn't true," Mollie said to Winks. "You didn't like pepper soup, so you shouldn't have asked for any."

"I was just being funny," said poor Winks.

"Well, *we* thought it was all very funny, especially when you took that spoonful," said Peter. "Now—can I get you a little mustard soup, Winks?"

But Winks had had enough of soups. "Let's leave this soup shop," he said. "What's in the next one?"

The next one was a baker's shop. There were iced cakes of all shapes and colours set in rows upon rows. How delicious they looked!

"Wouldn't you each like to take one home with you?" said Pipkin. "You don't have to pay for them, you know."

301

That was one of the nice things about the Land of Goodies. Nobody paid anyone anything. Mollie looked at the cakes. There was a blue one there, with yellow trimmings of icing sugar. Mollie had never seen a blue cake before.

"Can I have this one, do you think?" she said.

The baker looked at her. He was as plump as Pipkin and had a little wife as plump as himself. Their dark eyes looked like currants in their round little faces.

"Yes, you càn have that," said the baker. "What is your name, please?"

"Mollie," said Mollie. "Why do you want to know?"

"Well, it's to be *your* cake, isn't it?" said the baker. He dabbed the cake and suddenly in the very middle of the icing came the letters MOLLIE — Mollie! Now it really was Mollie's cake.

Peter had one with his name, and Pipkin had another. Chinky chose a pretty pink cake and his name came up in white icing sugar.

Winks' name came up spelt wrongly. The letters were WINXS, and Peter pointed out that that was not the right way to spell his name. Winks hadn't noticed. He was a very bad speller. But Peter noticed it, and Winks chose another cake on which his name appeared spelt rightly. It was all very queer indeed.

"Well, Pipkin, thank you very much for a most interesting and delicious afternoon," said Chinky, when they each had a cake to take home. "How I'm going to eat this cake I really don't know. Actually I don't feel as if I could ever eat *any*thing again."

They came to Pipkin's house and said good-bye to him. Then they went off to find their Wishing-Chair. Winks lagged behind, nibbling his cake. The others hurried on. They knew exactly where they had left the chair.

Suddenly they heard Chinky give a loud cry of anger. "Look! Winks is doing JUST what I said nobody was to do! He's breaking off bits of gate-posts to chew — and look, he's taken a bit of window-sill — it's made of gingerbread! And now he's throwing currant buns at that marzipan chimney to try to break it off!"

303

So he was! Poor Winks—he simply couldn't change from a bad brownie to a good one all at once. He was tired of being good and now he was being thoroughly naughty.

Crash! Down came the chimney, and Winks ran to it to break off bits of marzipan. And round the corner came two policemen! They had heard the crash and come to see what it was. When they saw Winks they blew their whistles loudly and ran up to him.

"Well—he's really got himself into trouble again now," said Chinky. "Isn't he silly?"

Winks was struggling hard with the two policemen. He called out to Chinky. "Save me, Chinky, save me! Mollie, Peter, come and help!"

"Oho!" said the bigger policeman of the two. "Are they your friends? We'll catch them, too! No doubt they are as bad as you."

"Quick! We must get in the Wishing-Chair and go!" said Chinky. "Winks will always get into trouble wherever he goes—but there's no need for us to as well. Where's the Wishing-Chair?"

They found it where they had left it, hidden well away under a bush. They climbed in, with Chinky at the back, just as the big policeman came pounding up.

"Hey! What's all this?" he called. "Is that chair yours?"

"YES!" shouted Chinky. "It is. Home, Chair, home. Good-bye, Winks. Say you're sorry for what you've done and maybe you'll be set free."

Off went the chair, high into the air, leaving the

big policeman gaping in surprise. He had never seen a Wishing-Chair before. They were soon out of sight.

That night, when the three of them were playing Snap in the playroom, the door opened cautiously — and who should come in but Winks! The others exclaimed in surprise.

"Winks! You didn't get put into prison, then?"

"Yes," said Winks. "But the walls were made of chocolate cake — so I just ate my way through and got out easily. But, oh dear — I feel as if I never want to taste chocolate cake again! What is for supper?"

"CHOCOLATE CAKE," roared everyone in delight, and Winks fled out into the night. No — he simply could not face chocolate cake again.

XVII

A MOST ALARMING TALE

For a week Chinky didn't see the children because they had gone to the seaside. They gave him all kinds of advice before they went.

"Now you see that you keep an eye on the Wishing-Chair for us, won't you?" said Peter. "And if it grows its wings, don't you go on adventures without us. And DON'T let Winks have the chair at all. I like Winks, and he's good fun, but he's dreadfully naughty. I shouldn't be a bit surprised if he isn't sent back to Mister Grim's school again some day."

"I know. I caught him practising magic with my wand last night," said Chinky. "He was trying to change the teapot into a rabbit. Silly thing to do."

"Yes, very," said Mollie. "You can't pour tea out of a rabbit. Now you be sure to keep an eye on Winks, Chinky."

"And don't sleep with the door or window open at night, in case the chair grows its wings when you're asleep and flies off by itself," said Peter.

"Oh dear — it's so hot now," said poor Chinky. "It's dreadful to have to sleep with the doors and windows shut. I've been tying the chair to my leg, so that if it does try to fly off, it will tug at my leg and wake me. Isn't that all right? I thought it was a very good idea."

"Yes, it is," said Peter. "Well, so long as you remember to tie your leg and the chair's leg together at night, you can sleep with the door and windows open."

"But watch that nobody slips in to steal the chair," said Mollie.

Chinky began to look very worried. "I'm beginning to feel you'd better not go away," he said. "Anyway, don't I always look after the chair at night for you? Nothing has ever happened to it yet!"

The others laughed. "We're being fussy, aren't we!" they said. "Good-bye, Chinky, dear. A week will soon go, so don't be too lonely. I expect Winks will be popping in and out to see you."

The children had a lovely week at the seaside and came back browner than ever. As soon as Mother would let them they rushed down to the playroom to see Chinky.

He wasn't there, so they looked for a note. There wasn't one. "Well, he's probably just gone out for a few minutes to see a friend," said Peter. "We'll hang up the seaweed we've brought, and tidy up the room."

So they spent a happy ten minutes nailing up the long fronds of seaweed they had brought back, and tidying up their playroom, which seemed to have got very untidy whilst they had been away.

"It's funny Chinky hasn't kept it tidier than this," said Mollie, pulling the rugs straight, and putting a chair upright.

Then she suddenly gave a cry. *"Peter!* Where's the Wishing-Chair? It isn't here!"

Peter looked round, startled. "Well! Fancy us not noticing that as soon as we came in! Where is it?"

"I suppose Chinky's gone off in it," said Mollie. "He might have left a note! I suppose he's at his mother's."

"He'll soon be back then," said Peter, going to the door and looking out. "He knew this was the day we were coming home."

But Chinky didn't come, and by the time tea-time came the children felt rather worried. Surely Chinky would have been back to tea on the day they came home? He always liked to spend every minute with them that he could, especially now that they had to go to boarding-school and leave him for months at a time.

They had brought their tea down to the playroom. They were sitting having it, rather solemnly, when a small mischievous face looked round the door. It was Winks.

"Hallo!" he said, but he didn't smile. He looked very grave and walked in quietly.

"Where's Chinky?" asked Mollie at once.

"And where's the Wishing-Chair?" said Peter.

"An awful thing happened two nights ago," said Winks. "I hardly like to tell you."

This was most alarming. The children stared at Winks in dismay. "For goodness' sake tell us," said Mollie.

"Well," said Winks, "I was staying here with Chinky that night. I was to sleep on that rug on the floor with a cushion, and Chinky was to sleep on the sofa as usual. When we were tired we got ready for bed."

"Go on," said Peter, impatiently. "I want to know what's happened to Chinky."

"I went to sleep," said Winks, "and I suppose Chinky did, too. I suddenly woke up to hear a terrible noise going on—Chinky shouting and yelling, and furniture being upset and goodness knows what. I put on the light, and what do you think had happened? Why, you know Chinky always ties a rope from the chair to his foot, don't you—well, the chair grew its wings that night and we didn't wake—so it tried to fly out of the door all by itself, and——"

"The rope pulled on Chinky's foot and woke him!" said Peter.

"Yes, the chair pulled him right off the sofa," said Winks. "He must have landed with an awful bump on the floor, and I suppose he thought someone had pulled him off and there was an enemy attacking him—so he was fighting the furniture and the rugs and shouting and yelling—and all the time the chair was tugging at his foot, trying to fly off!"

"Gracious!" said Mollie. "What happened in the end?"

"Well, when I put the light on I saw the chair struggling to get out of the door, and it was dragging Chinky along," said Winks. "I ran to stop the chair, but it rose into the air, dragged poor Chinky out into the garden, and flew up into the sky!"

"What about Chinky?" asked Mollie in a trembling voice.

"Oh, Mollie—poor, poor Chinky had to go, too, hanging upside-down by one foot," said Winks blinking away tears. "I couldn't do anything about it, though I did try to catch hold of Chinky. But he was too high up by that time."

"This is awful," said Mollie. "Whatever are we to do? Has the chair gone to his mother's, do you think?"

"No. I thought of that," said Winks. "I went next day to see, but Chinky's mother said she hadn't seen either Chinky *or* the chair. She's very worried."

"But *why* didn't the chair go to Chinky's mother?" wondered Peter. "Chinky would have been sure to yell out to it to go there."

"Well, I think the chair was frightened," said Winks. "It didn't know it had got Chinky by the foot, you see. It couldn't understand all the yelling and struggling. It just shot off into the night, terrified."

"This is awfully bad news," said Mollie. "Both Chinky *and* the chair gone. And we don't know where. How can we find out?"

"I don't know," said Winks, who looked very tired. "I've been all over the place, asking and asking."

"Poor Winks," said Mollie. "You do look very tired. I suppose you've been worried to death about Chinky."

"Yes, I have," said Winks. "You see, I've been teasing him rather a lot—and I hid his wand and made him cross—and I broke a cup—and now I feel awfully sorry I was such a nuisance to him."

"You're really not very good at times, Winks," said Peter, sternly. "You ought to be careful, in case you get sent back to Mister Grim."

"Yes, I know," said Winks.

"The awful part is, even when we do find out, if ever we do, we haven't got the Wishing-Chair to fly off in to rescue him," said Peter, gloomily.

"Shall we go and ask Mr. Spells if he can help us?" said Mollie, suddenly. "He's awfully clever. He might think of some way of finding out where Chinky's gone."

"Yes—that's a very good idea," said Peter. "You've heard about Mr. Spells, haven't you, Winks? Shall we go straight away now? I think I remember the way. We have to go to the Village of Pin first, and then take the bus, and then a boat."

"Yes," said Winks, cheering up. "I feel much better since I've talked to you."

They set off. Down the garden they went, and through the gap in the hedge. Into the field, and across to find the dark patch of grass. It was still there. They all sat down in it and Mollie felt about for the little knob that set the magic going.

She found it and pressed it. Down shot the ring of grass, much too fast, and they all tumbled off in a heap below. "Gracious!" said Winks. "You might have warned me what was going to happen. I nearly died of fright when the earth fell away beneath me!"

"Come on," said Peter. "We have to go down this passage now—past all these doors. We really *must* find Mr. Spells as soon as possible."

They went on down the twisting passage, which was still lighted clearly by some light nobody could see. Winks wanted to stop and read the names on each door.

" 'Dame Handy-Pandy'," he said. "Whoever is she? And this name says 'Mr. Piggle-Pie.' Oh, let's knock and see what he's like."

"Winks! Come along at once," said Mollie. "We're in a hurry!"

"Wait!" cried Winks. "Look at this door! Look

at the name. Hey, Mollie. Peter—it says 'MRS. SPELLS!' Do you think she's anything to do with *Mr.* Spells? Let's find out."

And he banged hard at the little green door. "RATTA-TATTA-TAT!" Oh, Winks—now what have you done?

XVIII

MR. SPELLS' MOTHER

RATTA-TATTA-TAT!

The echo of Winks' knocking at Mrs. Spells' door filled the underground passage and made the children jump. They turned round angrily.

"Winks! You shouldn't do that!"

"But I tell you, it says '*MRS.* Spells' on this name-plate," began Winks. Just then the door opened and a black cat stood politely there, with a little apron round its tubby waist.

"If you've brought the papers, please don't knock so loudly again," said the cat, politely but crossly. "We were in the middle of a spell, and you made my mistress upset half of it. Now we've made a spell to make things small instead of big. It's most annoying." He slammed the door, almost hitting Winks' nose. The children came running up, Peter calling out breathlessly:

"I say! I do believe that was old Cinders, Mr. Spells' cat! He had such enormous green eyes— like green traffic lights shining out!"

"Was it really?" said Mollie. "Well, let's ask him if he is. Why, Mr. Spells might be here himself! It would save us quite a long journey."

"Dare we knock again?" said Peter. "That cat was really very cross."

"I'm not afraid of a cross cat!" said Winks boldly, and he lifted the knocker and knocked again. He also found a bell and rang that, too.

"RATTA-TATTA-TAT! JINGLE-JANGLE-JING!"

Mr. Piggle-Pie's door flew open and a cross voice called, "Who's making that row? Just wait till I get dressed and I'll come and chase you!"

"That must have been Mr. Piggle-Pie," said Winks. "Bother! He's shut his door again. Now I shan't know what he's like!"

Then Mrs. Spells' door flew open, and the cat appeared again. But this time it behaved much more like a real cat. It spat at Winks and scratched him on the hand.

It was just about to shut the door again when Peter called out, "I say, aren't you Cinders?"

The cat stared at him. "Yes, I'm Cinders. Oh, I remember you. You're the boy who came with a girl to rescue Chinky—and I helped my master do a spell to wake him up. What are you doing here, hammering at our door?"

"Well, we were really on our way to see Mr. Spells," said Peter. "But Winks here noticed the name 'Mrs. Spells' on the door, and he knocked. He thought she might be some relation to Mr. Spells."

"She is. She's his mother,". said Cinders. "I came here to help the old lady with a new spell — the one you spoilt by making her jump. My master is coming to call for me in a few minutes."

"Oh, *is* he?" cried Peter joyfully. "Then do you think we might stay and see him — we do so badly want his help."

"Well, come in, then," said the cat. "I don't know about this brownie though — Winks, do you call him? Banging and ringing like that. You wait till Mr. Piggle-Pie is dressed and comes after him. He'll get such a spanking."

"I don't want to stay out in the passage," said Winks, nervously. "I'll be very good and quiet and helpful if you'll let me come in."

"Who is it standing gossiping at the door?" suddenly called an annoyed voice. "Tell them either to go or to come in."

"You'd better come in and wait for Mr. Spells," said Cinders. So they all trooped in and Cinders shut the door. Winks was quite glad to be out of the passage, away from a possibly furious Mr. Piggle-Pie.

The cat led them into a remarkably big room, with three windows. The children were so astonished to see what the windows looked out on that they quite forgot their manners for the moment, and didn't greet the bent old lady who sat in a chair in the middle of the room.

One window looked out on the sea! Yes, the sea, as blue as could be! Another looked out on a sunny hillside. The third looked out on an ordinary backyard, where washing was blowing in the wind. Most extraordinary.

"Well!" said rather a peevish voice, "have the children of to-day no manners at all? Can't you even say how do you do to an old lady?"

"Oh, dear," said Mollie, ashamed of herself. "Please, Mrs. Spells, I'm so sorry—do forgive us —but it did seem so extraordinary seeing three windows like this—in an underground room—and one looking out on the sea, too. Why, I thought the sea was miles and miles away!"

"Things aren't always what they seem," said Mrs. Spells. "What is miles away for you, may be quite near for me. Now, what was all this noise about at my front door? When I was younger I would have turned you all into pattering mice and given you to Cinders, for making a noise of that sort in a respectable place like this!"

"Madam," said the cat, seeing that the old lady was working herself up into a temper, "Madam, these children know Mr. Spells, your son."

The old lady beamed at once. "Oh, do you know my son? Why didn't you tell me that at once? Cinders, some strawberryade, please, with strawberry ice, and some strawberry biscuits."

This sounded exciting—and when it came, beautifully arranged on a large silver tray by Cinders, it was just as exciting as it sounded!

It was a pink drink made of strawberry juice. In it were pieces of ice shaped like strawberries, and the biscuit had tiny sugar strawberries in the middle!

"This is lovely," said Peter. "Thank you very much."

There came the sound of a key in the door. "Ah—my son, Mr. Spells!" said Mrs. Spells. "Here he is!"

And there he was again, just the same as before, tall and commanding, but this time dressed in a long green cloak that shimmered like water. He looked very surprised indeed to see the visitors.

"Why—I've seen you before!" he said to the children. "How are you? Quite well, I hope. And let me see—have I seen this brownie before? Yes—I have. Aren't you the bad fellow who turned all his grandmother's pigs blue? Isn't your name Winks?"

"Yes, Mr. Spells, sir," said Winks.

"I hope you got spanked for that," said Mr. Spells. "I had a terrible job turning the pigs back to their right colour again. I believe they've still got blue tails."

Winks wished the floor would open and swallow him up, but it didn't. Mr. Spells turned to Peter.

"Well, have you come visiting my dear old mother?" he said.

Peter explained how it was they were in his mother's room. Then he told the enchanter about poor Chinky and the chair.

"Good gracious!" said Mr. Spells. "We must certainly find out where that chair has gone. If it falls into the hands of some rogue he can use it for all kinds of wrong purposes. And Chinky, too —what a silly thing to do, to tie his foot to the chair! Why didn't he tie the chair to the door-handle, or something like that?"

"We didn't think of that," said Peter. "Can you help us to find out where the chair is, and Chinky, too, Mr. Spells?"

"Of course," said Mr. Spells. "Now, let me think for a moment. This happened at night, you say—and the chair, as usual, flew up into the sky?"

"Yes," said everyone.

"Well, then—who was about that night in the sky, who might possibly have seen the chair and Chinky?" said Mr. Spells thoughtfully.

"Hoot, the owl," said the old lady at once.

"Quite right, Mother," said Mr. Spells. "Splendid idea. We'll call Hoot, the owl, and see if he knows anything about this. He's a very wise and observant bird, you know," he said, turning to the children. "Never misses anything that goes on at night."

"Shall we go and ask him if he knows anything, then?" said Mollie. "Where does he live?"

"Oh, we'll get him here," said Mr. Spells. "That's the easiest way. I'll go and call him."

He went to the window that looked out on the sunny hillside. He clapped his hands three times and muttered a word so magic that Winks trembled in his shoes. And a very curious thing happened. The sunny hillside went dark—as dark as night—and behind the trees shone a little moon! It was all very peculiar, especially as the sun still shone out in the backyard and on the sea that could be seen from the other windows!

"I must make it dark, or the owl won't come," explained Mr. Spells. "Now I'll call him."

He put his hands up to his mouth, placed his thumbs carefully together, and blew gently—and to the children's delight and surprise, the hoot of an owl came from his closed hands. "Ooo-ooo-oooo-oooh! Ooo-ooo-ooh!"

An answering hoot came from outside the window. A dark shadow passed across the room. Then a big owl flew silently down and perched on Mr. Spells' shoulder. He caressed the big-eyed creature, whilst Cinders looked on rather jealously.

"Hoot," said Mr. Spells. "Listen carefully. Two nights ago a Wishing-Chair flew off into the sky, and hanging to it by a rope tied to his foot was a pixie called Chinky. Did you see anything of this?"

"Ooooooo-ooo-ooo! Oooooo-oo! Ooooh! Ooo-oo-oo-oo-oo-oo-oo-oo-ooooooooooh!" answered the owl, hooting softly into Mr. Spells' ear.

"Thank you, Hoot," said Mr. Spells, looking grave. "You may go."

The owl flew off silently. Mr. Spells waited a moment and then muttered another magic word. The moonlit hillside grew lighter and lighter—and, hey presto, it was the sun behind the trees now and not the moon—daylight was everywhere!

"What did the owl tell you?" asked Peter.

"Oh—I forgot you couldn't understand," said Mr. Spells. "Well, he saw the chair—and Chinky, too, dangling by his foot. He followed them out of curiosity—and he says they flew near the

318

Wandering Castle, where Giant Twisty lives, and the giant must have seen them and captured them. He saw no more of them after that."

This was very bad news indeed. "Oh, dear— whatever are we going to do, then?" said Peter at last. "Poor little Chinky!"

"I must help you;" said Mr. Spells. "I can't let Twisty own that chair. Sit down. We must think of a plan!"

XIX

AWAY ON ANOTHER ADVENTURE

"We can't do anything this evening," said Mr. Spells. "That's quite certain. Anyway, the first thing to do is to find out where the Wandering Castle is."

"Don't you know?" said Mollie, in surprise, as she thought Mr. Spells knew everything.

"I know where it was last year, and the year before, and even last month," said Mr. Spells, "but I don't know where it is now. It may have wandered anywhere."

"Oh—does it move about?" asked Peter in amazement.

"Good gracious, yes! It's always wandering," said the enchanter. "One day it may be here, the next it's somewhere else. Giant Twisty finds that very useful because he's always getting into trouble because of his bad ways, and it's very convenient to have a castle that can slip away in the night."

"It's going to be very difficult to find, isn't it?" said Mollie. "I mean, even if we find out where it is now, it may not be there when we get there."

"True. But there's a chance it may rest in the same place for some weeks," said Mr. Spells. "*Winks*, what are you doing?"

Winks jumped. "Just—just stirring this stuff in the pot," he said.

"Look at your hands!" thundered Mr. Spells. "You've been dipping them in—and now see what you've done! Meddlesome little brownie!"

Winks looked at his hands. Oh, dear, they were bright blue! He stared at them in horror.

"Now you know what your grandmother's pigs must have felt like when you turned them blue," said the enchanter. "Well, keep your blue hands. Every time you look at them you can say to yourself, 'I must not meddle. I must not meddle.'"

Winks put his hands into his pockets, looking very doleful.

"Well, children," said Mr. Spells, "I think you'd better leave things to me to-night. I'll do my best to find out where the Wandering Castle happens to be at the moment and we will make a good plan to get back the chair and Chinky. Can you come along early to-morrow morning?"

"Yes. We'll ask Mother to let us go out for the day," said Peter. "Come on, Mollie. Thank you, Mr. Spells, for your help. Good-bye, Mrs. Spells. Good-bye, Cinders."

"You can go out of this door if you like," said the enchanter, and the children suddenly saw a small silver door gleaming in the wall near the window that looked out on the hillside. They were sure it hadn't been there before. Cinders opened it for them.

He bowed politely to the children, but dug a claw into Winks, who yelled and shot outside in a hurry. Winks shook a bright blue fist at the cat.

"Where are we?" said Peter, as they walked down the hillside, now filling with shadows as the sun sank low. "Goodness—why, there's our garden!"

So it was, just nearby. How very extraordinary. "If only people knew how near their gardens are to curious and wonderful places, how surprised they would be!" said Mollie, walking in at their side-gate, and going to the playroom. "Well, we can take that short cut to-morrow. I do wonder how it is that the sea is outside that other window. I just simply can't understand that!"

They said good-bye to Winks, who had tried in vain to wash the blue off his hands under the garden-tap. Then off they went to ask their mother if they could have the whole day to themselves to-morrow. She said, Yes, of course they could! It would do them good to go into the country in the lovely summer weather they were having now.

"Well, I don't know what Mother would say if she knew we were going to hunt for Giant Twisty in his Wandering Castle!" said Peter. "I suppose she just wouldn't believe it."

The next day the children had breakfast very early indeed, and then set off down the garden to collect Winks. His hands were still as blue as ever, so he had put on a pair of gloves.

"Oh—you've borrowed them from my biggest doll, Winks," said Mollie. "You might have asked permission first. I should have said, 'No, certainly you can't have them.'"

"Yes. I felt sure you wouldn't let me," said Winks. "That's why I didn't ask you. I'll take great care of them, Mollie, I really will. Your doll doesn't mind a bit."

They went out of the garden gate and looked round. Where was that short cut now? They couldn't find it at all! But Winks spotted it.

"I've better eyes for strange things than you have," he said. "I can see a little shining path in the grass that you can't see. Follow me."

"Well, you must be right," said Peter, as Winks led them straight over the grass to the same trees on the same sunny hillside as they had seen the day before. "And there's the little silver door!"

Cinders opened it as they came near. Winks shot in so quickly that he hadn't time to scratch the brownie, though he did try!

Mr. Spells was there, surrounded by papers and old books of all kinds. "My mother is still asleep in bed," he said. "I'm glad you're early. We can start off straight away."

"Oh—have you found out where the Wandering Castle is?" asked Mollie, in delight. "Did your magic books tell you?"

"They helped," said Mr. Spells. "And Cinders and I did a little Find-Out Spell we know. Wandering Castle is now on the island belonging to Giant Small-One, Twisty's brother."

"Giant Small-One—that's a funny name," said Mollie.

"Not really," said Mr. Spells. "He's small for a giant, that's all. Well, we'd better start."

"But how can we get to an island?" said Peter. "We haven't a Wishing-Chair to fly over the sea!"

"That doesn't matter," said Mr. Spells. "Cinders has been getting my ship ready."

He pointed to the window that so surprisingly looked out on the sea. The children stared in wonder and delight. A most beautiful ship rocked gently on the calm blue sea, a picture of loveliness with its big, white sails. Mollie cried out in joy. "Oh—what a beauty! And it's called *The Mollie*!"

"Just a little compliment to you," said Mr. Spells, smiling. "Also it's supposed to be lucky to sail in a ship bearing one of the passengers' names. Well—shall we set off? The wind is just right."

Cinders opened the window. Just outside was a stone ledge, with steps leading down to a tiny jetty. Cinders went first and helped Mollie down.

They all stepped aboard the beautiful white-sailed ship. Mr. Spells took the tiller.

"Blow, wind, blow.
And on we will go
Over the waters blue,"

323

he sang, and the white ship leapt forward like a bird.

"Is that a spell you sang?" said Mollie.

"Oh, no—just a little song," said Mr. Spells. And he began to sing again, whilst the ship sailed lightly over the blue waters. The children and Winks enjoyed it very much. Mollie trailed her hand in the water.

"Did we bring any food?" asked Mollie, suddenly. "I'm hungry!"

"No," said Mr. Spells, and everyone at once looked rather gloomy. "Enchanters don't need to," he went on. "I always carry a spell in my pocket that I use when I need any food."

Soon they were all eating and drinking, as the ship sped on and on.

For two hours the ship sailed on—then Cinders gave a shout. "Land ahoy! It's the island, Mr. Spells, sir."

"Aha!" said the enchanter. "Now we must be a bit careful." They all looked hard at the island that was rapidly coming nearer as the ship sped over the water. It didn't look very big. It was crowded with tall buildings, some of them looking like palaces, some like castles.

"Which is the Wandering Castle, I wonder?" said Mollie.

"Can't possibly tell," said Mr. Spells. "Now here we go towards this little jetty. We'll land there. You'll have to watch out a bit, because several giants live here and you don't want to be trodden on like ants."

Mollie didn't like the sound of this much. She was determined to keep very close to Mr. Spells. Cinders was left with the ship, much to Winks' relief. They all set off up an extremely wide street.

"We shall be all right if we keep to the narrow pavements that run beside the walls of the building," said Mr. Spells, guiding them to one. "There are plenty of small folk living here, as well as giants."

So there were — pixies and brownies and goblins and elves — but there were also giants, and Mollie suddenly saw a most enormous foot, followed by another one, walking down the street! She shrank close to Mr. Spells.

When the giant came by the children tried to see up to the top of him, but he was too tall. "That's a large-sized giant," said Mr. Spells. "I know him — nice fellow called Too-Big. Here's a smaller one."

It was exciting and extraordinary to see giants walking about. Mr. Spells guided them to a palace not quite so tall as some of the buildings.

"This is where Giant Small-One lives — the giant the island belongs to," he said. "Come along — we will ask him whereabouts his brother's Wandering Castle is. Don't be afraid. I am much more powerful than he is and he knows it."

They went up a long, long flight of steps. At the top was a big open door, leading into a vast hall. At the end of the hall sat a giant — but he was such a small one that he wasn't more than twice the size of the enchanter himself!

"Advance, Mr. Spells, and pay your respects to Giant Small-One," boomed an enormous voice from somewhere.

And Mr. Spells boldly went forward. Now to find out what they all wanted to know!

XX

WANDERING CASTLE AT LAST

Mr. Spells made a small bow. "Greetings, Giant Small-One," he said. "I see you have not yet found a spell to make you Tall-One instead of Small-One. I come to ask you a question. We want to find your brother, Giant Twisty. Is Wandering Castle on your island?"

"I believe so," said the voice of Giant Small-One, rather a feeble voice for a giant. "Go to High Hill and you will see it there. Why does Mr. Spells, grand enchanter, want my brother?"

"That is my own business," said Mr. Spells. The children thought he was very bold indeed to speak to a giant like that.

"Pray stay to a meal," said Small-One, and he clapped his big hands, making a noise like guns cracking. "I have few guests as important as you."

"Thank you, no," said Mr. Spells. "Our business is urgent. We will go."

He walked back to the children and Winks, and they made their way to the door. But it was shut! They couldn't open such a big door themselves, so they had to go all the way back to Small-One and ask for a servant to open the door.

It took a long time to find a servant, which was strange, considering how many there had been in the hall a few minutes before. "He is delaying us," said Mr. Spells angrily. "He wants to get a message to his brother, before we reach him, to warn him that we are on his track!"

At last a servant was found, the door was opened and they all trooped down the endless steps. They made their way down the street, came into a wide lane, lined with hedges as high as trees, and then found a sign-post that said "To High Hill."

"There's High Hill," said Peter, pointing across the fields to a very tall hill. "There are quite a lot of buildings on it. I wonder which is Wandering Castle?"

They came to High Hill at last and toiled up it. They met a small pixie running down, and Mr. Spells hailed her.

"Hey, little pixie! Where's Wandering Castle?"

"Let me see, now—I saw it yesterday," said the little pixie. "Yes, I remember now. It's in the Silver Buttercup Field, sir."

"*Silver* Buttercups!" said Mollie, astonished. "I've never heard of those. I don't think I should like them. The golden ones are just right."

"I agree with you," said Mr. Spells, guiding them round a big house. "But some enchanters are very silly—always trying out novelties, you know. Well, here we are—here is Silver Buttercup Field."

So it was. Silvery buttercups nodded in a great shimmering carpet. "Beautiful, but washed-out looking," said Mr. Spells. "The thing is—where's Wandering Castle? It's certainly not here! It's wandered away again. Small-One got a message to his brother in time—whilst we were trying to get that door open. Well, where has it wandered to now?"

"Please, sir, I know!" said a small goblin, running up. "It's gone to Loneliness! I don't know if you know that country, sir. It's over the sea to the east—a very, very lonely place, where nobody ever goes if they can help it. It is going to hide itself there till you've given up looking for Twisty and his castle."

"How do you know all this?" demanded Mr. Spells.

"Because I was lying resting in these buttercups when a servant from Giant Small-One came running up to warn Twisty that you were after him," said the goblin. "And I heard Twisty say where he was going."

"Right. Thank you very much," said Mr. Spells. "Come along, children—back to the ship. We must sail off to Loneliness at once. Twisty could easily hide himself in that strange, desolate land without anyone finding him for years."

"Oh, dear—we really must find him, because of Chinky," said Mollie. They went back to the ship. Cinders was so pleased to see them back so soon that he quite forgot to try and scratch Winks as he got on board.

They set off again, the wind filling the sails and making the ship fly like a bird. She rocked up and down lightly as she went, and the children began to feel very sleepy.

They fell asleep. Mr. Spells awoke them after a time. "Mollie! Peter! We're here. Wake up, both of you."

They sat up in the ship. It was moored to a small pier. Mollie looked out on the land of Loneliness. It was a gloomy, desolate place, with enormous trees growing in thick masses. "There are forests and forests of those," said Mr. Spells, looking as gloomy as Loneliness looked. "How we shall ever know where the Wandering Castle is, I can't imagine!"

They landed, and walked towards the nearest forest of trees. Just as they got there they heard a voice shouting furiously.

"No peace anywhere! None at all! I come here, where nobody ever goes—and what comes walking almost on top of me but a castle! A CASTLE! Just when I thought I was going to sleep alone in peace!"

And out of the trees burst Chinky's cousin, Sleep-Alone! He was just as surprised to see the children and Winks and Mr. Spells as they were to see him.

"Sleep-Alone! Oh, Sleep-Alone, you're just about the *only* person who would come here!" cried Peter. "Where is that castle you've been

complaining about? It's Giant Twisty's, and he's got Chinky a prisoner there."

"Good thing, too," grumbled Sleep-Alone. "Mischievous creature, always coming and disturbing me at night!"

"Listen, Sleep-Alone," said Mr. Spells. "If you will lead us to that castle, we plan to rescue Chinky and the Wishing-Chair—and we will turn the wicked Twisty out of his castle. Then it will be empty, in the middle of the land of Loneliness. And *you* shall have it for your own! Think of being alone there, with no one to wake you at night, no one to bother you!"

Sleep-Alone listened to all this in delight.

What, have a large empty castle all to himself, with a thousand rooms to sleep in—lost in the middle of a forest in the land of Loneliness? Wonderful!

"I'll show you where it is," he said eagerly.

They followed him. He darted in and out of the trees, following no path that they could see—and then at last they saw Wandering Castle! It stood there, rocking a little in the wind, for it had no true foundations as other buildings have. It was tall and dark and gloomy—and it hadn't a single window of any kind!

"There you are!" said Sleep-Alone. "A very fine castle, too—only one door—and no windows. Just the place for me!"

Mr. Spells looked at the castle in silence. One door—and no windows. A very difficult place to escape from if they got inside. But they must get inside. There was no doubt about that.

"Stay here by the door, Sleep-Alone," said Mr. Spells at last. "We're going in." He went up the broad steps to the great studded door.

The door opened. A giant stood there, a cross-eyed fellow, with a twisted smile on his face.

"Come in," he said. "So you've found me, have you? Well, I'm not going to deny that I've got the Wishing-Chair—yes, and Chinky, too—and now I'll have you as well."

To the children's surprise, Mr. Spells didn't run away. He stepped inside and the children and Winks went, too, all feeling rather scared. Twisty laughed.

"This is easier than I thought!" he said. "How are you going to get out again, Mr. Spells? There is now no door—and, as I dare say you have seen, there are no windows at all!"

The children turned and looked behind them. The door had vanished. They were indeed prisoners. But Mr. Spells didn't seem at all disturbed.

"Where is Chinky?" he said.

"Follow me," said Twisty, and he went down a long, dark passage and through a door. He crossed the room beyond the door, and came to another one. The door to this was locked and bolted. He opened it.

Inside was Chinky, sitting miserably in the Wishing-Chair! He leapt up in the greatest joy when he saw the others. Mollie ran to him and flung her arms round him.

"Chinky! You're safe! Oh, Chinky, we've come to rescue you!"

Peter slapped Chinky on the back and Winks pumped his hand up and down, yelling, "Chinky, good old Chinky!"

In the middle of all this there came the sound of the door being slammed and bolted. Then they heard Twisty laughing loudly.

"Easy! Too easy for words! You can't get out, Mr. Spells, however powerful you are. This door has a Keep-Shut Spell in it that I bought from an old witch years ago. And it's the only way out! You can go free if you give me some spells I've wanted for years."

"You'll never get them from me, Twisty," called Mr. Spells. "Never!"

"Mr. Spells! You *are* going to get us out of here, aren't you?" begged Mollie.

"Sh! Don't get alarmed," said Mr. Spells. "I am going to do a spell on us all. Yes, and on the Wishing-Chair, too. Now, where's my chalk?"

He found a white chalk in his pocket and a blue one, too. He drew first a white circle and then a blue one inside it. He made the children, Chinky and Winks sit down in the middle of it.

Then he got inside the circle himself, and sat down in the Wishing-Chair.

"I'm going to say very magic words," he said. "Shut your eyes, please — and don't be surprised at whatever happens!"

XXI

A VERY EXCITING TIME

The children, Chinky and Winks shut their eyes. Mr. Spells began to mutter some magic words under his breath — then he spoke some aloud and then he suddenly shouted three spell-words at the top of his voice, making everyone jump violently.

There was a silence. Then Mr. Spells spoke in his ordinary voice. "You can open your eyes now. The spell is done."

They opened their eyes and looked round them

in wonder. They were in the very biggest room they had ever seen in their lives. The floor stretched endlessly away from them. The walls seemed miles away. Not far from them was. a colossal wooden pillar—or what looked like one. The ceiling seemed to have disappeared or else was so far away that they couldn't see it. Certainly there was no sky above them, so probably the ceiling was still there!

"What's that enormous wooden post?" said Peter in wonder. "It wasn't here just now."

"It's the leg of the table," said Mr. Spells surprisingly.

"What do you mean?" said Peter. "It's much too big for that—look, that's the wooden pillar I mean—over there. And where are the chalk circles gone?"

"We're still standing in the middle of them," said Mr. Spells with a laugh. "Do you mean to say you don't know what has happened?"

"No," said Peter. "I feel funny, you know—but except that we appear to be in quite a different place now I don't know what's happened."

"*I* do," said Chinky. "You've used a very powerful Go-Small spell, Mr. Spells, haven't you? Goodness, I was awfully afraid you weren't going to stop the spell soon enough—I thought we were going to shrink to nothing. How big are we?"

"Smaller than mice," said Mr. Spells. "I wanted to make us small enough to creep under the door, you see."

"How clever of you!" said Mollie joyfully. "I

see what has happened now—why the ceiling seems so far away, and why that table-leg looks like a great pillar—and why we can't see the chalk circles—we'd have to walk a long way to get to them now!"

"Quite right," said Mr. Spells. "Now I think we'd better make a move, in case the giant comes back and guesses what I've done. I'm glad the spell went so well—sometimes a powerful spell like that makes loud noises, and I've known it to make lightning come round the circle."

"Gracious!" said Peter. "I wish it had. I'd have enjoyed our own private little storm!"

"Now the thing is—where's the door gone?" said Chinky. "We've gone so small that the room is simply enormous, and the wall where the door is seems miles away. We'd better begin walking right round the walls till we come to the door!"

But Mr. Spells knew where the door was. Carrying the Wishing-Chair, which had gone small, too, he led them for what seemed miles over the floor, and they at last came to where the door was fitted into the wall. A draught blew at them as they came near to the enormous door.

"That's the draught blowing under the bottom of the door," explained Mr. Spells. "Now—I'm going to squeeze under first to see that everything is safe. Be ready to follow me when you hear me call."

He disappeared under the door, bending himself double. Soon they heard his voice. "Yes—come along—it's all right."

335

One by one they squeezed under the door, and found themselves in what they supposed must be the room outside — but now, of course, it seemed a very vast dark place indeed. "Shall I make us our right size again — or shall I keep us small?" wondered Mr. Spells. "On the whole, I think I'll keep us small."

He led them across the room and down a passage, making them all keep very close to the bottom of the wall. It was a very good thing he did, too, because round the corner they heard the sound of tremendous footsteps that shook the floor and made it tremble — the giant coming along the passage!

In a trice Mr. Spells pulled them all into what appeared to be some kind of mouse-hole — it seemed as large as a cave to the children! They crouched there till the thundering footsteps had gone by. Then out they went as fast as they could.

"I want to find the front door if I can," said Mr. Spells. "We can easily slip under that. It must be at the end of this passage."

But before they reached it a thunderous noise made them all jump nearly out of their skins.

BANG-BANG-THUD-RAT-TAT-TAT!

"What is it?" cried Mollie, and caught hold of Mr. Spells. "What can it be?"

Mr. Spells laughed. "I think I can guess what it is," he said. "It's Chinky's cousin, Sleep-Alone. He's got tired of waiting for the castle, and he's knocking at the door to see what's happened! Oh dear — now I don't know *what* will happen!"

336

Plenty happened. When the knocker banged again on the door, an answering roar came from inside the castle, and Twisty the giant came pounding along the passage in a fine temper.

"Who's that knocking at my door? How dare you make this noise?"

The door was swung open and a wind blew down the passage at once, almost blowing the five tiny people over. Sleep-Alone stood outside, a small figure compared with the giant, but seeming like a giant now to the tiny children!

"Quick!" said Mr. Spells, "they are going to have a quarrel. Now's our chance to escape out of the door—but keep away from their feet. We're so small that neither of them will notice us."

The children ran with Chinky and Winks out of the door, keeping well to the side. But they couldn't possibly go any further than the top step because the drop down to the second step seemed like a cliff to them!

"I'll have to take a chance now and change us back to our right size," said Mr. Spells. "Otherwise we'll have to stand on this top step and sooner or later be trampled on. Shut your eyes, please, take hands, and keep together. I haven't got time to draw chalk circles, so this spell will happen very quickly. As soon as you're the right size, run down the steps as quickly as ever you can, and go to that tree over there. I'll bring the Wishing-Chair, and we'll soon be off and away!"

"What about Sleep-Alone?" said Chinky. "We promised he could have the castle."

"He'll look after that all right," said Mr. Spells, with a laugh. "Sleep-Alone is bolder than I thought he was! Now—eyes shut, please, and hold hands hard."

They all obeyed. Mr. Spells said the words that undid the Go-Small spell, and allowed them to shoot up to their right size again—but, as he had said, it happened very suddenly indeed, and all five of them gasped, felt giddy and fell over.

"Quick—get up—he's seen us!" shouted Mr. Spells. He picked up the Wishing-Chair which had also gone back to its right size, and ran down the steps with it. Everyone followed.

Sleep-Alone and the giant had been having a real rough and tumble. The giant was stronger and bigger than Sleep-Alone—but Chinky's cousin had got in so many sly jabs and punches that the giant had completely lost his temper.

He lashed out at Sleep-Alone, who ducked—but the blow just caught him on the top of his head. He stumbled—and that would have been the end of him if the giant hadn't, at that very moment, caught sight of the five prisoners tearing down his steps!

He was so tremendously astonished that he forgot all about Sleep-Alone and simply stood there, staring out of his saucer-like eyes!

Then, with a bellow, he was after them. "How did you escape?" he roared. "Come back—or I'll throw you all up to the moon!"

Mr. Spells put down the Wishing-Chair. He sat in it quickly and pulled Peter and Mollie on his knee. Winks and Chinky sat on the back. "Home, Chair," ordered Mr. Spells, and at once the obedient Wishing-Chair rose into the air.

The giant made a grab at it, but the chair dodged, and Mr. Spells hit the giant smartly on his outstretched hand. The giant yelped.

"Good-bye!" called Chinky, waving his hand.

Meanwhile what had happened to Sleep-Alone? Plenty! When he saw the giant rushing after the others, he stood and stared for a moment. Then he grinned. Then he hopped into Wandering Castle and shut the door very quietly.

And when Twisty turned round to go back and finish his quarrel with Sleep-Alone, there was no castle there! It had gone on its wanderings again!

"Oh dear—I wish we could stay and see the giant looking for his castle," said Mollie. "What a shock he's having! His prisoners all escaping, the Wishing-Chair gone—and his castle wandering away in the forest with Sleep-Alone in charge. Won't your cousin be thrilled to have such a fine place to sleep in, Chinky?"

The Wishing-Chair didn't go back to the playroom—it went to Mrs. Spells' room.

They went in to see Mrs. Spells, and told her their extraordinary adventures. To their surprise, Cinders was there and produced some excellent fruit buns that Mrs. Spells said he had just made. He really was a most remarkable cat.

Mollie glanced out of the window that looked out on the sea. "Oh, look!" she cried, "there's our ship! *The Mollie!* I wondered what would happen to her. She's come back, Mr. Spells."

"Cinders brought her back," said Mrs. Spells. "He knew the ship wouldn't be needed again."

"It was a grand adventure," said Mollie. "I was scared at times, you know—but somehow I knew everything would be all right with Mr. Spells there. Thank you, Mr. Spells, for being such a good friend."

"Delighted," said the enchanter. "Now it's time you went home."

The children went to find the Wishing-Chair, which was still in the back yard. They climbed into it with Winks and Chinky.

"Take us home, Chair!" cried Peter—and up into the air it rose, flapping its big wings—and in five minutes' time they were all back in the playroom once more.

XXII

WINKS AND CHINKY ARE SILLY

The Wishing-Chair seemed tired with all its adventures. It stood in its place for ten whole days and didn't grow its wings.

"We've only got a week and two days left before we go back to school," said Mollie, who was a bit worried. "I do hope we have another adventure before we have to say good-bye to you, Chinky. Where's Winks?"

"I don't know. He was here last night, looking

very mysterious," said Chinky. "You know, the way he looks when he's up to some kind of mischief. I just hope he won't get into trouble."

"You know he lost my doll's gloves on the last adventure? He says he dropped them into the sea," said Mollie. "Now his hands show up again — that awful blue colour!"

"I know. The things he loses!" said Chinky. "He came in without his shoes the other day, and said he'd lost them. I said: 'Well, where did you take them off, Winks?' And he said he'd lost them without even taking them off. How could anyone do that?"

"Sh! Here he is!" said Mollie. "Oh, *Winks!* Your hands aren't blue any more! They're the right colour! How did you manage that?"

"Aha-ha-ha!" said Winks. "I've got a secret."

"What is it?" asked Chinky at once.

"Well, it won't be a secret if I tell it," said Winks annoyingly.

"Have you been to see Mr. Spells?" said Mollie.

"No. I went to see Witch Wendle," said Winks. "I borrowed her wand — it's got very good magic in it."

"Do you mean to say old Witch Wendle lent you her wand?" said Chinky disbelievingly. "Why, it was only last week you told me you put her chimney pot upside down so that her smoke blew down into her kitchen. I don't believe you!"

"All right, then — but here's the wand, see?" said Winks, and he suddenly produced the wand from under his coat. It was a small, neat wand, not

341

long and slender like Chinky's. He waved it about. Mollie and Peter stared in surprise — and Chinky jumped up in alarm.

"WINKS! You took it without asking? I know you did. Witch Wendle would never lend her wand to you — why, look, it's absolutely *full* of magic!"

So it was. All wands glitter and shine and gleam and shimmer when they are full of magic, and this one was quite dazzling.

"I just borrowed it for a little while," said Winks. "The witch has gone to call on her sister. She won't miss it. I'll take it back soon. I wished my hands the right colour again — wasn't I pleased when they came all right!"

"You're a very bad, naughty brownie," said Chinky. "You ought to go back to Mister Grim's school. I've a good mind to make you go back!"

"Don't you talk like that to me, or I shall lose my temper," said Winks, crossly, and he poked the wand at Chinky.

"Stop it," said Chinky. "You should never poke people with wands. Surely you know that? And let me tell you this — I shall talk to you how I like. You take that wand back to Witch Wendle AT ONCE!"

"I don't like you, Chinky," said Winks, looking suddenly cross. "I shall wish for a Maggle-Mig to chase you!"

He waved his wand in the air — and goodness gracious, whatever was this extraordinary creature running in at the door?

It was rather like a small giraffe, but it had feathers, and it wore shoes on its four feet. It galloped round the room after Chinky. The children fled to a cupboard. If this was a Magglemig, they didn't like it! Winks sat down on the sofa and roared with laughter. Chinky was furious.

He rushed to the toy cupboard and felt about for his wand. He waved it in the air. "Magglemig, change to a Snickeroo and chase Winks!" he cried. And at once the little giraffe-like creature changed to a thing like a small crocodile with horns. It ran at Winks, who leapt off the sofa in a hurry.

Winks waved his wand at the Snickeroo and it ran into the fireplace and completely vanished. Winks pointed the wand at Chinky.

"Horrid Chinky! Grow a long nose!"

And poor Chinky did! It was so long that he almost fell over it! Winks took hold of it and pulled it.

Chinky hit out at Winks with his own wand. "Grow a tail!" he yelled.

And, hey presto! Winks grew a tail—one like a cow's, with a tuft at the end. It swung to and fro, and Winks looked down at it in alarm. He tried to run away from the swinging tail, but you can't leave a tail that's growing on you, of course, and the tail followed him, swinging to and fro.

"Ha, ha!" said Chinky. "A brownie with a tail!"

Winks was crying now. He picked up his wand, which he had dropped. He and Chinky hit out at each other at the same moment.

"I'll change you into a puff of smoke!" shouted Winks.

"I'll change you into a horrid smell!" cried Chinky.

And then they both disappeared! Mollie and Peter stared in the utmost dismay. A little puff of green smoke blew across the room and disappeared out of the door. A horrid smell drifted about the room for a few minutes and then that went, too.

Mollie burst into tears. "Now look what's happened!" she sobbed. "We've lost both Chinky and Winks."

Peter saw that the two wands were on the floor. He picked up Chinky's and put it into the toy cupboard. Then he picked up the one Winks had taken from Witch Wendle's and looked at it. Mollie gave a cry.

"Don't meddle with it, Peter. Don't!"

"I'm not going to," said Peter. "I'm just wondering what to do about all this. It's very serious. I think we ought to take this wand back to Witch Wendle."

"Oh, let's take it back quickly then," said Mollie. "And perhaps if we do she'll tell us what to do about Chinky and Winks. How shall we find the way?"

"We might ask Mr. Spells," began Peter, and then suddenly stopped in delight. He pointed behind Mollie.

She turned and saw that the Wishing-Chair was growing its wings again! The buds on its four legs burst into feathers, and soon the big green and yellow wings were waving gently in the air.

"Oh! *What* a bit of luck!" cried Mollie. "Now we can get in the Wishing-Chair and just tell it to go to Witch Wendle's!"

Peter sat in the chair and pulled Mollie down beside him. He had the witch's wand in his hand.

"Wishing-Chair, we want to go to Witch Wendle's," he said. "Go at once!"

The chair rose into the air, and made for the door. Out it went and up into the cloudy sky. It made for an opening in the clouds and shot through it. Now the children were in the sunshine above.

They flew for a long way, and then Mollie shouted in surprise, and pointed. "Look! What's that? It's a castle in the clouds!"

Both children stared. It was a very surprising sight indeed. A big purple cloud loomed ahead, thick and gloomy. Set in its depths was what looked exactly like a castle, with towers and turrets. The chair flew straight to the cloud and stopped. It hovered just above the cloud, and the children couldn't get down.

"Go lower, Chair!" cried Peter. But the chair didn't. A head popped out of a window of the castle.

"Wait! I'll get you cloud-shoes! If you walk on the cloud without them you'll fall."

The head disappeared. Then out of the castle came Witch Wendle, a bright star glinting at the top of her pointed hat. She carried what looked like snowshoes, big flat things, to fasten to their feet.

"Here you are!" she said. "Put these on your feet and you will be able to walk easily on the clouds. That's why your Wishing-Chair wouldn't land—it knew it would be dangerous for you without cloud-shoes."

"Oh, thank you," said Mollie. She liked Witch Wendle very much, because her face smiled and her eyes twinkled. The children put on the cloud-shoes and then stepped down on the cloud. Ah, they could get along quite well now—it felt rather as if they were sliding on very, very soft snow.

"What a strange home you have, set high in the clouds," said Peter.

"Oh, people often build these," said the witch. "Have you never heard of people building castles in the air? Well, this is one of them. They don't last very long, but they are very comfortable. I've had this one about two months now."

She led the way to her curious castle. "We've come to bring you your wand," said Peter. "I must tell you all that happened."

So he did, and the witch listened in silence. "That tiresome Winks!" she said. "He should never have left Mister Grim's school."

"What can we do about Chinky and Winks," said Mollie, "now that they are a puff of smoke and a horrid smell? Where have they gone?"

"To the Land of Spells," said the witch. "We'll have to get your Wishing-Chair to go there—come along!"

XXIII

WHAT HAPPENED IN THE
LAND OF SPELLS

The witch led the way to where the Wishing-Chair stood waiting patiently on the edge of the cloud, its wings flapping gently.

"That's a really wonderful chair of yours," she said. "I only wish I had one like it!"

They all sat in it. "To the Land of Spells!" commanded the witch, and the chair at once rose into the air. It left the cloud and the curious castle built in the air, and flew steadily to the north.

"I'm very glad to have back my wand," said Witch Wendle. "Luckily it is only my third best one. If it had been my best one, the magic would have been so powerful that it would have shrivelled Winks up as soon as he touched it."

Mollie and Peter at once made up their minds that they would never, never touch any wand belonging to a witch or wizard. Goodness — what a blessing that it had been the witch's third best wand and not her best one!

The chair flew on for a long while and the witch pointed out the interesting places they passed — the Village of Stupids, the Country of No-Goods, the Land of Try-Again, and all kinds of places the children had never heard of before. They stared down at them in interest.

347

"What's the Land of Spells like?" asked Mollie.

"It's a strange land, really," said the witch. "All kinds of spells wander about, and bump into you — Invisible Spells to make you invisible, Tall Spells to make you tall, Laughter Spells to make you laugh — they've only got to touch you to affect you at once."

"Oh dear," said Mollie in alarm. "I don't like the sound of that at all."

"You needn't worry," said Witch Wendle. "They only affect you whilst they bump into you — as soon as they drift away you're all right again. We shall have to look for a puff of smoke and detect a horrid smell — then we shall know we've got Winks and Chinky and I must do my best to put them right for you."

The chair flew rapidly downwards, and landed in a very peculiar place. It was full of a blue-green mist and queer sounds went on all the time — sounds of rumbling, sounds of music, of bells, and of the wind blowing strongly.

They got off the chair. "Now take hands," said the witch. "And keep together, please. You're all right so long as you're with me, because I am a mistress of all spells — but don't slip away for goodness' sake, or you may get changed into a white butterfly or a blue beetle, and I would find it difficult to know you again."

Mollie and Peter held hands very hard indeed, and Mollie took the witch's hand, too. And then all kinds of extraordinary things began to happen.

A little trail of yellow bubbles bumped into

Mollie—and, to Peter's great alarm, Mollie's neck grew alarmingly long, and shot up almost as tall as a tree! She was very alarmed, too.

"It's all right," said Witch Wendle. "It will pass as soon as the trail of bubbles goes."

She was right. When the bubbles flew off in another direction. Mollie's neck came down to its right size! "You did look queer, Mollie," said Peter. "Don't do *that* again!"

It was queer to think of spells wandering about like this. Mollie began to look out for them and try to dodge them. She dodged a silvery mist, but it wound itself round Witch Wendle—and she at once disappeared completely.

"Where's she gone?" cried Peter in fright.

"I've still got hold of her hand," said Mollie. "I think she's only invisible—but she's here all right."

"Yes, I'm here," said the witch's voice. As soon as the silvery mist cleared away she became visible again and smiled down at the children. "I didn't see that spell coming or I would have dodged it," she said. "Oh dear—here's an annoying one coming!"

Something that looked like a little shower of white snowflakes came dropping down on them. The witch changed into a big white bear, Peter changed into a white goat and Mollie into a white cat! That lasted about two minutes, and they were all very glad when they were back to their right shapes again.

They went wandering through the queer misty

349

land, listening to the queer noises around, trying to dodge the spells that came near them. The witch put out her hand and captured a tiny little spell floating through the air. It looked like a small white daisy.

"I've always wanted that spell," she said to the children. "It's a good spell—if you put it under a baby's pillow it makes a child grow up as pretty as a flower."

Suddenly Peter stopped and sniffed. "Pooh! What a smell of bad fish!" he said. "I'm sure that must be Winks. Can you smell a horrid smell, Witch Wendle?"

"I should think I *can*," said the witch. She took a small bottle out of her pocket and uncorked it.

"Come here to me, you bad little smell,
Into this bottle you'll fit very well!"

she sang. And the children saw a very faint purplish streak streaming into the bottle. The witch corked it up.

"Well, we've got Winks all right," she said. "Now for Chinky. Look—here comes a puff of green smoke. Would that be him?"

"Yes!" said Peter. "I'm sure it is. He and Winks would be certain to keep together."

The witch took a small pair of bellows from under her long, flowing cloak and held them out to the puff of green smoke, which was hovering near. She opened the bellows and drew in the puff of smoke! She hung the bellows on her belt again.

"And now we've got Chinky," she said. "Good! We'd better get back home now, and see what we can do with them. It's so easy to change people into bad smells and green smoke—any beginner can do that—but it takes a powerful witch or wizard to change them back to their own shapes again."

They walked back to find the Wishing-Chair, still bumping into curious spells every now and again. Mollie walked into a Too-Big spell and immediately towered over the witch and Peter. But she went back to her own size almost at once.

The witch bumped into a train of bright bubbles that burst as they touched her. When they looked at her they saw that she had changed into a beautiful young girl, and they were amazed. But she was soon her old self again.

"That was a nice spell," she said with a sigh. "I should like to have caught that spell and kept it. Ah, is that the Wishing-Chair?"

"Yes—but there's only half of it!" said Mollie, in surprise. "Oh, I see—it's just been touched by an invisible spell—it's coming all right again now."

Soon they were sitting in the chair. "To the children's playroom," commanded the witch. "And hurry! The puff of smoke in the bellows is trying to get out. We'll lose Chinky for ever if he puffs himself out, and gets lost on the wind."

"Oh dear!" said Mollie. "Do hurry, Wishing-Chair!"

The Wishing-Chair hurried so much that the witch lost her hat in the wind and the chair had to go back for it. But at last they were flying down to the playroom, and in at the door. Thank goodness!

.The witch got carefully out of the chair. She took the bellows from her waist. "Is there a suit of Chinky's anywhere?" she asked. Mollie got Chinky's second-best one from the cupboard. "Hold it up," said the witch. "That's right. Now watch!"

Mollie held up the little suit. The witch took the bellows and blew with them. Green smoke came from them and filled the little suit, billowing it out, and—would you believe it?—it was Chinky himself filling it out, growing arms and legs and head—and there he was standing before them in his second-best suit, looking rather scared after his curious stay in the Land of Spells!

Then it was Winks' turn. The witch asked for the teapot and took off the lid. She uncorked the bottle in which she had put the bad smell, and emptied it into the teapot. She put on the lid.

Then she lifted up the teapot and poured something out of the spout, singing as she did so:

"Teapot, teapot, pour for me
A brownie naughty as can be,
He's not as clever as he thinks,
That wicked, wilful little Winks!"

And before the children's astonished eyes the teapot poured out Winks! He came out in a kind

352

of stream, which somehow built itself up into Winks himself!

When Winks saw Witch Wendle he went very red and tried to hide behind the sofa. She pulled him out, saying, "Who stole my wand? Who changed Chinky into a puff of smoke?"

"Well, he changed me into a bad smell," said Winks, beginning to sniff.

"He at least used his own wand to do it with," said the witch. "Winks, I'm sending you back to Mister Grim's school. You've a lot to learn."

Winks howled so loudly that Mollie felt very sorry for him.

"Please," she said, "could he just stay with us till we go back to boarding school? We might have another adventure, a nice one."

"Very well," said Witch Wendle. "One week more. Don't sniff like that, Winks. You bring all your trouble on yourself."

"I'm sorry, Witch Wendle," wailed Winks.

"You'll be sorry till next time — then you will do something tiresome once more and be sorry all over again," said the witch. "I know you, Winks! Well, good-bye, children. I'm very pleased to have met you — and, by the way, may I sometimes borrow that Wishing-Chair of yours when you are at school? It would be such a treat for me to do my shopping in it sometimes."

"Oh, yes, please do," said Mollie at once. "It would be a nice return for all your help. You'll have to go to Chinky's mother to borrow it when we're at school. He keeps it there."

"Thank you," said the witch, and off she went. Chinky turned to Winks. "We were silly to quarrel like that," he said. "I'm sorry I turned you into a bad smell, Winks. Go and wash. I still think you smell a bit horrid."

So he did—and it was two or three days before he smelt like a brownie again. You just can't meddle with spells, you know!

XXIV

THE ISLAND OF SURPRISES

"You know," said Mollie to Chinky, "we've only one more day before we go back to school. Mother has already sent off our trunks."

"Oh dear," said Chinky, sadly. "The holidays have simply flown! I do wish you didn't have to go to school."

"Well—we love being at home—but we really do love school, too," said Peter. "It's great fun, you know—and it's so nice being with scores of boys and girls who are our own age. I'm awfully glad we do go to boarding-school, really, though, of course, I'm sorry to say good-bye to Mother and Daddy and you and the garden and Jane and the Wishing-Chair, and everything."

"We never went to the Land of Goodness Knows Where," said Mollie. "I'd like to go before we leave for school."

"Wishing-Chair, you *might* grow your wings

quickly," said Peter, looking at the chair standing quietly in its place. "You really might!"

And, dear me, for once in a way the chair was most obliging and began to grow them! Unfortunately the children didn't notice that it was actually doing what it was told, and they went out into the garden to play.

The next thing that happened was the chair flying out of the door of the playroom, its wings flapping strongly! Luckily Chinky caught sight of it, or goodness knows where it would have gone by itself. He felt the swish of the big wings, and looked up. The chair was just passing by his head!

He gave such a yell that Mollie and Peter jumped in fright. They turned, to see Chinky making a tremendous leap into the air after the chair. He caught one leg and held on. "Help! Help!" he yelled to the children. "Come and help me, or the chair will go off with me like this."

However, the chair went down to the ground, and allowed Chinky to sit in it properly. Mollie and Peter ran up eagerly.

"Gracious! Whatever made us leave the playroom door open?" said Peter. "The chair might have flown off anywhere and not come back. We shall really have to get a watch-dog for it."

"It was lucky I just saw it," said Chinky. "Well now — shall we go to the Land of Goodness Knows Where or not? Is there anywhere else you'd like to go?"

The children couldn't think of anywhere else, so the chair was told to go there. It flew off in the

355

right direction at once. It was a lovely, clear day, with hardly any cloud at all. The children and Chinky could see down below them very clearly indeed.

"Go lower, Chair," said Chinky. "We'd like to see the places we're flying over." The chair obediently flew down lower still, and then Chinky gave a shout.

"Look—there's Winks! Isn't it Winks?"

It was. He, too, saw the chair and waved madly.

"Shall we take him with us?" said Chinky.

"Well—it's his last chance of coming with us for a long time," said Mollie. "We said we'd let him come with us once more, didn't we, before he goes back to Mister Grim's school. We'll take him."

So they ordered the chair to go down to the ground to fetch Winks. He was simply delighted. He clambered on to it at once. "Did you come to fetch me?" he said. "How nice of you."

"Well, actually we weren't fetching you," said Chinky. "The chair suddenly grew its wings, flew out into the garden, and I just managed to grab it in time. It was a bit of luck, catching sight of you like that. Winks, you must try and be good to-day—don't spoil our last adventure by being silly or naughty, please. We're going to the Land of Goodness Knows Where."

"That's a silly land," said Winks. "Why don't you go somewhere more exciting—the Land of Birthdays, or the Land of Treats, or the Village of Parties—somewhere like that."

They were just passing over a big blue lake. They came to an island in the middle of it, and as they flew over it a surprising thing happened. Fireworks went off with a bang, and coloured stars burst and fell all round the chair. It was startled and wobbled dangerously, almost upsetting the children.

"Gracious!" said Mollie. "What a surprise! What island is that?"

"Oh!" cried Chinky, in great excitement, "I do believe it's the Island of Surprises! Isn't it, Winks? I really think it is."

"Yes," said Winks, peering down. "It is! Look out, here comes another rocket or something. My word—what a lovely shower of coloured stars!"

"Can't we go to this island?" said Mollie. "Chinky, let's go."

"Right," said Chinky. "Mind you, the surprises may not all be nice ones—but if you're willing to risk that, we'll go."

"Of course we'll go!" said Winks. "Chair, go down to the island at once, please."

Down went the chair, dodging another rocket. It landed on a patch of green grass, which at once changed into a sheet of water! The chair almost sank, but just managed to get itself out in time, and flew to a little paved courtyard.

"First surprise," said Chinky, with a grin. "We shall have to be careful here, you know. Winks, you mustn't be an idiot on this island—you'll get some unpleasant shocks if you are."

"Can we leave the chair here?" said Mollie

357

doubtfully. "It would be a horrid surprise if we found it gone when we came back for it."

The chair creaked and flew towards Mollie. "It says it's not going to leave us!" said Chinky, with a grin. "Very wise of it. Right, Chair, you follow us like a dog, and we'll all be very pleased."

So the chair followed them closely.

The first really nice surprise came when they saw a table set out in the sunshine, with empty dishes and plates in a row. The children, Chinky and Winks stopped to look at them. "Is there going to be a party or something?" said Peter.

A small goblin came up and sat himself down on the form by the table. He stared earnestly at the plate and dish in front of him. And, hey presto, on the dish came a large chocolate pudding, and on his plate came a big ice-cream to match. He began to eat, beaming all over his ugly little face.

"Oooh," said Winks at once, and sat down at the table. So did the others. They all stared hard at their dishes and plates.

Mollie got a pile of sausages on her dish and some fried onions on her plate. Peter got a big trifle on his dish and a jug of cream on his plate. Chinky got strawberries on his dish and found his plate swimming in sugar and cream to go with them.

They looked to see what Winks had got. That bad little brownie, of course, had been tricky as usual. He had put *two* plates and *two* dishes in front of him!

But he wasn't looking at all pleased! On one

dish had appeared a wonderful-looking pie — but when he cut the crust there was nothing in the pie. On the other dish had appeared a chocolate cake — and, as we know, that was the one cake that poor Winks simply couldn't bear to eat.

On one plate had come some steaming cabbage and on the other two prunes. How the others laughed!

"A pie with nothing in it — a cake he hates — cabbage — and prunes! Oh, Winks, what a horrid surprise. It serves you right for being greedy!" cried Chinky.

Winks was cross. He stood sulkily whilst the others tucked into their exciting food. Mollie was sorry for him and offered him a sausage.

The next surprise was also a very nice one. They finished their meal and then suddenly heard the sound of loud music coming from round the corner. They hurried to see what it was.

It was a roundabout! There it stood, decorated with flags that waved in the wind, going round and round, the music playing gaily. How lovely!

"How much is it to go for a ride on this roundabout," asked Chinky, feeling in his pocket.

"Oh, nothing!" said the pixie in charge of it. "It's just a nice surprise for you. Get on when it stops."

When the roundabout stopped, the children saw that there were all kinds of animals and birds to ride, and each of them went up and down as well as round and round. The brownies, goblins and pixies who had had their turns got off, and the children, Chinky and Winks looked to see which animal or bird they would choose to ride.

"I'll have this pony," said Mollie, who loved horses and always wanted one of her own. She climbed on to a dear little black pony.

"I'll have this camel," said Peter. "It's got two humps, and I'll ride between them!"

Chinky chose a snow-white gull with outstretched wings that flapped as the roundabout went round. Winks chose a big goldfish. Its fins and tail moved in a very life-like manner. Winks cut himself a little stick from the hedge nearby. "Just to make my fish swim well on the roundabout," he said to the others as he climbed on.

"No whipping allowed!" shouted the pixie in charge. "Hey, you—no whipping allowed!"

The roundabout started off again. The music blared gaily, the animals, fish and birds went round and round, up and down, flapping their wings and fins, nodding their heads and waving tails—all very exciting indeed.

And Winks was disobedient—he whipped his goldfish with his stick! "Gee up!" he cried.

Then he got such a shock. The goldfish suddenly shot right off the roundabout through the air and disappeared! The roundabout slowed down and came to a stop. The pixie in charge looked very angry.

"He whipped his goldfish and I told him not to. Now I've lost the goldfish, and my master will be very angry with me."

"Oh *dear!*" said Mollie, getting off her pony.

360

"I'm so very sorry. Winks did promise to be good. Where has he gone, do you think?"

Then there suddenly came the sound of a terrific splash, and a loud wail came on the air. "That's Winks," cried Peter, beginning to run. "Whatever has happened to him?"

XXV

HOME AGAIN – AND GOOD-BYE!

The yells went on and on and on. "Help me! I'm drowning! Help, help, HELP!"

The children and Chinky tore round the corner. The sea lay in front of them, blue and calm. The goldfish was swimming about in it, looking enormous. Winks was splashing and struggling in the water, and every time he tried to wade out, the goldfish bumped him with his nose and sent him under.

There was a crowd of little people yelling with laughter. Peter waded in and pulled Winks out. The goldfish flapped out, too, and lay on the beach. It didn't seem to mind leaving the water at all – but then, as Mollie said, it wasn't a *real, live* fish. It was just a roundabout one.

"Winks, we're not a bit sorry for you," said Peter. "As usual, you brought your trouble on yourself. Now, just pick up that fish and take it back to the roundabout."

The fish was big but not heavy. Winks groaned

and put it on his shoulder. It flapped its fins and made itself as difficult to carry as it possibly could. Winks staggered back to the roundabout with it.

But the roundabout was gone. It had completely disappeared.

"Well," said Winks, dumping the fish on the ground at once. "I'm not carrying this fish any longer, then."

But the others made him. "We might meet the pixie in charge of the roundabout," said Peter. "And you could give it him back then. He was very upset at losing it."

So Winks had to stagger along carrying the goldfish. Still, as Peter said, if he was going to make trouble, he could jolly well carry his own troubles!

It certainly was an Island of Surprises. There was a surprise round almost every corner! For one thing, there was a wonderful Balloon Tree. It had buds that blew up into balloons. Under the tree sat a brownie with a ball of string. You could choose your own balloon, pick it off the tree, and then get the neck tied with string by the brownie. They all chose balloons at once.

Winks stayed behind and they had to go back and fetch him. He had done a very surprising thing. He had picked six of the biggest balloons and had got enough string from the brownie to tie each of them to the big goldfish. And just as Chinky and the children reached the Balloon Tree again they saw Winks set the goldfish free in the wind — and the breeze took hold of the balloons and carried goldfish and all high up in the air. "Oh, Winks!" said Mollie. "Now look what you've done!"

Winks grinned. "Just a little surprise for the goldfish," he said. "Thank goodness I've got rid of him."

Well, what can you do with a brownie like that? The others gave him up in despair and walked on again. The Wishing-Chair followed them closely, as if it was a bit afraid of the Island of Surprises.

Round the next corner was another surprise. There were a dozen small motor cars that seemed to go by magic. "Come and race, come and race!" chanted a little goblin. "The winner can choose his own prize!"

The prizes were as exciting as the little cars. There was a purse that always had money in it no matter how many times you took it out.

There was a little clock that didn't strike the hour, but called them out in a dear little voice. "It is now twelve o'clock!" And there was a teapot that would pour out any drink you liked to mention.

"Ooooh—do let's try a race!" cried Winks, and he leapt into a fine blue car. "I want one of those prizes!"

They all chose cars. The goblin set them in a row and showed them how to work them. "Just press hard on these buttons, first with one foot and then with the other," he said. "Now—are you ready—one, two, three, GO!"

And off they went. Winks bumped into Chinky and both cars fell over. Mollie's foot slipped off one button and her car stopped for a moment or two. But Peter shot ahead and won the race, whilst all the little folk cheered and clapped.

"Choose your prize," said the goblin. Peter chose a little dish with a lid. It was a wonderful dish. Every time you lifted the lid there was some titbit there — a sausage or a bar of chocolate or an orange, or an ice-cream — something like that. Peter thought it would be very useful indeed to keep in the playroom.

They had a wonderful time that day. Once the surprise was not very nice. They went to sit down for a rest on some dear little rocking chairs. The chairs at once began to rock as soon as everyone was sitting in them — and they rocked so violently that everyone was thrown roughly out on the ground.

The goblin in charge laughed till the tears ran down his cheeks. "*Not* a very pleasant surprise," said Mollie, picking herself up and running after her balloon, which was blowing away. "Funny to watch, I dare say — but not funny to do!"

They kept having titbits out of the Titbit Dish, but Mollie wished there were more ice-creams. So it was a lovely surprise when they came to a big public fountain, which had a tap labelled: "Ice-cream Tap. TURN AND SAY WHAT KIND."

Mollie turned it at once. "Chocolate ice-cream," she said, and out came a stream of chocolate cream that ran into a small cornet underneath and froze at once.

"Oh, look!" cried Peter. They had come to the little field, and in it were big white swans waiting to take people for flights in the air.

"Shall we have a fly?" said Peter. "Do you think the Wishing-Chair will be jealous if we do?"

"I think one of us had better stay down on the ground with the chair, whilst the others are having a turn at flying on the birds," said Mollie. "Just in *case* it flies off in a huff, you know."

So Mollie sat in the Wishing-Chair whilst the others chose swans and rose up in the air on the backs of the beautiful white birds.

When it was Winks' turn to sit in the Wishing-Chair and stay with it, whilst the others rode on the swans, he thought he would get the chair to chase the swans and make them fly faster!

And up went the Wishing-Chair into the air and began to chase the swans, bumping into their tails and creaking at them in a most alarming manner. One swan was so startled that it turned almost upside down trying to get away from the Wishing-Chair—and the rider on its back fell headlong to the ground.

It was a witch! Fortunately she had her broomstick with her and she managed to get on that as she fell.

She was so angry with Winks! She called the Wishing-Chair to the ground at once and scolded Winks so hard that he tried to hide under the chair in a fright. Mollie, Peter and Chinky flew down at once, angry, too, because of his mischievous trick.

"Ha, Chinky!" said the angry witch, "is this brownie a friend of yours? Who is he?"

"He's Winks," said Chinky.

"What—Winks, who turned his grandmother's pigs blue?" cried the witch. "I thought he was at Mister Grim's school. Well—it's time he was back there. Swan, come here!"

A big white swan flew down to her. The witch picked up Winks as if he were a feather and sat him firmly down on the swan's back.

"Now," she said to the swan, "take Winks to Mister Grim's school and deliver him to Mister Grim himself."

"Oh, no, oh, no!" wailed Winks. "Mollie, Peter, don't let me go."

"You'll have to, Winks," said Mollie. "You really are too naughty for anything. Try to be good this term, and perhaps you'll be allowed to spend your next holidays with Chinky and us. Good-bye."

"But I shan't get enough to eat! I always have to go without my dinner!" wailed Winks.

Peter couldn't help feeling sorry for him. "Here—take the Titbit Dish," he said, and pushed it into Winks' hands. "You'll always have something nice to eat, then."

Winks' tears dried up at once. He beamed. "Oh, *thank you*, Peter—how wonderful! Now I don't mind going back a bit! I'll be as good as anything. I'll see you all next holidays. Good-bye!"

And off he went on the swan, back to Mister Grim's school for Brownies, hugging the Titbit Dish in joy.

"He's very, very naughty, and I can't help thinking that Mister Grim's school is the only place for him," said Mollie. "But I do like him very much, all the same."

"Look, the sun's going down," said Chinky suddenly. "We must go. They say the Island of Surprises always disappears at sunset, and we don't want to disappear with it. Quick—it's disappearing already!"

So it was! Parts of it began to look misty and dream-like. The children and Chinky went to the Wishing-Chair at once. "Home, Wishing-Chair," said Mollie. "Quick, before we all disappear with the Island. That witch has vanished already!"

And home to the playroom they went. They heard Mother ringing the bell for bedtime just as they arrived.

"Oh dear—our very last adventure these holidays, I'm afraid," said Mollie. "Chinky, you'll take the chair to your mother's won't you, and take great care of it for us? You know the date we come back home from school. Be here in time to welcome us!"

"We'll slip in and say a last good-bye before we leave for school," promised Peter. "Don't be lonely without us, Chinky, will you? And couldn't you go and see Winks once or twice at school—in the Wishing-Chair—just to cheer him up?"

"I'll see if my mother will let me," said Chinky. "She doesn't like Winks, you know. Anyway, he will be quite happy with the Titbit Dish, Peter. It *was* nice of you to give it to him."

"Good-bye, Wishing-Chair," said Mollie, patting it. "You've taken us on some wonderful adventures this time. Be ready to take us again next holidays, won't you?"

The chair creaked loudly, as if it, too, were saying good-bye. The bedtime bell rang again, this time quite impatiently.

"We must go!" said Mollie, and she gave Chinky a hug. "We *are* lucky to have you and a Wishing-Chair, we really are! Good-bye!"

Good-bye, too, Mollie, Peter, Chinky, Winks and the Wishing-Chair. We'll see you all again some day, we hope!

BOOK THREE

More
Wishing Chair
Tales

I

THE WITCH'S CAT

ONE afternoon Mollie and Peter were talking to Chinky the pixie in their playroom. Mollie was sitting in the magic chair, knitting as she talked. She was making a warm scarf for Chinky, who often used to go out at night and talk to the fairies in the garden. It was still very cold, and Mollie was afraid he would get a chill.

Peter and Chinky were not looking at Mollie at all – and then a dreadful thing happened! The chair grew its red wings all of a sudden, spread them out, and flew straight out of the open door! Yes – with Mollie in it, all alone! Peter and Chinky gave a shout of dismay, and rushed after it. They were too late – the chair rose over the trees, and the last they saw of Mollie was her pale anxious face looking over the arm at them.

"I say! The chair oughtn't to do that!" said Peter. "Now what are we to do?"

"We can't do anything," said Chinky. "We must just hope that the chair comes back safely, that's all."

Mollie had the surprise of her life when the chair rose up so suddenly. She wondered where in the world it would take her to. It flew a long way, and when it came down Mollie saw that a very thick dark wood lay beneath her.

The chair squeezed its way through the trees, and Mollie crouched down in the chair, for the branches

370

Mollie peeped into the cottage, and inside she saw an old witch.

scratched against her face. At last she was on firm
ground again, and she jumped off the chair to see
where she was. She saw, not far off, a beautiful little
cottage, and to her surprise, there were pink and red
roses out all around it – which was very astonishing,
for it was only the month of February.

"Perhaps a fairy lives there," thought Mollie, and
she went up to the cottage. The door was shut, but
there was a light in the window. Mollie thought she
had better peep into the cottage and just see who
lived there before she knocked at the door. So she did
– and inside she saw an old witch, standing before a
curious fire whose flames were bright purple, stirring
something in a big green pot.

"Ooh!" thought Mollie. "It's a witch. I don't think
I'll go in!"

Suddenly the witch looked up – and she saw Mollie

peeping in. In a trice, she threw down the ladle she was using and ran to the door.

"What are you spying on me for?" she shouted, in such a rage that her face went red as a sunset. "Come here! Let me see who you are! If you are a spy, I'll soon deal with you!"

"But I'm not!" said poor Mollie. She thought she had better run away, so she turned – but the witch caught hold of the sleeve of her frock.

"You go indoors," she said, and pushed Mollie into the cottage. She slammed the door and went back to her green pot, which was now singing a curious tune to itself, and puffing out pale yellow steam.

"Go and help the cat to make my bed," ordered the witch. "I won't have you peeping round whilst I make this spell!"

Mollie looked round for the cat. There was one in the corner, busily washing up some dishes in the sink. It was a black cat, but its eyes were as blue as forget-me-nots. How strange!

The cat put down the tea-cloth and ran into the next room. There was a bed there, and the two set to work to make it. As they were in the middle of it, the witch called sharply to the cat:

"Puss! Come here a minute! I need your help."

The cat at once ran to her – and Mollie took the chance to look round. She saw that the bedroom window was open. Good! It wouldn't take her long to slip out of it and run back to her chair!

She climbed out – but in doing so she knocked over a big vase on the window-sill. Crash! The witch at once guessed what was happening. She rushed into the bedroom, and tried to get hold of Mollie's leg – but she was too late! Mollie was running between the trees!

"Cat! Chase her! Scratch her! Bring her back at once!" yelled the witch.

The blue-eyed cat at once leapt out of the window and rushed after Mollie. How they ran! Mollie reached the wishing-chair, jumped into it, and cried, "Home, quickly!"

It rose up – but the cat gave an enormous leap and jumped on to one arm of the chair. Mollie tried to push it off, but it dug its claws into the arm, and wouldn't leave go.

"You horrid creature!" said the little girl, almost in tears. "Get off my chair!"

But the cat wouldn't move. The chair rose higher and higher. Mollie wondered what she should do if the cat flew at her – but it didn't. It crawled down into the chair, hid behind a cushion there, and seemed to go to sleep!

After a while Mollie saw that she was near her own garden. She was glad. The chair went down to the playroom, and Peter and Chinky rushed out excitedly. Peter hugged Mollie, and so did Chinky. They had been so worried about her.

Mollie told them her adventure. "And the funny thing is," she said, "the witch's cat is still in the chair! He didn't scratch me – he hid behind the cushion!"

Chinky ran to the chair and lifted up the cushion – yes, there was the cat! It opened its great blue eyes and looked at Chinky.

The pixie stared hard at it. Then he ran his hands

over the cat's sleek back, and shouted in surprise.

"Come here, children, and feel! This isn't a proper witch's cat! Can you feel these bumps on its back?"

Sure enough, Peter and Mollie could quite well feel two little bumps there.

"This cat was a fairy once," said Chinky, in excitement. "You can always tell by feeling along the back. If there are two bumps there, you know that that was where the wings of the fairy grew, once upon a time. I say! I wonder who this fairy was!"

"Can't we change the cat back into its right shape?" asked Peter, in great excitement.

"I'll try!" said clever Chinky. He drew a chalk circle on the floor, and then put a chalk square outside that. He stood between the circle and the square, and put

Both children poured water on the silent cat, whilst Chinky chanted a string of strange words.

374

the cat in the middle. Then he told the children to pour water on the cat whilst he recited some magic words.

Peter got a jug of water, and Mollie got a vase. Both children poured water on the silent cat, whilst Chinky chanted a string of strange words.

And then a most peculiar thing happened! The cat grew larger – and larger. The bumps on its back broke out into a pair of bright blue wings. The cat stood upright on its hind legs – and suddenly the whole of the black fur peeled away and fell off – and inside was the most beautiful fairy that the children had ever imagined!

He had the brightest blue eyes, and shining golden hair, and he smiled in delight at Chinky.

"Thank you!" he said. "I am Prince Merry, brother to the Princess Sylfai. The witch caught me and changed me into a cat at the same time as she caught my lovely sister. She sold her to the Green Enchanter, and she is still a prisoner."

"Oh, your highness!" cried Chinky, bowing low before the beautiful prince. "It is such an honour to have returned you to your right shape. What a good thing Mollie flew to the witch's house!"

"It certainly was!" said Prince Merry. "I suddenly saw she had a wishing-chair out in the wood, though, of course, the witch didn't know that! I was determined to come with her in the magic chair – but I only just managed it! It is the first time I have had a chance to escape from the witch!"

"I wish we could rescue your sister, the Princess!" cried Peter.

"That *would* be splendid!" said the Prince. "If we only could! But before we can get to the hill on which the Green Enchanter lives, we have to get a map to find it – and there is only one map in the world that shows the Enchanter's Hill."

"Who has it?" asked Chinky excitedly.

"The Dear-Me Goblin has it," said Merry. "He lives in the caves of the Golden Hill."

"Then we'll go there the very next time the chair grows wings!" shouted Chinky, Mollie, and Peter.

II

THE DEAR-ME GOBLIN

PRINCE MERRY lived with Chinky in the playroom, waiting for the chair to grow its wings again. Chinky made himself Merry's servant, and did everything for him gladly and proudly. Peter and Mollie thought they were very lucky children – to have a wishing-chair of their own, a pixie for a friend, and a fairy prince living in their playroom. Nobody would believe it if they told the story of their adventures.

It was a whole week before the chair grew its red wings. It was one evening after tea, when Peter, Mollie, Chinky, and the Prince were sitting round the playroom fire, having a game of snap. All four had cards in front of them, when suddenly a draught blew the whole lot together!

"I say! Is the window open?" cried Peter, jumping

up. But it wasn't. He couldn't think where the draught came from when he suddenly saw that it was the chair, flapping its red wings again! Of course! They made the wind that blew the cards together!

"Look!" cried Peter excitedly. "The chair's ready again! Come on! Is there room for us all?"

"No," said Chinky, "but the Prince has wings. So he can fly beside us. Come on – get in! I say, though – hadn't we better take a rug? It's an awfully cold night."

The children pulled a rug from the sofa, and then they and the pixie climbed in the chair, wrapping the rug closely round them. The prince opened the door, and the chair flew out at once. Merry followed it, and held on to one of the arms as he flew, so that he should not miss the way.

The Prince opened the door, and the chair flew out at once.

377

"I told the chair to go to the Dear-Me Goblin's cave," said Chinky. "I hope it knows the way."

It did! It flew to a hill that looked dark and lonely in the starlit night; but as soon as the chair had flown inside a big cave, and come to earth there, the children exclaimed in delight. The inside of the cave shone with a golden light, though there was no lamp of any sort to be seen.

"That's why it's called the Golden Hill," said Merry. "The whole of the hill shines like gold inside. So plenty of goblins live here because they are mean fellows, you know, and are only too pleased to live in a hill where they do not need to buy candles by which to see!"

The children and Chinky explored the golden cave. There was a passage leading away into the heart of the hill, and the four of them walked down it, able to see everything quite clearly.

Along the passage were many doors of all colours. Each door had a little notice on it, giving the name of the goblin who lived there. The children looked at them all, but could not see the name of Dear-Me. At last they came to the end door, and that had no name on at all.

"*This* must be Dear-Me's cave," said Merry. "It's the only one left!"

So they knocked, and the door opened. A queer-looking goblin poked out his head. He wore a wastepaper basket for a hat, and had a pencil in his mouth at which he kept puffing as if it were a pipe!

"Hallo!" he said.

"Hallo!" said Chinky. "What is your name?"

"It's on the door," said the goblin. "I've forgotten what it is."

"But it isn't on the door," said Peter. "There is no name there at all."

"Oh," said the goblin. "Well, come in, whilst I think of it."

They all went in. There was a large and cosy room made out of the cave behind the door. A fire glowed in one corner, and a small bed stuck out of the other. There was a table in the middle, and two or three stools stood here and there. There was no lamp, for the curious golden light shone here too.

"Is your name Dear-Me?" asked Chinky.

"Of course it is," said the goblin. "Every one knows that!"

"Well, *you* didn't seem to know it," said Merry.

"Only because it wasn't on the door," said the goblin. "What have you all come for?"

"Well, we wanted to know if you have the map that shows the hill on which the Green Enchanter lives," said Chinky.

"Yes, I have," said Dear-Me. "But, dear me! I couldn't tell you where it is at the moment!"

"Did you put it in a safe place?" asked the Prince.

"Of course!" said the goblin. "But it is always so difficult to remember safe places, isn't it?"

"Well, tell us one of your safe places, and we'll look there," said Mollie.

"It might be in that drawer," said the goblin, pointing to a drawer in the kitchen table. Mollie opened it, and then stared in the greatest surprise. It was full of pea-pods, turned brown and dry!

Mollie opened the drawer, and then stared in the greatest surprise.

"Dear me!" said the goblin. "So that's where those pea-pods went to last summer. Well, look in the teapot, then, and see if the map's there."

"In the *teapot!*" said Peter, thinking the goblin must be quite mad. However, he looked in the teapot on the dresser, and found it full of safety-pins. The goblin was so pleased to see them.

"I couldn't think *where* I'd put those pins!" he said.

"You know, buttons are always coming off my clothes and I have to pin them up such a lot. So I bought a whole crowd of safety-pins and thought I'd better keep them somewhere safe in case I lost them. So I put them in the teapot – and then I couldn't remember where they were."

"Tell us another of your hiding-places," begged Chinky patiently.

"You might look in the boot-box," said the goblin.

380

They all looked for it.

"Where *is* the boot-box?" asked Peter at last. "Have you put that in a safe place too?"

"Oh, no," said the goblin. "Now let me think. Yes! I remember now – when the laundry came, the carrier wanted the basket back, so I put the clean clothes into the boot-box."

"You do think of some surprising ideas!" said Merry. "I don't suppose the washing will be clean any longer. I suppose this is it, under the mangle."

He pulled out a dirty old box in which clean shirts and collars were stuffed – but except for some old potatoes at the bottom, there was nothing else in the box at all.

"I suppose you use the boot-box for your vegetables as well," said Chinky, shaking the potatoes about.

"Oh, are there some potatoes there?" cried the goblin, pleased. "I'll cook them for my dinner then. I was just going out to buy some, but I couldn't find my hat."

Chinky, Merry, and the children started at the wastepaper basket on the goblin's head. "Well," said Chinky, "you've got *something* on your head – we thought it was meant for a hat."

The goblin took the basket off and looked at it in surprise.

"It's my waste-paper basket!" he said. "Now how did that get there? I spent all the morning looking for it."

"Is *this* your hat?" asked Chinky, picking up something stuffed full with old newspapers.

381

*Chinky, Merry, and the children stared at the waste-paper
basket on the goblin's head.*

382

"Dear me, yes!" said the goblin, pleased. "I must have mistaken it for the basket. I do get into such muddles sometimes. I have so much to do, you know."

"What do you have to do?" asked Mollie curiously.

"Oh – there's getting up – and having meals – and dressing – and dusting – and going to bed," said the goblin. "That reminds me – it's time for something to eat. Will you have a bit of cherry-pie?"

He darted to a cupboard, opened it, and brought out a pie; but as he went to put it on the table he fell over the waste-paper basket, and smash! the pie fell to the floor and the red juice flowed out on to the carpet!

"Dear me!" said the goblin. "That's the end of the pie, I'm afraid. Well, it wasn't a very good pie. Now, what shall I wipe up the mess with?"

He went to the cupboard and caught up the piece of paper that lined the shelf. He was just about to mop up the mess with it when Chinky gave a cry: "Wait!"

The pixie took the paper from him and shouted loudly:

"It's the map! Look! Fancy the goblin using it to line a shelf with! Just the sort of thing he *would* do!"

At that moment another goblin came rushing into the room, crying, "Your chair's flapping its wings!"

"We must go!" shouted Chinky, "or our chair will leave us behind! Good-bye, Dear-Me! Thanks for all the help you didn't give!"

Out they all ran and flung themselves into the chair. Prince Merry had the map safely in his pocket. To think how nearly they had lost it!

"Home, chair!" cried Peter, and off it went!

III

THE ADVENTURE OF THE GREEN ENCHANTER

PETER, Mollie, Prince Merry, and Chinky the pixie all looked eagerly at the dirty old map.

"See!" said Chinky, pointing. "There is the Enchanter's Hill. I will tell the wishing-chair how to get there as soon as it grows its wings again."

"Then we will rescue Sylfai!" cried Merry.

"You can live here with Chinky," said Mollie, looking round the playroom. "I will bring you an old rug, Prince. Let us know when the chair grows its wings again."

But a dreadful thing happened when the chair next grew its pretty red wings and flapped them in the playroom – for Peter was in bed with a cold! When Chinky came climbing up the window to peep into the bedroom (the playroom was at the bottom of the garden, you remember), Mollie was ready to go – but Peter was much too sneezy and snuffly, and he was sure that his mother would be very angry if she came and found him gone. So it was decided that Mollie, Merry, and Chinky should go alone, and Merry promised to look after Mollie. They all said good-bye to Peter and left him. He felt very sad and lonely.

The chair was anxious to fly off. Mollie sat in the seat with Chinky squeezed beside her. The Prince flew near them, holding on occasionally when the

They all said good-bye to Peter and left him.

chair went very fast.

"To the Green Enchanter's Hill!" cried Chinky to the chair. "Go by way of the rainbow, and then over the snowy mountains of Lost Land."

The chair flapped steadily up into the air. The sun shone out. Then there came a big cloud, and rain fell. The sun shone through the rain and made a glorious rainbow. At once the chair flew towards it, higher and higher into the air.

It came to the topmost curve of the glittering rainbow. It balanced itself there – and then, WHOOOOOOOOOSH! It slid all the way down it! What a slide that was! Mollie held her breath, and Merry's hair flew out behind him!

They slid down to the bottom of the rainbow, and then the chair flew steadily on towards some high mountains, whose snowy tops stood up through the clouds.

"There's Lost Land!" cried Chinky, pointing. "If we got lost there, there'd be no finding us again."

"Ooh!" said Mollie, shivering. "I hope the chair doesn't go down there."

It didn't. It flew on and on. Presently a big mountain-top loomed up in the distance, sticking its green head up through the clouds.

"The Green Enchanter's Hill!" cried Chinky, in delight. "We haven't taken long! Now, we must be careful. We don't want the Enchanter to know we're here."

The chair flew downwards. It came to a beautiful garden. It settled down on the ground in a sheltered corner, where high hedges grew all round. Nobody could possibly see them there.

"Now, how can we rescue the Princess?" asked Chinky.

"She and I know a song that our pet canary whistles at home," whispered the Prince. "If I whistle it, she will answer if she hears it, and then we shall know where she is."

He pursed up his lips and began to whistle just like a singing canary. It was wonderful to hear him. When he had whistled for half a minute, he stopped and listened – and, clear as a bird, there came an answering song, just like the voice of a singing canary!

"That's Sylfai!" said Prince Merry joyfully. "Come on – let's go towards the whistling. It's over there."

He and the others crept round the tall hedge and looked about. Stretching in front of them was a small bluebell wood, and in the midst of it, gathering bluebells, was a dainty little Princess!

"Sylfai!" cried Merry, and ran to her. She hugged him and then looked around her nervously.

"The Green Enchanter is somewhere near," she whispered. "He hardly ever leaves me. How are you going to rescue me, Merry?"

"We have a magic wishing-chair behind the hedge," whispered back Merry. "Come along, Sylfai. Come with me, and with Mollie and Chinky. They are my good friends"

The four hurried out of the wood to the hedge; but when they reached it, they stopped – for they could hear an angry voice shouting loudly:

"Come here, chair, I tell you! Come here!"

"It is the Enchanter, who has found your chair!" whispered Sylfai frightened. "Now what shall we do?"

Mollie and the others peeped through the hedge – and they saw a very strange sight! The Enchanter was trying to catch hold of the chair, and it wouldn't let him! Every time he came near it, the chair spread its red wings and flapped away from him. Then it settled down and waited till the angry Enchanter ran at it again. Once more it spread its wings and dodged away.

And then suddenly a most dreadful and surprising thing happened! The chair, tired of dodging the Enchanter, suddenly flew straight up into the air,

"Come here, chair, I tell you! come here!" shouted the Enchanter.

made for the clouds – and disappeared!

"It's gone without us!" said Merry, in dismay. "Whatever shall we do now?"

"Quick!" cried Sylfai, in fright. "The Enchanter will come to look for me, and he'll find you three too. Then he'll make you all prisoners, and it will be dreadful!"

"Where can we hide?" said Mollie, looking round.

"There's an old hollow tree in the wood," said Sylfai, and she ran with them to the middle of the wood. She showed them an enormous oak tree, and in a trice the Prince had climbed half-way up, and was pulling Mollie up. They slipped inside the big hollow, and waited for Chinky to join them. He soon came.

The Prince poked his head out and called to Sylfai: "Can't you join us, Sylfai?"

"Sh!" said the Princess. "The Enchanter is coming!"

Sure enough, a loud and angry voice came sounding through the wood.

"Sylfai! Where are you, Sylfai! Come here at once!"

"I'll see you when I can!" whispered the Princess. "All right, I'm coming!" she called to the Enchanter, and the three in the tree heard the sound of her feet scampering off.

They looked at one another.

"Whatever are we to do?" groaned Chinky. "I don't see how in the world we are to escape now our chair is gone! We *are* in a fix!"

IV

PETER'S OWN ADVENTURE

PETER lay in bed, wishing very much that he could have gone off in the wishing-chair with the others. He dozed for a little while, and then woke up feeling so much better that he decided to get up. He jumped out of bed and ran to the window to see what sort of afternoon it was.

And, as he looked out of the window, he saw something that made him stare very hard indeed! He saw something strange flying high up in the sky – not a bird – not an aeroplane – not a balloon! What could it be?

It came down lower – and then Peter saw that it was the magic wishing-chair!

"But it's empty!" said Peter to himself, feeling very much afraid. "Where are the others? Oh dear, I do so hope that the Green Enchanter hasn't caught them! However will they escape, if the wishing-chair has come back without them?"

He dressed quickly, watching the wishing-chair as it came down to earth and flew in at the open door of the playroom at the bottom of the garden.

He slipped downstairs and ran to the playroom. The chair was there, making a curious noise as if it were out of breath!

"Wait a minute, chair, before you make your wings disappear!" cried Peter, flinging himself into the seat.

"You must fly back again to Mollie and the others! Do you hear? I don't know where they are – but you must go to them, for they will be in a great fright without you!"

The chair made a grumbling, groaning sort of noise. It was tired and didn't want to fly any more. But Peter thumped the back of it and commanded it to fly.

"Do you hear me, chair? Fly back to Mollie!" he ordered.

The chair flapped its wings more quickly and flew out of the door with a big sigh. It flew steadily upwards, found a rainbow and slid down it, much to Peter's delight. Then it came to the Lost Land, and Peter saw the snowy tops of the mountains sticking up through the clouds, just as the others had done. The chair was very tired as it flew over these mountains, and, to Peter's dismay, it began to fly downwards as if it meant to rest itself on one of the summits.

"You mustn't do that!" cried Peter. "No one is ever found again if they go to the Lost Land."

But the chair took no notice. It flew down to a snowy peak and settled itself there. Almost at once Peter spied some bearded gnomes coming up the mountain towards them, and he knew they were going to catch and keep him and the chair. He jumped off the chair, picked it up, and waved it in the air until it started flapping its wings again. Then the little boy jumped into it, and up they flew once more, leaving the disappointed gnomes behind them.

"This is my own adventure!" thought Peter. "But

it's lonely, having adventures all by myself."

At last he saw the green peak of the Enchanter's high hill poking up through the clouds. Down flew the chair to the castle on the top. It came to rest in the very same place where it had rested before – in the sheltered place between high hedges. Peter jumped off and looked round. He thought it would be a good idea to tie the chair up, as Chinky had once done before – then it couldn't fly away without him. So he tied a string from its leg to the hedge, then left it.

As he was creeping round the hedge he saw a little figure running nearby. It was the Princess Sylfai, though he did not know it. He gave a low whistle, meaning to ask her if she knew where his friends were. She heard him and looked round. When she saw him, she gave a scream, for she did not know who he was.

"I say! Don't be frightened! Come here!" cried Peter. But she ran away all the faster. So Peter gave chase, thinking that he really must catch her and ask her if she knew where Mollie and the others were. The little fairy raced along, panting, and disappeared into the bluebell wood.

She ran to the hollow tree where Mollie, Prince Merry, and Chinky the Pixie were hiding, and called for help.

"There's an enemy after me!" she panted. Prince Merry heard his sister calling for help, and he at once climbed out of the hollow tree and drew his sword. He would kill the enemy!

Sylfai ran to him, and pointed behind her. "He is coming!" she panted. "Hide behind this tree, Merry and jump out at him as he runs by!"

"I say! Don't be frightened! Come here!" cried Peter.

So Merry hid behind the tree, waiting, his sword drawn. Peter came up, panting and puffing, wondering where the little fairy had gone.

"*Now* I've got you!" shouted Prince Merry in his fiercest voice, as Peter ran by the tree behind which he was hiding. He pounced at the surprised boy with his sword ready to strike – and then stopped in amazement!

"Peter!" he cried. "I nearly wounded you! How did you get here?"

"I came in the wishing-chair!" said Peter. "I saw it

"Now I've got you!" shouted Prince Merry, as Peter ran by the tree.

come home alone, and I was afraid something had happened to you all. So I made it come back again. I saw this little fairy and wanted to ask her where you all were, but she ran away."

"This is my sister, Princess Sylfai," said Merry, "and this, Sylfai, is Peter. Hi, Mollie and Chinky! Come out! Here's Peter – and he's got the wishing-chair!"

"What's all this NOISE!" an angry voice suddenly shouted. "Sylfai! WHERE ARE YOU?"

"There's the Green Enchanter!" said Sylfai, in dismay. "What shall we do?"

"Run for the chair!" cried Peter. "Come on!"

All five of them ran out of the wood towards the hedge behind which the chair was tied – but will you believe it, when they crept round the hedge, there was the Enchanter sitting in their chair, a wicked grin on his face, waiting for them to come!

"Peter! Chinky! There's only one thing to do!" whispered Merry desperately. "We'll run at him, tip him off the chair, and, before he knows what is happening, we'll be off into the air. Mollie and Sylfai, keep by us!"

Then, with a loud whoop, Peter, Chinky, and the Prince hurled themselves at the astonished Enchanter, tipped up the chair, and sent him sprawling on his face! The Prince quickly picked up the Enchanter's cloak and wound it tightly two or three times round the angry man's head, so that he could not speak or see!

Whilst the Enchanter was trying to unwrap himself, Mollie and Sylfai squeezed into the chair. Chinky sat on one arm, and Peter sat on the other. Merry cut the rope, and cried, "Home, Chair!"

It rose up swiftly into the air, with Merry guiding it, flying beside it.

"We're safe!" cried Merry. "Thank you, Peter, for daring to come on an adventure by yourself!"

V

THE OLD, OLD MAN

THE wishing-chair had not grown its wings for a long time. Chinky and the children had become quite tired of waiting for another adventure. Mollie thought perhaps the magic had gone out of it, and it might be just an ordinary chair now. It was most disappointing.

395

It was a lovely fine day, and Peter wanted to go for a walk. "Come with us, Chinky," he said. "It's no use staying in the playroom with the chair. It won't grow its wings today!"

So Chinky the pixie squashed his pointed ears under one of Peter's old caps, put on an old overcoat of Peter's, and set out with the children. Jane the housemaid saw them going, and she called after them:

"If you're going out, I shall give the playroom a good clean out. It hasn't been done for a long time."

"All right!" called back Mollie. "We won't be home till dinner-time."

They had a lovely walk, and ran back to the playroom about dinner-time. It did look clean. Jane was just finishing the dusting. Chinky waited outside, for he did not want to be seen. But suddenly Peter turned pale, and said, "Oh, where's the chair? Mollie, where's the chair?"

"Oh, do you mean that old chair?" said Jane, gathering up her brushes. "An old, old man came for it. He said it had to be mended, or something. He took it away."

She went up to the house, leaving the two children staring at each other in dismay. Chinky ran in, and how he stared when he heard the news!

"I know who the old man must have been!" he cried. "It's old Bone-Lazy, who lives at the foot of Breezy Hill. He hates walking, so I expect he thought he'd get hold of our wishing-chair if he could. Then he'd be able to go everywhere in it!"

"How can we get it back?" asked Mollie, almost in tears.

"I don't know," said Chinky. "We'll have a try anyhow. Come back here after dinner, and we'll go to his cottage."

So after their dinner the two children ran back to their playroom. They found a most astonishing sight. There was no Chinky there – only an old woman, dressed in a black shawl that was drawn right over her head!

"Who are you?" asked Mollie. Then she gave a cry of surprise – for, when the old woman raised her head, Mollie saw the merry face of Chinky the pixie!

"This disguise is part of my plan for getting back our magic chair," explained Chinky. "Now I want you to go with me to Bone-Lazy's cottage, and I shall pretend to fall down and hurt myself outside. You will run up and help me to my feet – then you will help

"Who are you?" asked Mollie.

397

me to BoneLazy's cottage, knock at the door, and explain that I'm an old lady who needs a drink of water and a rest."

"And whilst we're in the cottage we look round to see if our chair is there!" cried Peter. "What a marvellous plan!"

They set off. Chinky took them through a little wood they never seemed to have seen before, and, when they came out on the other side of it, they were in country that looked quite different! The flowers were brighter, the trees were full of blossom, and brilliant birds flew here and there!

"I never knew it was so easy to get to Fairyland!" said Mollie, in surprise.

"It isn't!" said Chinky, with a grin, lifting up his black shawl and peeping at the children merrily. "You couldn't possibly find it unless you had me with you!"

"Is that Bone-Lazy's cottage?" asked Mollie, pointing towards a cottage at the foot of a nearby hill.

Chinky nodded.

"I'll go on ahead now," he said. "Then you must do your part as we have planned. Good luck!"

He hobbled on in front, looking for all the world like an old woman. When he came just by the cottage, Chinky suddenly gave a dreadful groan, and fell to the ground. At once the children rushed up and pulled the pretended old woman to her feet. From the corner of his eye Peter saw some one looking out of the window of the cottage at them.

"Quick! Quick!" he cried very loudly to Mollie. "This poor woman has fainted! We must take her into

"Is that Bone-Lazy's cottage?" asked Mollie, pointing towards
a cottage at the foot of a nearby hill.

399

this cottage and ask for a drink of water for her. She must rest!"

They half-carried Chinky to the cottage door and knocked loudly. An old, old man opened it. He had narrow cunning eyes and the children didn't like the look of him at all. They explained about the old woman and took her into the cottage. "Could you get a drink of water?" said Mollie.

The old chap left the room, grumbling. "I shall have to go to the well," he muttered crossly.

"Good!" thought Peter. "It will give us time for a look round."

But, to their great disappointment, their wishing-chair was not to be seen! The cottage only had one room, so it did not take them long to hunt all round it. Before they had time to say anything the old, old man came back with a jug of water.

Mollie took it from him – and then she suddenly noticed a very curious thing. A great draught was coming from a big chest-of-drawers standing in a corner. She stared at it in surprise. How could it be making such a wind round her feet? It was only a chest-of-drawers!

But wait a minute! *Was* it only a chest-of-drawers? Quick as lightning Mollie upset the jug of water, and then turned to Bone-Lazy in apology. "Oh! I'm so sorry! I've upset the water! How very careless of me! I wonder if you'd be good enough to get some more?"

The old man shouted at her rudely, snatched up the jug, and went down the garden to the well. The others stared at Mollie in surprise.

"Whatever did you do that for?" said Peter.

"There's something queer about that chest-of-drawers," said Mollie. "There's a strange wind coming from it. Feel, Chinky! I upset the jug just to get the old man out of the way for a minute.

"Stars and moon! He's changed our chair into a chest!" cried Chinky. "It must have grown wings, but we can't see them because of Bone-Lazy's magic! Quick, all of you! Jump into a drawer, and I'll wish us away!"

The children pulled open two of the enormous drawers and sat inside. Chinky sat on the top, crying "Home, wishing-chair, home!"

The chest groaned, and the children heard a flapping noise. Just at that moment the old man came into the room again with a jug of water. How he stared! But, before he could do anything, the chest-of-drawers rose up in the air, knocked the water out of his hand, almost pushed him over, and squeezed itself out of the door.

"You won't steal our chair again!" shouted cheeky Chinky, and he flung his black shawl neatly over Bone-Lazy's head.

The chest rose high into the air, and then a funny thing happened. It began to change back into the chair they all knew so well! Before they could think what to do, the children found themselves sitting safely on the seat, for the drawers all vanished into cushions! Chinky was on the top of the back, singing for joy.

"That *was* a marvellous plan of yours!" said Peter.

"Well, Mollie was the sharpest!" laughed Chinky. "It was she who noticed the draught from the chest. Good old Mollie!"

401

VI

TOPSY-TURVY LAND

ONCE the wishing-chair played a very silly trick on Mollie. The children were cross about it for a long time, and so was Chinky the pixie.

The chair had grown its wings and the children sat on the seat as usual with Chinky on the back.

"Where shall we go?" asked Peter.

"Let's go to Topsy-Turvy Land," said Chinky with a laugh. "It's a funny place to see – everything wrong, you know! It will give us a good laugh!"

"Yes, let's go there!" said Peter, pleased. "It would be fun."

"To Topsy-Turvy Land, chair!" commanded Chinky. The chair rose up in the air and flew off at once. It flapped its wings fast, and very soon the children had flown right over the spires of Fairyland and were gazing down on a strange-looking land.

The chair flew downwards. It came to rest in a village, and the children and Chinky jumped off. They stared in surprise at the people there.

Nobody seemed to know how to dress properly! Coats were on back to front, and even upside down. One little man had his trousers on his arms! He wore his legs through the sleeves of his coat. The children began to giggle, and the little man looked at them in surprise.

"Have you had bad news?" he asked.

"Of course not," said Peter. "We shouldn't laugh if we had!"

You would if you lived in Topsy-Turvy Land," grinned Chinky. "Look at this woman coming along, crying into her handkerchief. Ask her what's the matter."

"What is the matter?" asked Mollie. The woman mopped her streaming eyes and said, "Oh, I've just found my purse, which I lost, and I'm so glad."

"There you are!" said Chinky. "They cry when they're glad and smile when they're sad!"

"Look at that man over there!" said Mollie suddenly. "He's getting into his house by the window instead of through the door; and do look! his door has lace curtains hung over it. Does he think it's a window?"

"I expect so," said Chinky, with a grin. "Do you see that little boy over there with gloves on his feet and

"What is the matter?" asked Mollie.

shoes on his hands? I must say I wouldn't like to live in Topsy-Turvy Land!"

The children didn't want to live there either – but it really was fun to see all the curious things around them. They saw children trying to read a book backwards. They watched a cat crunching up a bone and a dog lapping milk, so it seemed as if even the animals were topsy-turvy too!

Suddenly a policeman came round the corner, and, as soon as he saw the children and Chinky with their chair, he bustled up to them in a hurry, taking out a notebook as large as an atlas as he did so.

"Where is your licence to keep a chair?" he asked sternly. He took out a rubber and prepared to write with it.

"You can't write with a rubber!" said Mollie.

"I shall write with whatever I please!" said the policeman. "Yes, and I shall rub out with my pencil if I want to. Now, then, where's your licence?"

"You don't need to have a licence for a chair," said Chinky, impatiently. "Don't be silly. It isn't a motorcar."

"Well, it's got wings, so it must be an aeroplane chair," said the policeman, tapping with his rubber on his enormous notebook. "You have to have a licence for that in this country."

"We haven't a licence and we're not going to get one," said Peter, and he pushed the policeman's notebook away, for it was sticking into him. The policeman was furious. He glared at Chinky. He glared at Peter. He glared at Mollie – and then he glared at the chair. The chair seemed to feel uncomfortable. It hopped about on the pavement and tried to edge away from the policeman.

"I shall take your chair to prison," said the policeman, and he made a grab at it. The chair hopped away – and then hopped back unexpectedly and trod hard on one of the policeman's feet. Then off it went again. Chinky ran after it.

"Hie, come back, chair!" he yelled. "We can't have you going off like this. Don't be afraid. We won't let the policeman get you! Come on, Mollie and Peter – jump into the chair quickly, and we'll fly off."

Peter ran after the chair – but the policeman caught hold of Mollie's arm. Chinky and Peter jumped into the chair before they saw what was happening to Mollie – and, dear me, before they could get off it again, the chair spread its red wings and rose up into the air!

"Peter! Chinky! Don't leave me here!" shouted Mollie, trying to wriggle away from the policeman.

"Chair, fly down again!" commanded Chinky.

But, do you know, the wishing-chair was so scared of being put into prison that it wouldn't do as it was told! It flew on, straight up into the air with Peter and Chinky, and left poor Mollie behind. Nothing Chinky could say would make that disobedient chair go down again to fetch Mollie. It flew on and on and was soon out of sight.

Mollie was terribly upset. She began to cry, and the policeman stared at her. "What is amusing you?" he asked. "What are you glad about?"

"I'm *not* amused or glad!" said Mollie. "I'm not like you silly topsy-turvy people, crying when I'm glad, and laughing when I'm sad. I don't belong to this horrid, stupid country at all!"

"Dear me, I didn't know that," said the policeman, putting away his notebook. "Why didn't you say so before?"

"You never asked me," said Mollie, half angry, half frightened. "My friend, the pixie who was here just now, will probably tell the pixie King how you kept me here, and he will be VERY ANGRY INDEED."

"Oh, you must go home at once," said the policeman, who was now shaking like a jelly with fright. "You shall catch a bus home. I will pay your fare myself. I will show you where the bus is."

He took Mollie to a stopping-place – but as the buses all went straight on, and passengers had to jump on and off whilst it was going, Mollie thought it was silly to call it a stopping-place! It was a comical-looking bus, too, for although the driver drove it by a wheel, he had a whip by his side and cracked it loudly whenever the bus seemed to slow down, just as if it were a horse!

The policeman put Mollie on the bus as it came past the stopping-place and threw some money at the conductor. He picked it up and threw it back. Mollie thought that the topsy-turvy people were the maddest she had ever seen.

She sat down on a seat. "Standing room only in this bus," said the conductor. "Give me your ticket, please."

"Well, you've got to give *me* one," said Mollie. "And what do you mean by saying 'standing room only?' There are heaps of seats."

She sat down and the conductor glared at her. "The seats will be worn out if people keep sitting on them," he said. "And where's your ticket, please?"

"I'll show it to you when you give me one," said Mollie, impatiently. "Give me a ticket for home. I live in Hilltown."

"Then you're going the wrong way," said the conductor. "But as a matter of fact no bus goes to Hilltown. So you can stay in my bus if you like. One is as good as another."

Mollie jumped up in a rage. She leapt out of the bus and began to walk back to where she had started from. What a silly place Topsy-Turvy Land was. She would never get home from here!

Just as she got back to the street from which the bus had started, Mollie saw Chinky! *How* pleased she was. She shouted to him and waved. "Chinky! Chinky! Here I am!"

Chinky saw her and grinned. He came over to her and gave her a hug.

"Sorry to have left you like that, Mollie," he said. "The wishing-chair did behave badly. I've left it at home in the corner! It is very much ashamed of itself."

"Well, if you left the chair at home how did you come here?" asked Mollie in astonishment.

"I borrowed a couple of Farmer Straw's geese," grinned Chinky. "Look! There they are, over there. There's one for you to fly back on and one for me. Come on, or Farmer Straw will miss his fat old geese."

"Chinky, quick! There's that policeman again!"

407

cried Mollie suddenly. "Oh – and he's going to the geese – and getting his big notebook out – I'm sure he's going to ask them for a licence or something! Let's get them, quick!"

Chinky and Mollie raced to where the two geese were staring in great astonishment at the policeman, who was looking all around them, trying, it seemed, to find their number-plates! Mollie jumped on to the back of one and Chinky on to the other.

"Hie!" cried the policeman, "have these geese got numbers and lamps?"

"I'll go and ask the farmer they belong to!" laughed Chinky. The geese rose up into the air and the wind they made with their big wings blew off the policeman's helmet.

"Hie!" cried the policeman, "have these geese got numbers and lamps?"

"I'll take your names, I'll take your names!" he yelled in a temper.

He scribbled furiously in his notebook – and Mollie laughed so much that she nearly fell off her goose.

"He doesn't know our names – and he's trying to write with his rubber!" she giggled. "Oh dear! What a topsy-turvy creature!"

Peter was delighted to see Chinky and Mollie again. The two geese took them to the playroom door, cackled good-bye to Chinky, and flew off down to the farm.

The wishing-chair stood in the corner. Its wings had disappeared. It looked very forlorn indeed. It knew it was in disgrace.

Chinky turned it round the right way again. "We'll forgive you if you'll behave yourself next time!" he said.

The chair creaked loudly. "It's sorry now!" grinned Chinky. "Come on – what about a game of ludo before you have to go in?"

VII

THE CHAIR RUNS AWAY AGAIN

ONE afternoon Mollie, Peter, and Chinky were in the playroom together, playing at Kings and Queens. They each took it in turn to be a King or a Queen, and they wore the red rug for a cloak, and a cardboard crown covered with gold paper. The wishing-chair was the throne.

It was Peter's turn to be King. He put on the crown and wound the red rug round his shoulders for a cloak. He did feel grand. He sat down in the wishing-chair and arranged the cloak round him, so that it fell all round the chair and on to the floor too, just like a real king's cloak.

Then Mollie and Chinky had to curtsy and bow to him, and ask for his commands. He could tell them to do anything he liked.

"Your Majesty, what would you have me do today?" asked Mollie, curtsying low.

"I would have you go and pick me six dandelions, six daisies, and six buttercups," said Peter, grandly, waving his hand. Mollie curtsyed again and walked out backwards, nearly falling over a stool as she did so.

Then Chinky asked Peter what *he* was to do for him. "Your Majesty, what would you have me do?" he said, bowing low.

"I would have you go to the cupboard and get me a green sweet out of the bottle there," said Peter commandingly. Chinky went to the cupboard. He couldn't see the bottle at first. He moved the tins about and hunted for it. He didn't see what was happening behind him!

Peter didn't see either. But what was happening was that the wishing-chair was growing its wings – under the red rug that was all around its legs! Peter sat in the chair, waiting impatiently for his commands to be obeyed – and the chair flapped its red wings under the rug and wondered why it could not flap them as easily as usual!

Mollie was in the garden gathering the flowers

that Peter had ordered. Chinky was still hunting for the bottle of sweets. The wishing-chair flapped its wings harder than ever – it suddenly rose into the air, and flew swiftly out of the door before Peter could jump out, and before Chinky could catch hold of it. It was gone!

"Hie, Mollie, Mollie!" yelled Chinky in alarm. "The wishing-chair's gone – and Peter's gone with it!"

Mollie came tearing into the playroom. "I saw it!" she panted. "Oh, why didn't Peter or you see that its wings had grown? Now, it's gone off with Peter, and we don't know where!"

"We didn't see its wings growing because the red rug hid its legs!" said Chinky. "It must have grown them under the rug and flown off before any of us guessed!"

"Well, what shall we do?" asked Mollie. "What will happen to Peter?"

"It depends where he's gone," said Chinky. "Did you see which way the chair went?"

"Towards the west," said Mollie. "Peter was yelling and shouting like anything – but he couldn't stop the chair."

"Well, we'd better go on a journey of our own," said Chinky. "I'll catch Farmer Straw's two geese again. They won't like it much – but it can't be helped. We must go after Peter and the chair somehow!"

He ran off down to the farm. Presently Mollie heard the noise of flapping wings, and down from the sky came Chinky, riding on the back of one of the geese, and leading the other by a piece of thick string.

411

The geese hissed angrily as they came to the ground.

"They are most annoyed about it," said Chinky to Mollie. "They only came when I promised them that I wouldn't let Farmer Straw take them to market next week."

"Ss-ss-ss-ss!" hissed the big geese, and one tried to peck at Mollie's fat legs. Chinky smacked it.

"Behave yourself!" he said. "If you peck Mollie I'll change your beak into a trumpet, and then you'll only be able to toot, not cackle or hiss!"

Mollie laughed. "You do say some funny things, Chinky," she said. She got on to the goose's back. Up

"Ss-ss-ss-ss!" hissed the big geese, and one tried to peck at Mollie's fat legs. Chinky smacked it.

in the air it went, flapping its enormous white wings.

"We'll go to the cloud castle first of all," said Chinky. "The fairies there may have seen Peter going by and can tell us where they think the chair might have been going."

So they flew to an enormous white cloud that towered up into the sky. As they drew near it Mollie could see that it had turrets, and was really a cloud castle. She thought it was the loveliest thing she had ever seen.

There was a great gateway in the cloud castle. The geese flew through it and landed in a misty courtyard. Mollie was just going to get off when Chinky shouted to her.

"Don't get off, Mollie – you haven't got cloud-shoes on and you'd fall right through to the earth below!"

Mollie stayed on her goose. Small fairies dressed in all the colours of the rainbow came running into the courtyard, chattering in delight to see Mollie and Chinky. They wore cloud-shoes, rather like big flat snow-shoes, and with these they were able to step safely on the cloud that made their castle.

"Come in and have some lemonade!" cried the little folk. But Chinky shook his head.

"We are looking for a boy in a flying chair," he said. "Have you see him?"

"Yes!" cried the fairies, crowding round the geese, who cackled and hissed at them. "He passed about fifteen minutes ago. The chair had red wings and was flying strongly towards the west. Hurry and you may catch it up!"

"Thank you!" cried Chinky. He shook the string

reins of his goose, and he and Mollie flew up into the air once more, and went steadily westwards.

"There is a gnome who lives in a tall tower some miles westwards," said Chinky. "It is so tall that it sticks out above the clouds. We will make for there, and see if he has seen anything of Peter and the wishing-chair."

The geese flew on, cackling to one another. They were still in a bad temper. Chinky kept a look out for the tall tower – but Mollie saw it first. It looked very strange. It was sticking right through a big black cloud, and, as it was made of bright silver, it shone brilliantly.

There was a small window at the top. It was open. The geese flew down to the window-sill and Chinky stuck his head inside.

"Hie, gnome of the tower! Are you in?"

"Yes!" yelled a voice. "If that is the baker leave me a brown loaf, please."

"It isn't the baker!" shouted Chinky. "Come on up here!"

"Well, if it's the butcher, leave me a pound of sausages!" yelled the voice.

"It isn't the butcher!" shouted back Chinky, getting cross. "And it isn't the milkman or the grocer or the newspaper boy or the fishmonger either!"

"And it isn't the postman!" cried Mollie. "It's Chinky and Mollie!"

The gnome was surprised. He climbed up the many steps of his tower till he came to the top. Then he put his head out of the window and gaped in amazement to see Mollie and Chinky on their two geese.

"Hallo!" he said. "Where do *you* come from?"

"Never mind that," said Chinky. "We've come to ask you if you've seen a boy on a flying chair."

"Yes," said the gnome at once. "He passed about twenty minutes ago. I thought he was a king or something because he wore a golden crown. He was going towards the land of the Scally-Wags."

"Oh my!" said Chinky in dismay. "Are you sure?"

"Of course I am," said the gnome, nodding his big head. "I thought he was the baker coming at first."

"You think everyone's the baker!" said Chinky, and he jerked the reins of his goose. "Come on, goose! To the land of the Scally-Wags."

The geese flew off. The gnome climbed out on the window-sill and began to polish his silver tower with a big check duster.

"Does he keep that tower polished himself?" said

The gnome climbed out on the window-sill and began to polish his silver tower with a big check duster.

Mollie in surprise. "Goodness, it must keep him busy all the week!"

"It does," said Chinky, grinning. "Because as soon as he's done it all and reached the top, the bottom is dirty again and he has to begin all over again!"

"Chinky, you didn't sound very pleased when you knew that Peter and the chair had gone to the Land of the Scally-Wags," said Mollie. "Why weren't you?"

"Well, the Scally-Wags are horrid people," said Chinky. "You see, to that land go all the bad folk of Fairyland, Goblin-Land, Brownie-Town, Pixie-Land, Gnome-Country, and the rest. They call themselves Scally-Wags, and they are just as horrid as they sound. If Peter goes there he will be treated like a Scally-Wag, and expected to steal and tell fibs and behave very badly. And if he doesn't, they will say he is a spy and lock him up."

"Oh, Chinky, I do think that's horrid," said Mollie in dismay. "Peter will hate being in a land like that."

"Well, don't worry, I dare say we shall be able to rescue him all right," said Chinky – though really he had no idea at all how to save Peter. Chinky himself had never been to the Land of Scally-Wags before!

The geese cackled and hissed. They were getting tired. Chinky hoped they would be able to go on flying till they reached Scally-Wag Land. Mollie leaned over and looked down.

"Look, Chinky," she said. "Is that Scally-Wag Land? Do you see those houses down there – and that funny railway line – and that river with those ships on?"

"Yes," said Chinky, "that must be Scally-Wag Land. Down, geese, and land there!"

The geese flew downwards. They landed by the river, and as soon as Chinky and Mollie had jumped off, the two geese paddled into the water and began to swim. Chinky tied their strings to a post, for he was afraid they might fly off.

A Scally-Wag ran up to him.

"Where do you come from?" he asked. "Are you messengers from anywhere?"

"No," said Chinky. "We've come to look for some one who came to this land by mistake. We want to take him back."

"No one leaves this land once they are here," said the Scally-Wag. "I believe you are spies!"

"Indeed we are not!" said Mollie. The Scally-Wag drew a whistle from his belt and blew on it loudly. Chinky looked alarmed. He caught hold of Mollie's hand.

"Run!" he said. "If they think we are spies they will lock us up!"

Off went the two, running at top speed, with the angry Scally-Wag after them.

Off went the two, running at top speed, with the angry Scally-Wag after them. They didn't know where they were going! They only knew that they must run and run and run!

VIII

THE LAND OF SCALLY-WAGS

MOLLIE and Chinky ran down the river-path, the Scally-Wag shouting after them.

"Spies!" he called. "Stop them! Spies!" Chinky dragged Mollie on and on. They were both good runners. Another Scally-Wag, hearing the first one shouting, tried to stop Chinky – but the pixie gave him a fierce push and he toppled into the river, splash! How he spluttered and shouted! That gave Chinky an idea.

He squeezed through a hedge and pulled Mollie after him. Then he lay in wait for the shouting Scally-Wag. As soon as he was through the hedge Chinky gave him a push too – and into the river he went, head-first, squealing like a rabbit! Mollie couldn't help laughing, for he seemed all arms and legs. The water wasn't deep, so he couldn't drown – but dear me, how he yelled!

"Come on, Mollie," said Chinky. "We seem to be behaving just as badly as Scally-Wags, pushing people into the river like this!"

They ran on. They seemed to run for miles. They

asked every Scally-Wag they met if he had seen a little boy in that land, but nobody had. They all shook their heads and said the same thing.

"There is no little boy in this land."

"Well, it's really very peculiar," said Chinky to Mollie. "He must be *some*where here!"

"I say, Chinky, I'm getting so hungry," said Mollie. "Aren't you?"

"Yes, very," said Chinky. "Let's knock at this cottage door and see if they will give us something to eat."

So he knocked – rat-a-tat-tat. The door opened and a sharp-eyed little goblin looked out.

"What do you want?" he asked.

"We are hungry," said Mollie. "Could you give us anything to eat?"

"Look!" said the goblin, pointing down the lane to where a baker's cart was standing, full of loaves. "Go and take one of the baker's loaves. He's gossiping somewhere. He won't miss one!"

"What do you want?" asked the goblin.

419

"But we can't do that!" said Mollie in horror. "That's stealing!"

"Don't be silly," said the goblin, looking at her out of his small, sharp eyes. "You don't mind stealing, do you? I've never met a Scally-Wag who minded stealing yet! *I'll* steal a loaf for you if you are afraid of being caught!"

He set off towards the cart, keeping close by the hedge so that he wouldn't be seen. Mollie and Chinky stared at one another in dismay.

"Chinky, what horrible people live in this land," said Mollie. "Stop him! We can't let him steal like that. I would never eat any bread that had been stolen."

"Let's warn the baker," said Chinky. But before they could find him, the goblin had sneaked up to the little cart and had grabbed a new loaf. Then back he scurried to Mollie and Chinky and gave them the loaf, grinning all over his face.

"I'm sorry, but we couldn't have it," said Chinky. "Stealing is wrong."

"Not in Scally-Wag Land," said the goblin, his cunning eyes twinkling.

"It's wrong *any*where," said Mollie firmly. "Come on, Chinky. We'll put this loaf back into the cart."

They set off to the cart – but do you know, just as they were putting the loaf back, that horrid little goblin began to shout for all he was worth. "Baker, Baker! Thieves are at your cart! Look out!"

The baker came hurrying out. He caught hold of Chinky and began to shake him. "You bad Scally-Wag!" he cried.

"I'm not a Scally-Wag! I was just putting back

420

a loaf that the goblin stole!" cried Chinky.

"You are a fibber!" said the baker, and he shook Chinky again until his teeth rattled. Mollie ran to the rescue. She tried to catch hold of the baker's arm – but he pushed her and sent her flying. She caught at the little cart to try and save herself – and it went over! All the loaves rolled out into the road.

The baker gave a loud yell and ran to his cart. The watching goblin shrieked with delight. Mollie and Chinky ran off as fast as they could, crying, "We're so sorry! But it was your own fault for not believing us!"

They ran until they came to a field of buttercups. They squeezed through a gap in the hedge, and sat down to get their breath.

"I'm thirsty as well as hungry now," said Mollie. "Where can we get a drink? If we went and asked for a drink of water surely no Scally-Wag would want to steal that for us! Look, there's a cottage over there, Chinky. Let's go and ask."

They went to the cottage, hot and thirsty and tired. A brownie woman came to the door. She was a cross-looking creature.

"I thought you were the milkman," she said.

"No, he's just down the road there," said Chinky, pointing. "Please, Mam, may we have a drink of water."

"I'll get you a drink of milk!" said the woman, and to Chinky's surprise she darted down the road to the milkman's little hand-cart, and turned on the tap of the churn. The milk ran out of the tap on to the road.

"Come on!" said the woman. "Drink this!"

"But we can't do that!" cried Mollie in surprise

421

and disgust. "That's stealing. Oh, do turn off the tap. The milk is all going to waste!"

The milkman could be heard coming down some one's path, whistling. The woman ran back to her house, leaving the tap turned on. The milkman heard his milk running to waste and ran to turn off the tap, shouting angrily, "Who did this? Wait till I catch them!"

"They did it, those children did it! I saw them!" cried the brownie woman from her door. The milkman saw Chinky and Mollie standing nearby and made a dart at them. But this time they got away before they were caught. They ran down the lane and darted inside a little dark shed to hide.

"It's too bad," said Mollie. "These Scally-Wags keep doing horrid things and blaming them on to us. I do hate them!"

"Sh!" said Chinky. "There's the milkman coming after us. Cover yourself in this old sack, Mollie, and I'll do the same."

They lay down in a corner, covered with the sacks. The milkman looked into the shed and ran on. Mollie sat up. She looked at Chinky and laughed.

"You do look dirty and hot and untidy," she said.

"So do you," said Chinky. "In fact, we look like proper little Scally-Wags. They all look dirty and untidy too! Now, where shall we go next! If only we could find Peter!"

They went out of the shed. The hot sun shone down on them. They felt thirstier than ever. They saw a little stream running nearby, looking cool and clear.

"What about getting a drink from that?" said Mollie.

"Well, I don't like drinking from streams," Chinky said. "But really, I'm dreadfully thirsty! Let's try it. But don't drink too much, Mollie."

The two of them knelt down by the stream, took water into their cupped hands and drank. Ooooh! It was so cold and delicious. Just as they finished, and were feeling much better, they heard a voice behind them.

They turned and saw a wizard behind them.

423

"That will be twopence each, please. You have drunk from my stream."

They turned and saw a wizard behind them, in a tall, pointed hat, and cloak embroidered with stars.

"We haven't any money," said Chinky.

"Then you had better come with me and work for me for one day to pay for the drinks you have had," said the wizard. He tried to grab hold of Mollie – but quick as thought Chinky lifted his fist and brought it down on the wizard's pointed hat. It was crushed right down over his long nose, and he couldn't see a thing!

Once more Mollie and Chinky ran. "Oh dear," panted Mollie, "we really are behaving just like Scally-Wags, Chinky – but we can't seem to help it!"

"Look! There's the river again!" said Chinky in delight. "And there are our two geese. Let's get on their backs, Mollie, and go away from this land. I'm sure Peter isn't here. No one seems to have seen him. I'm tired of being here."

"All right," said Mollie. They ran down the river-bank and called to the geese.

"Come here! We want to fly farther on!"

And then, to their great surprise, a witch in a green shawl stood up on the bank and cried, "Hie! Leave my geese alone!"

"They are not yours, they are ours!" yelled Chinky in anger. He cut the string as the geese came swimming to the bank. The witch tried to grab the two big birds – and in a fright they spread their big wings, flew up into the air and away! Mollie and Chinky watched them in the greatest dismay. Their way of escape had gone!

Chinky was furious with the witch. Before Mollie could stop him he gave her a push, and she went flying into the water. Splash!

"Chinky! You mustn't keep pushing people into the water!" cried Mollie, turning to run away again – but this time it was too late. The witch shouted a few magic words as she made her way out of the river – and lo and behold, Chinky and Mollie found that they could not move a step!

"So you thought you could push me into the river and run away, did you?" said the witch. "Well, you were mistaken! I shall now take you before our King – and no doubt he will see that you are well punished. March!"

The two found that they could walk – but only where the witch commanded. Very miserable indeed they marched down a long, long road, the witch behind them, and at last came to a small palace. Up the steps they went,

The guards cried, "advance!" and the three of them walked down a great hall.

425

and the witch called to the guard there.

"Two prisoners for the King! Make way!"

The guards cried, "Advance!" and the three of them, Mollie, Chinky, and the witch, walked down a great hall. Sitting on a throne at the end, raised high, was the King, wearing a golden crown and a red cloak.

And oh, whatever do you think! Mollie and Chinky could hardly believe their eyes – for the King was no other than Peter – yes, Peter himself! He was still wearing his golden cardboard crown and the red rug for a cloak – and his throne was the wishing-chair. Its wings had disappeared. It looked just like an ordinary chair.

Peter stared at Mollie and Chinky in amazement – and they stared at him. Mollie was just going to cry, "Peter! Oh, Peter!" when Peter winked at her, and Chinky gave her a nudge. She was not to give his secret away!

IX

THE PRINCE'S SPELLS

FOR a minute or two Peter, Mollie, and Chinky gazed at one another and said nothing. Then the witch spoke.

"Your Majesty, here are two prisoners for you. They pushed me into the river after they had tried to steal my geese."

"Leave them with me," said Peter in a solemn voice. "I will punish them, Witch."

426

The witch bowed and went out backwards. Mollie wanted to giggle but she didn't dare to. Nobody said a word until the big door closed.

Then Peter leapt down from the chair and flung his arms round Mollie and Chinky. They hugged one another in delight.

"Peter, Peter! Tell us how it is you are King here!" said Mollie.

"Well, it is quite simple," said Peter. "The chair flew off with me as you know. It flew for some time, and then began to go downwards. It landed on the steps of this palace, which had been empty for years."

"As soon as the Scally-Wags saw me, all dressed up in my crown and cloak, sitting on the flying chair, they thought I must be some wonderful magic king come from a far-off land to live here. So they bowed down before me, and called me King. I didn't know what to do because the wishing-chair's wings disappeared, of course, so I couldn't escape. I just thought I'd better pretend to be a King, and wait for you to come along – for I guessed you and Mollie would find some way of getting to me! Now, tell me *your* adventures!"

How Peter laughed when he heard what a lot of people Chinky had pushed into the water! "You really are a bit of a Scally-Wag yourself, Chinky," he said. "That's the sort of thing the Scally-Wags love to do!"

"Peter, how can we all escape?" asked Mollie. "If only the wishing-chair would grow its wings again! But it never does when we really want it to!"

"What will Mother say if we stay away too long?" said Peter, looking worried.

"Well, a day here is only an hour in your land," said Chinky. "So don't worry. Even if we have to be here for two or three days it won't matter, because it will only be two or three hours really. Your mother won't worry if you are only away for a few hours."

"And by that time perhaps the chair will have grown its wings again," said Mollie, cheering up.

"Look here," said Chinky, "I think you ought to make up some sort of punishment for us, Peter, or the witch will think there is something funny about you. Make us scrub the floor, or something. Anything will do."

"But do give us something to eat," said Mollie. "We really are very hungry."

Peter clapped his hands. The door swung open and two soldiers appeared. They saluted and clicked their heels together.

"Bring me a tray of chocolate cakes, some apples, and some sardine sandwiches," commanded Peter. "And some lemonade, too. Oh, and bring two pails of hot water and two scrubbing-brushes. I am going to make my two prisoners scrub the floor."

The guards saluted and went out. In a few minutes two Scally-Wags, dressed in footmen's uniform, came in with the tray of food. How good it looked! Behind them followed another Scally-Wag carrying two pails of steaming hot water, two scrubbing-brushes, and some soap.

"Your Majesty, is it safe for you to be alone with two prisoners as fierce as these?" asked one of the Scally-Wags.

"Dear me, yes," said Peter. "I would turn them both

into black-beetles if they so much as frowned at me!"

The Scally-Wags bowed and went out. Mollie and Chinky giggled. "Do you like playing at being a King Peter?" asked Mollie.

"I'm not playing at it, I *am* a King!" said Peter. "Come and help yourselves to food, you two. I'll have some too. It looks good."

It *was* good! But in the middle of the meal there came a loud knock at the door. Mollie and Chinky flung down their sandwiches in a hurry, caught up scrubbing-brushes and went down on their hands and knees! They pretended to be hard at work scrubbing as three Scally-Wags entered with a message.

Mollie and Chinky pretended to be hard at work scrubbing.

"Your Majesty!" they said, bowing low till their foreheads bumped against the floor. "His Highness, the Prince of Goodness Knows Where, is coming to see you tomorrow, to exchange magic spells. He will be here at eleven o'clock."

"Oh," said Peter. "Thanks very much."

The three Scally-Wags looked angrily at Mollie and

Chinky scrubbing the floor, and said, "Shall we beat these prisoners for you, Your Majesty? We hear that they have pushed three people into the river, and smashed down the old wizard's hat on to his nose, and . . ."

"That's enough," said Peter in a fierce voice. "I punish my prisoners myself. Any interference from you, and you will scrub my floor too!"

"Pardon, pardon, Your Majesty!" cried the three Scally-Wags, and they backed away so fast that they fell over one another and rolled down the steps. The two children and Chinky laughed till their sides ached.

"Oh, Peter, you do make a good King!" said Mollie. "I do wish I could be a queen!"

"I say! What about this Prince of Goodness Knows Where," said Chinky. "If he is really coming to exchange magic spells with you, Peter, you will find things rather difficult. Because, you see, you can't do any spells at all."

The three stared at one another. Then Peter had an idea.

"Look here, Chinky, couldn't you change places with me tomorrow, and do spells instead of me?" he asked. "I'll say that I will receive the Prince alone – so that none of the Scally-Wags will know it's you and not me."

"Good idea!" cried Chinky at once. "I don't know anything about the Prince, but perhaps I can manage to satisfy him. That's just what we'll do – change places!"

That night Mollie and Chinky slept in the kitchen of the palace. They were quite comfortable on a big sofa there, though the two kitchen cats would keep on lying down on top of them. They were nice, warm cats, but very fat and heavy. Peter slept on a golden bed in a big bedroom – but he said he would much rather have slept with Molly and Chinky on the kitchen sofa with the cats. It was lonely in the golden bed.

Peter told the soldiers that he meant to keep the two prisoners, Mollie and Chinky, as personal servants, and therefore they were to bring him in his breakfast. You may be sure that the two of them piled the trays up well with food of all kinds when they took the breakfast in! They laid it on a table, and then they all ate a good meal, though Mollie and Chinky had to eat theirs standing behind Peter's chair, in case some one came in suddenly.

As the morning went on and the time came nearer for the Prince to come, the three began to feel rather excited. Peter gave orders that he was to be alone with the Prince.

"See that no one comes into the room whilst His Highness is here," he said to the soldiers. They saluted and went out smartly. Peter said it was fun to have two soldiers obeying him like that.

"Now here's the crown, Chinky," he said, handing him the golden cardboard crown. "And here's the red rug for a cloak. Get on to the wishing-chair throne. I guess the old wishing-chair never thought it was going to be used as a throne!"

Chinky put on the crown and sat down on the chair, pulling his cloak round him. Mollie and Peter stood behind him as if they were servants. Eleven o'clock struck.

"Here's the crown, Chinky," said Peter, handing him the golden cardboard crown.

The door was thrown open and in came a tall and grandly dressed Prince. He swept off his feathered hat and bowed to Chinky. Chinky bowed back. The door shut.

Chinky and the Prince began to talk.

"I was on my way through your kingdom," said the Prince, "and thought that I would come to exchange spells with you. I have here a spell that will change all the weeds in a garden into beautiful flowers. Would you care to exchange that for a spell of your own?"

"No, thank you," said Chinky. "I have no weeds in my garden. It would be of no use to me."

"Well," said the Prince, bringing out a bag embroidered with little golden suns, "here is another spell, really most useful. Put a bit of the shell in this bag into an egg-cup and say 'Toorisimmer-joo-joo,' and you will see a beautiful new-laid egg appear. You can have it for your breakfast. There is enough shell in here to make one hundred thousand eggs."

"I can't bear eggs for breakfast," said Chinky. "Show me something else."

432

"Well, what about this," said the Prince. He showed Chinky a strange little cap with three red berries on it. "Put this cap on and you will know immediately who are your enemies and who are not, for the three red berries will wag about when enemies are before you."

"I know who are my enemies and who are not without wearing any cap," said Chinky. "It's no good to *me*! You have no spells at all that are of any use, Prince!"

"Well, what spells have *you?*" asked the Prince rather impatiently.

Chinky waved his hand in the air and a most delicious smell stole all around. It seemed like honeysuckle one minute – like roses the next – like carnations the next – then like sweet-peas – so that all the time you were sniffing and smelling in delight. The Prince was most excited.

"That is a most unusual spell," he said. "I should like that to take home to my Princess. She would be pleased."

"Well, I will give it to you if you will give me a spell that is useful to me," said Chinky. "Can you, for instance, make wings grow on this throne of mine?"

The Prince looked at the wishing-chair and rubbed his hand down its legs.

"Yes," he said at once. "I can easily do that. If I am not mistaken that throne of yours was once a flying chair! I will work the flying spell on it!"

He took from his pocket a little blue tin. He took off the lid and dug his finger into the tin. Mollie saw that his finger was covered with green and yellow ointment. The Prince smeared it down the legs of

*The Prince showed Chinky a strange little cap with
three red berries on it.*

434

the chair. Then he stood back and chanted a curious magic song. The children and Chinky watched in excitement. They saw the familiar red buds come – and break out into feathers! The chair was growing its wings! It spread them out – it flapped them and a draught came!

"Quick!" shouted Chinky, jumping on to the top of the chair's back, "get in, Mollie and Peter. We can fly off, now!"

But the Prince gave a shout and snatched Chinky's cardboard crown from his head.

"You are not a real king!" he cried. "Your crown is only cardboard! Stop! Soldiers, soldiers! Come here at once!"

The big door burst open. In came the soldiers and stared in amazement at the chair holding the two children and the pixie.

"Home, chair, home!" yelled all three in the chair. "Fly out of the window!"

The chair rose into the air, kicked out at the Prince, and knocked him over. Peter kicked out at the soldiers and knocked their helmets off! The chair flew out of the window and up into the air. Hurrah! They were leaving the Land of the Scally-Wags – and a good thing too; for, as Peter said, they stood a good chance of becoming as bad as Scally-Wags themselves if they stayed there very much longer – pushing people into rivers, kicking them over, and banging their hats over their noses!

"But I quite enjoyed being a bit of a Scally-Wag for once," said Chinky, as the chair flew in at the playroom.

"It was a good thing for me that we had been playing at Kings and Queens before the chair flew to the Land of Scally-Wags," said Peter. "It was jolly nice every one thinking I was a king, I can tell you!"

X

THE LAST ADVENTURE OF ALL

CHINKY was reading by himself in the playroom, curled up on the couch. He was waiting for Mollie and Peter to come and play with him. They were going to set out the railway lines all over the room, and run the two engines round and round. It would be fun, Chinky thought.

Chinky was reading by himself in the playroom, curled up on the couch.

He listened for the two children to come along. Soon he heard them. But they were not running merrily along as usual. They were coming slowly.

Chinky wondered if anything had happened. Usually the children only walked slowly if they had been in disgrace, or were sad about something. He ran to the door and looked out.

Yes – it *was* Mollie and Peter – but they did look miserable. Chinky ran to them and took their hands.

"What's the matter?" he cried. "Have you been punished for something?"

"No," said Peter. "But Mother has just told us some bad news."

"What?" cried Chinky.

"She has told us that Mollie and I are to go away to school," said Peter.

"But you go to school now," said Chinky, puzzled. "You like school."

"Yes, but this is a new school – it is called a boarding-school," said Mollie. "We go there and *live* there – sleep there, have our meals there, and everything! We shan't be able to pop down to our playroom and play with you, Chinky."

The pixie stared at the two children in dismay. "But won't you ever come back again?" he asked. "Won't you ever see your mother and father even?"

Peter laughed. "Oh, yes," he said. "We shall see them often. We shall come home for holidays and at half-term too. So it isn't really so bad, I suppose. But it means we shan't be able to see you every day as we do now, Chinky. You will have to wait many weeks before we come back again."

"Oh dear!" said Chinky. "I do hate the idea of that! But perhaps it will be a good thing; because, you know, my mother is rather lonely living by herself in

Fairyland. I ought to go and live with her a bit. Then I could come and live with you in the holidays, couldn't I?"

"Yes," said Peter. "But I say, Chinky – what about the wishing-chair? We can't leave it here by itself. It might fly away and not come back."

"Or get stolen by someone," said Mollie.

"Yes, that's true," said Chinky. "Well, I think I'd better take it home with me, don't you? My mother will keep it safely for us till we need it. We will see that it doesn't fly off."

"That's a good idea," said Peter.

"When are you going to school?" asked Chinky.

"Tomorrow," said Mollie. "I am going to a girls' school and Peter is going to a boys' school. We shall miss one another dreadfully. But I expect it will be fun to live with lots of other children."

"Perhaps the wishing-chair will grow its wings once more before we have to say good-bye to it," said Peter. "But anyway, we'll go off adventuring in the holidays when they come. And, oh, Chinky! I suppose you couldn't come in the chair to school one night? It would be so exciting!"

"I'll see," said Chinky. "I don't want the other children to know about the wishing-chair – and they would see it if I came."

"Look!" said Mollie suddenly. "The chair is growing its wings! It must have heard what we were saying. It wants to take us on a last adventure. Come on, you two, get in!"

Chinky sat in his usual place, on the back of the chair. Mollie and Peter squeezed into the seat. The chair flapped its wings strongly and flew off into the air. Up it flew and up, and went due south.

"We haven't been this way before," said Chinky, peering down. "We pass over some strange lands hereabouts, I know. Chair, you are not to go down anywhere here. We might find it difficult to get away."

The chair obeyed Chinky. It flew on, keeping quite high. The children leaned over the arms to see what they were passing. They saw that they must be flying over Giantland, for the people looked very big and tall. Some of the giants saw them and waved to them to come down. But the chair flew on. It came to yet another land.

This was a peculiar-looking place. The people seemed to have no legs, but rolled about here and there on their round, fat little bodies.

"That's the land of Rollabouts," said Chinky, pointing. "I once went there when I was little, and dear me, how I kept falling over those Rollabouts. They will keep rolling in between your feet!"

Mollie laughed. She thought she would like to fly down and see the Rollabouts – but the chair kept on, flying strongly.

"Now what is this land, I wonder?" said Chinky, looking down. "Oh, my word! I know! It's where the Chatterboxes live! Dreadful people, they are! They talk all the time, and simply won't let you get a word in!"

"I don't like chatterboxes," said Peter. "They are dull and tiresome, and just talk about themselves all the time. Oh, I say, Chinky! The chair's going down!"

"Keep up, chair!" commanded Chinky. The chair

swung itself upwards. But the Chatterboxes had seen it and they called to it.

"Hie, chair, chair, chair! Come on down here! We've lots to say to you, and we'd like to hear all your adventures, and see your wonderful wings, and . . ."

"And, and, and!" said Chinky. "They'll go on talking for ever!"

The Chatterboxes grew angry when they saw that the chair was not coming down. One of them ran indoors and fetched a long rope. He rolled it round in rings on his arm. Then, taking careful aim, he threw it up at the chair, as a cowboy throws a lasso. The loop of rope fell right round the chair. The Chatterbox gave a yell of delight. He pulled the rope tightly. Chinky and the children were caught neatly, for the rope was round them, too!

The Chatterbox began to haul on the rope, and although the chair flapped its wings as hard as it could and tried to fly

The Chatterbox began to haul on the rope.

440

upwards, there was no help for it – it had to come down!

Bump! It was down on the ground.

The Chatterboxes undid the rope, talking all the time. "You should have come down when we called you! You see, you had to come down anyhow! Where were you going to? Where did you come from? What are your names?"

"My name is Chinky," began the pixie – but the Chatterboxes did not want to listen to anything. They just went on talking, all of them at once.

"They sound like the monkey-house at the Zoo!" said Peter in despair.

"LISTEN, CHATTER-BOXES! LET US GO ON OUR JOURNEY!"

Peter shouted as loudly as he could – but the Chatterboxes took no notice. They pulled the two children and Chinky along to a little cottage, saying, "You must come and have some lemonade! You must have some biscuits!"

"Oh, well," said Peter to Mollie. "I can always do with lemonade and biscuits. I don't like leaving the chair behind, though. I say, Chatterboxes, can we bring the chair with us?"

"Oh yes, we will send some one back to fetch it," said the little folk. "You go, Lollipop! You go, Twisty! You go, Knobbly!"

Lollipop, Twisty, and Knobbly all began to tell why they didn't want to go – and in the end nobody went at all. They were most annoying little people, all talk and nothing else!

They sat down in the little kitchen, and went on

441

talking, whilst the children and Chinky waited patiently for the lemonade and biscuits. But every one wanted to talk, and no one fetched anything to eat or drink.

"You know, when we saw your chair we thought 'What a wonderful thing!' And we did want to see it and see you too, so we called you, but you wouldn't come down, and then we had to lasso you, and you came down, and what nice people you are, and we are so pleased to have you here, and to give you lemonade and biscuits, and to be your friends, and listen to all you have to tell us of your wonderful adventures, and . . ."

"Oh, do be quiet for a minute," said Mollie, putting her hands over her ears. "You go on and on and on."

"And what about some lemonade and biscuits," said Chinky.

"Oh yes, lemonade and biscuits, of course you shall have some, and we will all have some, too!" cried the Chatterboxes. "How nice it is to have you here eating and drinking with us, and telling us all your adventures, and sharing your wonderful journeys, and . . ."

"Well, we haven't told you ANYTHING so far!" said Peter, getting annoyed. "I say, Chinky, let's get back to our chair. I'm tired of waiting here for lemonade and biscuits that don't come!"

They pushed aside the silly little Chatterboxes and went to get their chair – but it was gone! They saw it high in the sky, a little black speck, flying away to the north!

"Bother!" said Chinky crossly. "Now we've got to go back by train! Do get away, Chatterboxes, and don't talk so loudly in my ears all the time. You make me quite deaf!"

"Hurry!" called Mollie. "There's a train over there in that station!" The three ran fast, with the stupid Chatterboxes chattering hard behind them all the time, saying something about lemonade and biscuits!

They jumped into the train, and only just in time too! It was a funny train – a wooden one, with open trucks. In Chinky's carriage there was a hedgehog, a Chatterbox, and a mole who was fast asleep.

The Chatterbox was talking as usual. The hedgehog spread out his prickles and pricked him. The Chatterbox looked at him angrily.

"Every time you open your mouth I shall prick you," said the hedgehog in a hoarse, cross voice. The Chatterbox glared at him, but didn't dare to say another word.

The hedgehog spread out his prickles and pricked the Chatterbox.

"It's a pity that a hedgehog doesn't travel with every Chatterbox," whispered Mollie to Chinky. The train clattered on, and stopped at funny stations. The Chatterbox waited until the hedgehog got out and then began rattling on about all sorts of things, never stopping for a moment. The mole snored loudly. Chinky, Mollie, and Peter turned their backs on the silly Chatterbox and pretended not to listen. How glad they were to get to their own station and jump out.

"Well, I hope *I* shall never be a chatterbox!" said Mollie.

"We won't let you be!" said Peter. "Come on – let's go home and see if the wishing-chair is safely back."

They ran through the wood and down the lane and into their garden. But do you know, the wishing-chair was not there! It hadn't come back!

"Oh, do you suppose it has gone away for ever?" cried Mollie. "Do you think it heard what we were saying and ran away?"

"It's funny," said Chinky, puzzled. "I shouldn't have thought it would leave us like that! Oh dear – and you're going away to school tomorrow! It might have let you say good-bye to it!"

Just then a tiny fairy came knocking at the playroom door with a note for Chinky. He opened it and read it – and his face broke into smiles. "Just listen to this!" he cried. "It's from my mother. She says: 'Dear Chinky, this is just to let you know that the wishing-chair arrived here by itself today. I don't know why. – Your loving Mother.'"

"Oh, the clever old chair!" said Peter. "It heard us say that you would live with your mother and keep it there – so it has gone there itself! Well, you must say good-bye to it for us, Chinky – and we'll hope to see it when we come home for half-term."

A bell rang at the top of the garden. Mollie ran to Chinky and hugged him. "That's the bell to tell us to go in," she said. "We'd better say good-bye now, dear, dear Chinky, in case we can't get down to the playroom tomorrow before we go. Good-bye and don't forget us!"

They all hugged one another. Chinky waved to them as they ran up the garden. He felt rather sad – but never mind, there would be more adventures when the holidays came! He would wait for those.

Chinky caught the bus to Fairyland and went to Mrs. Twinkle, his mother! The children packed their last things. Everything was ready for school. They couldn't help feeling rather excited.

The playroom was empty. The wishing-chair was gone. Ah – but wait till the holidays! What fine adventures they would all have then!

XI

HOME FOR HALF-TERM

A LITTLE pixie peeped anxiously into the window of a small playroom built at the bottom of a garden. A robin flew down beside him and sang a little song.

"What's the matter, Chinky? What do you want? What are you looking for?"

"I'm looking for Mollie and Peter," said Chinky. "I've got the wishing-chair hidden under a bush just near here, and I'm waiting for the children to come home, so that I can get into this playroom of theirs and put the chair safely in its corner."

"But you know that the children are away at boarding-school," said the robin, with a little trill. "How foolish you are!"

"I'm *not*," said Chinky. "They're coming home at half-term, just for a few days. They told me so – and I promised to bring the chair from my mother's, where I've been looking after it – hoping that perhaps it would grow its wings just for their half-term. So I'm not foolish, you see!"

"Sorry," said the robin. "Shall I go and find out if they are up at the house? I haven't *heard* them yet – and usually they make a lot of noise when they come home. Wait here, and I'll find out."

He flew off. He peeped into all the windows, his perky little head on one side. There was nobody to be seen at all except the cook in the kitchen. She was busy making cakes.

446

"What are you looking for, Chinky?" asked the robin.

"Ah – the children's favourite chocolate buns!" thought the robin. "I can hear them now, banging at the front door. What a pity their mother isn't here to welcome them!"

Mrs. Williams, the cook, hurried to the front door. Two children burst in at once, each carrying a small case. It was Mollie and Peter, home for the half-term!

"Hallo, Mrs. Willy! Where's Mother?" cried Peter.

"Welcome home, Master Peter," said Mrs. Williams, "and you, too, Miss Mollie. Your mother says she's very, very sorry, but she's had to go off to your Granny, who's been taken ill. But she'll be home before you have to go back to school on Tuesday – and I'm to look after you."

"Oh," said the children, disappointed. Home didn't somehow seem like home without Mother there. They felt rather miserable.

"What about Daddy?" asked Mollie.

"He's away," said Mrs. Williams. "Didn't your mother tell you that in her last letter?"

"Oh, yes," said Mollie, remembering. "I forgot. Oh dear – half-term without either Mother or Daddy – how horrid!"

"I've made you your favourite chocolate buns," said Mrs. Williams, following them indoors. "And I've got ice-cream for you, too, and honey in the comb. And your mother says she has ordered twenty-four bottles of ginger-beer and orangeade for you this weekend, and you can take it down to your playroom."

"Oh, well – that sounds good," said Peter, cheering up. "We'll just pop upstairs with our things, Mrs. Willy – and then what about your honey in the comb and chocolate buns? We're starving! We simply *never* get enough to eat at school, you know!"

"Rubbish!" said Mrs. Williams. "You're both as plump as can be!"

The two children went up the stairs two at a time. They stood at a landing window, looking down to the bottom of the garden. They could quite well see the roof of their playroom there. They looked at each other in excitement.

"I hope Chinky is there," said Mollie. "Because if he is, and has got the Wishing-Chair with him, we shall be able to fly off on an adventure or two without bothering about anyone! It's always difficult to slip off in it when Mother and Daddy are at home – and we just *have* to keep the chair a secret. It would be too dreadful if it was put into a museum, and taken right away from us. It must be very, very valuable."

"Yes. We're really very lucky to have a wishing-chair of our own," said Peter. "It's a long time since we got it now. Come on – let's put our things in our bedrooms, and then ask Mrs. Willy to let us take our tea down to the playroom. Perhaps Chinky is there."

"He may be waiting outside," said Mollie. "He can't get in because the door is locked. I shall love to see his dear little pixie face again. We're lucky to have a pixie for a friend!"

Mrs. Willy was quite pleased to let them have a tray of goodies to take down to the playroom with them. She piled it with buns and new bread and butter, and a slab of honey in the comb, biscuits, and ice-cream out of the fridge. It did look good!

Mrs. Willy gave them a tray of good things for tea.

"I'll take some ginger-beer down under my arm," said Peter. "I can manage the tray, too, if you'll bring the biscuits and ice-cream – they look as if they might slip about!"

"I'll get the key of the playroom, too," said Mollie, and she took it off its hook. Then, feeling excited, the two of them went carefully down the garden path, carrying everything between them. Would Chinky be waiting for them?

He was, of course, because the robin had flown down to tell him that the children were coming. He hid behind some tall hollyhocks, and leapt out on them as they came up to the door of the playroom.

"Mollie! Peter! I'm here!"

"Chinky! We *are* glad to see you!" said Mollie. "Wait till I put down all this stuff and I'll give you a hug! There!"

She gave the little pixie such a hug that he almost choked. He beamed all over his face. "Where's the key?" he said. "I'll open the door. I want to get the wishing-chair inside before anyone sees it. There's a tiresome little brownie who keeps on wanting to sit in it."

He unlocked the door of the playroom and they all went in. Chinky helped them with the food, and then ran to get the wishing-chair. He staggered in with it, beaming.

"I tipped that tiresome brownie off the seat, and he fell into some nettles," said Chinky. "He shouted like anything. Well, does the chair look just the same as ever?"

"Oh, *yes!*" said Mollie, in delight, looking at the

polished wooden chair. "Your mother does keep it well polished, Chinky. Did it grow its wings and fly off at all, while we were away at school this term?"

"It grew its wings once," said Chinky, "but as I was in bed with a cold I couldn't fly off anywhere exciting in it – so I tied it to one of the legs of my bed, in case it tried to do anything silly, like flying out of the window."

Mollie giggled. "And did it try?" she asked.

"Oh, yes – it woke me up in the middle of the night, flapping its wings and tugging at my bed," said Chinky with a grin. "But it couldn't get away, and in the morning its wings had gone again. So that was all right."

"I do so hope it will grow its wings this weekend," said Peter. "We've only got a few days' holiday, then we go back to school again – and as Mother and Daddy are both away we really could go off on an adventure or two without any difficulty."

"I expect it will," said Chinky, looking at the chair. He felt its legs to see if there were any bumps coming, which meant that its wings were sprouting. But he couldn't feel any. What a pity!

Soon they were all sitting down enjoying Mrs. Williams's buns and ice-cream. It was a hot day, so they drank rather a lot of the ginger-beer.

"It won't last long if we drink it at this rate!" said Peter. "I say – I wonder if Mrs. Willy would mind if we lived down here in the playroom all this weekend – slept here, too?"

"That *would* be fun!" said Mollie. "I don't see why we shouldn't. You could come too, Chinky."

451

It was very easy to arrange. Mrs. Williams smiled and nodded. "Yes, you do that," she said. "Your mother said I was to let you do what you liked, so long as it wasn't anything silly. I'll take down bedding for you."

"Oh, no," said Peter, hurriedly. "We'll take it all down, Mrs. Willy." He didn't want any questions about the wishing-chair! "And Mrs. Willy, we could have all our meals down there, if you like. We don't want anything hot, you know, this weather. If you could give us some tins and a bottle of milk, we could pick our own fruit and salad out of the garden. We shouldn't be any bother to you at all then."

"You're no bother!" said Mrs. Williams. "But you do just what you like this weekend, so long as you're good and happy. I'll give you tins and milk and anything else you want – and don't be afraid I'll come bothering you, because I won't! I know how children like to have their own little secrets, and I shan't come snooping round!"

Well, that was grand! Now they could go and live in the playroom, and sleep there, too – and if the wishing-chair grew its wings at any time, they would know at once! They would hear it beginning to creak, and see the bumps growing on its legs and the wings sprouting. Not a minute would be wasted!

It was fun taking down everything to the gay little playroom. Chinky kept out of sight, of course, because nobody knew anything about him. He was as much of a secret as the wishing-chair!

"There now," said Mollie, at last. "Everything is ready for us – food – drink, too – bedding – and a cushion and rug for you, Chinky. We're going to have a lovely time! Wishing-chair, grow your wings as soon as you can, and everything will be perfect!"

The wishing-chair gave the tiniest little cree-ee-eak. "Did you hear that?" said Chinky. "Perhaps it *will* grow its wings soon. We'll have to keep a watch. Where shall we go to, if it does grow its wings?"

"Wishing-chair, grow your wings as soon as you can," said Mollie.

"Is there a Land of Lost Things, or something like that?" said Peter. "I got into awful trouble this term because I lost my watch. Or what about going to a Land of Circuses or Fairs? I'd love to see a whole lot of those at once."

"I never heard of those lands," said Chinky. "Why don't we just let the chair take us somewhere on its own? It would be fun not to know where we are going!"

"*Oooh*, yes," said Peter. "That would be really exciting. Chair, do you hear us? Grow your wings and you can take us anywhere you like. But do, do *hurry up*!"

XII

CREE-EE-EAK

MOLLIE and Peter spent a very jolly evening with Chinky, down in the playroom. They played snap and happy families and ludo, and all the time they watched the wishing-chair to see if it would grow its wings.

Mollie, Peter and Chinky spent a jolly evening playing snap.

454

They did so long to fly off on an adventure again.

But the chair stood there quietly, and when it was half-past eight the children were so sleepy that they felt they really must go to bed.

"We'd better go and have a bath up at the house," said Peter. "I feel dirty, travelling all the way home by train. We'll dress properly again, just in case the wishing-chair grows its wings and flies off with us. We'll say good-night to Mrs. Willy, too, so that she doesn't feel she's got to come down to see if we're all right."

Just as they went out of the door they saw somebody disappearing round the corner. "Who was that peeping?" said Mollie at once. "Quick, run and see, Peter."

Peter raced round the corner of the playroom and saw a little brownie dive into a bush. He yelled at him.

"Hey, what do you think you are doing, peeping about here? You wait till I catch you!"

A cheeky face looked out of the bush. "I just want to see your chair grow wings, that's all. It's a wishing-chair, isn't it? Can't I watch it grow wings?"

"No, you can't," said Peter. "No peeping and prying in *our* garden, please! Keep out!"

The brownie made a rude face and pulled his head back into the leaves. Chinky ran out of the playroom to see what the shouting was about.

"It's that brownie you told us about, the one who sat in the wishing-chair," said Peter. "Keep an eye open for him, Chinky. We don't want him telling everyone our secret."

"I'll watch," said Chinky. He yelled at the bush where the brownie had gone.

"Hey, you little snooper! If I see you again I'll tie you to a witch's broomstick and send you off to the moon!"

There was no answer. The children went off to the house to have their bath and Chinky went back to the playroom.

Mrs. Willy gave Peter and Mollie a jam sponge sandwich she had made, and another bottle of milk. "Could you give us some eggs, too?" asked Peter. "Then we could boil them ourselves for breakfast on our own little stove. We wouldn't need to come in for breakfast then."

Mrs. Willy laughed. "You're not going to bother me much, are you?" she said. "Well, here you are, four new-laid eggs – and you'd better take a new loaf down with you, and some more butter. You're sure you'll be all right?"

"Oh, *yes*," said Mollie. "We love being on our own like this with Ch—"

Peter gave her such a nudge that she almost fell over. She stopped and went red. Goodness gracious, she had almost said Chinky's name! Mrs. Williams didn't seem to have noticed anything, though. She added a pot of marmalade to the tray, and Peter took it.

"Well, I suppose I'll see you when you want more food!" she said. "And not before. Have a nice time – and don't get into mischief!"

Peter and Mollie went down the garden path with the tray. Good! Now they wouldn't need to go up to the house for breakfast, so if the chair grew its wings

456

that night they would have time for a nice long adventure!

Just as they got near the playroom they heard a noise of shouting and slapping.

"I told you I'd smack you if I found you peeping again!" they heard Chinky say. "Coming right into the playroom like that!" Slap, slap, slap! "Howl all you like, you'll get a worse smacking if you come back again. What's up with you that you won't do as you're told?"

"You horrid thing!" wept the little brownie. "Your hand's very hard. You hurt me. I'll pay you out, yes, I will!"

Slap! Yell! Howl! Then came the sound of running feet and the little brownie almost bumped into the two children. He knocked the tray and an egg leaped right off it and landed on his head. It broke, and in an instant he had a cap of yellow yolk!

The little brownie knocked the tray and an egg fell on to his head.

457

Mollie and Peter laughed. The little brownie couldn't think what had happened to him. "I'll pay you out," he cried. "I will, I will!"

He disappeared into the tall hollyhocks, grumbling and wailing. Dear, dear – what a silly little fellow he was, to be sure!

"Well, he's gone," said Peter. "And so is one of our eggs. Never mind, we've still got three left, one for each of us. Hey, Chinky, you've been having more trouble with that brownie, I see."

"Yes. But I don't think he'll be back again in a hurry," said Chinky. "I smacked him hard. I know who he is now. He's little Nose-About, a spoilt little brownie who sticks his nose into everything. His mother didn't spank him enough when he was little, so people have to keep on spanking him now. I say – what a lovely sponge sandwich! Are we going to have some now?"

They sat down to have their supper. It was a lovely summer's evening, still quite light. As they sat by the doorway, munching big slices of jam sandwich, a purple cloud blew up. Big drops of rain fell, and yet the sun still shone brightly, for it was not covered by the cloud.

"There's a rainbow, look!" said Mollie, and they all gazed at the lovely, shimmering rainbow that suddenly shone out in the sky. "I do wish the chair would grow its wings, because I'd love to go to the rainbow and see if I could find a crock of gold where it touches the ground."

"Yes, I'd like that, too," said Chinky. "I don't believe anyone has ever found the crock of gold yet.

They say you have to slide right down the rainbow itself and land with a bump on the patch of ground where the crock is hidden."

"Let's go right into the garden and see if we can spot where the rainbow-end touches," said Mollie. So out they went, but as the end of the rainbow disappeared behind some high trees they couldn't make up their minds where it touched.

"It's miles away, anyhow," said Peter. "Isn't it a lovely thing? It's like a bridge of many colours."

They heard a sudden little scuffling sound and turned quickly. "Was that that tiresome brownie again?" said Chinky, frowning. "Anybody see him?"

Nobody had. Nobody had spied him scuttling into the playroom. Nobody saw where he went. Peter felt uneasy. "I believe he's slipped into the playroom," he said. "We'd better look."

They went in and hunted round. They looked into every corner, and Mollie even looked inside the dolls' house because she thought he *might* have been able to squeeze himself in at the door.

"He's not in the playroom," said Peter at last. "We've looked simply everywhere. Let's shut the door now, and keep him out. It's still very light, and the rainbow is still lovely, though not so bright as it was. We'd better go to bed. I'm really sleepy."

Mollie looked longingly at the wishing-chair. "If only it would grow its wings!" she said. "I just *feel* like an adventure!"

The two children had mattresses to lie on. Chinky had a cushion and a rug. They all settled down, yawning. How lovely the very first evening was! Half-term seemed to be quite long when it was still only the first day.

Mollie fell asleep first. Chinky gave an enormous yawn, and then he fell asleep, too. Peter lay watching the rainbow fading gradually. He could see part of it through the window.

His eyes fell shut. His thoughts went crooked, and he was *almost* asleep when something woke him.

"Creeeee-eak!"

Peter opened his eyes. What was that noise that had slipped into his first moment of dreaming? His eyes shut again.

"Cree-ee-ee-EAK!"

Ah! That woke up Peter properly. He sat up quickly. He knew that noise all right! It was made by the wishing-chair. It was about to grow its lovely wings of green and yellow! He sat and stared at the chair.

Could he see bumps coming on its legs? He was almost sure he could. Yes – there was a big one on the right front leg – and now another on the left. He could see bumps on the back legs, too.

Then one bump sprouted a few red feathers! Hurrah! The wishing-chair *was* growing its wings for them. What luck!

Peter reached over to Chinky and gave him a little shake. He did the same to Mollie. "Wake up! The chair's growing its wings. We can fly off in it tonight!"

Both Mollie and Chinky woke up with a jump. Chinky leapt up and ran to the chair. His face beamed at them.

The Wishing-Chair flew up into the sky. Mollie, Peter and Chinky felt very excited

"Yes! Look at its lovely wings sprouting out – good big ones! Quick, open the door, and we'll all get into the chair – and away we'll go!"

Peter flung the door open. Chinky and Mollie were already sitting in the chair. It flapped its wings and rose a few inches. "Wait for Peter!" cried Mollie, in a fright. Peter leapt across to the chair and sat himself firmly on the seat. Chinky sat himself on the back to make more room. Ah – they were off!

"Tell the chair where to go," said Peter. "Or shall we just let it take us where it wants to?"

"Chair, go to the rainbow!" suddenly cried a voice, and the chair, which was flying in the opposite direction, changed its course and flew towards the almost-faded rainbow. It had flown right out of the door and up into the air, the children and Chinky holding fast to it, all feeling very excited.

"Who said that?" asked Peter. "Did you, Mollie? Or you, Chinky?"

They both said no. All three gazed at one another, puzzled. Then who *had* said it? There was nobody on the chair but themselves. Whose voice had commanded the chair to go to the rainbow?

"I expect it was that silly little brownie, calling from the ground," said Peter at last. "He must have seen us flying off, and yelled out to the chair to go to the rainbow. Well – shall we go?"

"Might as well," said Chinky. "Go on, Chair – go to the rainbow!"

And immediately a voice chimed in: "That's what *I* said! Go to the rainbow, Chair!"

Who could it be? And where was the speaker? How very, very peculiar!

XIII

AN ADVENTUROUS NIGHT

"THERE must be somebody invisible on the chair with us!" said Chinky. "Quick – feel about on the seat and on the arms and back. Feel everywhere – and catch hold of whoever it is."

Well, they all felt here and there, but not one of them could feel anybody. They heard a little giggle, but it was quite impossible to find whoever it was giggling.

"Surely the chair itself can't have grown a voice – and a giggle," said Peter at last.

462

"Of course not. It wouldn't be so silly," said Chinky. "Gracious – here we are at the rainbow already!"

So they were. They landed right on the top of the shimmering bow. "It's like a coloured, curving bridge," said Mollie, putting her foot down to it. "Oh, Peter – we can walk on it. I never, never thought of that."

She jumped down to the rainbow – and immediately she gave a scream.

"Oh, it's slippery! I'm sliding down! Oh, Peter, help me!"

Sure enough, poor Mollie had sat down with a bump, and was slithering down the curving rainbow at top speed. "Follow her, Chair, follow her!" yelled Peter.

"No, don't!" shouted the strange voice, and the chair stopped at once. That made Peter angry. He began to yell at the top of his voice.

"You do as *I* tell you, Chair. Follow Mollie, follow Mollie, follow Mollie, follow . . ."

And because his voice was loud and he shouted without stopping, the chair couldn't hear the other little voice that called to it to stop. It slid down the rainbow headlong after Mollie, who was now nearly at the bottom. Chinky held on tightly, looking scared. Would the chair be able to stop at the bottom of the rainbow?

It wouldn't have been able to stop, that was certain – but before it reached the bottom it spread its red wings and flew right off the rainbow, hovering in the air before it flew down to Mollie.

"That was clever of it," said Peter, with a sigh of relief. "Mollie, are you all right?"

"I fell on a tuffet of grass, or I'd have had a dreadful bump," said Mollie. "Let me get on to the chair again. I don't want it to fly off without me. Oh – what's this?"

She pointed to something half-buried in the grass. It had a handle at one side and she gave it a tug. Something bright and shining flew out of it.

"Mollie! It's the crock of gold!" shouted Peter. "The one that is hidden where the rainbow end touches. We've found it! All because you slid all the way down and landed by it with a bump. Let's pull it up."

He and Chinky jumped off the chair to go to Mollie. All three took hold of the handle of the crock and tugged. It came up out of the ground with a rush, and all three fell over.

"There it is – and, my word, it's *full* of gold!" said Peter. He put his hand into the crock and ran the gold through his fingers. "Who would have thought we would be the first to find the gold at the rainbow's end?"

"Let's carry it to the chair and take it with us," said Mollie. "I don't know what we're going to do with it, though! We could give it away bit by bit to all the poor people we meet, perhaps."

They lifted the gold on to the seat of the nearby wishing-chair. They were just about to climb on beside it when the strange little voice cried out again.

"Off you go, wishing-chair! Go to the Brownie-Mountain!"

The chair rose up, flapping its wings. It almost got away – but Peter managed to catch hold of the

*Mollie carefully lifted
the crock of gold.*

bottom of its right front leg. He held on for all he was worth, and Mollie helped him. They pulled the chair down between them, and climbed on to it.

"This is amazing!" said Chinky. "Who is it that keeps calling out? Where *can* he be? Even if he is invisible we should be able to *feel* him! He nearly got away with the chair, and the gold, too. My word, if I get hold of him I'll turn him into a fly and blow him into a spider's web!"

"Chair, go to the Old Woman Who Lives in a Shoe!" cried the voice suddenly, and the chair shot off to the east.

"Oh, no!" yelled Peter, angrily. "We're not going there for the Old Woman to get hold of us. Chair, go where you like!"

The chair set off to the west, then, changing its course so suddenly that Chinky almost fell off the back. It flew over a land of gleaming towers.

Chinky peered down. "This is the Land of Bells, I think," he said. "There are bells in every tower. Yes, listen – you can hear them."

"Ding-dong, dong-dong, dell!" rang dozens and dozens of bells, echoing all through the sky round them. The wishing-chair didn't attempt to go down. It kept high above the tall, gleaming towers, and soon it had left the Land of Bells far behind.

"It's beginning to get really dark now," said Peter, peering down. "Where do you suppose the chair is going to?"

"I think it's rather cross," said Chinky. "It's begun to creak a bit. I wonder why? We haven't done anything to make it angry. I wish it wouldn't swing about so. It feels as if it's trying to shake us off."

"Yes, it does," said Mollie. "Hold tight, everyone! I say, look – is that a town down there? Chinky, do you know what it is?"

Chinky peered down. "Yes – it's the Town of Bad Dreams. Gracious, I hope we don't go there. We don't want to fall into a bad dream and not know how to get out of it!"

"Go on farther, Chair," commanded Peter at once. A little voice called out, too, "Go farther! Go to the Brownie Mountain!"

"There's that voice again," said Chinky crossly. "Chair, take no notice. You belong to *us* and you have to do what *we* say! Go farther – but go where you like. We want an adventure before we go back home."

The chair suddenly began to drop downwards.

Two stern-looking brownies came up.

Chinky peered to see where they were going. "We've passed the Town of Bad Dreams. We're dropping down to the Village of Gobbo. Yes – that's right. Dear me, I wonder why? Gobbo is the head of all the brownies, and bad ones are sent to him to be punished."

A loud wail rose on the air. "Oh my, oh my! Chair, go to the Brownie Mountain, I tell you!"

But the chair took no notice. It flew right down to the ground, and immediately two stern-looking brownies came up, both with long beards and shaggy eyebrows.

"Who has been brought to be punished?" said one. "Which of you is a bad brownie?"

"Not one of us," said Peter, puzzled. "Mollie and I are children – and Chinky here is a pixie."

"Well, go away again, then," said one of the brownies. "Landing is not allowed here unless naughty brownies are to be taken before our chief, Gobbo."

"Right. Chair, fly away again," said Peter. Up flew

467

the chair – but one of the brownies suddenly gave a loud cry and caught hold of the right-hand wing. The chair almost tipped over, and Chinky fell right off the back. He landed with a bump on the ground.

"What did you do that for?" he shouted to the brownie. Then he stared in surprise. The two brownies pulled the children off the chair, which was now back again on the ground – and then they turned the chair upside-down! It creaked angrily.

"Don't do that!" said Peter, astonished. Then he stared, even more astonished! Underneath the chair, clinging desperately to it, was the naughty little brownie who had peeped and pried outside the playroom!

"Look at that!" cried Mollie. "It's Nose-About, the tiresome brownie! He must have slipped into the playroom and clung to the underneath of the chair so that we couldn't see him. And he flew off with us, and tried to make the chair go where *he* wanted to."

"And when we found the rainbow gold he wanted to go off to Brownie Mountain with it. That's where he lives, I expect," said Peter. "It was his voice we kept hearing! He was underneath the seat of the chair all the time."

"No wonder the chair took us to the Village of Gobbo, then," said Chinky. "It knew he was under it and wanted him to be punished. Brownies, take him away. He's a nuisance."

"No, no! Mercy, Mercy!" wept the little brownie. "Forgive me! I just wanted a ride, that's all. And when I saw the gold I thought I'd make the chair go to my home with it – then I'd be rich all my life."

"You're very bad and you want punishing," said Peter. "I'm not at all sorry for you."

"One spanking every day for a month," said one of the brownies, solemnly, clutching hold of the frightened brownie. "And he will never be allowed to go back home."

The little brownie wailed loudly. "But my mother will miss me so. She loves me, she does really. I do lots of jobs for her. And my little sister loves me, too. I take her to school each day. Do, do let me go. I only wanted the gold for my mother."

Mollie suddenly felt sorry for him. She knew how much *her* mother would miss her if she were taken away. And perhaps this naughty little brownie was quite good and kind at home.

She put her hand on the arm of one of the brownies. "Let him go, please. He's sorry now. He won't be bad again."

"Oh, yes he will," said the brownie. "His mother didn't spank him when she should, so he's growing into a perfect nuisance. We'll soon cure him."

"No, no, no," wailed the little brownie. "I'll tell my mother to smack me, really I will. Let me go. I want my mother, I do, I do."

"How much will you charge us for letting him go?" asked Mollie, much to Peter's surprise.

The two brownies talked together about this. "Well," said one at last, "our master, the Great Gobbo, is laying out some wonderful rose-gardens, but he hasn't enough money to finish them. We will let this brownie go if you pay us a fine of one thousand gold pieces. And that's cheap!"

"It isn't," said Mollie. "Peter, help me to count out the gold in this crock. I don't think there are as many as a thousand pieces, though. We'll just see."

They all began to count, the little brownie too. They counted one hundred – then two – then three and four and five – and, will you believe it, in that rainbow-crock there were exactly one thousand and one pieces of gold!

"There you are – a thousand pieces," said Peter, handing them over. "We'll have the odd one – and the crock, too, because it will look nice on our play-room mantelpiece. Now can we go?"

"Yes, certainly," said the brownies, delighted. "But we must warn this little brownie that *next* time the fine will be *two* thousand pieces! Good-bye!"

"Good-bye," called everyone, and up went the

"There you are – a thousand pieces of gold," said Peter.

wishing-chair into the air again. Where to next?

"Thank you," said the small brownie, in a humble voice. "Thank you very much. Please drop me at Brownie Mountain, will you?"

XIV

LAND OF WISHES

"WELL, brownie, you were lucky to have a kind friend like Mollie to pay your fine," said Chinky, who wasn't really very pleased about it at all. "Behave yourself, please – or I shall tell your mother all about you."

The chair was a bit crowded now, with the two children, the brownie, and the pixie, and the empty crock as well. Peter had the one piece of gold that was left. He had put it into his pocket.

"I'll take you to the Land of Wishes if you like," said the small brownie, humbly. He was very anxious to please them all now. "You can have as many wishes as you like this weekend because it's the Princess Peronel's birthday. I've an invitation ticket. Look."

He pulled a rather crumpled ticket from his pocket. It certainly was an invitation.

"But it's for you, not for us," said Peter.

"It says 'For Brownie Nose-About *and Friends*,' " said the brownie. "I'm Nose-About – and you're my friends, aren't you? Oh, please do say you are!"

"Well – all right, we're your friends then," said Peter. "Mollie certainly *was* a friend to you in the Village of Gobbo! Chinky, shall we go to the Land of Wishes? I know quite a few wishes I'd like to wish!"

"Yes, let's go," said Chinky. "Nose-About, *you'd* better tell the chair to go, because you're the only one that has the invitation."

471

"I've got an invitation ticket to The Land of Wishes,"
said Nose-About.

So, in rather an important voice, Nose-About told the chair where to go. "To the Land of Wishes, please," he said. "To the Princess Peronel's birthday party."

The chair gave a little creak and flew straight upwards. It was very dark now and stars were out in the sky. Mollie began to feel sleepy. She nodded her head and leaned against Peter. Peter nodded his head, too, and both of them slept soundly. Chinky and Nose-About kept guard. The chair flew all night long, for the Land of Wishes was a long, long way away.

The sun was up and the sky was full of light when at last the two children awoke. Below them was a land of flowers and lakes and streams and shining palaces. How lovely!

"Does *everyone* live in a palace here?" asked Mollie, marvelling at so many palaces.

"Oh, yes. It's easy enough to wish for one," said Nose-About, peering down. "And then when you're tired of living in an enormous place with windows everywhere, you just wish for a rose-covered cottage.

472

Would you like a palace for a bit? I'll wish you one!"

The chair flew downwards. It landed in a field of shining, star-like flowers. "Here we are," said the brownie. "I'll wish for a palace to begin with – and then we can be princes and a princess, and go to the Princess Peronel's birthday party. I wish for a palace with one thousand and one windows!"

And silently and shimmeringly a tall, slender palace rose up around them. The sun shone in through hundreds of windows.

"I'll just count if there *are* a thousand and one," said Nose-About.

"Oh *no*! We simply *can't* count up to a thousand and one all over again!" groaned Peter. "I say – look at the wishing-chair. It's standing on that platform there wishing it was a throne!"

"I wish it *was* a throne!" said Mollie at once. And dear me, the good old wishing-chair changed into a gleaming throne, with a big red velvet cushion on its seat and tassels hanging down its back. It looked very grand indeed.

Peter went and sat on it. "I wish I was a Prince!" he said. And to Mollie's enormous surprise her brother suddenly looked like a very handsome little prince, with a circlet of gold round his head and a beautiful cloak hanging from his velvet-clad shoulders. He grinned at Mollie. "Better wish yourself to be a Princess before I order you about!" he said. "I feel like giving a whole lot of orders! Where's my horse? Where are my dogs? Where are my servants?"

Well, before very long Mollie was a Princess, and looked quite beautiful in a dress that swept the

473

ground and twinkled with thousands of bright jewels as she walked. Chinky wished himself a new suit and a new wand. Nose-About still felt very humble so he didn't wish for anything for himself but only things for the others.

He wished for horses and dogs and cats and servants and ice-creams and everything he could think of.

"I think we've got enough dogs, Nose-About," said Peter at last. "And I'd rather not have any more ice-creams. I feel rather as if I'd like a good breakfast. All the clocks you wished for have just struck nine o'clock. I feel hungry."

The brownie wished for so much porridge and bacon and eggs that there was enough for the cats and dogs too. The servants had taken the horses out of the palace, which made Mollie feel more comfortable, because when the brownie had first wished for them they kept galloping round the enormous room. She was afraid of being knocked over.

That was a most exciting morning. When the children got into the way of wishing there was no end to the things they thought of!

"I feel like snowballing! I wish for plenty of snow!" said Peter, suddenly. And outside the palace windows fell the snowflakes, thick and fast. There was soon enough for a game. It was very easy to wish the snow away when they were tired of snowballing and wish for something else – an aeroplane they could fly, or a train they could drive.

"I wish this would last all over our weekend," sighed Mollie. "I'm enjoying it so."

"Well – I suppose it will," said Peter, "now you've

*Mollie and Peter and Chinky wished for everything
they could think of!*

wished it, the wish will come true. But what about Mother? She won't like it if we stay away all the time."

"I'll wish *her* here, then," said Mollie. But Peter wouldn't let her.

"No. Don't," he said. "If she's with Granny she wouldn't like leaving her – and it would upset Granny to see Mother suddenly disappear. We'll just enjoy ourselves here, and then try and explain to Mother when we get home."

The Princess's party was wonderful. It began at four o'clock that afternoon, and lasted till past midnight. There was a birthday cake that was so very big it took six little servants to cut it into slices. One hundred candles burned on it! How old Peronel must be!

"A hundred years old is *young* for a fairy," said Chinky. "See how beautiful the Princess still is."

She certainly was. Peter wished hard for a dance with her – and at once she glided over to him, and danced as lightly as a moth. "Now I can say I've danced with a princess!" thought Peter, pleased.

The next day came and slid away happily. Then the next day and the next. The children grew used to having every single wish granted.

"A big chocolate ice at once!" And hey presto, it came. "A tame lion to ride on!" There it was, purring like a cat. "Wings on my back to fly high above the trees!" And there they were, fluttering strongly, carrying Mollie high in the air. What a truly lovely feeling.

On that fourth day the children didn't wish quite so many things. "Tired of wishing?" asked Chinky, who hadn't really wished many things. "Ah – people always get tired of wishes coming true after a time."

"I can't seem to think of any more," said Peter.

"*I* keep thinking of Mother," said Mollie. "I do so hope she isn't worried about us. We've got to go back home today, Peter – do you realise that? It's the day we have to go back to school. It's a pity we've had so little time at home. We shall hardly have seen Daddy and Mother at all."

"Oh goodness – how the weekend has flown," said Peter. "I wanted to do quite a lot of things at home, too. I wanted to get out my electric train – and didn't you want to take your dolls out just once in their pram, Mollie?"

"Yes. I did," said Mollie. "Oh dear – I do wish we had the weekend in front of us still, so that we could enjoy being at home, too! I feel as if we've rather wasted it

The beautiful wings carried Mollie high in the air.

now. Peter, I think we ought to go back. We've a train to catch, you know. We mustn't be late back for school."

"All right. Chinky, we'd better change the throne back to the wishing-chair," said Peter. "Wish for its wings, will you? They've gone, but a wish will bring them back, in the Land of Wishes!"

It did, of course. As soon as the throne had changed back into the wishing-chair they knew so well, Chinky wished for the wings to grow – and they sprouted out gaily, at once, looking bigger than ever.

"You coming, Nose-About?" said Peter to the little brownie.

"No. I'm going back home to my mother," he said. "Good-bye. Thank you for being kind to me."

"Well, you've certainly repaid our kindness!" said Mollie. "I've never had such a wonderful time in my life. Now – are we all ready? Wishing-chair, home, please, as fast as you can!"

It was a long, long way back from the Land of Wishes. They all three went sound asleep, and the chair was careful not to jolt them at all in case they fell off. It flew down to the playroom at last, and went in gently at the door. It tipped out Mollie and Peter on to their mattresses, and Chinky on to his cushion. The crock that had contained the rainbow gold tipped out, too, and fell on to the carpet. Luckily it didn't break.

The children groaned a little, and then slept on soundly, curled up on their mattresses. The chair stood still. Its red wings disappeared gradually. It was just a chair.

And then there came a loud knocking at the door, and a loud voice, too.

"Master Peter! Miss Mollie! How late you are sleeping! Haven't you had your breakfast yet? Your mother has telephoned to say that Granny is much better and she'll be home to lunch. Isn't that good news?"

The children woke up with a jump and stared at Mrs. Williams' smiling face. She was looking in at the door. Peter sat up and rubbed his eyes.

"Well, I declare!" said Mrs. Williams. "You are not in your night-things! You don't mean to say you didn't go to bed properly last night? Do wake up. It's half-past ten already!"

"Half-past ten?" said Mollie, amazed. "What day is it, Mrs. Willy?"

"Saturday, to be sure!" said Mrs. Williams, surprised. "You came home yesterday, that was Friday – and so today's Saturday!"

"But – but surely it's Tuesday or perhaps even Wednesday," said Mollie, remembering the wonderful weekend in the Land of Wishes. "Aren't we due back at school?"

"Bless us all, you're asleep and dreaming!" said Mrs. Williams. "Well, I must be getting on with my work. It's Saturday morning, half-past ten, and your mother will be home for lunch. Now – do you understand *that*?"

And off she went, quite puzzled. She hadn't seen Chinky on the cushion. He was still fast asleep!

Mollie looked at Peter and her eyes shone. "Peter, oh Peter!" she said, "do you remember that I wished we had the weekend in front of us still? Well, that wish has come true, too. We've *had* the weekend once in our palace – and now we're going to have it all over again at home. Could anything be nicer!"

"Marvellous!" said Peter, jumping up. "Simply marvellous! Wake up, you lazy old Chinky. We've good news for you. It's not Tuesday – it's only Saturday!"

So there they are, just going to welcome their mother back again, and looking forward to a wonderful half-term.

"Crreee-eee-eak!" says the good old wishing-chair, happily.

XV

SANTA CLAUS AND THE WISHING-CHAIR

I AM sure you have not forgotten the adventures of Peter and Mollie with their wishing-chair! Well, one Christmas they had a fine adventure with Chinky, their pixie friend, and the good old chair.

Christmas was coming. Peter and Mollie were home from boarding-school and were very excited.

"Two more days till Christmas!" said Peter. "Then stockings, and crackers, and pudding, and Christmas tree, and parties. Oooh!"

The next day came – and that was Christmas Eve. "Only today," said Mollie, "then Christmas!"

They went down to their playroom, which was built at the bottom of the garden. The wishing-chair was there, but Chinky, their friend, was not. He had gone Christmas shopping.

"Chinky said he would hang his stocking up on the back of the wishing-chair," said Mollie. "Then Santa Claus would fill it for him. Where shall we put the presents we have bought for him, Peter?"

They put them on the sofa in the corner, and then ran back to the house. They had not been for any rides on the wishing-chair so far these holidays – but they had been so busy doing their Christmas shopping that they had hardly paid any attention to the magic chair.

The children hung up their stockings that night at the end of their beds. Mother tucked them up, kissed them, and put out the light.

"Now, go to sleep quickly," she said. "No staying awake and peeping."

So they went straight off to sleep, and began to dream about parties and presents. But in the middle of the night Peter suddenly woke up. He had heard a queer noise in his sleep. What could it be?

It was some one tapping on the window-pane outside. Tap-tap-tap! Tap-tap-tap!

"Mollie! Wake up!" cried Peter. "There's someone knocking at the window."

Mollie sat up, rubbing her eyes.

"Do you suppose it's Santa Claus?" she said, in an excited voice.

"Of course not! He comes down the chimney," said Peter. "Come on. Let's see who it is."

They went to the window and opened it – and in popped Chinky the pixie, shivering with cold, and panting with excitement.

"Mollie! Peter! Something's happened! I was asleep

in the playroom when I heard a galloping noise – and I looked out of the window. And I saw Santa Claus and his reindeer in the sky, and the reindeer were running away. Something had frightened them. Then I heard a crash, and I'm sure the reindeer have galloped into some trees, and broken the sleigh. Will you come with me and see?"

The children dressed quickly, for it was a cold night. They put on their warmest coats and crept downstairs. Soon they were at the bottom of the garden. The moon came out from behind a cloud and lighted up everything for them.

"It's nearly midnight," said Chinky. "I do hope Santa Claus hasn't been hurt."

He hurried them into the field at the back of the garden and ran towards some big elm trees – and there they saw a strange sight.

The sleigh and the reindeers had got caught in the trees. The children and Chinky could quite clearly see them in the moonlight.

"Oh dear," said Mollie, half-frightened. "I wonder where Santa Claus is?"

"There's somebody climbing down the tree – look!" said Chinky. So there was – and even as the children watched, someone jumped down from the tree and came towards them.

"It's Santa Claus," said Peter. Sure enough, it was. There was no mistake about it, for there were the bright twinkling eyes, the snow-white beard, and the red, hooded coat.

"Good evening, sir," said Chinky. "I'm afraid you've had an accident."

"I certainly have," said Santa Claus, in a worried voice. "Something frightened my reindeer and they ran away at top speed. They ran into the top of that tall tree and wrecked my sleigh. Now what am I to do? It's Christmas night and I've thousands of stockings to fill."

Santa Claus still had his sack with him, and it was bulging full of toys. He put it down on the ground and wiped his hot forehead.

"What will happen to the poor reindeer?" asked Mollie.

"Oh, I've sent a message to my reindeer stables, and they will send along two or three men to free them from the branches and take them home," said Santa Claus. "And now the next thing is – what will happen to *me*? Here am I, Santa Claus, with a big sack of toys to fill every one's stockings – and no way to get to those stockings."

It was then that Peter had his wonderful idea. He nearly cried with excitement as he spoke.

"Santa Claus, oh, Santa Claus! *I* know what you can do. Borrow our wishing-chair."

"Whatever is the boy talking about?" said Santa Claus, puzzled. "Wishing-chair! There aren't such things nowadays."

"Well, *we've* got one," said Mollie, overjoyed at Peter's idea. "Come on, Santa. We'll take you to where we keep it, and then you'll see for yourself. You could fly in it to every chimney quite easily."

They dragged the big jolly man across the field and through the hedge into their garden. Chinky was just as excited as everyone else. They all went into the playroom and Chinky lighted the lamp.

"There you are," he said proudly, holding the lamp over the old wishing-chair. "There's the wonderful chair. And look! It's grown its wings all ready to take you, Santa. It might have known you were coming."

Santa stared at the rose-red wings that were slowly

They dragged the big jolly man across the field.

484

flapping to and fro on the legs of the chair. His eyes shone in the lamplight.

"Yes," he said. "Yes. The very thing. I didn't know there was a wishing-chair in the world nowadays. May I really borrow it, children?"

"Yes," said Mollie.

"On one condition," said Peter suddenly.

"What's that?" asked Santa Claus, putting his great bag over his shoulder.

"Take us with you in the chair for just a little while, so that we can see how you slip down the chimneys and into the bedrooms," begged Peter. "Oh do!"

"But will the chair hold all of us?" said Santa doubtfully. "I'm rather heavy, you know."

"Oh, the chair is as strong as ten horses," said Chinky eagerly. "You don't know the adventures it has had, Santa. Get in, and we'll go."

Santa sat down in the chair. He filled it right up. He took Mollie on his knee. Chinky climbed to the back of the chair, where he always sat – and Peter sat on the sack of toys. The chair gave a creak, flapped its wings fast, and rose into the air.

"We're off!" cried Mollie, in excitement. "Oh, who would have thought that we'd be flying to the house-tops with Santa Claus tonight. What a fine adventure we'll have!"

485

The wishing-chair rose high into the air once it got out-of-doors. Mollie shivered, for the air was frosty. Santa Claus covered her up with part of his wide coat. They passed the elm tree where the sleigh and the reindeer had got caught. "Look," said Peter. "There are your men freeing the reindeer from the branches, Santa Claus."

"Good!" said Santa. "They will be quite all right now. Hallo, the chair is flying down to this roof. Who lives here, children?"

"Fanny and Tommy Dawson," said Peter. "Oh, have you got presents for their stocking, Santa? They are such nice, kind children."

"Yes, I know," said Santa, looking at a big notebook where many names were written down. "Ah! Fanny wants two twin dolls and a puzzle, and Tommy wants a train and some lines. Put your hand into the sack, Peter, please, and take them out."

Peter put his hand into the enormous sack, and the first things he felt were the dolls, the puzzle, and the train with lines! He pulled them out.

"You might see if there are any oranges and nuts

there too," said Santa. "I always like to give a little extra something to good children."

Peter put his hand into the sack again and felt a handful of nuts, apples, and oranges. He gave them to Santa. The chair flew down to a flat piece of roof just by a big chimney. Santa put Mollie off his knee and stood up.

"Watch me slip down this chimney!" he said – and in a second he was gone! It was astonishing how such a big man could get down the chimney.

"Watch me slip down!" he said – and in a second he was gone!

"Quick!" said Chinky, patting the chair. "Get in, Mollie. We'll fly the chair down to Fanny's window and peep in to see what Santa Claus does there. He won't mind."

The chair rose off the roof and flew down to a little window. It put two of its legs there and balanced itself most unsafely, flapping its wings all the time so that it wouldn't fall. Chinky and the children peered in at the window.

487

Fanny and Tommy always had a night-light, and they could see the room quite clearly. Fanny was asleep in her cot, and Tommy was asleep in his small bed.

"Look! There's Santa's feet coming out of the fireplace!" said Chinky excitedly. "Don't they look funny! And now there's his knees – and his waist – and all of him. It's funny he doesn't get black!"

Santa Claus slipped right out of the fireplace and tiptoed to Fanny's bed. There was a stocking hanging at the end. Santa put the oranges, apples, and nuts at the bottom, and then stuffed in the puzzle and the twin dolls.

Fanny didn't stir! She was quite sound asleep. Santa Claus went to Tommy next and filled his stocking too. Then he tiptoed back to the chimney, put his head up, and was soon lost to sight. The wishing-chair flew back to the roof and waited there for Santa. Up he came, puffing and blowing.

"*I* saw you peeping in at the window!" he said. "You gave me quite a fright at first. Come along now – to the next house where there are children!"

It was not far off, for Harry and Ronald, two big boys, lived next door! Santa looked them up in his notebook and found that they were good, clever boys. Neither of them had asked for anything in their stockings. They had just left it to Santa Claus to choose for them.

"Now, let me see," said Santa. "*Clever* boys, my notebook says. What about a book on aeroplanes for Harry, and a big meccano set – and a book on ships for Ronald, and a really difficult puzzle? Put your hand in the sack, Peter, and see what you can find."

Peter slipped in his hand – and, of course, he found the books, the meccano, and the puzzle at once! It almost seemed as if the toys arranged themselves just right for Santa Claus! It was part of his magic, Peter supposed.

He handed the things out to Santa Claus, and then took apples, nuts, oranges, and a few crackers from the sack too. Santa Claus got off the chair and went down the chimney again.

"Come on, chair," said Mollie. "Let's go and peep in at the window again!"

So the chair flew down to the window-sill and tried to balance itself. Harry and Ronald had no night-light, but the moon shone well in at their window, and the children and Chinky could easily see what was happening inside.

They saw Santa creep

So the chair flew down to the window-sill and tried to balance itself.

489

out of the chimney, and go to Harry's stocking – and then, just as Santa was turning to go to Ronald's bed, the wishing-chair fell off the window-sill! The sill was very narrow indeed, and the chair simply couldn't stay there!

The children gave a small squeal, for they were frightened when the chair fell. Of course, it at once rose up again to the roof, flapping its strong wings. But the noise had awakened Ronald, and he sat up!

The children didn't see what happened, but Santa Claus told them when he at last came up the chimney once more.

"You shouldn't have made such a noise," he said. "You woke Ronald, and I had to hide behind a chair till he lay down and went to sleep again! I might have had to wait for an hour!"

"We're very sorry," said Chinky. "The chair slipped and we thought we were falling! Perhaps we'd better not peep in at the windows any more."

"I suppose we couldn't come down a chimney with you, could we?" asked Mollie longingly. "I've always wanted to do that."

"Yes, you can if you like," said Santa; "but you mustn't make any noise. Now who's next on the list? Oh, Joy Brown, seven years old."

Nobody said anything, but Mollie and Peter thought a lot. Joy was not a bit like her name – she was a spiteful, unkind child, who didn't bring joy to anyone. Mollie was surprised that Santa Claus should take presents to Joy.

But he wasn't going to! He read a few lines out loud and then pursed up his mouth. "Dear, dear! Joy seems to be a bad girl. Listen to this! 'Joy Brown – unkind, selfish, and never gives any happiness to any one. Does not deserve any toys this Christmas.' Well, well, well – we must miss her out, I'm afraid."

So the wishing-chair flew past Joy's house. There was nothing in that naughty little girl's stocking the next morning!

"This is George's house," said Peter eagerly, as the chair flew down on to a sloping roof. It was so sloping that they all had to hold on to the nearest chimney. "Can't we go down with you, Santa?"

Santa nodded, so Mollie tried to get into the chimney. But she stuck fast and couldn't go down! Then Peter tried, but he stuck fast too, and so did Chinky. Santa Claus laughed softly.

"Ah! You don't know my trick! I could never get down some of these narrow chimneys if I didn't use some magic oil to make the chimney slippery! In the

Santa nodded, so Mollie tried to get into the chimney.

491

old days chimneys were very wide and there was no difficulty, but nowadays the chimneys are narrow and small. Stand back, Chinky, and I'll pour a little of my oil down."

Santa Claus tipped a small bottle up, and a few drops fell down the chimney. "Now try, Mollie," said Santa.

So Mollie tried again, and this time she slid down the chimney quite easily, and crept out of the bottom into George's bedroom! It did seem queer! There was George in bed, and he was snoring very gently, so Mollie knew he must be asleep.

Then Peter slid down, then Chinky, and last of all Santa Claus. "You can fill George's stocking if you like," he whispered to Peter. "You're a friend of George's, aren't you? I know you like him very much."

"Yes, he's a fine boy," said Peter, and he took the books, the fruit, and the box of small motor-cars

"Yes, he's a fine boy," said Peter, and he took the books, the fruit, and the box of small motor-cars.

492

that Santa gave him. Soon George's stocking was full to the top!

"It's fun playing at being Santa Claus!" said Peter. Then they all crept up the chimney again, but Chinky had a dreadful time trying not to sneeze, because the soot got up his nose and tickled it.

"A-tishoo!" he said, when he stood on the roof again, holding firmly to a chimney. "A-tishoo!"

"Sh!" said Santa in alarm. "Don't do that!"

"A-tishoo!" said poor Chinky. "I can't help it. A-tishoo!"

Santa Claus bundled him into the chair and they all flew off to another house. "Now this must be the last house you visit with me," said Santa Claus, seeing Mollie yawning and rubbing her eyes. "You must be fresh and lively on Christmas Day, or people will wonder what is the matter with you. You may come down the chimney here, and then I shall fly back to your own house with you, and go on my journey by myself!"

The children and Chinky were disappointed, but they knew Santa was right. They really were beginning to feel very sleepy. They slipped down that chimney with Santa, and Mollie filled Angela's stocking herself with all kinds of exciting things. Mollie wondered what Angela would say if she knew that she, Mollie, had filled her stocking and not Santa Claus. It wouldn't be any use telling her, for she wouldn't believe it!

Then Santa Claus told the wishing-chair to fly back to the playroom, and very soon it was there, standing on the floor.

"Good-bye, dear old Santa!" said Mollie, and she gave the jolly old man a hug. So did Peter. Chinky shook hands with him very solemnly. Then they watched him fly off in their chair to fill hundreds more stockings. He waved to them as he went out of sight.

"Oh, I'm *so* sleepy!" said Mollie. "Good-night, Chinky dear – see you tomorrow!"

They ran up the garden, crept into the house, and were soon fast asleep. And in the morning, what a wonderful surprise!

Santa Claus had come back at the end of his journey, and his last visit had been to Mollie and Peter. He must have climbed down their chimney whilst they slept, and he had filled their stockings from top to toe! They were almost bursting with good things!

"Oh, here's just what I wanted!" cried Mollie.

The presents had even overflowed on to the floor! "Oh, here's just what I wanted!" cried Mollie, picking up a book. "*Mr. Galliano's Circus*! And here's a doll that opens and shuts its eyes – and a toy typewriter – and a doll's bathroom – and, oh look, Peter, you've got six different kinds of aeroplanes!"

Peter had plenty of other things beside those. The two children were very happy indeed. Mother was most astonished when she saw all their toys.

"Why, anyone would think you were great friends of Santa Claus, by the way he has spoilt you with so many presents!" she said.

"We *are* friends of his!" said Mollie happily.

After breakfast they went down to the playroom to wish Chinky a merry Christmas – and do you know, he had as many things as they had, too! So you can guess what a fine Christmas morning they had, playing with everything.

"Good old Santa Claus, and good old wishing-chair!" said Peter, patting the chair, which was safely back in its place. "I do hope Santa Claus is having as good a Christmas as we are!"

Well, I expect he was, don't you?

XVI

MORE ABOUT THE WISHING-CHAIR

YOU remember the wishing-chair, don't you, that Mollie and Peter had, with Chinky the pixie?

Well, Mollie and Peter went to boarding-school,

and Chinky took the chair home to his mother until the holidays came. And you can guess that the very first day of the holidays Mollie and Peter rushed down to the playroom at the bottom of the garden to see if Chinky was there!

"Chinky's not here!" said Mollie, in disappointment.

"Nor is the chair!" said Peter.

But just at that very moment there came a whizzing noise, and in at the door flew the good old wishing-chair, with Chinky sitting as usual on the back, grinning all over his merry pixie face.

"Chinky! Oh, Chinky!" yelled Mollie and Peter, in delight. Chinky leapt off the chair and ran to the two children. They flung their arms round one another and hugged like bears.

"Oh, it's good to see you again, Chinky," said Mollie happily.

"You don't know how I've missed you and Peter!" said Chinky. "Now we'll have some more adventures!"

"Well, first of all, tell us any news you have," said Peter. But Chinky pointed to the wishing-chair.

It was flapping its red wings as hard as ever it could, making quite a draught.

"The chair's glad to see you, too!" said Chinky, laughing. "And it badly wants to take us somewhere. Come on – let's get in and go whilst the chair has its wings."

Mollie and Peter sat on the seat as they always used to do, and Chinky sat on the back. The chair flapped its wings, rose into the air, and flew off.

"Oh," said Mollie. "What fun it is to fly off in the wishing-chair again! I do so like it!"

The children leaned over and looked at the towns and villages they were flying over. They knew exactly when they came to the borders of Fairyland, for Fairyland always had a soft blue mist hanging around it.

"Where are we going?" asked Peter.

"Don't know," said Chinky. "This is the first time the chair has had a fly since you went to school. It's been a proper well-behaved, ordinary chair in my mother's house for weeks – now it's enjoying a good fly!"

The chair flew on and on. The children watched the towers of Giantland pass – the blue seas of Pixieland – the hills of the Red Goblins – and still the chair flew on.

At last it flew downwards. The children felt excited. Chinky looked down to see where they were going.

"I've never been here before," he said. "I don't even know the name of the land."

The chair came to rest in a little town. The children jumped off, but Chinky still sat on the back of the chair, trying to think where they had come to.

A lot of little folk came running up. They had very wide-open eyes, long ears, long noses and no chin at all. Mollie wasn't sure that she liked the look of them.

"What is this land?" asked Chinky.

"It's Disappearing Land," said one of the little folk, smiling. "You'll have to be careful you don't vanish."

Mollie remembered the Disappearing Island. It had disappeared suddenly just as they were going to land on it. Would this country disappear suddenly too? She asked Chinky.

"No," said Chinky. "But *we* may disappear if we

don't look out! I think we'd better go off again. I don't want to vanish somewhere!"

The children sat down in the wishing-chair once more. But its wings had gone. It wouldn't fly at all.

"Oh!" said Chinky. "First disappearing trick! I suppose they've done that to keep us here. Now, hold hands, all of us – then if one of us vanishes the others can still *feel* him and take him along. We may as well have a look round whilst we are here. We'll remember where the chair is – just by that yellow lamp-post. Come on!"

They went down the little, winding street. The strange little folk hurried everywhere, nodding and smiling. There was a market nearby, and the children and Chinky went to see what was being sold.

It was a strange village. Mollie was looking at a crooked little house with twisty chimneys when it quite suddenly disappeared and she was staring at nothing. It gave her such a shock.

Peter got a shock too. A dog with big pointed ears came running up to him and licked his fingers. Peter bent down to pat it – and found he was patting air! The dog had vanished under his very nose!

Even Chinky got caught too – and he was used to strange things! He went to buy three rosy apples off a stall. He gave the old dame there three pennies – but just as he took the apples from her they disappeared into nothing! There was Chinky, his three pennies given to the old dame, and his hands trying to take hold of three apples that had disappeared!

"I want my money back," he said to the old woman, who was grinning widely. "I haven't got my apples."

There was Chinky trying to take hold of three apples that had disappeared.

"Well, I gave them to you," said the old woman. "They are not here! You can't have your money back."

Chinky was angry. He stalked off down the street with Peter and Mollie. He kicked crossly at the kerb. At once it disappeared!

"I say! Don't do that," said Peter, in alarm. "You might kick the whole street away!"

Chinky was pleased to find he could kick things away. He kicked very hard indeed at a lamp-post. But that didn't disappear! It just stood there, as solid as ever – and Chinky gave a loud yell and hopped about holding his poor toe!

Mollie and Peter couldn't help laughing. Peter leaned against a shop window and roared at Chinky – and then, very suddenly, the window behind him vanished and he fell over backwards! The whole shop had disappeared!

499

Peter stopped laughing and picked himself up. Then it was Chinky's turn to laugh. Peter did look so very much astonished!

"This is a funny sort of town," said Mollie, looking round her carefully, not quite certain what was going to disappear next. As she spoke, three chimneys disappeared off a cottage, and a door nearby vanished as well. It seemed as if everything that she looked at disappeared!

"I *am* hungry," said Chinky, wishing he had the three apples he had bought. "Look! There's a shop selling buns. I wonder if *they*'ll disappear if I buy some!"

He walked into the shop. A pointed-eared girl sat knitting behind the counter. She put her knitting down as Chinky went in, and immediately the needles disappeared. But she didn't seem to mind at all.

"Have you any currant buns?" asked Chinky,

Chinky walked into the shop.

500

looking round, hoping the whole shop wouldn't disappear before he had bought the buns.

"Yes, fresh made today," said the girl, and she pointed to some fine big ones, with plenty of currants in, and looking nice and sticky on the top.

"I'll take three, please," said Chinky. He didn't give the girl the pennies until he had the bag of buns safely in his hand. Then he ran out of the shop and showed the buns to the others.

"Look at the lovely, juicy currants!" he said. "Come on – let's sit down on this seat and eat our buns."

They sat down on the seat – but it at once vanished under them, and the three of them rolled over on the path. How all the little folk of the village laughed and laughed!

"I do think the way things disappear here is silly!" said Chinky, rubbing his head. "Where are the buns?"

"In the bag," said Mollie. "Good thing they are, or they would have rolled in the road!"

But the buns had disappeared out of the bag, which was quite empty. The children stared into it in disgust. "Oh, let's go back to the wishing-chair," said Peter. "I'm tired of this place."

"Oooh, Peter!" said Mollie suddenly. "Look! Your feet have disappeared!"

Peter stared down at his feet – and it was true, they had gone!

"Well, I can still walk all right," he said. "So they must be there although we can't see them. Thank goodness for that! Oooh, Chinky! Where's your mouth?"

Chinky hadn't got a mouth! It had disappeared!

A big wind suddenly swept round the corner of the street and took off Chinky's cap. He ran after it, and Peter ran too – and do you know, when they turned round to go back to Mollie, *she* had disappeared as well!

"Oh! Mollie! Mollie!" cried Peter, in alarm. "Where are you?"

But there was no answer. Peter turned to Chinky. "Chinky! Did you see where Mollie went?"

But Chinky had now gone too! There was nobody at all where Chinky had been standing, putting on his hat again. Peter felt more alarmed than ever. This would never do!

"Bother!" he said fiercely. "Chinky said we'd better keep hold of each other's hands, in case this happened – and we all forgot about it – and now, on our very first holiday adventure, this has happened! Mollie! Chinky!"

Nobody answered Peter. And then a strange thing happened. Peter disappeared too! He felt as if he was there all right – but he couldn't see himself! He held out his hand and it wasn't there! He kicked up a foot – and it wasn't there either! Then he knew that he was invisible too.

"*Now* what am I to do?" he thought. "This is dreadful. Let me think."

He stood and thought. Little folk came up and bumped into him for they couldn't see him. At first Peter was cross – then, as he saw their astonished faces, he remembered that he couldn't be seen. He ran and stood in a doorway where no one would bump into him.

"What's to be done, what's to be done?" thought Peter. "The others are in the same fix as I am. What will they do? Why – they will try to get back to the wishing-chair, I expect! That's what I must do too! We left it by the yellow lamp-post!" And off he went to find it.

XVII

THE END OF THE ADVENTURE

PETER made his way back to where they had left the wishing-chair. He did hope he might meet Mollie and Chinky there. He soon saw the yellow lamp-post in the distance, where the chair had been left.

"Good!" thought Peter, hurrying. "I'll soon be back with the chair again – and I'll sit in it and wait there till the others come."

But as he got nearer he could see a crowd round the chair. The strange little folk of the village were shouting to one another about it, and two of the pointed-eared men had hold of the chair.

"I tell you *I* shall have this chair!" yelled one man, and he pulled hard.

"I tell you I shall have this chair!" yelled one man.

"And I tell you *I* want it!" shouted the other, angrily, and he pulled the other way.

"Goodness! The chair will be in bits soon," thought Peter, and he ran at top speed to the crowd of people.

"Leave that chair alone!" he shouted. "It's *not* yours – it belongs to *me*!"

Every one looked round – but, of course, they couldn't see Peter, for he was quite invisible. They only heard his voice.

"Who are you?" they said.

"I'm Peter, and I want my chair," said the little boy. he pushed his way through the crowd and took hold of the chair firmly. At once the other two who were holding it began to pull away hard. But Peter didn't let go.

"Show yourself, show yourself!" shouted the crowd.

"I don't know how to," said Peter. "I suddenly

disappeared, and I can't even see myself. But I'm real enough, and if anyone begins to be horrid to me I've got fists that can hit hard. And you won't see them coming, either! Now, let go my chair, please."

"We don't believe it's yours, we don't believe it's yours!" cried everyone, siding with the two men who had got hold of the poor wishing-chair.

Peter didn't know what to do. He certainly couldn't get the chair away by himself. "Oh, wishing-chair, we *are* in a fix!" he groaned. "Our very first holiday adventure, too! It's bad luck!"

Suddenly the wishing-chair decided to help matters itself. It grew its wings very fast. It flapped them strongly. It rose into the air – and with it it took Peter, who was holding it – and the two little men as well!

The crowd shouted in surprise to see the chair rise up. The two little men were full of fear. They hung on with all their might. Peter climbed up and sat safely in the chair. He had got away from the crowd, at any rate. He wondered what to do with the little men who were hanging on to the chair. He couldn't make them fall – they might be hurt.

The chair rose high up. Peter suddenly cried out in alarm. "Hie, wishing-chair! Don't go home yet! We've left Mollie and Chinky behind! Fly down again, quickly."

The chair flew down at once. As soon as it was safely on the ground the two little men began to quarrel again about who was to have the chair. Peter got really angry. He pushed them both hard. They fell over.

"I wish you'd stop this," said Peter. "What's the

good of quarrelling about *my* chair? *I'm* going to have it, not you, Leave go!"

But they wouldn't. Peter picked up a twig and rapped their hands sharply. They let go at once – and before they could take hold again, what do you think happened? Why, the wishing-chair most obligingly disappeared! Peter blinked in surprise, for he still wasn't used to seeing things disappear so suddenly.

Then he knew what to do. If he picked up the chair and ran off with it, the two little men wouldn't know where it had gone – for they could see neither Peter nor the chair, now! So Peter felt for the chair, and, quick as lightning, snatched it up and ran down the street! The two little men stared all round in astonishment, and then began to slap each other hard.

"Just what they both want!" thought Peter, pleased. He ran on and on and then stopped. He put the chair down just inside a field gate, sat down in it firmly, and tried to think what to do. How in the world could he find Mollie and Chinky?

"If I go through the village again, yelling out Mollie

and Chinky's names, maybe they'll hear me and come to me," thought Peter. "They must be very worried, because they don't know where the chair is!"

Back he went to the village, carrying the chair on his shoulder. As he went he shouted loudly, "MOLLIE! CHINKY! MOLLIE! CHINKY!"

Suddenly he heard Mollie's voice, answering. How glad Peter was! It came from the other side of the road. "Peter! I can hear you! I'm still invisible. Where are you?"

"I'm standing by the fruit-shop here!" yelled back Peter. "I've got the chair, too!"

In half a minute he felt Mollie's hands touching him, and then she hugged him and felt for the good old wishing-chair too. "Now we must get Chinky," said Peter. "What have you been doing all this time, Mollie?"

"Oh, I've been looking for you," said Mollie. "I went back to the yellow lamp-post but the chair was gone."

Just then someone they couldn't see bumped into them. He couldn't see them either, for they were still invisible. As soon as the person who bumped into them felt the chair, he gave a yell, and caught hold of it.

Peter snatched at the chair too. He pulled and Mollie helped him. They were not going to lose their precious chair! But the one who was pulling against them was very strong, and suddenly the chair was tugged right away, and they could no longer feel it. They couldn't see it either, of course – it was gone!

"Oh, it's gone, it's gone!" cried Mollie, almost in tears. "Oh, Peter, what shall we do now?"

"Mollie! Peter! Is it you!" cried a voice gladly. "It's me, Chinky! I didn't know I was pulling against *you*! I just came along the street, bumped into the chair, felt it was ours and grabbed it. When I felt someone pulling hard against me, I jerked till I got it! Hurrah! We're all together again!"

How pleased everyone was! "I've been looking everywhere for you," said Chinky, climbing on to the back of the chair. "My word – fancy the chair disappearing, too! This is a most uncomfortable sort of place. Come on – let's get away as soon as we can."

They all got on to the chair. It flapped its wings and rose up suddenly into the air. "Oooh!" said Mollie, "that was quick – it felt like a lift going up!"

"Chinky, how are we going to get ourselves right again?" asked Peter. "We can't go home like this."

"I can get some of that magic paint we once used at Witch Snippit's spinning house," said Chinky. "Then we'll paint ourselves back again. That's easy. I'll send one of my friends to get the paint for us."

The children flew on and on through the air until at last they were over their own garden once more. They flew down – and right through the open door of their playroom at the bottom of the garden. They were just going to shout and jump off – when they saw someone there!

It was their mother. She had come to look for them. The children sat perfectly still on the chair. They knew they were invisible and couldn't be seen. If Mother heard their voices, she would get such a shock, for she wouldn't be able to see them! Chinky sat still too. He had always made the children promise

508

that they would never, never say a word about him to any grown-up.

Mother looked round the playroom. "I wonder where those children are," she said. Then she walked out, almost, but not quite, bumping into the wishing-chair as she went.

"My goodness! That was a narrow escape!" said Peter, when Mother had gone. He jumped out of the chair. "What a good thing the chair and all of us couldn't be seen today! Mother *would* have got a fright if she had suddenly seen a chair come flying through the doorway with us in it!"

"She certainly would," said Chinky, grinning. "So would anyone! Now, I'll just send for that paint."

He ran out. In a few minutes he was back and said that a friend of his had flown off to Witch Snippit's at once. "Let's play a game of ludo whilst we're waiting," he said. "I haven't played since you went away to school. I've forgotten what a lovely feeling it is to throw a six!"

It was rather peculiar to play with people you couldn't see. It was even funnier to see counters moving by themselves, as the children pushed them round the board. They just had time to play one game, when there came a knock at the door.

"The paint!" said Chinky. He opened the door. On the step stood a large tin of Witch Snippit's magic paint. "Good!" said Chinky. "Now, what about brushes?"

"There are some in our paint-boxes," said Mollie, and she fetched them. "They are very small – it will take us ages to paint ourselves right again!"

They began. They each had a paint-brush and they set to work. Chinky painted the wishing-chair back first. Mollie began to paint herself back. Wherever she ran her brush full of paint a bit of her appeared! It was funny.

Mollie ran her brush over her left hand. At once it appeared. It was nice to see her fingers again!

"You haven't painted that little nail on your fingers," said Peter. "Look!"

"And *you*'ve painted all your face back except your left eyebrow," laughed Mollie. "You look funny!"

The wishing-chair was soon back again. Then Chinky began to paint himself back. They all had to help each other when they came to bits of themselves that they couldn't reach. They had great fun.

"We're quite done except that Peter hasn't got his feet yet," said Chinky, and he stepped back to look at him – and do you know, he stepped right on to the tin

Chinky stepped right on to the tin of paint and upset it.

510

of paint and upset it. It ran all over the floor and the floor disappeared! The paint always acted both ways – it made things disappear, or it made them come back if they had vanished.

"Chinky! You *are* clumsy!" cried Mollie, in horror. "We shan't be able to do Peter's feet! Whatever will Mother say?"

Peter caught up a rag and mopped up the spilt paint as fast as he could. He squeezed it from the rag into the tin, and then looked at the little bit there anxiously.

"Do you think there's enough for my feet?" he said. Chinky, who had gone very red, nodded his head, and took up his paint-brush again. Without a word he began to paint in Peter's feet, being very careful not to waste a drop of the precious paint. Mollie was very glad to see that there was enough.

"What about that hole in the floor?" said Peter. "Is there enough paint left to paint it back again?"

"Just!" said Chinky – and there was! My goodness, there wasn't a single drop over.

"Well," said Mollie, as she heard a bell ring to call them indoors, "we always seem to have narrow escapes and exciting times when we begin going off in the wishing-chair. I *did* enjoy this adventure, now it's all over and we're safely back again, looking like ourselves!"

"Good-bye," said Chinky. "See you tomorrow, I hope! It's been lovely to go adventuring again!"